THE BLUE BENCH

Paul Marriner

Bluescale Publishing

www.bluescalepublishing.co.uk

Cover artwork by Linda Laurie and Catherine Murray

Cover design by Catherine Murray at www.piggledesign.co.uk

Bluescale Publishing

ISBN   978–0–9929648–8–7

For the unknown warriors:

May your cause have been just,
May you rest,
May those that love you find peace,

THE BLUE BENCH

Patrick, London,
Thursday 14th November 1940

I waited outside the west doors of Westminster Abbey. The relentless comings and goings were unnerving. I had visited the abbey often before the war, usually for study, and enjoyed inspiration and peace in the resolute calm and dignity founded within its stone. But the war had come to London, to Westminster. Workmen came and went under the west towers, dodging around and between the procession of building materials and sandbags being ferried past the tall, dark doors. It was hard to tell the men apart – mostly they wore heavy wool jackets over blue dungarees, under grey or brown caps – and I didn't think them the cheery Londoners of the newsreels, making good and the best of it with patient smiles. But there was comfort in the defiance of their dogged and measured activity.

There had been rumours of looting from the mangled wreckage of bombed out stores and houses but I couldn't believe anyone would steal from the abbey and it was known most of the treasures had been moved from the city. Was it possible the grave just inside the west door was gone? Surely it would have been impossible to move, so I prayed it was protected, perhaps by some divine respect for the contents.

I watched the workmen and deliveries, checking my old watch often, concerned for the ladies I was meeting.

The damage to the windows above the abbey's west doors was recent. Many panes had been blown in by the Luftwaffe, and, as if needed, it was a reminder of these

1

days. There were others: the workmen's uniforms, of a sort, were echoed in the Service khaki and blues that mingled with the civilian browns and greys. They moved with a purpose that hadn't been there a year ago, the last time I'd visited the abbey, the last time of our pilgrimage. But a year ago the air raid siren blew for practise or false alarms. These days the sirens announced the urgent, terrifying, indiscriminate violence of bombs. I looked up to the jagged windows and tried to remember last year. Today the sky was clear – a beautiful crisp November day. A good day for the Luftwaffe? I worried about the ladies I was to meet in case the sirens should howl and they were caught without cover. How would they know where to shelter? Perhaps this was the year they should have missed their pilgrimage. An older man looked at me and did not look away when I caught his eye. He might have shaken his head and I supposed it was because I wore civvies – ill–matching brown trousers and jacket. I looked towards Victoria Street. The ladies weren't late and there were no sirens but I checked my watch again, Edward's old Elgin, refurbished at the ladies' expense. They'd presented it to me before I went up to Cambridge a couple of years earlier. I lit a cigarette – Embassy, more expensive than my usual brand but I had the feeling I might not see the ladies for a long while after today; melodramatic, I know. Catherine would laugh at such thoughts but Evelyn would have patted my arm. My cigarette offered no comfort.

The flow of workmen and materials into and out of the abbey slowed and stopped as another set of uniforms arrived. Older men in long black coats under black top hats or homburgs, with pale, drawn faces, strolled from the Houses of Parliament or were delivered in black cars. They milled round the abbey. I watched them and saw I was wrong; they didn't stroll, they walked slowly and carefully but also careworn; if a stroll implies a casual enjoyment, these men did not stroll. I checked my watch again – 11:40 a.m. A woman carrying a reporter's notebook stood near

Dean's Yard and scribbled notes. I walked over to her and she replied to my question by nodding upwards to the half–mast flag on the tower over the Houses of Parliament. 'Funeral. Neville Chamberlain. Noon.'

'Oh, thanks. I didn't know it was today. I only travelled down this morning,' I explained, though she didn't care. I turned to go back to waiting but she took a step toward me.

'I don't suppose you've heard anything about Birmingham being hit yesterday. A daylight raid?'

'No, I'm sorry.'

'There's been talk.'

'Uh–uh,' I murmured vaguely, not wanting to repeat the conversation I'd overheard on the way down from Cambridge that morning. I had paid little attention on the train and perhaps there was something to know but the poster at the station in Cambridge had proclaimed 'Careless Talk Costs Lives', next to a picture of an alluring but somehow menacing young woman. I felt some small pride at not repeating the gossip I'd heard.

The reporter returned to her scribbles.

A group of clerics in bright ecclesiastical robes welcomed Winston Churchill. I had never seen him in person before and was careful not to stare. Another man, in army uniform with braid and stripes, joined them. I understood the ecclesiastical garb but the military flashes were a mystery which I supposed I'd need to learn. The group made their way into the abbey. Policemen in heavy coats and blue steel helmets watched.

Looking back up Victoria Street I saw the ladies walking my way and felt pride in their manner and appearance, though I was in no way responsible. Catherine walked on their left, she always did, while Evelyn, I knew, would have set the pace, trying to slow the other woman. They both wore blue; Evelyn in a long, dark coat and Catherine in lighter, three quarter length, with slim, belted waists and padded shoulders. They appeared the same height. As usual, Catherine wore taller heels than Evelyn. Catherine's grey hat was perched to the back of her head while Evelyn's dark hair was uncovered. Though they were up from the coast for the day they were indistinguishable from London's most fashionable dressers, which was no surprise.

They were often taken for sisters.

'Here's our young man. Hello Patrick.' Catherine said to me.

The greeting was supported by Evelyn touching my arm. They took turns to stretch up and peck my cheek, Evelyn whispering, 'Our young man.' Though it wasn't a secret it was all the more true for the discretion.

'Hello, my ladies,' I said.

Though they had both used the term 'our', there was not a hint of ownership or possession. Before being 'our' young man I had been 'our' lad and before that 'our' boy and before that 'our' joy – and the 'our' was never possessive, in the same way though they were now 'my' ladies, there was no claim or hierarchy implied. We were 'ours' and 'my' and bound by time, love and circumstance. No, not bound, that implies against our will and it was never that – better to say bonded.

'Sorry we're late, the trains are … difficult, at the moment,' said Evelyn.

'Full of bloody soldiers, though they gave up seats for us and brought a cuppa from the buffet car,' said Catherine.

'After we offered to pay for theirs,' Evelyn added.

'We had to fib at the station though. The ticket office said all travel is restricted to essential only. Evelyn told them we were coming up for a funeral. Apparently we shared an aunt. I never knew. I hope she's left us something in the will.'

'And we had to show our identity cards to the conductor.'

It was nearly noon and I pointed to the abbey as the

doors closed. 'Well, there is a funeral, but not an aunt. It's Chamberlain's. It looks like we can't enter.'

'But we will go in later?' asked Evelyn.

'Of course,' said Catherine. 'We've not missed a year. Have you a cigarette Patrick? I gave my last one to a young soldier on the train, just a boy. Poor Chamberlain. Do they all have funerals here?'

'Who?' I asked.

'Prime ministers.'

'I don't know. Perhaps because he was a man of peace?'

'That wasn't a choice he was free to make, was it?' said Evelyn and, as so often, she understood instinctively that which many others did not.

'I know, let's have tea and come back later. I want to see what the Nippies are wearing this year.' Catherine took my left arm, Evelyn my right, and we turned away from the abbey to walk through St James's Park.

It was as pleasant a walk in London as any I could recall. We ambled through the park. I answered their questions on how I was getting on at Cambridge and deflected comments on how much I was missing Isabella, without giving away my immediate plans, then caught up on their news. It had been only six weeks since I'd last seen them but time was compressed in these days; the events of the summer were both old and new. For a few days in late May and early June, during the evacuation of Dunkirk, our county, Kent, was the centre of the war. And our home town of Margate was invaded by thousands of troops, except it was a retreat, not an invasion, no matter how glorious we pretended it to be. Evelyn and Catherine owned two hotels in Margate but the wartime restrictions deterred holidaymakers. The empty rooms were taken by officers managing the evacuation through the town. The kitchens prepared meals and hot drinks non–stop for nearly a week while an army washed through town, soldiers were lost and found and regiments reformed and

5

removed by rail to home bases. And when the appeal was made for all and any vessels to help with the evacuation I easily found a friend with a small fishing boat who would take me. Catherine and Evelyn were unusually accepting when I told them I was going. We followed the Margate lifeboat across the channel and made our own way back with a full load of men. Being able to slip in close to the beach we picked up ten or so tired and sodden soldiers who waded out to meet us. We finished the last pack of cigarettes when little more than a couple of miles on the voyage home and the men were silent and haunted. They looked to the skies and I kept busy making tea when not throwing up over the side – despite my beloved steamer trips I'd grown to be a fragile sailor, even in the calmest of seas. The men didn't laugh and I wished they had. We brought them home to Margate. They left us at the quayside with barely a smile, though I'd thought we had shared something to celebrate. On the harbour wall they merged with the horde of lost soldiers and we turned our little boat back to the channel, returning to Dunkirk.

Foolishly, I wasn't scared on the journeys to or from Dunkirk and couldn't deny the excitement of playing some small part in the war. It was the first time I had doubts about going back to Cambridge.

As June eased into July the sky above our town and fields was filled with noise and violence. It was easy to take pride in the graceful defiance of the Spitfires and Hurricanes whilst ignoring the reality of explosive, eviscerating death and burning agony in the clear blue air. Many of the men dying in those skies were younger than me and the thought of returning to Cambridge in the September became more unsettling, as if it might be an irrelevance. I went back anyway, for a few weeks, but always with the feeling this trip to London, 14th November, would be a crossroads.

On the walk through the park I tried not to glance skyward; it would be a futile gesture – if the Luftwaffe came the sirens would warn before we heard the aircraft.

From St James's Park we made our way towards Piccadilly and the Lyons Corner House on Coventry Street. The café was crowded and noisy and we were escorted to a table on the second floor, on the balcony from where we could look down to the other floors. A piano played somewhere but I couldn't see and it was hard to hear over the constant chatter. The waitress was the cheeriest of Nippies and Evelyn talked to her while Catherine took a small pad and pencil stub from her purse and made a sketch of some of the details of her uniform. It was comforting to hear Catherine and Evelyn chat so easily with the waitress and conclude such a uniform would look right on the staff in their own, new tea shop, down on the front at Margate, but wouldn't suit the hotel staff, the reasons for which were joyously arcane to me. The Nippy brought a large pot of tea and two plates of sandwiches and Evelyn asked her to tell the manager we were impressed with the fare in these days of rationing. Catherine made some notes which I knew she would use later in their own hotels and tea shops to make the rations go further. I wondered to what extent they relied on the black market to keep going – in the summer I had noticed, or perhaps imagined, stilted conversations with strangers that stopped as I walked into the kitchens.

We ate the Lyons sandwiches, talking loudly to be heard over the noise of the other customers. Enlisted personnel and civilians mixed and, though conversation was difficult because of the volume, I enjoyed the atmosphere, more raucous than last year.

As Catherine had said, they had not missed this pilgrimage in twenty years. In that time I had joined them on seven or eight occasions and never under duress. We usually took tea after visiting the abbey but the change of routine this year didn't bother them and they spoke more of their plans for another tea room and the possibility of buying another hotel, renovating it for when war ended and people wanted, needed, to holiday again. I smoked between sandwiches and Evelyn commented I hadn't used to smoke so much. I shrugged and there was an unnatural silence until Catherine took the cigarette I offered, saying, 'Evelyn wants to know why you've come again this year …'

'Not that we didn't want you to,' interrupted Evelyn, '… but …'

'… you came last year and don't need to join us every time …' said Catherine.

'And we thought you'd be busy, at Cambridge …'

'… which made Evelyn … wonder …'

'… as she does,' I said, leaning forward to light Catherine's cigarette. 'Nothing to wonder about. It just seemed, with all that's going on, the war and bombs, I should be here, and to make sure you're both safe if there's a raid. That's all.'

'Sure? Nothing to do with William dying last month?' Catherine looked to Evelyn as she asked.

'No, nothing to do with William.'

'He served, you know. In the last war. Of course you know. Just before he died he wrote that the cancer was from the mustard gas, but that was over twenty years ago.'

I hadn't seen William or Georgette for months before the funeral. Georgette was my mother and, apart from William's interment, the only time we'd met that year was in the spring, for a weekend at their new semi in Malden. I'd visited them rarely over the years, even when much younger. William wasn't my father and his death a month earlier from lung cancer was sad, but of course more for Georgette, my mother, than me.

'We did see William shortly before he died. He came down to see us,' Evelyn said and looked to Catherine who gave a slight nod. 'He was very poorly and we had tea but he wouldn't stay over. He insisted he must get back to Georgette.'

'I'm not sure really why he came to see us,' said

Catherine. 'To say …'

'… goodbye, most probably.' Evelyn completed Catherine's sentence.

'No nothing to do with William,' I repeated. 'I just wanted to make sure you're both all right, in case I'm not back here for a year or two.'

Silence.

'Oh my God, you've come down to enlist, haven't you?' gasped Evelyn, shocked at the sudden realisation. She looked to Catherine who looked at me before speaking.

'No, he hasn't, and why would he come here? He could enlist in Cambridge. And if you're going to be an army chaplain you must finish your studies. And the war will be over before then.'

I hesitated. Evelyn understood. 'Our Patrick isn't going to be a chaplain.'

'Royal Fusiliers, London Regiment, I hope,' I said as lightly as possible.

'Oh, like Edward,' said Catherine.

I nodded and nearly apologised but didn't know if I would be sorry for enlisting or for joining Edward's regiment. In truth, it didn't have to be the Royal Fusiliers but they had been good enough for Edward.

'Does Isabella know?'

'Not yet.'

'Should we tell her?'

'No, I'll be back home in the next few weeks. Please don't say anything to her before I've had the chance. It must be to her face.'

Evelyn nodded. 'But that's a terrible secret with which we're burdened.'

'I'm sorry.'

I poured tea for us all. We ate the next sandwiches without talking but not in silence, thanks to the other customers and pianist, now playing something more modern than the light classical of earlier. Catherine made a show of listening carefully to the piano before casually remarking, 'Edward was much better.'

Catherine insisted on settling the bill and on the way out Evelyn asked, 'Do we have time to visit the Royal College of Music? I'd like to.'

'You're not still writing to them, asking for Edward's name on their war memorial?' I asked.

'Of course Patrick. Once a year, in the spring. Then if they do add Edward, when we make the November trip we can see it for ourselves. They always kindly respond to say it's under consideration,' said Catherine.

'I'll write again next April,' added Evelyn.

'I don't think you have time to go there today.' I used the 'pulpit' voice I was developing. 'We've still to get back to the abbey and I want you to be going back home before the raids come, probably tonight again.'

'And you'll need to get to the recruitment office in Whitehall before it closes, I suppose,' said Catherine.

We went in through the west door of the abbey. Though the sky outside was clear and the doors open, the sun was low and the tomb poorly lit. There were few people in the abbey; some clerics repositioning chairs used earlier for Chamberlain's funeral, and a couple of workmen rearranging sandbags. Evelyn, Catherine and I stood at the foot of the grave, further reducing the light reflecting from the black stone but the polished brass lettering was clear. Catherine and Evelyn linked arms and stood tall but relaxed. There was no tension in their bodies and when they looked at each other to smile it was to share something I knew little of and only by way of hearsay.

The warrior in the grave was unknown, of course, but I could say for sure it wasn't my father – he had died at Mons in 1914, shortly after I was born and there was a cross with his name on it in Saint Symphorien Cemetery.

Nor, of course, was it Edward. He had been taken back to his hometown, Lincoln, for burial, in 1920, but Evelyn and Catherine both understood what this grave had meant to Edward – they had been there with him that first time and returned every year since, on the anniversary of Edward's death.

I had been just six when Edward came into their lives – as did I – in the summer of 1920. I have few memories of that time and most of them come from Catherine's and Evelyn's stories. Some of the gaps have been filled by my mother or William but I'm not sure of their truth, and there are many events I've satisfied with imagination over the years, hoping Edward would have approved.

(

The Blue Bench

Edward, Vimy Ridge, France
Monday 9th April, 1917

The barrage stopped. A whistle blew. Lieutenant Edward Thompson checked his watch, from habit, drew his revolver and stepped up out of the trench and onto the soft mud. The sleet dragged in the cold air of a pale dawn and packets of smoke drifted across the scarred brown earth. He looked to his left where twenty or so of his men walked alongside him, rifles ready though targets could not yet be seen. To his right were another twenty or thirty men, moving in a line at the same pace. He felt, rather than heard, the movement to his right and turned to see Sergeant William Burrslow running to catch up. Burrslow had stayed behind in the trench for half a minute to make sure no one else did. Now their platoon was complete. Edward was terrified, of course – as much as any of them. Private Kayst, to his left, smiled at him. Edward nodded back just as the silence was shattered by the German machine guns, rifles and mortars. Edward had played this moment in his mind many times and, though he was scared, there was some comfort in the decision he had taken. How horrific it would be he could not say, but if and when it was enough, he knew what he had to do and prayed for courage to see it through.

The Blue Bench

Edward, Margate, Friday 30th July 1920

'Already past ten thirty,' Edward said with his slight lisp. He tapped his watch.

'You sure? You can't trust that Yankee watch, especially where you've worn it. It's 'ad an 'ard life. C'mon, let's find a caff.' William was dismissive.

Edward followed William from the side street, turning north east onto Marine Drive, where the wind was strong in their faces. Edward looked behind, to the junction with Marine Terrace and checked his watch against the clock in the tower standing there. His watch no longer kept good time but he was loathe to give it up, or even part with it for repair. The Elgin had been through much with him, and was a reminder both of where they had been and, running fast, for what time might be left. It was a present from an American aunt, his father's side, back in 1915, and though they had never met, she was still family, of which he saw little these days. He turned the watch back a few minutes.

From the beach the wind carried welcoming sounds of children shouting and laughing. The cloud was low and it was colder than summer should be but the sand was still crowded with holidaymakers. Most were down from London for their annual break and if the cold North Sea was no deterrent to the swimmers jumping from the bathing carts wheeled into the water, then the possibility of light drizzle was no threat. But Edward was no beach lover, nor a swimmer. He wore his light summer day suit and his favourite homburg – the rim was wider than

15

typical, though not obvious to the casual observer. He pulled his hat down a little more, for security against taking flight in the wind, and carried on along the promenade. They had come to Margate from Hackney that morning, in Edward's Wolseley, though William drove, as always. Edward had hidden from William his excitement at the journey, anxious to leave the cloying brown and grey smoke of London's East End. William had seemed less enthusiastic to be leaving. They had travelled through the farmland and hop fields of north Kent in the early hours. The sun struggled through the cloud but its weakness didn't detract from the clear air and open spaces compared to London. And though the Kent countryside had gentle hills and was unlike Lincolnshire, where he grew up, simply being out of town was a reminder of home. He hadn't been there since 1917 when he'd taken leave, just before the trip to Le Havre, just before Vimy Ridge. His mother wrote often, the letters always found him, and he planned to visit, perhaps next spring.

William needed cigarettes and found a tobacconist a few shops along. Edward waited outside, turning away and looking at the shop window as a family group, three generations, ambled by, both excited and calm with ice cream. In the reflection of the shop glass Edward could see the crowded beach. The water was high though he couldn't tell if the tide ebbed or flowed. Children dug in sand and jumped waves. Clothed adults sat in deckchairs; others, in full bathing suits, swam – some out to the wheeled cart fifty yards off shore, to climb up and jump into the cold sea. A little further inshore was a cluster of bathing huts, their wheels half submerged. Four donkeys clustered together, stoically waiting their next set of riders. Perhaps it was simply because it wasn't Hackney, or perhaps because the drive down had been an escape, of sorts, but he liked Margate already. He liked it being summer but not so hot the straw boater was ubiquitous; he liked his homburg. He liked the way crowds shared so many common, diverting joys when on holiday. He liked the anticipation of playing for new audiences and the chance he might feel the need to compose something, anything. It had been a long while since he'd written anything new and though the desire was there, the compulsion had been missing.

He liked that Margate was both old in its roots and renewed by its shifting, transient tourist population.

He flicked open his silver cigarette case. It was nearly empty so he followed William into the tobacconist. On seeing Edward, William nodded towards the counter at the back where an argument was simmering – a shopkeeper barely keeping his anger quiet and a younger man barely containing the fear that might burst to rage. The shopkeeper held the other man by the arm and called through the door at the back of the shop, 'Go find the constable. I'll hold the bugger.'

'Bastard. Let go.' The man called, but not as a shout and struggled to break free. The two fell against a glass display cabinet of pipes which toppled, the glass shattering as it exploded on hitting the floor with a sudden, violent burst of bright, piercing noise. William looked to Edward who stood frozen in the doorway, one eye wide with fright, the other pale and frozen. His hands shook, he held a breath. The tobacconist and other man grappled in a confused huddle. The shopkeeper was up first and kicked the man back down as he grabbed at the counter, struggling to pull himself up. The movement caught Edward's eye and he gasped air, as if remembering to breathe. William took a step back toward Edward who shook his head and nodded to the fight by the counter. The younger man wore a soldier's tunic and a crutch lay beside him; he had only one leg but with the other trouser leg flapping it was not possible to see how much was missing. The shopkeeper was no longer kicking out, but stood over the man, holding what Edward thought first to be a cosh but on second look was the man's false lower arm. The shopkeeper had been holding it tight enough that when they fell he'd ripped it from the sleeve. The tobacconist saw William and Edward and explained in short bursts. 'Bastard thief. Five fags and an ounce. And maybe a silver lighter. I'll 'ave 'im done.'

Edward looked at the other man and saw embarrassment.

'William,' said Edward, closing the shop door behind him. The door's blind was lowered and the shop, already dark with heavy wooden shelving and floor, was darker still.

William smiled, 'Of course,' and moved to help the disabled ex–soldier stand, passing him the crutch.

'He owes me for what he took, and now the breakages,' said the shopkeeper, nodding to the fragmented display cabinet on the floor.

'He's already paid.' William took a step towards the shopkeeper, broken glass crunching under his polished Oxfords. The shopkeeper raised the false arm threateningly. It was comical and William laughed but without humour.

'Thieving git. He owes me,' the shopkeeper insisted.

'Give me the arm and we'll be off and there'll be no more … damage.' William waved a hand around the shop but the tobacconist raised the prosthetic arm higher, placing it less like a weapon, more like a trophy. The shopkeeper was never going to be quick enough and William stepped in, slapped him across the face and stepped back out again before the false arm could be brought down. The shopkeeper cried out, more in shock than pain, and shook his head as if to clear it. The side of his face reddened.

'Thank you William.' Edward walked forward and, for the first time, the shopkeeper saw Edward's face behind the reflection in his spectacles. They stared at each other for a few seconds before the shocked tobacconist handed over the false arm. Edward passed it to the disabled man. William ushered him back out onto the seafront while Edward took a backward step into a shadow. The shopkeeper started to speak but Edward turned and left.

The disabled ex–soldier was agile on one leg and a crutch. Ignoring the curious stares of the promenaders they found a bench on which to sit while he took off his threadbare khaki tunic and re–attached the prosthetic arm using the complicated strapping. The pink and scarred stump of his arm was sore where the leather straps chafed and pulled. He was shaking but smiled a thank you to William. Edward looked down at the tunic on the bench. There were no badges or markings. He had no need to touch it to feel the coarse wool in his fingers and he wrinkled his nose at the memory of damp, rotting cloth. He wondered if it would be alive with lice before picking it up anyway, turning it over then rifling the pockets for the cigarettes, tobacco and lighter. He passed them to William before sitting next to the ex–soldier, who didn't shrink from Edward's face, close as it was. Edward started to speak but could offer only platitudes and knew their inherent condescension would be insulting, not comforting. They sat in silence for a few seconds, William standing beside them, glancing back towards the tobacconist.

'Best take those back to the shop,' Edward said to William, indicating to the stolen goods, adding, 'Oh, and get me a pack of Players would you?'

'They're mine.' The disabled man reached for the cigarettes now held by William.

'No.' Edward gave him some coins and stood to leave.

'Four shillings? That lighter's silver.' The man held Edward's arm.

'Go,' Edward said.

'It's not enough.'

'It never could be.' Edward tugged his arm free and

left the disabled ex–soldier sitting on the bench to walk along the promenade, towards the harbour, his head tipped down.

Edward was standing on his own by a newspaper kiosk, reading *The Times*, when William returned. Without looking up he told William, 'Someone called George Simpson was fined a pound at Brentford yesterday. He bit off a dog's tail.'

'Really?'

'I think so, they wouldn't make up something like that. Do you think it was our Corporal Simpson?'

'No. He copped it at Cambrai in eighteen.'

'Oh. Sounds like the sort of thing he'd do. He wasn't a dog lover, as I recall.'

'Nor cats. Remember that episode with the flare and the moggy? Simpson was a nasty bastard,' said William. 'Anyway, I left the tobacconist's stuff on the counter. He wasn't grateful. Not even when I bought these.' He passed a pack of Players Navy Cut to Edward. 'The constable wasn't there but he will be soon and, let's face it, you won't be hard to describe. I need a drink.'

'No rum, it's too early for our ration,' said Edward, transferring the cigarettes into his own case.

'Your ration maybe, not mine.'

Just a short walk further along Marine Drive it became The Parade, leading up to the harbour pier. There was another clock on a small square building, The Droit House, at the beginning of the pier. Edward checked his watch again before they turned right, away from the seafront and back into the side streets. They entered the first tea shop they found, two minutes from the seafront and a ten minute walk from the guest house where they'd rented rooms. William led Edward through the door and they took a second to choose a table. Edward was most comfortable with his back to the window and though he would have preferred both a corner table and stronger sun shining in behind, he found a place that would do. William sat on Edward's left, as usual, so the damaged hearing in William's left ear wouldn't be an irritation. A waitress handed them menus, returning William's smile. Edward looked away and, reluctantly, removed his hat, holding it in his lap while he read the menu. There was a small smudge on the right lens of his spectacles but though annoying he would not take them off to wipe clean. The tea shop was half full, good for this time of day, with a mix of ages, families, couples and class – holidays were almost a leveller, however brief. The children were loud and impatient to return to the beach. Cigarette smoke hung in the air and settled on the watercolours on the walls. They were mostly sea and beach scenes and well painted, the artist had an eye for composition and the drama of a sunset or sunrise. Edward thought them pretty enough for a parlour, perhaps even a gallery, and they brightened the otherwise dull grey of the walls, except for one in oils. It held a different tone. A dark night was broken by storm clouds, flashing lightning within, illuminating a grey warship as it tipped unnaturally down into thrashing waves. The bow was already engulfed and the dark waters would inevitably claim the vessel. The blackness in the foreground half–cloaked hints of faces, screaming with shock and fear and the white foam on the waves shrouded arms reaching up in desperation. The ship and the crew were doomed; there would be no rescue or salvation and death clawed at them from the depths. The scene was disconcerting, both for its content and being so out of place against the other pictures, and it emanated a despair and hopelessness that unsettled Edward. He looked away, disturbed, but the brighter paintings, some already losing their colour, were not diversion enough.

The waitress returned to the table and he turned in

his seat but she looked twice, not sure of Edward's face, partially silhouetted against the window. She might have looked again if William hadn't captured her attention with the order. 'Coffee for me please and tea for my colleague.'

'The coffee's good sir. We grind it ourselves nowadays, it's from Taylors, we have the roasted beans sent down from Yorkshire.' The waitress spoke to Edward who shook his head slightly and spoke with his slight slur,

'No thank you.'

'Or perhaps an ice cream if you're warm? We've just had a new machine installed. Three different flavours.'

'No, thank you.'

'Of course sir,' she said, taking a step back on catching proper sight of Edward's face.

William thanked her and, as if by way of explanation, added, 'He's not drunk coffee since nineteen seventeen.'

She nodded, pretending that made sense and made her way between the tables to the back of the shop and out to the kitchen. She wore a white blouse with a high neckline and a black skirt that reached her ankle. The waist band was unnaturally high. The skirt was no longer the fashion and fitted badly over her pregnancy. William turned to Edward. 'Pretty thing. Shame she's carrying.'

'We've not been here a day yet. Are you lonely already? And isn't she a little older than your usual ... friends?' Edward asked in his slow drawl.

'I wouldn't say I'm lonely, but I've not ... known ... a woman since ... since, the last Hackney Empire show, two months ago or more. And, to be honest, she wasn't as enthusiastic as she might've been.'

'Well choose the next one carefully. We're here for a while and I don't want any more vengeful husbands waiting backstage, never mind how enthusiastic the wife might be.'

'I'll pick careful.'

'Speaking of picking, I also don't want any

accusations of wallets or purses going … missing.'

'I know. It was me got this season sorted in the first place, wasn't it? You could have had Bournemouth, but you chose 'ere, with less money.'

Edward shrugged.

'Have a fag,' said William. He held a cigarette towards Edward.

'No thanks,' Edward said, tapping one of his own Players against the silver case from which he'd taken it.

'Until you run out of them,' William said, laughing and lighting the Woodbine Edward had refused.

'You were meant to return that.' Edward reached over to take the silver cased lighter William was using.

'It's nice ain't it? Swiss, I believe, Thorens.'

'The tobacconist will miss it.'

'The tobacconist does all right. They usually do.' William ignored Edward's look of disapproval. They sat in silence for a minute, Edward toying with the lighter, then saying,

'Didn't young Kayst's parents run a tobacconist?'

'In Herne Bay. A kiosk on the pier. You know,' said William.

'I thought so, but wasn't sure.'

Edward returned the lighter to William and lit his own cigarette from his old trench lighter, sucking noisily. The first drag was always loud while he worked out where to place the fag – the numbness in some parts of his face was unrelenting and still surprising. A small boy on the next table heard the suck and turned, as did his mother. She turned back quickly but the boy just looked. He didn't stare or betray any fear, he just looked, and Edward could see the questions playing in the boy's mind. Edward didn't mind and smiled. Before leaving Wandsworth General he had practised this smile in the mirror a hundred times, and though it wasn't natural at least wasn't the frightening grimace it had started out. The boy returned the smile and went back to his bun. William had seen and discreetly pulled a hip flask from his inside pocket. He took a swig and offered it to Edward, who shook his head. William raised the hip flask an inch or two saying, 'To Major Gillies.' He took another sip and held it out to Edward who shook his head again. William persisted, 'Come on Lieutenant. To Major Gillies.'

'I suppose.' Edward nodded and took the hip flask, adding, 'and to Derwent Wood,' before sipping the Old Orkney scotch.

The waitress brought their drinks. William sipped his coffee and made noises of appreciation while Edward waited for his tea to brew.

The other customers continued drinking, eating and talking and, as far as he could tell, and was able to tell himself, no one saw him, though the urge to put on his homburg was strong.

They drank slowly, their guest house rooms were not so enticing, and there was little for them to do until their lunch appointment at The Winter Gardens, early that afternoon. Although William had said the deal was done, Edward knew such things were not necessarily decided by his musical skills alone.

Between careful sips of tea Edward glanced at *The Times* he'd brought in and William made notes in the small book he carried everywhere. Edward had given up asking after the content.

The waitress came over to ask if their drinks were acceptable but was distracted by the entry of an old man and younger woman. The waitress directed them to the empty table next to Edward. The new customers sat, the woman placing a small suitcase by her legs and resting a green cloche hat on the table. Edward saw the old man's clerical collar. He wore a dark grey three piece suit with fraying cuffs but his collar was starched and clean and the polish on his shoes almost hid the scuffs. The waitress's welcome was formal but still warm and genuine. 'Reverend Coughston and Evelyn. It is so lovely to see you. You look so well.'

'And you Alice. How are you feeling? May I?' the younger woman, Evelyn, asked, placing a hand gently on the bump of Alice's pregnancy. Alice flushed slightly.

'What would you like?' Alice indicated to the menu. 'I'll be back in a minute, with Alastair.'

Edward watched the old man over his newspaper and wondered what type of reverend he was – had he lived the word or merely read it? Had he been one to carry news of broken and dead men to their loved ones in the counties, or one to hold pieces of the shattered man while he died in the mud? The distinction was unfairly black or white, Edward knew, and the reverend in front of him was much too old to have been in France, but he still found it hard to let go the difference.

While Edward watched, Alice brought a man to the reverend's table.

'Peter, so good to see you. How are you both?' said the man. They shook hands.

'We're well thank you, Alastair,' said the reverend, 'and so pleased to see you. It has been … too long. Letters are just not the same. You look well. Is business good? Is Alice well?'

Alastair looked around his tea shop, Edward followed suit. Alastair said, 'Not a busy summer, yet, but there is time. We get by … and of course, now Alice is expecting, she will soon need more rest.'

Edward thought the man's demeanour melancholy and so might have the older man as he said,

'More rest and, dare I say it, peace. Though of course that is hard to come by in these times. In any event, we are glad to help. Still painting, I'm glad to see. Do they sell?' Reverend Coughston pointed to the watercolours on the walls. 'They are … mostly … lighter than your work of old, much lighter.'

Alastair hesitated, 'A few sell. It helps. And your business?'

'There's always another soul to save.'

'How is the mission?'

'There's not much to be done at the moment, I'm just visiting for a couple of days to start organising accommodation and suchlike. There are a few families down, helping out with organising and some cleaning and fixing up the huts but the hop pickers won't be here for a few weeks yet. I'll go there this afternoon to see how preparations are coming along …'

'… and I'll stay on here,' said the young woman, Evelyn. There was a cheerful openness to her voice Edward enjoyed; he kept half an ear on her conversation while reading his newspaper.

By eleven forty Edward and William had made their drinks last long enough and the tea shop trade was turning to lunch. William put away his notebook and pencil and called for the bill while Edward was pleased to put on his hat and make his way to the door. He edged past the table where his elbow brushed the reverend's head. Edward's apology was instinctive and the older man reacted with a deep but quiet voice.

'No need sir. I should be paying more attention. I hope you can be well.'

The phrasing was unusual but Edward thought little of that, people were often tongue–tied or worse when they saw him. Edward could see the reverend's eyes were rheumy and they did not flinch. Like the little boy earlier, he held Edward's gaze until Edward nodded and moved on, suddenly conscious his left side was towards the younger woman by the reverend's side, though he didn't think she had looked up as he passed.

Edward left the tea shop while William went with Alice, the waitress, to settle the bill.

William joined Edward outside, asking, 'What were you talking to the vicar about?'

'Vicar?'

'The old man with the dog collar.'

'Oh, nothing. I just bumped him and apologised.'

'Reckon that's his wife with him? She looks far too young, don't you think? And pretty. Lovely eyes. I wonder if she can sing.'

'They usually can.'

'Who?'

'Wives and daughters of vicars. In my experience they sing well. Odd eh?'

'A gift from God perhaps.' There was sarcasm in William's tone.

'Perhaps.' Edward looked back through the tea shop window.

'Anyway, let's not keep The Winter Gardens waiting and I'm hungry.'

They made their way back to the seafront and turned north–eastwards. The sky was still grey, though the rain had not come. The tide was high and the brown waves uninviting. Further to the west there remained enough sand for beach lovers to enjoy but at this end of town it was all but lost to the sea and the crowds had moved up to the promenade. Edward and William meandered their way towards The Winter Gardens and they passed first the entrance to the harbour pier and then the jetty reaching out into the North Sea. The Winter Gardens was a ten minute stroll up Fort Hill, where the crowds lessened. To their right, rising above the town was Holy Trinity church tower, dominating the inland horizon.

They found the entrance to The Winter Gardens in an amphitheatre cut into the clifftop. Just inside was the ticket booth but at this time of day there were no queues and William smiled at the young woman behind the glass.

'Good morning. We've a meeting with Mr Taylor, the Bookings Manager.'

The young woman gave a practised smile and pointed to a door leading to a corridor on the other side of the entrance hall, saying, 'Third door along,' before turning back to last month's copy of *Vogue*.

William opened the door for Edward to go through, 'Pretty young thing,' and nodded back towards the ticket office.

'Don't tell me, she has lovely eyes.'

'So you noticed too. I wonder if she can sing.'

'You always do.'

'Edward, what are you suggesting?' William said, leading the way and knocking on the third door. A big voice called them in to a bright office with a desk facing the door. Behind the desk sat a large man, older than Edward and William, and a younger man sat doorside of the desk, but stood to leave as they entered.

'Mr. Taylor?' William asked.

'Yes. Mr. Thompson?' The large man asked after looking at his pocket watch.

'No. I'm William Burrslow. This is Mr. Thompson. Edward Thompson.' William stepped to one side, allowing Edward to enter. Edward hated the way William introduced him with a flourish, as if he should be known.

'Of course,' said Mr. Taylor as Edward removed his hat and his face was more visible, though Mr. Taylor did not flinch and introduced the other man. 'And this is Mr. Pine, down from London today to see if our auditorium is a good place to test some of his equipment. And I'm sure it is. He is experimenting with a new way of recording sound to make great performances available to all. After all, we book the finest acts in Europe and the acoustics are superb.'

Mr. Taylor's short speech was for the benefit of Mr. Pine, who appeared embarrassed and smiled awkwardly, nodding as he left, explaining he would be with his colleague in the main auditorium. The door closed behind Mr. Pine and Mr. Taylor rose from his chair, and kept rising. He was enormous, in height and girth, and used the desk to lever himself to stand before walking around it to shake his visitors' hands, 'Gentlemen. Please, be seated.'

He was the size of both Edward and William who sat while the big man perched on the edge of the table and looked down at them. The office shelves were packed with folders and against one wall stood a drinks cabinet. A bottle of Hennessy Cognac took pride of place next to a Johnnie Walker Black Label. The glasses alongside were heavy and fine cut. Dominating the room was the desk, the top of which was all but hidden under neat piles of paper, each weighted with a large pebble.

Mr. Taylor lit a cigarette without offering to his visitors. 'I'm not convinced myself. About the recordings, that is. I myself have a Columbia gramophone and even though there are many popular recordings it seems to me a poor substitute for our auditorium. It's a lot of trouble to get something even vaguely similar to the real performance. Still, we shall see what Mr. Pine can do. And then there's this new radio fad. Together they might put you fellows out of a job.'

'And you then,' said William.

'No. Holidaymakers will always need to be entertained, but we may need to find more acts an audience wants to see, not just hear. Talking of which ...' the big man nodded towards Edward, 'welcome to The Winter Gardens,' and went on to outline the days and times in the contract to which Edward was committed to perform.

'I thought we could finalise negotiations over lunch,' said William, lighting one of his own cigarettes.

'I'm afraid I can't. I have another meeting and we agreed terms in our letters.'

'Mostly, but there are one or two details. Mr. Thompson studied at the Royal College of Music,' William said, though Edward thought it unhelpful.

'I know, I read his credentials. It's a shame he didn't

finish his studies there.'

'Well he was rather busy … in France.'

'Indeed. Oh, and Mr. Thompson will be expected to play a few more popular pieces. We have the sheet music sent down from London.'

William started to speak but Edward put a hand on his arm and spoke directly to Mr. Taylor, 'Of course,' he lisped the 's' as he sometimes did when trying to speak a little more quickly, 'I'm happy to play as contracted but had hoped for two full evening performances during the week, when the house was full.'

Mr. Taylor looked at William and then back to Edward.

'Let's see how it goes. Perhaps we'll try a Wednesday night and see how it is received. Meantime, you can start the other agreed performances the day after tomorrow, Sunday. Now, if you'll excuse me.' He stood from the desk and walked past William and Edward to open the door. William rose but Edward remained seated.

'I really am busy,' said Mr. Taylor but Edward said nothing. William sighed and sat back down.

'Really, very busy,' repeated the big man.

There was an awkward silence until Edward said, 'Shall we say next Wednesday? I could play an extended intermission.'

Mr. Taylor came back from the doorway. 'Hmmm, but none of those newer classical pieces. We had someone in last year, played Rachmaninoff. Cleared the place. I prefer the lighter classics. Oh, and not too many German pieces. It's too soon.'

'No Rachmaninoff, not overly Teutonic, some lighter classical and whatever latest popular music you have had sent down, if you can provide a singer,' said Edward.

'We do have a choir once or twice a month. At least one of them must be able to sing.'

'Agreed,' said William, 'and we can talk about the

fee for the extra performance in a week or two, when you can see what a success it's been.'

'And I'd like to come in tomorrow morning to get used to the piano, if that's all right. Just for an hour.'

'I suppose. But I do need to go now.' Mr. Taylor ushered them to the door and walked them to the foyer.

'Well at least he didn't mention Major Gillies' or Derwent Wood's handiwork,' said Edward as Mr. Taylor left them and walked past the ticket booth and through another doorway.

'A good sign. It's going to be a successful season. We need your name bigger on these.' William tapped one of the posters on easels in the foyer, listing the acts and performance details over the coming weeks. He left Edward reading the posters to see if he recognised any of the other performers and went to the young woman at the ticket office.

'Hello miss, thanks for your help earlier. We found Mr. Taylor and we're all set for the season. Edward, Edward Thompson, will be playing. He starts on Sunday evening.' William spoke through the hole in the glass then nodded back towards Edward who heard his name but didn't look away from the poster. William turned his smile back to the woman; a winning, unthreatening smile that started with his dark eyes. He had shaved early that morning, before the journey down, and already the shadow of a beard was forming, darkening his skin. His hair was black, thick, slicked back with no parting and in need of a cut but not unruly. 'My name is William and you are …?'

'Catherine.'

'Lovely name. Are you working Sunday?'

Catherine nodded.

'We'll see you then.' William took a step away before asking, 'Oh, by the way. Do you sing?'

'A little.'

'I thought so. There's a nice rich tone to your voice. See you Sunday.'

Evelyn, Margate,
Friday 30th July 1920

'And Catherine here will look after her,' said the man whose name Evelyn didn't know.

Catherine caught Evelyn's eye, smiled and nodded, as if to confirm the man's assertion. Alice smiled at the man. Evelyn looked to her father, Reverend Coughston, who smiled at her. There was a lot of smiling going on and Evelyn felt she was a child again.

The small group stood in The Winter Gardens foyer.

'Thank you,' said Alice to Catherine. 'We do appreciate your help.'

'Indeed, thank you Catherine,' added Reverend Coughston.

'So all is agreed. Evelyn will work five evenings a week,' said Reverend Coughston.

'To start with,' said the man, 'beginning Monday. Regardless of the bank holiday, we will be open. Now, if you'll excuse us.' He drew Catherine's attention to the clock – half past three.

'See you Monday evening, Evelyn,' said Catherine, returning to the ticket booth. Evelyn watched her go. She guessed Catherine was close in age to herself but there was a hint of mischief in her smile and a confidence in her manner Evelyn envied. Catherine's uniform was functional but fitted well and the long necklace she wore lifted its tone while Evelyn was aware her summer dress had fallen out of fashion. Though she had shortened it a couple of inches the deep pointed collars on the v–neck were conspicuous.

'Good luck with the baby,' said the man whose name Evelyn didn't know. She thought it overly familiar when he touched Alice's bump.

They took the stairs back up to the promenade, Alice leading the way, explaining, 'It's all right Evelyn. That was my half–brother on my late mother's side.'

'Oh,' Evelyn was surprised her disapproval had shown, 'I didn't know. Father didn't say.'

'I'm sure I did,' said Reverend Coughston.

'No matter, and I should have mentioned it,' said Alice.

They walked back down Fort Hill to the entrance to both the jetty and harbour pier where Reverend Coughston checked his pocket watch. 'I need to go straight to the station. There is a train back to Herne Bay in twenty minutes and from there I still need to take a bus to the mission. Please say goodbye to Alastair for me and I'll return soon, for a proper visit.'

'Then you should take the tram to the station,' suggested Alice as one approached.

Reverend Coughston shook Alice's hand. 'I'm sure I'll be back soon.'

'Tell the ladies at the mission I'll visit before summer is over,' said Evelyn, with genuine sadness.

'Of course.' He pecked Evelyn on the cheek and met the tram at its stop. Alice and Evelyn waved as it pulled away.

'Thank you for staying,' said Alice, 'Alastair and I do appreciate it and I know you'll miss the mission. But your father thinks it's for the best, I'm sure.'

Evelyn took Alice's arm. 'Of course, I'm glad to be here. And the mission won't be busy for another month anyway. Come, let's get back and make sure Alastair is managing. And while there will always be another mission, you may not be with child again this time next year.'

Calling it a 'Mission' had always seemed to Evelyn an overstatement but her father, Reverend Coughston, insisted. Evelyn understood he used the term in an aspirational way, not out of arrogance, and she was proud of his ambition but when explaining its purpose found it better to emphasise the practical rather than spiritual elements. The mission was near Calcott, four miles south of Herne Bay, just off the Canterbury Road, and served four hop farms. At the moment the few families there were readying the camps for September. Most of the pickers came down to the fields of Kent from the poorer parts of London and settled in the countryside for a few weeks for their working holiday; it didn't pay much but travel and accommodation was arranged and the air was clear. The families would travel down by train or coach and settle into ramshackle huts, making them as homely as the dark, small terraces and tenements from which they came, often with their own furniture which they'd brought along. The men would work long hours, the women even longer, and the children could play from dawn to dusk unless being old enough to work, which was not at all the same as being of an age to stop play.

'You must be very proud of your father's work there,' said Alice as they walked back along the promenade to the tea shop.

'Oh yes. This is the fifth year and it's challenging, but gets easier. We're better organised every year and, in many ways, once there, it's easier than the parish work back at Spitalfields.'

'Easier?'

'We share everything with the families and get close to them. And the marquee for the services is less … intimidating … than even our modest church in town. And this year we've arranged with the farmer to use one of the huts as a clinic in the day and a social club in the evenings.'

'That sounds very ... modern,' said Alice. 'Your idea?'

'Some of the other missions already do it, but I suppose I can take a little credit for persuading Father. If the social club works well then the men will be less inclined to go to the pub in the village in the evening. The wives will like that ... mostly. And we were able to find two volunteers from the student doctors at the Royal London Hospital to come and work in the clinic. They'll be here when the picking starts, in a few weeks. The women will be suspicious but I'm sure the young doctors will win them over, though I'm not so sure about the men. But they won't have to pay to see the doctor and we hope to provide some medicine free and some cheap. They're good people and though the work is hard, it is a holiday of sorts. Not so different from these people.' There was enthusiasm in Evelyn's voice and she indicated to the busy promenade and beach.

'It sounds like you'll miss them. Are you sure you don't mind staying on with me and Alastair?'

'Not at all, and besides, after Father has made sure arrangements are in hand he'll be going back to London until September. I'd rather stay here. I'm happy to help.' Evelyn gestured to Alice's bump and, she hoped, hid her disappointment. In some ways the September weeks at the mission were the best of the year for her. Over the years she had become friends with many of the pickers, though few were members of the congregation back in Spitalfields, and helping in the fields gave her an appetite she never had at home. She would put on a few pounds and the fresh air and sun gave her pale skin a touch of colour, though that was not quite the fashion. Looking after the younger children was a joy though they were a reminder of her own childlessness; this year she had already passed twenty–six. Most of the men picking hops were older and married and the few single ones tended to be much younger. It was just two years since the war. During the previous year's hop harvest one of the older men – Mr. Tewson, a widower – had asked Evelyn's father if he might walk out with her. The Reverend Coughston had said Evelyn was a grown woman who could make her own choice, so Mr. Tewson built up the courage to ask Evelyn and she had said yes. It took just two occasions for her to realise she had agreed out of sympathy and spent the rest of the harvest avoiding poor Mr. Tewson, so perhaps it was just as well she wouldn't be at the mission this year.

'I'm sorry we can't afford to pay you,' said Alice.

'Don't worry. I earn nothing at the mission anyway and, besides, the evenings on the cloakroom desk at The Winter Gardens will bring in a few shillings. Thank you for speaking to your half–brother on my behalf. Actually, I think Father's pleased in some ways. At the mission I'm another mouth to feed, whereas here it's a privilege to help an old family friend.'

'A very old family friend,' said Alice.

'Oh, I didn't mean to imply you were … you know. I just meant, Father and Alastair have known each other so long … haven't they?'

'Of course. Since Cambridge. It's all right, I know people think I'm too old to have another child and, of course, Alastair is older still. And since we … lost Curtis … I don't know if it's the right thing.'

'I understand.' Evelyn patted her arm. She wasn't sure how old Alice was, perhaps late thirties, and if Alastair was at Cambridge with her father then he was late fifties, perhaps sixty. But perhaps the new baby was some recompense for the loss of their son, Curtis. 'God has his ways,' said Evelyn.

'Do you think so? Does your father think so?' Alice stopped walking and turned to face Evelyn. 'Since … losing Curtis … Alastair has avoided the church. I don't think he has told your father this in his letters but … it's hard for him, for us.'

'I'm sure Father would understand and perhaps the

baby is God's way of helping.'

'Perhaps.' Alice nodded unconvincingly. 'It's difficult. Did you know I lost a baby two years ago? I thought it might be because it was too soon after Curtis went down with his ship. I fell pregnant the following summer but lost the baby in the autumn. Alastair thinks it was because of the Spanish Flu but I don't see how. I didn't fall ill. I fear it was just too soon after Curtis died. Was God punishing us? And now I'm pregnant again. I don't know if it's right …' Her voice tailed away and Evelyn wished her father was there. What would he have said?

'We can't know God's purpose for us but if our hearts are true he will help us find a way,' Evelyn offered, though it would have been much better from her father. Alice looked down and stroked the heavy bump under her coat.

At the tea shop Alastair was barely coping and desperate for Alice and Evelyn's return. The sun had not found its way through the clouds, leading more holidaymakers to seek refreshment indoors, and nearly all tables were taken. Alastair was rushing between them and the kitchen, sweating in the heavy suit he wore. He looked up as he heard the door open. Evelyn sensed his relief as he interrupted the order he was taking to welcome them back. Evelyn took the small notebook and pencil Alastair had been using and finished taking the order while Alastair ushered Alice towards the kitchen.

The rest of the afternoon was as busy and it wasn't until past six o'clock, when the last customer had gone, they could clean and tidy the shop and kitchen and Alastair could properly welcome Evelyn. He gave a tour of the living accommodation and tea shop, starting in the kitchen with its three doors at the back. One led to the yard outside, one to a small room with a basin and tin bath standing upright in the corner, and the other to the stairs which served the upper floors. He showed Evelyn to her room on the first floor. Above her would be the nursery but Alice refused to have it decorated until the baby was born. Alice and Alastair lived on the topmost two floors. The baby was due in early October and it was assumed Alastair would be able to cope over the winter while Alice nursed and the tea shop was closed. Alastair gave Evelyn a key to the kitchen door from the yard and apologised that the nearest bathroom for washing was back on the ground floor and the nearest toilet was outside but Evelyn didn't mind. It was no different from her home in Spitalfields and more modern than the facilities at the mission.

Evelyn's room was sparsely decorated and dark. Its window was at the front of the building, above the entrance to the tea shop but the road was narrow, in shadows during the day and poorly lit at night. Alice made supper for the three of them after which Evelyn was grateful for her bed. She read for a while by the dim light of the single gas lamp but not even *Jane Eyre* could hold her attention when she was this tired and she soon slept.

The Blue Bench

Edward, Margate, Sunday 1st August 1920

'Look at this. The nineteen sixteen Christmas edition.' Edward had been hunting through the magazine rack in the guest house drawing room. There were several issues of *Tit–Bits* which he passed over, initially choosing an issue of *Nash's And Pall Mall Magazine*, but changing his mind on seeing the magazine underneath – *Blighty*, Christmas 1916 issue. 'Where were we?' He held it up to show William.

'Hadn't we just finished up at Ancre? Were we resting behind lines?'

'I think so. That was the last Christmas we were over there.'

'Your last Christmas. I had one other.' William reminded him.

'I'd have swapped, given the … circumstances.' Edward lisped the last word and flicked through the magazine. 'I remember this one. Didn't one of the men receive a couple of copies from his brother up at HQ, together with some French postcards?'

'That's so, though the ladies in the postcards didn't look particularly French, seeings 'ow they had no clothes on.'

'Still, brightened Christmas that year.'

'Though you wouldn't let the younger lads share round the postcards, as I recall. You made me confiscate them. Didn't young Kayst in particular have a right moan?'

'He did. You wanted to put him on a charge, insubordination or some such rubbish. I should have let all the lads see them. What happened to those postcards?'

'I've still got them,' said William.

'Those postcards were probably the closest young Kayst ever came to a fuck, before ...' Edward's voice tailed away.

'Poor Kayst,' said William.

'And I remember we had to explain a lot of the jokes in the magazine to him. Not the brightest lad, but a good heart.'

'I suppose.' William acknowledged. Edward flicked further through the magazine without paying attention and, after a minute, asked,

'Do you ever wonder if perhaps Kayst made it out?'

William shook his head. 'What? No, of course not. Don't be daft. He didn't. We saw.'

'Did we? See him? I don't think I did. One second he was there, then I looked away, to you, then looked back and he was gone. In a second ... less.'

'I saw.'

'Did you? You were looking at me, waving and shouting. Then I turned back and he was ... just gone, not there.'

'Does it matter?'

'No. But sometimes, I wonder, it might be easier, mightn't it? If I'd seen him ... go ... knew for sure ...'

'What, you mean maybe he somehow survived, hid, escaped and is living the life of Riley somewhere?'

'No, but, I didn't actually see him ... go. And sometimes I just ... I don't know.' Edward looked away, turned a few pages of the magazine then tossed it over to William, saying, 'I'm bored.'

'It's a beautiful day, we should go and explore Margate.' William stubbed out his cigarette and stood as if that might persuade Edward. The drawing room overlooked the back of the house where a gardener weeded the flower beds. The garden was partly in the shade of the house itself but the sun bathed the bottom half where a patch had been left to untended grass and wild flowers.

'We explored yesterday. And, while Margate is a nice town, I'm still bored.'

'You don't mean bored. You're missing your practise.' William sat back down.

That was nearer the truth and Edward nodded acknowledgement. 'All right. It is a beautiful day. We don't need to be at the auditorium until four this afternoon. What shall we do?'

'Five this afternoon will be plenty early enough.'

'I know, but I want to be there at four …'

'… in case the piano is free.'

'And I want to know if Mr. Taylor has resolved that problem. I told him there's something not right about the A six key, but I can't tell if it's a tuning issue or something wrong with the mechanism.'

'I'm sure he'll sort it.'

'And I do need the practise.'

'No, you don't.' William lit another cigarette as the maid entered. He caught her eye before she could begin plumping cushions on the settee in the window bay. 'Now, Georgette, I expect you know Margate. What should we do today? How can we entertain my friend on this fine Sunday morning?'

They had first met the maid on the Friday, when they arrived, then on the Saturday and Sunday mornings, when serving breakfast. Knowing they would be there for a while William had made introductions but Edward guessed she was not yet accustomed to his face as she looked away to answer. 'There is a new …' she hesitated over the unfamiliar words, '… scenic railway … at Dreamland. The ride opened a few weeks past. They say it is the biggest outside America. Maybe two kilometre long. I hear it's very … exciting.' Georgette's English was good and the French accent charming.

'There you are Edward. Scenic railway, Dreamland. Two kilometres, a proper mile, at least. Though I believe the ride would be more exciting with a French lass alongside.' He turned to Georgette. 'Your English is excellent. You've been here long?'

Georgette smiled. 'Oui, a long time. Or Monsieur might like the shell grotto. It is hundreds of years old, they say.'

'Edward, a shell grotto. We should see for ourselves. Or perhaps Georgette could show us.'

'Perhaps another day Monsieur.' She was still smiling and Edward thought the smile promised mischief. And there was no doubting the allure in her accent.

'Could we have a cup of tea, here in the drawing room?' Edward asked Georgette, looking down as he spoke.

'I am sorry Monsieur. There is no … refreshing … after breakfast and before lunchtime.'

'See Edward, no reason to sit here.' William stood again and this time Edward joined him.

Though the sun was warmer today the seafront was less crowded. There were few cars on Marine Drive and just a couple of trams and horse drawn carts. They crossed the road to the front, William pointing out to Edward the pile of manure in the gutter he should avoid. They found a bench overlooking the beach and sat.

'I wonder where the crowds are,' said William.

'Sunday services? It's about that time,' offered Edward.

'Who would go to church when they're on holiday?'

'Who would leave their faith at home?'

'Who could bother to bring it with them?'

'That doesn't make sense.'

'And faith does?'

Edward shrugged, 'It wouldn't be faith if it did.'

William returned the shrug and leafed through the copy of *Blighty* he'd brought along, with an occasional smile or short, knowing laugh.

'Something funny?' asked Edward.

'Not especially. They rarely were.'

'Then why the laughs?'

'They may not have been amusing, but they were all we had and helped us make each other laugh. That I remember.'

'True, I suppose. Though you never liked the lads.'

'And you did?' William closed the magazine and laid it in his lap. He took his notebook and pencil from a pocket and made a note of something while waiting for Edward to answer.

'I didn't know them. Who knew how long they would be there? It didn't do to like them too much, considering what we asked of them. We couldn't ask if we counted them friends.'

'So, like me, you didn't really like them.'

'Maybe not, but I suppose I loved them for what they did.'

'And they almost loved you, when you were their Lucky Lieutenant.' William passed the magazine to Edward as a family with four young children strolled closer.

'I wonder where young Kayst's parents' tobacconist is?' said Edward, opening the magazine and bowing his head to read but he was on the wrong side of the bench. One of the children, a teenage girl, was close enough to see him and shrank back to her mother. She saw Edward's face and called her other children closer, trying to subtly shepherd them past the back of the bench.

'Some of these benches should be painted blue,' said William. Edward nodded and kept his head lowered.

'Anyway, never mind that.' William lit a cigarette. 'For tonight's first appearance I thought you should wear dress uniform and when you're due on I'll walk you over from stage left, holding your arm. The women will swoon for the hero and the men will admire you, before you've even played a note.'

'No. You talked me into that at Brighton but not again. It's not as if I still have a commission and I don't need help walking. It's a fraud.'

'It went down well at Theatre Royal and those Brighton audiences are quite sophisticated.'

'No, they were just too polite to criticise.'

'All right, but at least enter from stage left. Show them you're a hero.'

'No.'

'I've been asking around and they say the crowds down here are tough. Having them on side early doors would be no bad thing.'

'You say that everywhere I play. It's not having them on side, it's pity. Not the same thing at all.'

'Well I still say it worked at Brighton.'

'No.'

'It's worth a try, isn't it? Even if only for first night.'

Edward ignored the comment by asking, 'Have you returned that lighter yet?'

'First job on the list today. Is it on the way to the shell grotto?'

'I've no idea. Perhaps we should save the grotto for another day.'

Edward looked at his wristwatch. William shrugged, stood and walked eastwards down the promenade. Edward closed the magazine and watched the boats leaving the small harbour though the tide was not yet at its highest. He thought he saw the young boy from the tea shop that had smiled at him and wanted to buy him an ice cream but couldn't be sure it was him and William wasn't back to ask.

The Sunday evening audience at The Winter Gardens was enthusiastic. A busy day on the seafront followed by tea had set them up for the evening's entertainment and they began filling the theatre from six o'clock. Parents had persuaded grandmothers to stay with the children in the guest houses, allowing mothers and fathers a rare night out. Edward watched from the edge of the auditorium, thinking through his choice of pieces. Though he knew this first slot was a warm—up for the entering audience he was keen to entertain and enjoyed the anticipation almost as much as the performance. William stood just behind him, making occasional notes in his pocketbook.

A few minutes past six o'clock the stage manager nodded to Edward. He walked from the side of the auditorium and up the steps to stage right without looking at the audience. There was polite applause as he sat, took some sheet music from an old leather briefcase and arranged it on the music rack. He removed his wristwatch and placed it on the top of the piano, clearly visible, before playing non—stop for half an hour. The auditorium was not laid out in the usual fashion – the stage was to one side, in the middle, and the chairs were lined across the length of the hall. Behind the audience was a row of floor to ceiling windows and doors looking out to sea. Behind the stage was a row of glass separating the back of the stage from the crescent amphitheatre, sunk into the clifftop.

Without pause Edward played extracts from Mozart, Strauss and Liszt that he thought the audience would recognise, before packing away his sheet music, taking his watch and giving a quick bow to lukewarm applause. He heard a few comments about his appearance as he left the stage, but no more than expected and he was happy enough with his playing, though Liszt's *Hungarian Rhapsody* needed a bit more energy and a quicker tempo at the finale – he made a mental note for the following evening. He went back to the dressing room he shared with the members of the Municipal Orchestra, where he removed and hung up his jacket and sipped scotch while smoking, waiting for the call to play in the interval. William left him to go and watch the orchestra from the side of the hall.

Edward's interval and closing performances passed with no drama but the highlight of the evening for him was the emptiness of the post–show auditorium and the chance to play as if the piano was his.

Evelyn, Margate, Monday 2nd August 1920

Evelyn's first shift at The Winter Gardens was on the Monday. She worked in the tea shop until five o'clock, washed, changed and was at the theatre in good time. She wore her favourite summer dress even though she would be given a uniform, it was her first night after all, and regretted not bringing her best shoes down from London. Outside The Winter Gardens the audience was already gathering and there were two young women in the ticket booth. One was Catherine who came out to greet her.

'Evelyn. I'm so glad you're starting. I think it's going to be busy. There's a new programme for tonight's show. Let's find your uniform. This way.' Catherine spoke quickly, but with a calm energy. Her uniform was spotless and not creased and her dark hair, cut to a bob but with curls, was topped by a cap. Evelyn followed her past the ticket office and into a labyrinth of corridors. They stopped outside a door signed *Staff Women* which Catherine opened, reaching for the pull cord under the bare bulb hanging from the centre of the room. There was a sharp 'clack' as the switch was forced and then a quiet buzz from the light fitting. The room was little more than a broom cupboard. There was no window and the harsh light bounced off the half–length mirror on the back of the door. Evelyn blinked, unused to electric lighting.

'The acts have their own dressing rooms, further down the corridor. This is where we change,' explained Catherine, 'though most of the girls take their uniforms home and wear them to and from work.'

On one side of the room was a small bench with hooks above, a couple with everyday clothes hanging and one with a uniform on a hanger. 'Try that. It's pot luck with size I'm afraid.' Catherine closed the door behind her, leaving room for three people at most. 'Take your time, I'll have a cigarette. It's not busy yet.' Catherine took a pack of Black Cats from the top of her stocking, explaining, 'It spoils the lines if I use the pocket,' patting the patch over her left breast. She offered a cigarette to Evelyn who shook her head. Catherine nodded to the uniform and prompted, 'Go on, try it on, it looks about your size. You're quite tall aren't you?'

'I suppose,' said Evelyn, a little sheepishly, uncomfortable at being expected to undress in front of a stranger.

'Oh, sorry,' said Catherine, sensing the tension and turning around, though it would be easy to see Evelyn in the mirror if she wished.

'Done,' said Evelyn a couple of minutes later and waited for Catherine to see before continuing, 'but it doesn't look like yours.' The light grey dress with cream pinstripes hung like a sack, pulled together by an oversize belt in the middle. It was big and shapeless.

'No, that looks fine, really. Very nice, you'll get a lot of tips appearing like that. I hear that look is all the rage in Paris this year. You're quite slim too.'

'You don't honestly think it looks all right, do you?' Evelyn said incredulously, checking again in the mirror.

'No, not really. Sorry. Though you can never tell about Paris. But in Margate … no.' Catherine started laughing and apologised again.

Evelyn looked from the mirror back to Catherine and back to the mirror. She was a similar shape to Catherine but a little taller. Neither had an hour glass figure but Catherine's uniform fitted hers and the belt didn't include a foot overhang. 'It just doesn't look much like yours.'

'Nor did mine, at first. It's all right, I'm good with a needle. I altered mine and can do yours. We'll come back here after the shift, I'll pin it and take it home. Tomorrow it will look fabulous, even with a cap.' Catherine took one from a hook and dropped it onto Evelyn's head. It squashed her hair down in front of her eyes and she joined Catherine's laugh.

'And is the cap necessary?' Evelyn's thick dark hair was her pride, though she rarely exploited it with any style other than a simple side parting and pulling it tight to a bun behind.

'I'm afraid so. The House Manager insists.'

Evelyn looked past Catherine at the mirror. 'In the war my aunt was a bus driver. They gave her a man's uniform and the cap was similar to this.'

'A driver? Good for her. I managed to get a job as a conductor. It was great fun, apart from the early starts. I learnt how to drive a bus but never with passengers and when the men returned they sacked the women.'

'Same for my aunt,' said Evelyn, still with an eye on the mirror. 'Is this the only uniform spare?'

'Sorry. But it's not that bad and we can sort it out later, we need to get back.' Catherine stubbed out her cigarette in the half full ashtray on the small table in the corner. She led the way back to the foyer and showed Evelyn the coat check desk, explaining what to do and how to accidently brush coats against the small 'tips' dish to make it jangle, without tipping out the few halfpennies lying inside.

The evening passed quickly for Evelyn, the work was much easier than the tea shop and she was being paid. After the initial rush at the ticket office Catherine came over a couple of times to make sure she was all right. The other girl on ticketing popped over when it was quiet and Evelyn felt welcomed – it was just a shame the uniform didn't fit. Half–way through the night Alice's half–brother, she now understood him to be Front of House Manager, came to see her and was officious but polite and his only criticism was for the cap being tilted too far back. Between the auditorium and the foyer there were two sets of doors and occasionally, if both opened in unison, the music and lights of the performance burst through and the audience's excitement escaped. She hoped staff were allowed to watch the concerts on their nights off. She rarely visited the concert halls near her home in Spitalfields – her father was ambivalent toward them; of course there was a time and a place for entertainment, though he believed it should supplement, not supplant, worship. But Evelyn felt sure her father would approve of the Municipal Orchestra. Shortly after eleven the orchestra stopped playing and the audience filtered out while a single piano played some popular Gilbert and Sullivan pieces. She only gave one person the wrong jacket and the man was kind and didn't mind. By half–past eleven there were no more customers at the coat check desk and the tips dish had collected perhaps three shillings. Behind Evelyn hung four unclaimed jackets and a stole. As the last of the audience drifted away Catherine closed her booth, cashed up the takings and took them through to the back. Then she returned to the foyer to collect Evelyn, telling her she should empty the tip dish, bar a couple of pennies, before leading her back to the staff changing room.

Catherine pinned Evelyn's dress to make it fit properly and turned away as Evelyn took it off and put back on her own clothes.

'I'll bring it back tomorrow, all done. You are coming back tomorrow, aren't you?' Catherine asked.

'Yes, and looking forward to it. I've never earned so much in an evening.' Evelyn showed the change from the tip dish in her hand.

'Oh,' said Catherine, 'didn't I tell you? The tips are shared between all of us. Then there's Maggie on the programme stall and Phoebe at the ice cream, so it's a six–way split.'

'Oh, no, I didn't know. Of course. That seems fair.' Evelyn held out her hand to Catherine, palm open, coins showing. Catherine went to take the money but closed her hand around Evelyn's, covering the change.

'You are sooo sweet,' she laughed. 'Of course it's yours. I was being cruel. The pay is less on the coat check than in the ticket booth, so you keep any tips. I'm sorry, I couldn't resist.' Her smile was broad and open and her dark brown eyes bright. She gave Evelyn's hand a squeeze before letting it go. 'Anyway, we should be going. The caretaker will be locking all the doors soon and this is the last place we want to be trapped. They say it's haunted.'

'Who do?'

'Those that have seen … it.' Catherine opened the door back out to the corridor, turning off the light in the changing room. Evelyn stepped through quickly behind her.

'It?'

'So some say. I've never seen … it … myself, but even so, doesn't do to tempt fate, does it?

'I suppose not,' said Evelyn.

'You don't believe me. I can tell. That's all right. I'm not sure I believe it myself, but still …' Catherine led the way, the pinned uniform draped over her arm. Back in the foyer the doors to the auditorium were open and music from a solitary piano floated through. It was a fragmented melody, not flowing but haunting and then frantic. An old man in blue overalls was standing by the open doors, listening. He saw the two women.

'Evening Cathy. New act. He's good.' He nodded towards the auditorium. 'Anyway, I'm just doing the rounds, the front doors will be locked in fifteen minutes. Who's this?' he asked.

'This is our new girl, Evelyn.'

'Good evening, Evie.'

'He always does that, shortens names. I told him I don't like Cathy, but he can't help it. It's why I call him

Willy.'

'Oi, cheeky, you know I don't like Willy. Now Bill I don't mind but not Willy.'

'All right … Willy. Anyway, Evelyn here is a reverend's daughter, so best behaviour please. She's not common like us.'

'Indeed. Evie, a pleasure to meet you and don't be led astray by young Cathy. G'night. Remember, doors locked in fifteen minutes,' said Bill, wandering off down another corridor to lock some other doors, Evelyn supposed.

The piano music from the auditorium stopped. There was brief silence then it continued, this time a slower, gentle piece. Catherine beckoned Evelyn to follow her and they went in to the auditorium. They turned left, to the back of the stalls and edged their way to the centre of the room. The chandeliers hanging in a line spanned the centre of the hall, illuminating the stalls. Footlights bathed the stage. There was a single audience member, sitting centrally in the front row. Stage right was a piano, the player facing across the stage. The pianist wore a black dinner jacket and black tie and sat upright but not stiff, playing effortlessly. Neither Catherine nor Evelyn recognised the music but it filled, and was part of, the auditorium rather than emanating from the piano. Its complexity was full of both energy and dread, and the pianist seemed to command the sound with gentle swaying, side to side, or occasionally a touch forward or back – they couldn't see his hands or face clearly. There was no discernible melody but the women stood behind the last row at the back of the stalls, listening for a few minutes until Catherine turned to go. Evelyn didn't move, feeling it would be rude to leave in mid–performance even though they were not known to be there. They waited until the last note faded and the solitary audience member applauded.

A voice from somewhere in the auditorium shouted,

'Is that it? Can I turn the bloody lights off now? I want to go home.'

'That voice is Frank, lighting man,' Catherine whispered to Evelyn.

The audience member shouted back, 'Sorry Frank. Of course. We're going now.' He stood, catching sight of Evelyn and Catherine as he did so. He smiled and waved. Catherine recognised him and waved back, still whispering to Evelyn, 'That's William. He's with the new piano player. Last night was his debut here.'

William beckoned the women down the aisle as he left his seat and went to the stage. 'Very nice Edward. As always. Major Gillies would be proud of you. Nothing like a touch of Rachmaninoff to cheer you up.'

Edward was still seated, gathering and sorting his sheet music then replacing his wristwatch.

'Good evening Catherine,' William said, standing in the aisle as the women reached him and slipping his notebook and pencil back into his pocket.

'Hello William. This is Evelyn.' Catherine made the introduction.

'Nice to meet you.' William shook hands with both women and called, 'Edward, come and say hello.'

The women looked to the stage as Edward stood, holding a thin, battered leather briefcase. Now they were closer, Evelyn could see he wore spectacles but still he was looking across the stage and it wasn't until he turned away from the piano she saw his face. The glare from the footlights reflected off the spectacles, partially hiding his upper cheeks and eyes but there was an unworldly imbalance to his features. Edward stepped forward, down the stairs to the stalls. He walked as upright as he sat and the tailored jacket gave him a taller appearance than was the case. His shoes were highly polished. The fringe of his dark hair flopped forward, over the left side of his forehead; his hair was parted on the side but not slicked back in the current fashion. Then, as he passed from the bright footlights into the houselights she saw through the spectacles. The soulless, menacing stare of his frozen, painted left eye was a shock and the dull sheen of the skin coloured plate around the eye and upper cheek a sudden abomination. The left side of Edward's face was unnatural, malign and disturbing. Edward gave his practised smile but it was not enough to counter the horror of the mask and, worse, the imagined horror of what was hidden. The mask, covering the top left half of the face, was attached to the spectacles, a novel method of keeping it secure. Evelyn felt Catherine stiffen beside her but recovered her own composure quickly and took a breath she hoped wasn't noticed. Disabled ex–soldiers were common sights these days and she shifted her gaze to Edward's right, natural eye. It was grey and she wanted to look back to the painted one to see if it matched but such curiosity was in morbid bad taste. Evelyn held out a hand as Edward approached, offering, 'You play … beautifully. Though it's a melancholy piece. I'm Evelyn.'

'Edward,' he answered, shaking her hand. 'Thank you, but it loses much without the orchestra support.'

'And Catherine you've seen before,' said William.

Catherine shook Edward's hand.

'Oi!' came the lighting man's voice from somewhere. 'I thought you were going.' The footlights went out and the stage all but disappeared.

'Sorry Frank. We're off,' shouted William, leading the way back up the aisle. 'Now, ladies,' he continued, 'I need an expert opinion on Edward's jacket. Tails or no tails?'

'It doesn't have tails,' said Catherine, her gaze scanning from Edward's face to his clothes.

'I know that,' said William, 'but the question is, should it? You both look ladies of sophistication. What do you think? What's the latest fashion? Catherine?'

'I prefer without but I'm not an expert. Evelyn, you're just down from the smoke. What's the latest up there?'

'I'm afraid I don't visit places where such clothes are required,' said Evelyn.

'That doesn't matter,' William said, 'I'm sure you have good taste. Go on, what do you think?' He pressed as they walked up the aisle.

'Well, I think without, as the tails look odd draped over the back of the stool when sitting and, if the tails aren't exactly the right length, they have the effect of making a man appear too short,' said Evelyn.

'Or too tall,' added Catherine.

'All right, without tails it is,' William said as they left the auditorium through the sliding doors at the back of the hall, leading onto the seafront. The chandeliers went dark behind them.

'And now, ladies. The night is still young. Is there a club or a bar where we can buy you a drink in return for your … what's the word … sartorial … advice?' William asked in a falsely aristocratic voice, lighting a cigarette and offering one to Catherine, who accepted, and Evelyn who refused.

'There are a couple of places open late, for members, and it's easy to become one, they're not fussy,' Catherine smiled and looked William up and down, 'so you'll be all right, but I need to go home, it's been a long day.' She drew on the cigarette.

'Perhaps a night cap at our guest house then?' William suggested, smiling.

'That's a shameful idea. No thank you.'

'Pity. Evelyn?'

'Evelyn and I are walking together,' said Catherine.

'Of course. And which way is that? Perhaps we can accompany you. We're going that way.' William pointed westwards. There were a few people still walking the seafront but they looked to be locals keen to be home from work rather than tourists eking the last moment from the day. The wind was chilly off the sea and the gas street lighting unconvincing under a dark, cloudy sky.

'That's my way too,' said Evelyn.

'And mine,' added Catherine.

There was an awkward silence. William took a hip flask from an inside jacket pocket and offered it round but there were no takers. He shrugged and sipped then asked Evelyn, 'Did we see you in the tea shop last Friday? With a Parson?'

'Yes, my father. Reverend Coughston.' She started walking and Edward fell into step beside her, on her left.

'And can you sing? Edward here wanted to know and he believes daughters of clergy have exquisite voices. And Edward is usually right in musical matters.'

Catherine butted in, 'I can. The choirmaster at my aunt's church wants me to join their choir, but I'm too busy.'

'Then one night, after the theatre is closed we should sing a few songs around Edward's piano, if we can get him to play *A Little Of What Yer Fancy*. He prefers more classical pieces but for you ladies I'm sure he'll make an exception.'

'Of course. I'm a great Marie Lloyd fan,' Edward said, deadpan.

The four had walked only a few paces when a police constable came towards them. He blocked their progress and addressed Catherine, 'Good evening Miss Burton, late to be out.'

'I'm just on my way home Constable.'

'And these gentlemen are?'

'William Burrslow,' said William.

'And I'm Edward Thompson. Good evening Constable.'

'Good evening.' The Constable studied Edward's face in the poor light. 'And how long have you been enjoying our resort?'

'Since Friday, Constable. We're here for the season,' William replied.

'And did you encounter some difficulties in the tobacconist on the front, on Friday?'

'Yes, we did Constable. But I believe all was sorted friendly like, in the end,' William answered confidently.

'Perhaps. Though the tobacconist sees things differently. He has raised a complaint.'

'Surely not against Lieutenant Thompson. He is a war hero.'

'Hmmm. We get a lot of those these days. In any event, we need to have a chat.'

The constable turned to Catherine. 'Miss Burton, if you'll excuse us, there's a few things we need to discuss. It may be a while. Perhaps you should go home, it's late, your aunt may be worried.'

Catherine and Evelyn walked on, down Fort Hill, and heard the call from William, ten or so yards behind them – 'Good night Catherine, good night Evelyn.' Catherine waved without turning; Evelyn turned to see Edward nod his goodnight, just visible in the dim street lighting.

'That's interesting,' said Catherine, 'I wonder what happened. Mind you, Constable Simms does tend to melodrama, I've found.'

'The constable knows you personally?' asked Catherine.

'More my Aunt Beatrice. She's a pillar of the local community and church and owns a guest house. Everybody in town knows her and I've lived there with her since I was nine. Seventeen years.' She sighed. 'It's about time I moved out, don't you think? It would be nice to have my own place. Anyway, you must come to tea, to meet her, she is lovely. Where are you staying?'

'I'm at Alice and Alastair's tea shop. They're old friends of my father and needed some help over the summer. Alice is having a baby.'

'Well that's good. We'll have the summer to get to know each other. And I'm sure the sea air will do wonders for your complexion. You have beautiful skin but it's a little too pale, if that's possible. Too much London air. You need some of our seaside wind and sun. Not that we've had a lot of sun this year yet. Meantime, what of Edward? I was quite shocked by his mask but you were a rock, didn't flinch. It is a little scary, isn't it? I wonder what's behind it. At first it looked quite real, but then I thought not. I wonder what it's made of. I wonder if he's really a hero.'

'My father says they all are, though they may not realise until they come home and then it's too late for them to learn how to be one.'

'I don't understand.'

'That's my father for you.'

'Anyway, the other one, William, doesn't strike me as heroic. The audacity to ask us to their guest house for a night cap.' Catherine pretended to be outraged then laughed, saying, 'He's certainly not my type. Good job they're not staying at my aunt's guest house.'

They passed the jetty and then the harbour, where boats lay on the low tide sand, their dark hulls just visible, and turned away from the front into the tea shop's side street. There was a corridor between two shops leading to the alley running behind the tea shop. 'I'll use the back door, the yard is down the alley,' explained Evelyn. 'I enjoyed this evening very much. Thank you so much for looking after me.'

'My pleasure,' said Catherine, 'and don't forget, tea at my aunt's guest house, soon, though as you're living above a tea shop perhaps that doesn't sound so enticing. Anyway, I have a feeling it's going to be a good summer. I'll get this dress sewn,' she indicated to the pinned uniform, still draped over her arm, 'and tomorrow it will look fabulous. Good night.' She squeezed Evelyn's hand and left.

Evelyn let herself in via the alley and yard at the back of the tea shop and crept to her room, anxious not to wake anyone. She undressed in darkness and tried to read in bed by the light of the desk lamp but she was neither able to concentrate nor tired enough for sleep.

The Blue Bench

Edward, Margate, Thursday 5th August 1920

The guest house was on Grosvenor Place, barely a quarter mile from Marine Drive and the seafront. Both Edward and William had rooms on the third floor, just below the attic. Much of the house had been modernised since the war. Edward's room had a small basin in the corner next to the dark wardrobe. There was a full bathroom with water closet down the hall and the owner talked of electric lighting within the year.

Edward had woken afraid, though he didn't know if from a nightmare. If so, he was grateful to be awake and not remember the dream but the fear tightening his chest would not abate, despite the sunrise pushing aside the darkness. The curtains were open, as always. He slipped from the sheets. Two sash windows overlooked Grosvenor Place and though the street was not yet in full light he could see the Wolseley below, parked outside the guesthouse front door. The sun was close to fully risen but not high enough to illuminate between the buildings and he guessed it was half five or thereabouts. He tried to slow his breathing. If he was lucky the feeling would pass. He snorted on thinking of luck – it was a long time since he'd been the Lucky Lieutenant. This wasn't an unknown way for his day to start and there would be perhaps an hour during which the pain might grow or, if it was to be a good day, decline. But, today, he felt it was probably too late as the ache began. He pressed the dry skin shielding the space where his left eye and cheek had once been and where pain now nagged.

An hour and four cigarettes later it was clear this episode was not going to subside but had not yet peaked. It was only six thirty. Soon he would be desperate for some relief before being swamped with both pain and frustrating despair and he regretted not bringing a stock of morphine from London. Though it had been four weeks since the last episode had he thought they were gone? He had been pleased with himself not to have taken any morphine for those weeks but now was angry at his poor judgement. There was a bottle of laudanum in his wash bag but its concentration of opium was low and, he knew, not nearly enough. From the attic room above he heard footsteps – Georgette, the guesthouse maid, was awake. There were muted voices which he didn't bother trying to decipher; all was irrelevant save the pain of the moment and the terror of the pain to follow.

William, Margate, Thursday 5th August 1920

The clinking of crockery disturbed the breakfast room peace – Georgette nearly dropping the plates she tidied from William's table. William smiled to show it didn't matter but several faces looked up from their food and papers.

'Could I have another pot of tea please?' William asked, turning over the *Daily Herald's* page and patting it into place with a heavy hand. Across the table from him lay the untouched crockery and cutlery at Edward's place, that day's copy of *The Times* folded on the table. William and Edward's table was in the corner of the room, furthest from the door to the hall but closest to the saloon doors to the small kitchen. Three other tables were occupied, two by couples and one by a solitary man – solitary in that he was both alone and avoided attempts at polite conversation. The couples at the other tables engaged in muted discussion with their partners but not with each other. In the quiet room William could hear all conversation, despite his left ear being more or less useless from artillery noise damage. An older lady pretended to listen while her husband read out a report from his paper on the Communist Party of Great Britain's first congress, the previous Sunday. The husband gave his views on the outrageous nature of the new party's intentions, but found it difficult to contain his outrage to almost whispered levels. William's smile was almost a sneer until the maid brought the new pot of tea.

'Thank you Georgette.' William poured himself a

fresh cup. 'By the way, have you seen Mr. Thompson this morning?'

Georgette nodded in acknowledgement of the thanks. 'Non Monsieur.'

William looked to the wall clock: 08:34. 'He's late, and I didn't hear him get up this morning.' Their rooms were side by side and the walls not substantial.

'I did hear him earlier Monsieur.'

'Georgette, no need for Monsieur, William will do. What time was that?'

Georgette thought for a short while, almost as if reluctant to share a secret, before saying in a quiet voice, 'It was very early Monsieur ... William ... perhaps half past five?'

'You heard him up and about that early?'

'Pardon?'

'You heard him moving around, in his room?'

'Ah, not moving, but I could hear ...'

'... hear?'

'Moaning ... not loud, but maybe as if in ... pain?' She finished it as a question, not wanting to be accusatory.

'And this was in the early hours.'

'Oui Monsieur.'

'William.' William touched her hand lightly, reassuringly.

'Yes, William,' she repeated.

'For how long?'

'It was in ... early hours, but stopped before I came down to ready breakfast.'

William added sugar to his tea and sipped. 'Thank you Georgette,' noticing the distaste apparent in the face of the man who had opined against the communists that William should be so familiar. After a couple more sips William left his tea and, on his way past, smiled at the couple, saying, 'Workers unite,' as he waved his newspaper.

Outside Edward's room William paused and held his breath to be able to listen at the door with his good ear.

He heard nothing. He knocked hard and, when there was no response and the door handle wouldn't turn, knocked harder. The door gave a little under his shoulder push but he was reluctant to cause damage and went back down two stairs at a time. He walked into the breakfast room shouting, 'Quick, the Bolsheviks are at the door!' and went through into the kitchen before anyone could make sense or respond. Georgette was washing up, her sleeves rolled and arms deep in steaming water.

'Georgette, did you hear Mr. Thompson go out this morning?'

'Non Monsieur,' she said hesitantly, appearing a little shocked a guest should be in the kitchen.

'Do you have a key to Mr. Thompson's room?'

'Oui.'

'Then you could let me in.'

'Monsieur? I don't think the mistress would like that.'

'Is she around? I can ask her.'

'She'll be here soon.' Georgette motioned towards the clock on the kitchen wall.

'So it's me and you then. Thompson may not be well. We should hurry.'

'Not well?'

'Poorly.'

'Poorly?'

'Perhaps.'

'But I must finish clearing the breakfast room.'

'Later, I'll help. Come.' William took Georgette's arm and grabbed a tea towel so she could dry her hands as he led her back into the room and past the disturbed breakfasters still there.

Upstairs they waited in the dim corridor outside Edward's room for perhaps half a minute, William still hoping for some noise but there was none. He took the key from Georgette to enter. Edward was not there and William was both happy not to find him unconscious, or worse, and worried he was not there at all. The room was uncharacteristically untidy; clothes on the floor and wash bag contents in the bathroom sink. William picked up the empty bottle of laudanum.

'You said you heard Mr Thompson moaning, as if in pain perhaps?'

'Oui, perhaps,' agreed Georgette, reluctant to be in the room and anxious to be away. There was noise from the room above and Georgette looked up. 'I must finish clearing the breakfast room. It's my day off and I will take my son to the beach. I promised. The mistress will be here soon.'

'Of course. You live upstairs, with your son?'

'Oui, Monsieur.'

'William.'

'Yes, William.'

'One last favour Georgette. Could you direct me to the nearest chemist shop?' He ushered her from Edward's room, locked the door and gave Georgette back the key. She didn't answer and the awkward silence was filled by the front door being opened, three floors below them.

'That's the mistress,' said Georgette.

'Let me speak to her. Come.'

Georgette looked along the corridor to the stairs leading to the floor above.

'It's all right,' William said, 'you'll be out with your son in minutes. Now, where's that chemist?'

Georgette gave him the directions as they descended to the hall and it took William but a minute to explain to the mistress how helpful Georgette had been.

Just as described by Georgette, the nearest chemist shop was close, back towards the front but not quite on it, in a side street. Its Georgian facade sat between a haberdashers and ironmongers and the sign above showed white lettering on a black background – Coperman's Druggist. It was not long past nine and a man in a grey suit was just inside the shop, sweeping glass and small pieces of wood into a dustpan held by a younger woman, bending down awkwardly in her long skirt. The glass and wood were from the shop's door – a single pane near the handle had been smashed and the door forced.

'Good morning,' William offered.

'Not so good,' the man replied, curtly.

'Trouble?' William feigned innocence.

'A little. Can I be of service?' The man passed the broom to the woman and stood aside to let William into the shop, following him to the counter.

'I hope so. My wife has suffered from a harsh headache this past week. We're down from London for a break. At home our doctor prescribes morphine sulphate. Do you have any soluble tablets?'

'Do you have a prescription?'

'No. Our doctor is in London.'

'Then I'm afraid I can't dispense.'

'Oh, but you do have a stock.'

'A little less than I did.' The pharmacist said, indicating to the cupboard behind him where a door swung loose, its lock ripped open.

'Is there a local doctor you'd recommend? For a prescription?'

'There's one or two. But there's a reluctance these days, since the war, especially if the patient is in the services.' The pharmacist stared at William who had the feeling his manner and stance was probably marking him out as military and the pharmacist was not to know he had been demobbed. 'I can offer some laudanum without prescription, though of course that's not the comfort it used to be, now it's weaker,' said the pharmacist.

'I don't suppose you mix your own?' William asked.

'With an increased concentration perhaps?' said the pharmacist, 'no, not these days.'

'That's a shame. I'll take a standard bottle. Oh, and

a bottle of syrup of figs.'

William carried the bottle of laudanum and the syrup of figs in a small paper bag from the druggist and stood next to the ironmongers next door, pretending to take note of the window display. But the wares were of no interest; he was thinking through various scenarios, guessing where Edward might have gone – he was sure Edward had broken into the pharmacy. The sensible thing would have been for Edward to take the morphine he'd stolen back to the guest house but he'd just left there. Where else might Edward go? William wandered onto the seafront and sat at a shoe polisher's stall on the pavement, watching as the beach began to fill with families. The polisher started cleaning William's shoes without speaking and, as it was early and no other customers waited, he worked slowly. The breeze off the sea cooled William but the irritation of not being able to second guess Edward's whereabouts was a frustration he took out on the polisher when a brush caught the ankle bone just above the shoe. He was insulting the old man when he saw Georgette walking from the promenade down to the beach, holding a young boy's hand. He stood, gave the shoe polisher a threepenny bit and walked after Georgette.

'It's a beautiful day isn't it?' William said to Georgette, interrupting her as she dressed the young boy in a heavy cotton all in one bathing suit. She was kneeling in the sand, fully clothed in a shapeless blue dress with low, hanging waist. Her arms were bare and the dress had a v–neck, exposing pale skin. William usually saw her in the dark maid uniform that kept her covered and the contrast with the casual dress was striking. Her dark hair was cut into a tight bob and there was an initial look of shock at being spoken to on the beach. William standing with the bright sun behind him and was starting to sweat in the growing heat. He was annoyed at the sand now covering his clean shoes but forced a smile as Georgette recognised him,

'Oui Monsieur ... Mr. William. A beautiful day. Did you find your friend?' She patted the young boy on the bottom and he ran off to paddle, oblivious to Georgette's shout to, 'Be careful!'

'No, not yet, but I know where he's been.'

'I'm sure he'll turn up,' Georgette said, sitting on a blanket she took from a bag.

'I expect so. May I?' William asked but didn't wait for an answer before sitting down – reluctantly – he didn't like sand and his jacket was uncomfortable attire for the beach. 'Handsome young man,' he said, nodding in the direction the boy had run. 'How old is he?'

'Patrick is six.'

'A good looking lad. He must take after his mother.' It was a cliché but usually worked and he smiled as Georgette blushed.

'No, not really, his father was very ... handsome.'

'You're too modest. And thank you for your help this morning. I insist on buying Patrick an ice cream.'

'I have until four this afternoon.'

'Excellent. Then I'll be back as soon as I find Edward. Speaking of which, where might a person go, in Margate, if they wanted, needed, a little peace and quiet and perhaps a place to rest and maybe even have a drink? At this time of day.'

'I don't know what you mean, Monsieur.'

'Please, once and for all, call me William. And, truth be told, I'm worried for my friend. As you've seen he ... carries a burden and often needs a little relief.'

'Relief?'

'Or ... looking after?'

Georgette edged away. 'Do you think I would know where a man might find ... relief ... just because I am a mother on her own?'

William laughed. 'No, you misunderstand.

Apologies if I've offended. I only meant somewhere a man could be left alone, away from crowds but find a drink perhaps. At this time of day.'

Georgette was placated. She looked eastwards, down the beach towards the harbour. The tide was out and a few fishing smacks rested on the mud there. 'The boats will have been in since the early hours and emptied. Some of the men will be in the backroom at The Compass. The landlord opens to his own hours, to suit the boats as they come and go, and the ... magistrate?' she made it a question and William nodded encouragement, '... magistrate turns a blind eye, I believe. It's off Market Street.' The sun was on her pale face and she squinted towards William. He almost asked her if she could sing, but instead thanked her and said she should think about the flavour of ice cream he could buy her and Patrick later.

The sand in William's shoes was irritating and needed three stops up on the promenade before being properly cleared. It was hot on the front and he was grateful to turn away from the sea into Market Street, carrying his jacket over his shoulder. The Compass was easy to find; a small pub in need of repair behind what might have once been a clean Georgian front. The doors were closed but there was a delivery of barrels being passed to the cellar through the hatch in the pavement. William asked the delivery driver if the publican was around and was pointed down a small alley in shadow next to the pub which ran round to the back. At the end was an unlocked door. He went through into a dark parlour. His eyes took a few seconds to adjust to the dim gas lights until he could make out a handful of men sitting around a dining table with a selection of half–filled glasses and bottles in front of them. They stopped talking as William stepped in but he wasn't intimidated and was about to ask after Edward when he saw him sitting side–on in a threadbare armchair in the corner, his right profile to the room.

'How long has he been here?' William asked. No one answered until a woman came in through an internal door. She carried a small crate of bottled beers and William took her for the landlady, asking the question again as he pointed to Edward.

'I don't know, my husband's been serving. You'll cover his bill?'

William ignored the question and kneeled in front of Edward, who held a tankard of dark beer but was in danger of letting it slip into his lap where a box of tablets lay. The top was open and the label showed 'morphine sulphate'.

'Edward, how many did you put in the drink?'

But Edward's head was bowed and his eye closed. He whispered, 'It hurts William. Bad.'

'I know Edward,' said William, gently checking the mask was in place and not damaged.

'No you don't. Not really.'

'I know that too. But you've a performance tonight.' William sighed. 'Let's get you back for some sleep.' William knew it unlikely Edward had drunk much but despite checking the box of tablets he couldn't tell how many of them he might have dissolved into the beer. He caught the attention of the woman handing out the bottles, 'How much does my friend owe?'

'Half a crown or thereabouts.'

'Hmmm. Let's call it a shilling and an extra threepence if you call a cab and help me get him into it.' William found the change in his purse and passed it over. The woman shrugged and watched William pocket the box of morphine sulphate tablets then went outside and was back in a minute.

'Cab arranged. Extra shilling.'

'Threepence.'

'Ninepence.'

'Tanner.'

'Done,' said the woman.

They each took one of Edward's arms, ignoring the moan of pain as he was lifted from the chair. Edward was a light load for two but as they opened the door and let in the daylight Edward groaned louder and his face was turned to the woman. As the light caught Edward's mask she gasped and nearly dropped him but recovered her composure.

'This would be the new pianist up at The Winter Gardens then. I heard he was ... marked, so to speak. I also heard he's good, not that I enjoy those sorts of tunes.'

William nodded. 'Oh yes, he's good, but he won't be tonight unless he can get some sleep.'

'And that happened to him in France?'

'Arras. Seventeen. Royal Fusiliers, London Regiment.'

'My old man was over in Gaza about then. Fifty third Welsh infantry. Madness to be so far from home, but we heard Arras was ... difficult.'

'Yes, difficult, and a little more. But no more than Gaza, I imagine.' William held out his free hand. 'I'm William.'

'Ceinwen.' The landlady shook it.

'Ah, hence the accent. Did your husband come home in one piece?'

'All his body, most of his mind and some of his soul.'

'You're a long way from Wales.'

'Not so far as to leave it all behind, be it Bala ... or Gaza.'

William nodded understandingly then asked, 'Tell me, do you know of anyone in town who might sell morphia solution and syringes? It may be my friend will need something stronger and quicker acting in future.'

The woman looked again at Edward's mask and winced. 'Rolf, back in the saloon, might help. He knows people with old war stocks of all sorts. I can point him out.'

'Rolf?'

'He's German.'

'German?'

'The war's over.'

'For some. Anyway, thank you. I might come back later in the week. I'm assuming Rolf won't need a doctor's note.'

She laughed, 'I expect not, though I daresay that will affect the price.' The woman helped carry Edward to the curb where the cab waited. As they started to load Edward she asked William, 'And can he play music hall songs and perhaps some ragtime?'

'He can play anything.'

'If he's free some evenings he can play here, for a pint or two, no more. We've a piano. It's not grand but your friend is welcome to knock out a tune on it.' She smiled – yellow teeth in a red face, warm eyes.

'In that little room?' William was sceptical.

'No, the public bar. The regulars like a tune they can sing to. Though we sometimes have a ragtime night, if there's a call for it.'

'And the piano's all right?'

'Not what he's used to, I shouldn't think, but if he's as good as they say then ...' She left it as a challenge.

'I'll ask him later. And thank you Ceinwen,' said William.

While Edward slept William went back to the beach. It was coming up to eleven and he found Georgette where he'd left her. She sat on the blanket and was still wearing the blue dress but had covered her face and head with a large brimmed sunhat. She was reading a copy of *Woman's Own* and Patrick sat beside her, alternately burying and digging up his feet in the soft sand. William was carrying his shoes and socks.

'Georgette. Still here. Good.'

Georgette and Patrick looked up. William moved so he no longer had the sun behind him.

'And thanks for pointing me to The Compass. Edward was there and now he's back in his room, sleeping. If not for you I'd be wandering the streets of Margate still. Hello Patrick.'

'And Mr. Thompson is all right?' Georgette asked.

'As well as can be expected. But now, I owe you an ice cream. What do you say Patrick? I know just the place.'

Patrick said nothing but looked at his mother who smiled at him.

The tea shop where Evelyn worked during the day had become William and Edward's favourite morning haunt. Evelyn guided William, Patrick and Georgette to William's favourite table, in the window. Patrick chose vanilla ice cream while Georgette and William ordered coffee.

'You know the waitress?' Georgette asked, noting Evelyn's familiarity with William on taking their order and asking where was Edward.

'That's Evelyn. In the evening she works at The Winter Gardens, where Edward is playing. We come here most mornings. Edward likes routine.'

Patrick flicked through a battered comic book, *Tiger Tim's Weekly*, and Georgette watched him for a short while before asking, 'Will Mr. Thompson be all right?'

'I expect he'll be all right for this evening's performance. He hates to miss a show, despite the … problems.'

'I mean, not just tonight but …?'

'Oh yes. Compared to when I dragged him back to the trench, he's practically brand new. He might not be a big lad but he's a tough bugger. Oh, sorry.'

Georgette waved a hand to show the bad language didn't offend. 'Patrick's papa was over there too. He didn't come home.'

'I'm sorry. So many didn't,' William said and looked at Patrick.

'It's all right. Patrick understands, I think. He's named after his papa.'

'A good Irish name?'

'For a good Irish man, though he served with the Royal West Kent. He didn't live past nineteen fifteen, Ypres. He was barely one.' She indicated to her son.

'I'm sorry.'

Evelyn delivered their order.

'Were you married long?' William asked when Evelyn had gone. He poured some scotch from his hip flask into his coffee.

Georgette reached to her bag and found a handkerchief to dab ice cream from Patrick's mouth; his attention didn't waiver from the book on the table in front of him. She didn't answer William's question and he said, 'It must be difficult, bringing him up alone.'

'Not so bad. We lodge for free at the mistress's and I get most of Thursday off. It's hard work and I know I'm not big, but I'm a … as you say, tough bugger,' Georgette said, taking William's hip flask and pouring a little into her tea, ignoring the disapproving 'tut' from the lady on the next table. William laughed.

Edward, Herne Bay, Thursday 12th August 1920

The Wolseley sped through the tight lanes. Edward kept a hand on his homburg as he looked over his shoulder to Evelyn and Catherine. William was driving. Edward sat up front and the ladies in the back. The canvas roof was down and though it was warm the wind buffeted the scarves secured around the ladies' heads. William was hatless but his eyes were shielded behind dark tinted spectacles, used only for driving in the sun – Catherine had giggled when he put them on after picking up her and Evelyn from Catherine's aunt's guest house. Catherine shouted something at Evelyn. She nodded. Edward smiled as Catherine nearly lost her scarf. The lane narrowed and the hedges closed in, emphasising the speed. Evelyn shrank a little in her seat.

They were driving to Herne Bay. Though it was a short distance to the west there was no direct coastal road, forcing a drive inland before turning north–west. Edward looked from Catherine to Evelyn. Both seemed to be enjoying the trip and he was glad they were there. It helped the journey make sense.

The previous Saturday afternoon, Edward and William had gone to The Winter Gardens. Edward's painful episode had been the Thursday before and though the morphine sulphate tablets had taken the edge off the pain he was not well enough to perform for a couple of days. They'd gone back to the auditorium on the Saturday to see Mr. Taylor,

Bookings Manager, and for Edward to practise for perhaps an hour. Catherine had been in the ticket booth when they arrived, William leading and Edward moving stiff and fragile behind, tired after the trudge up Fort Hill.

'Afternoon Catherine. Busy?' William's cheerfulness belied Edward's discomfort.

'Not particularly. Where have you two been?'

'Edward's been poorly, but feeling better now.'

'Are you sure?' Catherine's concern seemed genuine on seeing Edward's hunched demeanour. His mask was painted to match the usual colour of his natural cheek, but today that was noticeably more pale.

'Yes, thank you,' Edward said without looking at her.

'And how are you?' William asked her. 'You look well. New lipstick? Very ... alluring.'

'Ha, learnt a new word have we? What do you want William?' Catherine said, despite a slight flush.

The Bookings Manager entered the foyer. 'Thank you Catherine,' he said, with a tone just short of dismissive.

'Good afternoon Mr. Taylor.' William turned to him. 'Did you get our message on Thursday?' William had paid a lad threepence to tell Mr. Taylor of Edward's sickness.

'I did. Are you all right to perform today?' He asked Edward but William answered,

'Of course. And sorry to have been poorly but now raring to go. In fact, early, as you can see, to take some practise.'

'Good, though I'm afraid you'll have to wait a little while. I've brought a piano tuner down from London. We need it to be perfect if our auditorium is to be used for recording.' Mr. Taylor walked away but turned after a couple of yards to add, 'And I'm sorry but we can't pay you for the performances missed. As specified in the contract.' He was gone before William could respond.

'Miserable bugger. And he smelt of drink. At this time of day,' William said to Catherine.

'He is known to enjoy a brandy or two.' Catherine whispered.

William nodded and led Edward through to the auditorium.

The tuner's head was under the piano's lid. He surfaced occasionally to play one of the keys, listen to the note reverberate around the hall and then go back under the lid. Edward stood at the foot of the piano, partly silhouetted by the windows behind the stage. The next time the tuner raised his head Edward said, 'Good afternoon.'

'Good af ...' the piano tuner started but stopped on seeing Edward's face before completing, '... ternoon.' There was both shock and recognition in the tuner's face. 'You're Mr. Thompson.'

'I am. Is it A six that's out?'

'You have a good ear, but then you would, so I'm told.'

'Can it be fixed?'

'Of course sir. It's not out of tune as such, more a problem with the hammer. It's a little out of line and worn unevenly. Tonight it will sound fine and the acoustics in here are quite good aren't they?' He asked the last part as if needing Edward's assurance.

'Not bad.'

'It's a shame I won't be here to listen this evening. I've another job.'

'You're down from London?'

'For the day. There are a couple of jobs to complete. From here I need to set up a new Bechstein.'

'A new Bechstein?'

'At the Thanet Royal hotel, just outside Whitstable.'

'Did you hear that William?' Edward called down to the front row of seats.

'What?'

'A hotel nearby has a new Bechstein.'

'So?'

Edward and the piano tuner looked at each other and smiled, as if sharing a secret, before the piano tuner explained to William, 'All their property was seized back in sixteen, when they closed Bechstein Hall for being too ... German, I s'pose. Me and the lads heard rumours there were a few pianos taken. It appears at least one has found its way on to the market.' He turned to Edward. 'You should visit the hotel. Perhaps they'll let you play it sir. We hear you're good.'

'He is, but who do you mean by we?' asked William.

'There aren't many piano tuners in London these days. We tend to know each other. A colleague repaired the piano at the Hackney. He mentioned you were ... generous ...'

'Ha, I knew it,' said William. 'Edward, didn't I tell you not to tip that tuner? It's not even as if it was your piano. It was the theatre's.'

'He did a good job. Proper tuning and set up makes the pianist sound better,' said Edward.

'Of course,' William said sarcastically.

The tuner smiled and made another alteration before asking, 'Mr. Thompson, would you do me the honour of validating the adjustment?'

'My pleasure.'

Edward played an excerpt from Mozart's Piano Sonata no 11 before congratulating the tuner on a job well done and indicating to William a tip had been earned.

The following performances went well with Edward feeling better as the days passed and when William explained how Georgette had helped find him in The Compass, he insisted, through his embarrassment, that she accept a gift of a toy sail–boat for young Patrick.

On the Tuesday, after the evening performance,

Edward joined William on the seafront.

'You played well tonight Edward.'

'The piano here is good but I've been thinking. I'd like to try that new Bechstein. Why don't we take a trip to that hotel on Thursday?'

'Thursday? It's your day off. So of course, you want to play a piano.'

'What was the hotel called? Thanet Royal or something?'

'Something like that.' He caught sight of movement over his shoulder and raised his voice. 'A trip sounds a good idea and we should ask the ladies.'

Evelyn and Catherine joined them. It had become a habit to walk the ladies home after evening performances. Apart from William they were generally tired by that time and though the conversation was not sparkling there was comfort in the calm stroll; Edward all the more comfortable under the poor street lighting after the harsh stage lights.

'Ask which ladies and ask them what?' said Catherine, taking the cigarette William offered.

'You two ladies if you fancy a trip along the coast, to a hotel, on Thursday.'

'Oh really, a hotel?' Evelyn asked suspiciously.

'The Thanet Royal. I hear it's very classy. Just been remodelled in the manner of the best in New York and they serve cocktails at lunchtime.'

'What kind of ladies do you think we are?'

'Sophisticates.'

'Which is why we're unlikely to accompany you to the Thanet Royal,' said Christine. 'I doubt they'd even let you in. Is your family titled?' Catherine teased.

'My old man was a lord of the mines, like his old man before him and his before that. And there's no shame in working the seams.'

'Lords of the mines eh? Well, why didn't you say …'

'And, as such cultured ladies, you'll want to hear

Edward play a new Bechstein.'

'What's a Bechstein and where is the hotel?' Evelyn asked, looking at Edward. She had developed a knack for focusing on his good eye and not being distracted by the other's coldness.

'A piano at The Thanet Royal, or Royal Thanet, not sure which way round.'

'Some of the other girls have talked of it. There's a grand new ballroom,' said Catherine.

'Outside Whitstable, isn't it?' William asked.

'Just past Herne Bay,' said Catherine. 'Only a few miles along the coast. What do you think Evelyn?'

'Why not? As long as we're back for the evening shift.'

'We'll pick you up at, say, ten, from your aunt's guest house. Is that all right for you?' William turned to Evelyn who nodded. Edward lit a cigarette and was staring out at the darkness. The breeze and sea was loud enough their voices were raised a little, but there was little to see apart from the occasional flash of white water on top of a wave. Edward turned to Catherine, asking,

'Did you say Herne Bay?'

'Yes. We'll pass through it.'

'I'd like that. Perhaps we can stop there for refreshment. And perhaps pick up some cigars. Is there a tobacconist there, do you know? On the pier?'

'Why? Are Margate cigars not good enough for you Mr. Thompson?' Catherine put on a posh accent.

'No, I just … wondered …' said Edward, turning back to the water.

On the Thursday William and Edward enjoyed a leisurely breakfast, William taking the opportunity to annoy at least one of the other guests by loudly inviting Georgette to join them on the trip to Whitstable. But Georgette was needed despite it being her day off and, besides, young Patrick could not be left all day up in his room. Georgette was sad not to be joining them, but prepared a small hamper with flasks of hot tea and coffee for the journey.

Edward and William arrived outside Catherine's aunt's guest house just before ten. The ladies were waiting for them in the polished and well–ordered hall. William perched a pair of dark tinted spectacles on his head as he escorted them to the Wolseley and ignored Catherine's teasing over his modern eyewear as he pulled them down and sat behind the steering wheel. The ladies had borrowed driving coats from Catherine's aunt's friends, in the Ladies of St. John's, but the coats were for shorter and stouter women and hung sack–like. Catherine tightened first her own, then Evelyn's scarf as they settled into the back seats and there was a childlike excitement to Evelyn's smile that Edward tried to match. It took but minutes to leave Margate for the roads heading out of town.

William slowed the car as they drove along the front at Herne Bay and took Edward's pointed instructions to park next to the grass verge at the top of the beach, just past the pier. It was windy and the sun hadn't broken through the grey cloud, limiting the appeal of the sand, though many others were braver.

'Why have we parked?' Catherine asked as the clatter of the Wolseley died away.

William lifted his eyeshades. 'Edward wanted to pull over.'

'I felt a little sick. It's nothing. It'll soon pass. I'm not a good passenger.'

'Ever since that ambulance trip back in … sixteen was it?'

Edward shrugged, climbed from the car and went round to take the hamper from the back. He passed cups and flasks to the ladies in the back as William continued, '… yes, back in sixteen. We both ended up in an ambulance, crawling its way through the mud to a dressing station. What a fiasco. There was I, trying to help some poor chap on a stretcher keep his guts from falling out on to the floor with one hand while Edward pressed my other under his armpit to try and stop the blood seeping ...' William showed the ladies the scar on his left hand, where the little finger had been all but severed, '... and Edward was there because his big left toe had been pierced by some shrapnel and we didn't have any pliers in the trench toolbox to pull it out. And it would have been all right if not for that shell hole we fell down and the poor sod in the stretcher tipping out and covering the both of us with his foul smelling insides and liver and ... God knows what ... slimy, green, black ... It's no wonder we occasionally suffer from car sickness still. Mind you, that's the action where Edward came to be promoted to full lieutenant and earned his 'Lucky Lieutenant' nickname, and I became a sergeant. So it wasn't all bad.'

Catherine laughed nervously. Edward shook his head. Evelyn poured tea and William passed a cigarette to Catherine; Edward refused the offer, patted his own pockets to find them empty and said,

'Excuse me.' He stepped down from the car.

'Edward?' Evelyn asked.

'Just going for some fags,' he muttered, pointing towards the pier.

'I'll join you, I want a postcard to send my father.' Evelyn handed her cup to Catherine and left the car.

'Good idea. A short walk to clear the head and settle the stomach.' William shouted after them as they walked along the beach head. Twenty yards along Evelyn asked,

'Was that true? What William said? About the ambulance.'

'I suppose so. I don't remember all, or even much, of what happened, but I do have a piece missing from my toe so it could be.'

'And they called you the Lucky Lieutenant?'

'That's when it started. All nonsense of course, but we came through a few actions and hardly lost a soul, to start with. Men under fire invent superstitions. But the shrapnel in my foot didn't feel lucky.'

'The shrapnel is why they made you a full lieutenant?'

'What? Oh no, at least God I hope not. There must have been something else, or perhaps there was no one else left. It wasn't for a toe. Otherwise for this I'd be a field marshal.' He tried to joke and gestured to his mask, still walking. 'Ha, if you made full lieutenant for half a toe, half the bloody army would be generals or worse. And then who'd dig the trenches, let alone climb out of them to be slaughtered.' He stopped walking, realising his voice had risen. Evelyn stopped next to him, removing her scarf as it flapped about her face in the breeze.

'I'm sorry. No need to shout,' Edward said quietly.

Evelyn looked at his face. He was still wearing a hat and his head was tilted down but as he raised it she looked away. 'Come, let's find cigarettes,' she said, taking his arm and leading him on.

A few yards along they came to the entrance to the pier – a wooden building with a pitched roof straddling the timbers, acting as a barrier to the long stretch beyond, out into the North Sea. Although summer was high it was not busy and they stood looking through the doors of the building, to the pier beyond. The few people out there, small in the distance, seemed lost to the sea and Edward turned away. There was an ice cream kiosk and newsagent on the promenade side of the pier entrance but no tobacconist. Evelyn suggested they try back the other way but, before she could turn, Edward approached the newsagent, ignoring the shock in the face of the older man as he asked,

'Good morning sir. Do you know of a tobacconist on the pier? Perhaps further on if not here?'

The man seemed reluctant to answer until Evelyn

joined Edward's side.

'Ah yes, three or four days a week. They set up just inside the entrance there.'

'Is it Mr. Kayst?' asked Edward.

'Kayst? No, I'm afraid not.' The newsagent addressed Evelyn though Edward had asked the question.

'Are you sure?' Edward persisted.

'Quite sure. The Kaysts let the business run to ruin. The pitch was bought quite cheap as a result. I was tempted meself.'

'When?'

'Three or four years back. When their lad didn't come home.'

'Do you know what happened to them? The Kaysts?'

'No.' He looked over Edward's shoulder to another lady behind, fishing in her purse for change.

'I'm not sure the major is finished.' Evelyn said, retrieving the newsagent's attention and touching Edward's arm.

'Did the Kaysts go away?' Edward asked.

'I don't know. But the new tobacconist opens the kiosk some days, when he's well enough. He might know. Come back later.' The newsagent shrugged.

Edward turned, leading Evelyn back to the car but just as Evelyn began to ask a question Edward interrupted, 'I was never a major.'

'I know.'

'Oh. And we didn't find a postcard to send your father.'

But Evelyn didn't go back to the newsagent. 'It's all right. Another time. His mission is just a few miles from here anyway. Perhaps we should go and visit him when the hop picking starts.'

'Perhaps. Though William is not a fan of the clergy.'

'I suspect William is no fan of anyone not born and bred near his pits. Though it seems he is a long way from home these days.'

'The war gave many a way up as well as a way out. Some learnt to value themselves more, some less. In any event many will not be content to go back to the factories and pits. And I don't blame them. Have you seen it in London? Men coming back and wanting more?'

'Not many came back at all, though it could be some have gone to search for something better. May I ask, who were the Kaysts?'

'I didn't know them but their son was in my platoon … for a while … a young man. A good man. Ah, a hotel. Might they sell cigarettes do you think?' Edward held his hat against a stronger rush of wind from the sea and trotted over the beach road to the hotel on the other side. Evelyn caught up with him in the lobby, buying two packs of Players from the receptionist. By the time he'd lit one in the wind they were back at the car and Catherine poured both him and Evelyn fresh tea. William reached over to pour some scotch from his hip flask into Edward's cup. Evelyn declined.

'Well? Were they there?' William asked.

Edward shook his head and Catherine gave Evelyn a quizzical look but she said nothing. They sat without conversation, listening to the waves break on the sand and the gulls argue over scraps.

The Blue Bench

Evelyn, Whitstable, Thursday 12th August 1920

Whitstable was barely four miles along the coast, William driving faster on this part of the journey, Evelyn forsaking her scarf and enjoying the wind disarrange her hair. The Thanet Royal hotel was a quarter mile before entering Whitstable. It was recently built and even more recently modernised with a contentious art deco frontage and interior. William dropped his passengers at the hotel door which the bellboy opened for them. The grand lobby was well lit and three large multi–coloured glass uplighters hung from the tiered stucco ceiling. The brass fittings around the lobby gave the appearance of opulence and the marble floor bounced the light into confusing reflections. Hotel employees busied themselves back and forth, though not many guests were obvious, and as Catherine took out a cigarette another bell boy appeared with a match. Catherine smiled and caught Evelyn's eye. Edward removed his car coat and approached reception. The formal young man behind the tall desk didn't flinch as the light from a red and green desk lamp caught the dull sheen of Edward's mask.

'Can I help sir?'

'I wonder if you can. I'm told you have a new Bechstein and I'd love to see it, perhaps play it? Could that be arranged?'

'He does play rather well,' said Evelyn, over Edward's shoulder.

'A Bechstein, sir?'

'Yes, a piano?'

'Oh. I see. I'll tell the manager you're here but meantime, if you'd like to go through to the Moonlight Bar you'll find it there. The bar is closed for a further,' he checked the clock behind him, 'forty minutes, until twelve.'

The young man went out through a door behind him. Edward and the ladies followed the signs through to the Moonlight Bar, William joining them as they entered, disappointed to see no one serving.

'… until mid–day,' explained Catherine.

William's disappointment deepened and he found an armchair in which to sulk. He took out his notebook and flicked through before writing a few lines then sipping from his hip flask.

Edward inspected the highly polished grand piano, filling an ill–lit quarter of the room. He explained to Evelyn that though beautiful, it was too big for the bar, sonically. Evelyn reached to take his hat and coat from him and he sat on the piano's bench, adjusting the height before raising the fallboard. He played a succession of chords and scales before apologising, 'I'm sorry. What I'm going to play doesn't work without the orchestra, but I haven't played it in a while. Please forgive my indulgence,' and began Rachmaninoff's piano concerto number three. Catherine and Evelyn took seats at the bar as music burst from the piano and swamped the room. Evelyn could discern no melody nor feel any clear rhythm but the running notes and hammered chords were too intense to deny or ignore and, at their centre sat Edward, both mesmerised and mesmerising. He played effortlessly and flawlessly for ten or so minutes before Evelyn realised there was a small group of people standing in the doorway to the bar, watching and listening. He stopped at an appropriate place, embarrassed, but Evelyn walked over.

'I've no idea what you've just played, but it didn't sound like an accident.'

Edward looked down at the keys. 'It's been a long time since I played that. Sorry for the mistakes.'

'Ha, I thought so,' said Catherine, teasing, as William walked behind the bar and poured her a gin and tonic and a scotch for himself.

'Play more,' Evelyn encouraged.

Edward thought for a moment and began the refrain from Liszt's Hungarian Rhapsody number two. He was a couple of minutes through it, the audience at the door growing bigger and clapping along with the rousing chorus, when the young man from the reception desk pushed his way into the room, leading an older man, evidently the manager from his manner.

'Is he with you?' The manager asked William, talking over the music. Evelyn watched Edward, sitting side–on at the piano in the corner and in shadow but he didn't appear to hear.

'You are?' William asked back.

'The Day Manager. Is he with you?'

'Why do you ask?'

'I was not expecting anyone for audition today. And the bar isn't open yet.'

'I'm sorry sir, I thought …' the receptionist said, over the Day Manager's shoulder. He was waved away.

'Audition? For what?' asked William.

'The bar pianist.'

'Oh yes, he'd pass muster as a bar pianist, wouldn't you say?' William asked sarcastically as Edward finished playing and the crowd at the door applauded.

The manager looked at the crowd and William said, 'But, as it happens, I'm his agent. What terms would you offer?'

'What makes you think we'd want him?'

Evelyn moved closer to hear the conversation.

'Those people make me think you'd pay good money.' William pointed to the crowd dispersing from the doorway.

'But …' Evelyn said but was cut off by William's subtle shake of head.

'He's available at the right price. A very accomplished player,' William said and sipped on the scotch.

'And you're his agent? You can negotiate on his behalf?'

'It's my job. He's in a summer season at the moment but for the right money he might be persuaded to move. He would fill this bar lunchtimes and evenings. You name it, he plays it as the composer intended. Better.' William took a card from his inside pocket and gave it to the manager.

'I'd like to speak to him.' The manager looked over to where Edward was gently playing some minor scales.

'Of course. Edward, how's the Bechstein?' William called over.

'Marvellous. One or two actions are a little stiff but it will mature into a wonderful instrument. Of course, it needs more space to sing.'

'Come join us.' William beckoned.

Edward stood, still in shadow. The manager took a step toward him but stopped as Edward stepped into better light. The manager spoke quickly, 'You know, the problem is, we made a provisional offer to someone else. But I've got your card. If that falls through we'll be in touch,' and the manager was gone before Edward had even reached the bar.

William poured another scotch and passed it to Edward, 'Shame, I nearly bagged you a regular slot here. I think he would have paid well.'

'What happened?' Edward made a slight slurping sound as he sipped from the tumbler.

'He wasn't keen on your stage make–up. Perhaps you should have painted that piano bench blue.'

Edward downed the scotch in one. 'Well bugger him then. Though it is a nice piano.'

'The hotel doesn't deserve you. That's ... bullshit.' Evelyn exclaimed in frustration.

'Evelyn!' said Catherine, 'Where did you learn that?'

'One of the women at the mission married an Australian. And it's true. They should be begging Edward to play here.'

'Thank you, but anyway, I have a booking for the summer. Though that is a nice instrument.' Edward said, looking back towards the piano.

'It's a shame though,' said William, coming from behind the bar to follow. 'We might have earned as much here as from The Winter Gardens for less effort and a headline slot.'

'We?' said Catherine. 'It seems to me Edward is doing the earning.'

Edward started toward the door but Evelyn said, 'Why not play that first piece again.'

'The Rachmaninoff?'

'For me.'

'Really?'

'Yes please. I didn't understand it but it came alive in your hands.'

'Perhaps just the first couple of movements.'

Evelyn walked back with him to the piano. Edward played and, when she thought she saw the slightest tear under his right eye, focused on his hypnotic hands, caressing, driving and punishing the keys.

'Did you enjoy the trip ladies?' William asked as they settled in the front parlour of Catherine's aunt's guest house.

'Mostly,' said Evelyn, standing at the mirror over the fire place and fiddling with her dishevelled hair. 'It is a nice modern motor car.'

'You can thank Edward for that,' William said.

'More truthfully, my Aunt Maud, who passed away earlier this year and left me a modest sum. A lovely lady, though, to be honest I hadn't seen much of her since before the war.'

'A modest sum? Modest enough for an expensive motor car. And so William is sort of your … chauffeur, then?' Catherine said, with mischief.

'Please madam, manager or agent.' William said with exaggerated pomposity, 'and my dear client prefers to be driven.'

'My good eye isn't always good enough to let me drive with confidence,' said Edward, not looking up.

'Would you have left The Winter Gardens, a proper concert hall, for a hotel bar?' Evelyn asked.

'Probably not,' said William, filling the silence Edward left, 'but it's my job to make more money if we can.'

'And it was a Bechstein,' Edward added after a further pause.

'There you go again, saying we', said Catherine to William. 'So, what do you do? As Edward's … agent.'

William took a piece of homemade shortbread from the plate offered by Catherine and took a bite with his hand to his chin, capturing the crumbs to drop them on the small china plate in his lap. 'Well, as the late Major Price's pretty young wife once said, 'Sergeant Burrslow, the good doctors here have done what they can, now you need to find a place where Lieutenant Thompson can play his music and be whole.' And she was a clever lady.'

'Who is Sergeant Burrslow?' asked Catherine.

'Me,' said William, 'at least I used to be, though of course I wasn't by the time Major Price's good lady said that in the spring of nineteen.'

'I don't know what you're on about.' Evelyn poured Edward more tea.

'The late Major Price was the Discharge Officer at the tin nose hospital,' said Edward.

'He died under a train at Wandsworth station, last autumn,' William added.

Edward nodded, adding, 'He was a good man. He

was trying to stop a patient from throwing himself under and somehow got caught in the poor chap's bath chair apparatus. Apparently the patient survived.'

'I still don't know what you're on about,' Evelyn repeated.

'But I expect the late Mrs. Price has a string of suitors by now. She could sing well you know,' said William, ignoring Evelyn's apparent exasperation.

Edward picked up a piece of shortbread then appeared to think better of being able to eat it without mess and placed it untasted on the plate on the small table next to him.

The front parlour was newly decorated, bright and comfortable. The four of them sipped tea prepared by Catherine. Cook had baked shortbread to Catherine's aunt's recipe.

'What did you mean by tin nose hospital?' Evelyn asked. William looked to Edward as if asking permission to speak but Edward answered,

'It was our name for the wards at Wandsworth, third London General. It's where some of us went for … this sort of thing.' He indicated vaguely towards his face. 'Many of us were … patched up at Queens Hospital, Sidcup, then sent to Wandsworth where we were … finished off, so to speak.'

'Patched up?' William laughed. 'Oh yes, there was a quite a bit of patching to do. And then the craftsmen excelled.' He made a circle in front of his own face.

Edward looked down.

'How long were you there?' Evelyn asked.

'Sidcup or Wandsworth?' Edward asked.

'Both?'

'Perhaps eighteen months at Sidcup and a couple at Wandsworth.'

'It would have been longer if not for Major Price. After Derwent Wood's men had done their work it was Pricey …'

'… and his good lady,' Edward interrupted.

'… who coaxed the tin nosers back into the world. I'd kept in touch with the lieutenant throughout his time at Sidcup and they called me to help. Naturally, I was honoured and the late major's wife was right about Edward needing somewhere for his music.'

'And fortunate for you Edward's talent has such value,' said Catherine.

William pretended to appear offended.

'You knew of Edward's talents?' Evelyn asked.

'Ay, sharing a trench with a man you learn much about him and I knew Edward could tickle the ivories. But it wasn't until I visited him at Sidcup in late eighteen, after the, what, eighth operation, and heard him at an old upright in the social club I believed he'd studied at the Royal College of Music and for a reason. Not that I know much about proper music. But the major's wife was right. He needed to play, I knew that much.'

'For the right price,' added Catherine. William smiled acknowledgement.

Evelyn was looking at Edward while William spoke and stumbled over her next question, 'And what were … I mean, but why tin nosers? Yours … isn't.'

Edward's mask covered the upper part of his left cheek and the entire eye socket but much of the nose lipping underneath the mask was his own.

'A lot of the others didn't have their own noses,' said William.

'Though many still had their own eyes,' countered Edward.

'True, but not always in the right place on their face.' William said.

'That's not necessary,' Catherine spoke sternly. William shrugged and raised his cup of tea to Edward saying,

'To Gillies …'

'… and Derwent Wood,' finished Edward.

Evelyn looked to Catherine for some explanation. Catherine shook her head, understanding no more than Evelyn.

The Blue Bench

Evelyn, Margate,
Friday 13th August 1920

Evelyn had been working in Margate for two weeks, barely able to catch her breath. Crowded days in the tea shop, busy evenings at The Winter Gardens, new friends, a trip to Whitstable and helping Alice rest were full time tasks, both energizing and enervating by turn. She missed her father and worried she was being less useful here in Margate than she would be at the mission come September – and perhaps a little guilty at enjoying the company of new friends so readily – but there was little time for thinking. She checked the wall clock and saw it was close to Edward and William's habitual mid–morning visit. It was now a habit to place a 'reserved' sign on their table in the window, despite Alice's husband, Alastair's, hinted disapproval. But William's charm and Edward's promise that he'd purchase at least one of the watercolours were persuasive. Evelyn checked to ensure no customers were trying to attract attention before nipping out to the kitchen to check her reflection in the small mirror next to the coat rack. It would have to do, though she regretted the waitress dress provided by Alice fit less well than The Winter Gardens uniform, so expertly altered by Catherine. Alice was sitting on a chair at the back of the kitchen – she took advantage of any quiet moment to rest – sipping tea, watching Evelyn. They smiled at each other and Evelyn mouthed the question, 'All right?' Alice nodded and Evelyn hoped Alastair would be back soon. It was his habit to go for a walk after breakfast but he didn't say where and though Evelyn had asked Alice she said she didn't know. Alice seemed bigger even in the last fortnight and Evelyn was concerned at Alice's age; thirty–nine she had learnt. Back at their parish in Spitalfields Evelyn had known many of the women that gave birth and of one case where the mother had bled to death. Evelyn's father had said the mother's age, nearly thirty–five, was at least partly to blame. Evelyn was sceptical, death in childbirth was not unusual in their poor parish, but she had found her father was generally of sound opinion. The memory of that night, sitting with the disbelieving husband while her father attended upstairs and, after, when they cleaned the room, seeing the sheets stained a vivid blood red, was still a shock. Evelyn smiled again at Alice and went back out to the front, wondering on Alastair's morning walk and hoping he would be back sooner than usual. Perhaps he was painting or drawing? But most of the paintings here were sunrises or sunsets – save, of course, for the darker, powerful, disturbing oil painting of the sinking ship. Evelyn found herself staring at the shocked souls being sucked to their cloying, watery graves. The fear in their faces was compelling – it was a fear not of drowning but of being dead, for evermore; a fear of being lost by loved ones and of never being found by new loves; a terror of never having fully lived; a terror of eternity in empty darkness, filled with the torture of being surrounded by a blackness that loathed and taunted and clawed from inside.

'It's not for the faint–hearted.'

A voice spoke quietly in Evelyn's ear and she jolted with shock.

'I'm sorry, I didn't mean to startle you.' Edward took a step back. He had stood beside her unnoticed and she wondered how long he'd been there, looking at the picture with her.

'No, it's all right. I … I was just …'

'Watching?' Edward finished the sentence.

'Looking,' said Evelyn, 'at the painting.'

'I've generally avoided looking at it, when I come in

for tea I mean. But lately I find myself watching it. To see if anyone can escape.'

'I don't understand,' Evelyn said.

'Nor do I.' Edward admitted.

Though he had taken a step back he was still close to her. By now she was accustomed to his mask at a distance and the detail of the painting was remarkable at a few yards and behind the glass of the spectacles, but this close the pale grey eye carried menace and the dull sheen threatened a lifelessness that might creep unchecked. She avoided considering what might, or might not, lie underneath. She had seen the painted eye was usually a good match in shades of grey to the right eye, but occasionally, in a bad light or when Edward was tired, the colours were quite different. She hoped one day to ask him if he knew.

Edward asked, 'Is it true that Turner, the painter, might have drunk tea here? And, talking of which, may William and I have our usual?'

'Of course to the second question, but I've no idea on the first, I'm afraid. I don't know how long the tea shop has been here.'

'There's a guide book in our guest house and it seems Turner spent much time here, in Margate, I mean, not necessarily your tea shop.'

'We should ask Alastair. As the painter of these he might know. Alice tells me he has quite a reputation locally, as an artist.'

'And he did this?' Edward nodded at the sinking ship on the wall.

'Of course. See the initials A T. Alastair Trenter.' Evelyn pointed to the bottom right hand corner.

'I think I prefer the watercolours. Though I can't deny this speaks to me. Is it for sale?'

'I'm afraid not,' said a voice behind them. Alice had joined them unnoticed. 'The others are but not this one ... yet.'

'Hello Mrs. Trenter. How are you?' said Edward.

'Not enjoying the summer, if I'm honest, Mr. Thompson,' Alice said, stroking her pregnancy and looking at Evelyn rather than Edward.

'Not long to go. Is there anything we can do for you?' Edward asked and looked over his shoulder to where William sat.

'That's kind, but nothing at the moment thank you.'

'Well you must let us know. We enjoy our morning breaks here and I was wondering if, rather than impose on Evelyn's time, we shouldn't perhaps be more self–sufficient in serving ourselves, in some way.'

'Oh no Mr. Thompson. Mr. Trenter would not allow that.'

'Besides, I'm happy to bring your coffee and tea,' said Evelyn.

'I just thought I'd mention it. But if there's anything else.'

'Well, now you mention it, you did say a day or two ago you might be interested in a painting?'

'Of course. But I'm no connoisseur. Perhaps Evelyn can choose for me?' Edward said and left to rejoin William, ignoring his theatrical complaints over slow service.

The lunchtime business had subsided and Evelyn was clearing tables when she heard Catherine – she followed her aunt into the tea shop.

'So you honestly believe that, Aunt?'

'Well it is Friday the thirteenth my dear,' Catherine's aunt said as she gave Evelyn a wave and sat at the first empty table.

'And you think that's the cause?' Catherine asked, not hiding her incredulity.

'Well, let's ask Evelyn,' said the aunt, and Evelyn was happy to be involved.

'Evelyn's the daughter of a rector. I hardly think she'll subscribe to your theory of Friday the thirteenth.'

'As a rector's daughter I'm sure Evelyn understands more than most there is much we cannot explain within the confines of the world we can touch and see and little that can be excused as pure coincidence. Isn't that right dear?' she asked as Evelyn reached her table.

Catherine gave an exaggerated sigh.

'Hello Mrs.Blundell. How can I help?' asked Evelyn.

'Well, my neighbour's sister had a white cat she lost only last week and was found just this morning but had lost an eye and turned black.'

'Really?'

'Indeed. Now, if it wasn't Friday the thirteenth I'd be inclined to dispute it's the same cat but not only is the date apposite, it appears the cat answers to its correct name of Apollo and was able to paw at the precise jar where his treats have always been kept.'

'Aunt Beatrice, shouldn't it be considered fortunate if the cat were to return, and as the thirteenth is meant to be unlucky I don't see how that applies?' Catherine said, smiling at Evelyn for support.

'But the cat lost an eye, and if that's not to be considered unlucky then I don't know what is,' said Evelyn mischievously.

'Precisely, my dear,' said Catherine's aunt.

'Not to mention it has changed colour, to black. Absolutely in keeping with Friday the thirteenth,' Evelyn added. She liked Catherine's Aunt Beatrice. She was short and petite, exuded restless energy and was keen to share her gentle humour. She ran her guest house with a quiet determination for perfection and was as loyal to her staff as they were to her.

'You're impossible, both of you,' said Catherine, touching Evelyn's arm. She called to Alice, who stood in the kitchen doorway, 'Mrs. Trenter, please bring some sanity to our table.'

'And I'll bring some tea,' said Evelyn. Catherine and her aunt had only known the Trenters for a week, since Catherine took her aunt there for tea and to introduce her to her new friend Evelyn, but Catherine's aunt's knack for respectful familiarity meant Alice already seemed comfortable in her company.

'Mrs. Trenter. Do sit with us. I hear they serve an excellent afternoon tea here,' Aunt Beatrice complimented Alice as she sat, 'and you deserve a treat as I understand it's no easy matter to be with child in this heat.' Beatrice fanned first herself and then Alice with the menu. Beatrice's ready smile was infectious, laugh lines edging her eyes but making her appear younger, brighter.

'I'll help Evelyn,' said Catherine, placing the book she had been carrying on the table.

'Sadly, I have no children of my own and would not claim to appreciate what you're going through …' Beatrice was explaining to Alice as Evelyn and Catherine went to the kitchen, '… but I like to think of Catherine as more than a niece. And, of course, would dearly love to think she sees me as more than an aunt.'

'Do you?' Evelyn asked Catherine when they were in the kitchen, preparing tea, out of hearing range.

'Do I what?'

'See Beatrice as more than an aunt. She is quite lovely.'

'I suppose. And it's true she has been more than an aunt.'

'She raised you?'

'From nine years old.'

'I'm sorry,' said Evelyn, 'to lose your mother so young must have been difficult.'

'Not particularly.' Catherine shrugged but offered no more, instead asking, 'What about you? You don't mention your mother.'

'She died eight years ago.'

'I'm sorry.'

'As my father says, it was God's will to take her early.'

'Your father sounds … accepting.'

'Not for a while, but we had each other. I was eighteen, already grown, and we … managed. And his parish and the mission need him. And we'll be with her again one day.'

'But not soon, let's hope. May I ask, how did she die?'

'Consumption. I do wonder if Father's parish hadn't been in Spitalfields would it still have taken her? There was so much of it there. But we'll never know, so we … carry on. We have each other. And you have your aunt.'

'And perhaps that'll be enough.' Catherine shrugged and there was a hint of melancholy Evelyn wished to understand but before she could frame a question Catherine tugged at the black dress Evelyn wore. 'And meantime, let me alter this hideous hanging cloth.'

'Could you do anything with it?'

'What would you like?'

'Well the Nippies always look very smart in their uniform. Something like that?'

'Nippies?' asked Catherine.

'The waitresses in the Lyons Corner Houses. My favourite is just down from Piccadilly. I always make a point of going there when I'm in the West End. Though it's an indulgence and I avoid mentioning it to Father.'

'If you can get me a picture of what they wear I'll see what I can do. Meantime, at least let's put a belt around it.' Catherine pulled at the dress again. 'Is it one of Alice's from a previous pregnancy?'

'Maybe so,' Evelyn laughed, 'she had a child, before, a long time ago.'

'Oh, I didn't know she was already a mother. I did think she might be slightly … old … to be having a first. Though, of course, I'm not one to comment, unlikely as I am to be a mother soon. And Mr. Trenter is even older, I believe.'

'Sadly their son died, in the war.' Evelyn lowered her voice. 'Oh, and I've also just remembered, she miscarried, a little while ago. How awful of me to forget. Please, don't mention it to anyone, it may not be well known.'

'Of course, poor Alastair and Alice.'

They finished preparing tea and went back out front. Catherine's aunt was talking quietly to Alice and paused as Evelyn poured tea before saying, '… as Catherine and Evelyn may be able to elucidate. The sergeant down at the station tells me your new friends, Mr. Burrslow and Mr. Thompson, were in conversation with Constable Simms a few evenings ago?'

'Aunt Beatrice, spreading gossip?' said Catherine, with mock distaste, 'and yes, there was a conversation but, before you ask, I don't know what it was about and, as far as we know, both Mr. Burrslow and Thompson are gentlemen.'

'The constable may not be so sure,' said Aunt Beatrice.

'But that is his job,' said Evelyn.

'True. Anyway, I'm sure your new friends are, as you say, gentlemen,' said Beatrice, with a hint of mischief. 'Though I do fear my niece's judgement may be tainted by her choice of reading these days.'

'Aunt Beatrice, there is no shame in reading American novels,' said Catherine.

'Then why lay the book face down on the table? Is it the sort of book Mr. Thompson would read?' Aunt Beatrice turned the book the right way up: *This Side Of Paradise*, F. Scott Fitzgerald.

Catherine picked it up, saying, 'Last month there was an American gentleman in town who visited The Winter Gardens regularly. He made a special journey here from his own home town in America, which is also called Margate …'

'… presumably after our own …'

'… I expect so, Aunt. Anyway, he said this book is all the rage in New York and left me his copy. You might be interested to know the hero's mother is called Beatrice and is a little … eccentric.'

'Hmmm, proof surely Americans understand little about literature,' said Beatrice, laughing. 'In any event, I'm not sure it's proper to receive such a book as a gift from an American. Evelyn, what do you think?'

'I'm sure he was a perfect gentleman. Though I prefer reading the more traditional classics myself,' said Evelyn, taking the book to examine the cover. A fashionable and pretty young woman looked out from the cover and a slightly sinister looking, handsome and smartly dressed young man with slicked back hair hovered at her shoulder. It wasn't clear if the young woman knew the man was there.

'Indeed,' said Beatrice with exaggerated suspicion. 'I wonder what books Mr. Burrslow and Mr. Thompson read.'

'I should say both Mr. Burrslow and Mr. Thompson are welcome regulars here,' said Alice.

'Speaking of which,' said Evelyn, 'I need to choose one of Alastair's paintings for Edward. He has promised to buy one …'

'… or more …' interrupted Alice,

'… and has asked me to pick. Catherine, will you help me, before any new customers come in? It's quiet this afternoon.'

'And take it to him this afternoon. We should strike while the iron is hot, as Alastair would say,' Alice said.

Evelyn carried the parcel easily – it was a picture from the tea shop chosen with Catherine's help, though Evelyn had quietly insisted on the final decision. In truth it hadn't been hard as nearly all the paintings were sunrises or sunsets and all the same high quality. Alastair had returned as they'd taken the picture from the wall and Evelyn thought there was a hint of disdain for the choice they had made but he said nothing. It was a couple of minutes from the tea shop to the guest house where Edward and William stayed and Catherine joined her. The guest house front door was open and Catherine commented the building was neither as grand nor as clean as her aunt's as they went through. They didn't know Edward's room number and wouldn't have gone up if they did, but found the front parlour where William was sitting reading while a young woman dusted around him.

'Ladies,' William said, standing as they entered.

Both ladies smiled their greeting.

'What brings you here? Oh, and my manners. This is Georgette. Georgette, this is Catherine and Evelyn.'

This time all three ladies smiled at each other and Georgette went to leave but Evelyn spoke, 'Please Georgette, don't leave on our account. William has told us a little about you and your son. Patrick is it? It's good to meet you.' Evelyn thought she saw Catherine's natural smile freeze a little.

Georgette bowed her head slightly. 'And it's nice to meet you Mademoiselle. Can I get you anything?'

'Nothing for me thank you and your English is excellent, it puts my French to shame I'm afraid.'

'Evelyn's right. No need to leave on our account Georgette.' William reinforced the message as he invited the two visitors to sit before continuing, 'I was just trying to persuade Georgette to join Edward and me at Dreamland. To be honest I'm not sure Edward wants to go but the talk around town is the scenic railway is an exciting ride and I'm keen to try.'

'I do hope you were going to invite Evelyn and me too,' said Catherine.

'Of course.'

'In which case, How about Monday?' said

Catherine.

'Perhaps. But first, what's the present?' William asked, pointing to the parcel resting on the floor at Evelyn's feet.

'Edward wanted one of the paintings from the tea shop, one of Alastair's, and he wanted me to choose. So I did.'

'With some help,' added Catherine.

'True. But it's not exactly a present,' said Evelyn.

'Not exactly?' asked William.

'No. It's five pounds, a good price for such a painting. Mr. Trenter, Alastair, has a reputation in Kent for fine work. I understand when younger he was nearly accepted into the Royal Academy.'

William raised his hand, laughing, 'It's all right Evelyn, it's not me you're selling it to and I'm sure Edward will buy it, though I don't know where he'll hang it. Georgette, do you think your mistress will want guests banging nails in walls.'

'Perhaps it could hang in the breakfast room Monsieur.'

'Georgette, come on, William, not Monsieur just because we have visitors. Anyway,' he spoke directly to Evelyn, 'why don't you take it up to him. He's in his room.'

Georgette coughed and looked at William and coughed again until he looked at her.

'Oh Georgette, you're so discreet. Go on. What is it?'

'Monsieur Thompson might be resting. He often does in the afternoon when he's not performing. And he has a bad head, I heard him say earlier.'

'Then leave it with me.' William took the picture.

'That's probably best. In any case, it wouldn't do for me to call on him in his room.' Evelyn said, partly relieved the choice was taken from her but partly concerned the housemaid should know so much about Edward.

'Anyway, you'll see him later at The Winter Gardens,' said William, 'and I'm sure he'll pay you for it then.'

'I wasn't worried about the money,' said Evelyn.

'Good, because I'm not paying for him. I'm not at all interested in art. Mind you, a picture of a pretty girl can brighten a room. Talking of pretty girls, you three young ladies will accompany Edward and me to Dreamland on Monday then? Edward doesn't perform on Mondays.'

'I must be getting on,' said Georgette, heading for the door but William called her back,

'It's all right Georgette. We'd like you to join us, wouldn't we ladies?'

'Of course,' Evelyn said.

'I don't think my mistress would like it,' said Georgette.

'You've every right to a day off, you weren't given one yesterday, which you should have and besides, we'd like your company, wouldn't we ladies.' He made the last part a statement.

'Are you sure?' Georgette asked.

'Absolutely. I'll talk to the mistress of the house. I'm sure she'll let you have the day off.'

'But what about Patrick?'

'He'll come too.'

Georgette smiled, nodded and left the room.

That evening The Winter Gardens was busy. A soprano debuting there had sung at La Scala and though Evelyn couldn't hear properly from her coat check desk, she could hear the loud applause and cheers. The auditorium was crowded but as it was a warm evening few coats had been checked in, leaving Evelyn little to do. Halfway through the soprano's performance Catherine left the ticket booth and indicated that Evelyn should join her as she went outside for a cigarette. The cooler air in the gardens surrounding The Winter Gardens was welcomed and they stood a couple of yards outside the main entrance, protected from any wind off the sea by the amphitheatre cut into the cliff. The sun was low and in their sheltered bowl was cast the peaceful half–light of sunset. They listened to the muffled music and Catherine took a pack of cigarettes from the top of her stocking. She was about to light one when Edward came out, offering his trench lighter. Evelyn wondered if he had seen Catherine pull the cigarettes from under her uniform dress.

'Thank you,' said Catherine.

'She's very good,' said Edward, nodding back towards the auditorium, 'and the poster doesn't do her justice.' Inside the main entrance was an easel with a poster advertising the soprano's performances with a black and white picture. 'That's a lie,' he said, 'the poster is quite flattering. I'm thinking of getting one done for myself.'

'They say she's performed at Milan,' said Evelyn.

'Well I hope she had a better pianist than him.' He indicated back inside.

'Is he not good?' asked Evelyn.

Edward sighed and lit a cigarette. 'No, he's all right. He's better than all right. He's good. I'm just … I don't know, a bit … grey today.'

'Grey?' Evelyn repeated.

'I think … you know, not a black mood but maybe grey and less than charitable. I'm sorry.'

'Because of the other pianist?' Catherine asked.

'No,' Edward forced a half laugh, 'he's all right really, we met, earlier. He served, in Flanders. He was there. And he plays well enough, more than well enough.' He lit his own cigarette and drew deep. He was wearing his dinner jacket, having played earlier and being expected to play later, but seemed not to fill it this evening, as if it weighed heavily. 'And thank you for your choice of painting. I'll go to the bank tomorrow and bring the money to the tea shop. Is seven pounds enough?'

'I think the price is five,' said Evelyn.

'But it is a beautiful piece and you chose well. It's as fine and peaceful a sunset as fit to be the last a man might see.'

It was an odd phrase from Edward and even more odd for his usual slow delivery. There was a short pause, as if Evelyn and Catherine were thinking what it meant before Evelyn said, 'I saw it as a sunrise, not sunset.'

Edward shrugged. 'In any event, you chose well.'

'With Catherine's help,' said Evelyn, 'and I'm sure it was on sale for five pounds, not seven.'

'As you wish. I don't want to damage the walls so I'm thinking of hanging it in place of the mirror. Does that sound a good idea? I think so.' Edward said and lowered himself on to a small rock wall retaining a neat flower bed.

'Are you all right Edward? We met Georgette earlier, when bringing round your new painting. She mentioned you had a headache,' said Evelyn.

'Did she? Yes, I suppose so. It's … better now.'

'Do you get them often? Are they related to … your … wound?' Evelyn asked cautiously, not knowing how to refer to Edward's injuries.

'I expect so. They come and go. Anyway,' he nodded towards the auditorium, 'that's the opening bars to *Ave Maria*, I should go back inside,' said Edward, standing, stamping out his barely smoked cigarette and leaving the two ladies before they could respond. Evelyn watched his back, hoping she hadn't offended but also irritated perhaps he didn't feel he could explain further. She was annoyed that Georgette could know of the headache before she, not that there was any way she could have known earlier.

Just inside the foyer Edward was met by William. Evelyn watched as William took hold of Edward's wrist to check his watch, shrugged and took a step back. Edward pulled a small bottle from his jacket inside pocket, unscrewed the lid and took two or three tentative sips with the right side of his mouth. He then gave the bottle to

William and took out a handkerchief to wipe his mouth before going into the auditorium. William remained in the foyer for half a minute before turning to join him.

Catherine turned to Evelyn, 'Did we say something to offend? He didn't even finish his fag. And that appeared rather furtive, didn't it? Men do like their secrets. Not like us women, eh?' She touched Evelyn's shoulder.

Evelyn nodded. Catherine finished her cigarette and they went back in together.

The alley behind the tea shop was ill–lit and Evelyn was apprehensive about this part of the walk home. Living in Spitalfields she was used to dark alleys and narrow passages but there was always some noise or activity or other women on the streets, at least up until around midnight, and it felt safer than here. Yes, some of the women at home were prostitutes but she had come to know them, though not well enough to ask the questions she wanted – perhaps she would when next there. But here in Margate the alley was still and quiet when walking from The Winter Gardens and she missed the catcalls, arguments and crying children at home. She let herself into the yard and the tea shop's back door, then into the kitchen, moving cautiously in the poor light which barely reached the kitchen from the streetlamp out front. Usually, when back from working at The Winter Gardens, she felt a comfortable tiredness and was happy to be going to bed, but tonight there was a weariness she didn't recognise and a nervous train of thought that wouldn't be slowed.

She lit two gas burners on the hob, one for a kettle and the other for some meagre light and prepared a small pot of tea. Whilst waiting for the kettle to boil she went to change into her night dress and started up the stairs leading from the kitchen. As usual she could hear Alastair snoring from one of the rooms on the floor above but, unusually, there was a sliver of dim yellow light escaping from one of the doors on the next landing that was ajar. Assuming Alice must still be awake she went up and waited a few seconds, listening at the door. There were a few odd scratching sounds and the pouring of water into a receptacle. She knocked lightly and waited before moving a little closer and peeking through the thin gap between door and frame. Alice was standing at the far side of the room, back to the door, dusting a brush over an easel which held a half–finished painting of a sunset over the sea. Evelyn knocked again and watched as Alice startled and draped a cloth over the painting before coming to the door. Evelyn took a step back.

'Who's there?' whispered Alice.

'It's me. You're up late. Is everything all right?' said Evelyn wondering at the secrecy but not pushing open the door.

'Yes, thank you.' Alice spoke quietly.

'I'm making tea, would you like some?' Evelyn asked, hoping Alice would invite her in first.

'Yes please. I'll come down in a minute or two.'

Evelyn left, wondering, and by the time the kettle boiled Alice had joined her in the kitchen. They carried the pot and cups through to the front, sitting at the table favoured by Edward and William in the window. Alice seemed tense and Evelyn waited until she had sipped from her tea before asking her, 'It's late, are you sure everything is all right?'

The streetlamp gave some light to the shop and Alice's face was visible but not well lit. She was pale.

'Oh I'm fine. I'm usually awake when you come in, it's hard to sleep with Alastair snoring. How was work at The Winter Gardens? Perhaps Alastair and I will come one evening.'

'It was all right. Quite busy. I'm not sure Edward was at his best.'

'Did he mention the picture you chose for him? Did he like it?'

'He did and yes. He's hoping to hang it in his room and joked he might put it where the mirror is at the moment, but it wasn't amusing and he didn't seem himself.'

'It can't be easy for him.'

'No. And I think he's in pain some of the time.'

Alice nodded and sipped at her tea. As she raised her hand Evelyn saw a mark, just noticeable in the half–light.

'Have you a bruise?' Evelyn pointed to Alice's forearm.

'I don't think so.' Alice twisted her arm so she could see the mark better. It was a streak of red.

'Paint?'

Alice licked her hand, rubbed at the mark and it faded. 'Yes,' she said quietly.

'Are you decorating a nursery for baby?'

'Yes.'

Evelyn tried to read Alice's expression but the light was poor and Alice looked down into her cup and said, 'No,' before looking away and then up at the space on the wall where the picture they had sold to Edward had hung. 'I'm half–way through the latest watercolour.'

'Oh, some final preparation for Alastair's latest work?'

'Not quite.' Alice's voice, already quiet, dropped further. 'It's … I … Alastair doesn't, hasn't, painted all you see.'

'So you paint them together?'

'Not as such. It's been a long while … in fact it's been since our Curtis didn't come home … Alastair hasn't picked up a brush, or, rather, he did but …' Alice looked to the painting of the doomed warship, its dark images barely visible in the poor light.

'And all the others …?'

'I've been painting for many years, but of course nothing as good as Alastair … he was nearly accepted into the Royal Academy … did you know?'

'Yes. My father was … is … very proud of how good Alastair is.'

'And will be again. Perhaps when the new one arrives.' She touched her belly. 'But over the years I'd been trying and he has been teaching me … he's been a wonderful teacher you know … so encouraging … and we needed the money, so, they're not as good but … some sell.'

'But they have Alastair's initials.'

'It helps them sell, and they are the same as mine, after all.'

'Oh, I see.' Evelyn was unsure what to make of the revelation.

'You think I've done wrong,' said Alice.

'No. They're wonderful paintings, but why not let people know. You should not be ashamed of them.'

'Do you know how hard it is for a woman to be accepted as a serious painter?'

'It has been known.'

'And what of Alastair?'

'He should be proud of you …'

'… and he would be, if he could bring himself to pick up a brush again. But since Curtis … didn't come home.' Alice's voice trailed away and she sipped on her tea again then said, 'Alastair shouldn't know that you … know.'

'Of course, I understand.' Evelyn nodded and squeezed Alice's hand. 'But they are good, very good.'

'It's enough for the paintings to be well regarded. You're sure Mr. Thompson liked it?'

'Yes, he said so and I'm sure he does.' There was an awkward silence until Evelyn spoke quickly, with the idea that had just occurred to her. 'I know, you could paint his poster for The Winter Gardens. He could have one in the foyer, like the more famous performers, and you would be perfect for it.'

'I'm not very good at portraits.'

'It wouldn't be a formal portrait, but a picture to be made into a poster, and I could ask if The Winter Gardens would pay you for it. And Edward would trust you to provide a ... sympathetic portrayal. I could ask him tomorrow.' Evelyn was excited by the idea but Alice looked doubtful, saying,

'I don't think Alastair would approve.'

'You don't have to tell him.'

'I don't like secrets from Alastair.'

'But Alastair doesn't mind keeping them from you?' Evelyn asked in as kindly a fashion as she could and was reminded of Catherine's comments earlier that evening about men and secrets – though Alice's painting couldn't be considered open knowledge.

'What do you mean?' Alice asked.

'His morning walks. You don't know where he goes.'

'Oh.'

'He keeps it a secret, even from you.'

'No, not really.'

'I thought you said you didn't know.'

'I did, but ... I'm sorry ... I do know. It's just ... you'll think it odd, or Alastair mad.' Alice's voice dropped to a sad whisper.

'I'm sorry, I shouldn't have said anything.' Evelyn was ashamed to be the cause of Alice's sadness.

'No, it's all right. Perhaps I should have told you, but I'm not sure Alastair would want your father to know.'

'Know what?'

'Where he goes?'

'I won't say. I promise.'

Alice paused and looked behind her, towards the door out to the kitchen, then back to Evelyn. 'He doesn't go far, just past Cliftonville. There is a quiet spot, up on the cliffs, somewhere near Hodges Bridge, which affords a clear view out to the sea ...'

'… and …'

'… Alastair can't help but look out for Curtis. He has nowhere else to watch.'

'To watch?'

'For Curtis. In case … he comes home. You see, he has nowhere else. But you'll think him … mad. I'm sorry.'

'Oh Alice, for what? You shouldn't be, and nor should Alastair.'

Alice sipped on her tea. 'There's a lady, close by, who they say can help you contact loved ones that didn't come back.' She spoke slowly, measuring each word.

'And does Alastair think she can help him, you?'

'I don't know. But what if she could? We should try, shouldn't we? And then Alastair wouldn't need to go for his … walks.'

'You know my father wouldn't approve. There are many charlatans and liars.'

'I know, but if there's a chance … shouldn't we try? Sometimes I fear Alastair and I won't know how to stop missing Curtis so we can love …' Alice rubbed her belly.

'You will find a way. I'm sure.' Evelyn offered sincerely.

'Will we? It's been more than three years already since Curtis …' Alice failed to stifle her tears.

'A short time to think such great pain might subside even a little. But you have room in your heart to love another as much.' Evelyn left her chair to kneel next to Alice and hold her.

Edward, Margate, Monday 16th August 1920

Edward had been amused over the weekend by William's efforts to charm the mistress of the guest house into giving Georgette the Monday from work. William's campaign had started badly on Saturday morning. He had antagonised one of the other guests in an argument over the Labour Party's declaration the previous Thursday. The Party had called for a general strike if the government declared war on Russia following the Bolsheviks successes there; William was in favour of a strike. The guest and his wife were regular visitors to the house and had complained to the mistress of William's disregard for usual standards and decency. A bunch of flowers and a promise to avoid political discourse in the breakfast room had recovered some goodwill but the mistress was not to be moved on giving Georgette Monday off work. William resorted to purchasing ten Margate postcards and addressing them to friends and family around the country, each one extolling the virtues of the guest house's comfort and attractions; though he didn't stick any stamps on them until she agreed to give Georgette the day off. Edward teased William while watching the drama play out.

So, by Sunday evening, before leaving for The Winter Gardens, William had placated the guest house mistress. He'd also pleased both Georgette and Patrick, though it was considered prudent they meet Edward and William at the Clock Tower where Marine Terrace met Marine Drive. This was also where Evelyn and Catherine would meet them.

It was mid–morning and Edward was reading *The Times* while William smoked and occasionally wrote in his small notebook, waiting under The Clock Tower. William saw Georgette and Patrick first, Georgette almost trotting to keep up with the excited child, his baggy shorts flapping as he ran. Though it was warm he wore a dark jumper with a collarless shirt underneath and long woollen socks. He slowed as he neared the two men and, on reaching them said, 'Bonjour, thank you for taking us to Dreamland.' He spoke slowly and formally, trying to cover his accent, and looked William in the eye before switching to Edward, whose gaze he held even longer. Edward folded his newspaper and gave his practised smile. Georgette joined them and repeated the thank you for herself, without holding Edward's good eye for as long as her son, but for longer than she usually managed, which pleased Edward. Patrick stood quietly while William and Georgette chatted and Edward watched for the other two ladies. They soon arrived, talking to and over each other with a freedom Edward envied. Evelyn seemed especially pleased to see them and greeted all with equal enthusiasm, shaking Patrick's hand and being, 'very pleased to meet you.' Catherine was equally enthusiastic except perhaps, thought Edward, towards Georgette. Evelyn had brought sandwiches and a bottle of Schweppes ginger ale while Catherine had baked a fruit cake. Edward took the hamper from them.

They walked in two groups, men at the front and ladies behind, with Patrick in between. It was barely a five minute walk to Dreamland, despite the tourists, motor cars, trams and horse drawn carts and having to skirt around the small crowd building in front of a trestle table. The banner above it declared *National Council Of Women Of Great Britain And Ireland* and a group of young women were handing out leaflets, trying to interest other women, while three policemen stood nearby, watching. Edward recognised one of them, the constable that had spoken to them that first night on the way home from The Winter Gardens. The constable saw them and spoke to the sergeant next to him.

Dreamland was marked by a sign in a semicircle above the main doors to the hall which opened onto Marine Terrace. Edward's party joined the flow of holidaymakers from the town and the railway station down to the turnstiles – Edward being sure to put William to the front and giving him the money to pay for all six of them. He ignored Evelyn and Catherine's protestations and accepted Georgette's thanks with a nonchalant wave, hoping she wouldn't feel obliged in any way. Once past the turnstiles Patrick ran to the front and led the way, heading straight to the Scenic Railway. The Dreamland park was a haphazard collection of attractions and rides, dominated by the new Scenic Railway, opened that summer. As they neared the undulating wooden trellis structure they could hear the screams of riders and the rhythmic clack–clack of the carriages as they rushed around the oval track's concentric rails. It was almost a mile in length and its peaks and troughs came at the riders with indecent speed. The three ladies increased their pace as they approached the back of the queue, trying to catch Patrick, but on seeing the height of the ride's peaks and speed of the cars Edward slowed. William didn't realise and joined the ladies in the queue. It was Evelyn who first noticed Edward wasn't with them. She left the queue to go back to him.

'Edward, is everything all right?'

'Of course, you go on. I'll catch up.'

'But we should all sit together.'

'Yes, of course, but …' he touched his spectacles, securing the mask.

Evelyn looked at his good eye. 'I'm sure it will be fine. It fits well, doesn't it?'

'Of course,' agreed Edward, not wanting to admit to the redness of the skin being chafed underneath and which was made more sore by sweating under a hat in the sun. At least out on the seafront there was a breeze but here, in the sheltered gardens and park, it was too hot, even though there was cloud cover.

'Or are you concerned the wind might take your hat?'

'No, the hat's not a problem, I can hold it. It's just … sometimes my … spectacles slip forward and it wouldn't be right for others to see … underneath … not here. You go on. Besides, someone needs to look after the hamper.' He held up the wicker case he had been carrying. 'I'll watch, from there.' Edward pointed to a bench nearby from where he would see the cars as they reached the top of the first peak. 'You go on,' he repeated and walked away before Evelyn could respond.

Edward sat on the bench, smoking and watching the cars on the Scenic Railway track thunder past and wondering why he had mentioned his concern over the mask slipping to Evelyn. It was always a worry but he had never spoken of it to anyone. He watched the crowded cars as they crawled up the first incline and on the fifth set saw William, the ladies and Patrick. William and Georgette sat in a middle car with Patrick between them and Evelyn and Catherine sat behind them, arms linked, leaning nervously into each other as the car crept higher. It hung at the top just as Evelyn seemed to look down at him and both she and Catherine screamed with delight as the car tipped over the peak and careered down the track, thrilling with its speed and danger. Edward laughed out loud, forgetting that stretching his face would hurt so much, but this pain felt good.

The group came out of the ride, excited and chattering, apart from William, of course, and Catherine exclaimed it was 'the berries' and then had to explain the phrase as one given to her by the American visitor of last month. Edward suggested they go back on, making them promise next time to wave as they screamed. Then, when they came out again, he insisted they ride twice more before Patrick said he wanted to try the miniature railway and William wondered what the midget town show might present.

By early afternoon they were hungry and Patrick was tired so William led them from the park. They walked towards the harbour where a few smacks bobbed in the high tide water, sails furled. They had planned to lunch on the jetty, just past the harbour. It stretched a quarter of a mile into the North Sea, but was crowded and the wind was picking up. Ladies clutched hats with one hand and kept skirts low with the other. So Evelyn suggested they take their picnic past Cliftonville, near Hodges Bridge. She had heard the views were lovely; Catherine agreed. Halfway up Fort Hill William put Patrick on his shoulders and carried him the rest of the way up to the cliffs and a mile outside Margate. Edward still carried the hamper.

Hodges Bridge was an iron structure spanning a gap in the cliffs. Below was a cutting that led down to the beaches at the foot of the cliffs. Just the other side of the bridge they found a flat, grassy spot, far enough away from the tea rooms to be quiet. Evelyn took a rug from the hamper and spread it on the grass before unwrapping and handing round sandwiches as the group sat. Edward was uncomfortable on the ground in his summer suit but supposed the ladies must be more so in their calf length skirts and though Evelyn's rode up to expose slightly more of her legs he was careful not to be found looking. Patrick picked at the ham sandwich, being more interested in the bottle of ginger ale William opened.

'This reminds me of the Fortnum and Mason hampers some of the lads received at the front,' said William, 'not that I ever had one. The most I received was a jar of jam from an aunt that was cracked by the time I opened the parcel and I had to lick it off the newspaper it was wrapped in. Nearly cut my tongue off.' He passed the ginger ale to Patrick who waited for Georgette to nod before taking a gulp and declaring it to be 'the berries', his new favourite phrase.

Patrick handed it back then shouted, 'Look, it is *Royal Sovereign*,' pointing back towards Margate. From where they sat a toy–like paddle steamer was docking at the extension to the jetty's end.

'Patrick knows all the steamers that come down from London,' said Georgette proudly, 'even this far away.' They all agreed it was an impressive feat at what William reckoned was getting on for two miles. When Patrick asked how he knew, William was happy to draw on his wartime stories of estimating distances between lines, especially during his time with the Royal Horse Artillery, though Edward knew it had been but a few weeks before he was transferred into the Royal Fusiliers, London Regiment, in Edward's platoon.

While William entertained Patrick, the others settled into gentle conversation. Edward had half an ear on the war stories William was telling Patrick but when William finished telling one theory as to why Edward had been called 'The Lucky Lieutenant' and started the tale about the Christmas pudding and grenade that would lead to Corporal Wile's decapitation he edged over to them, still sitting on the rug, and interrupted, 'Perhaps another time William.'

William looked at Patrick and whispered, 'Later,' before starting a less gruesome story about the new recruit surprised to wake up cuddling a rat the size of small terrier. Edward smiled at the denouement, even though he knew it, saying, 'Poor young Kayst. Didn't he give the rat a name?'

'George.' William remembered.

'After the King. We could have charged him for that.' Edward laughed, but his mask made it awkward, more so if also speaking, and though Patrick laughed too Edward could tell the boy was watching him, but with interest, not fear. Edward hadn't seen himself laugh in a mirror but could guess the difference between the two halves of his face was exaggerated by one being animated while the other remained frozen. The sun was warming, the breeze from the sea was refreshing and he felt no judgement from his fellow picnickers. It was a good afternoon. He rolled off the rug to lay flat on his back on the grass, trying not to consciously remember the last time his mother and father had taken him on a picnic – it was not that he didn't want to remember; on the contrary, he hoped to, but his best chance lay in simply letting his concentration drift with the few clouds above and his mind wander in and out of the conversations around him.

Catherine was asking Georgette, 'Does Patrick go to school?'

'He should have, last year but ... I ... do not think he was ready. Perhaps he will start in September, the school at St. John's church.'

'Well he speaks very good English and will do well there. I know that school and my aunt prepares the flowers for the church. Which reminds me. William, Edward, do you know Reverend Railton? He's the new man looking after St. John's and I think my aunt has rather taken a fancy to him. In the right way, of course.'

'Should we know him?' William asked.

'He was in France, during the war.'

'I don't recall meeting him. But then I didn't spend much time with any of the clergy over there. Not that they often came by our way in the trenches,' said William.

'I think what William means is there were a lot of trenches and not many clergymen to go around,' said Edward, softening William's remark.

'Well my aunt thinks Reverend Railton may have spent quite some time in the trenches and saw some terrible things. It seems he doesn't sleep well since he returned from France and often walks Margate late at night, stopping at the police station to share a cocoa with the duty sergeant.'

'How does your aunt know?' Georgette asked.

'Oh, she's friendly with the sergeant.'

'As well as the constable?' said Evelyn.

'There aren't many don't find time to talk with my aunt. She likes a good chat, as I believe you men might say. Oh, and speaking of which, I noticed earlier the sergeant paying close attention to you gentlemen as we passed on the way to Dreamland. My aunt has already mentioned he is not trustful of you. Something to do with an altercation in a tobacconist?' Catherine let the statement hang as a question.

'We are as innocent as any soldier can be,' said William, winking at Patrick, then pulling his hip flask from an inside pocket and taking a gulp before offering it to Edward, who propped up on one elbow and took just a sip. Edward started to speak but stopped on hearing the low throbbing sound. Recognising it he looked skyward, scanning the horizons first to the sea and then inland where he saw, far in the distance, the silhouette of a bi–plane, heading their way. Anxious, he stood and went to pull his field glasses from their case, hanging at his right hand side, except it wasn't there.

'Sergeant Burrslow, where are my ...' he stopped himself.

'William was now also standing and moved to Edward. 'It's all right ... sir. One of ours.'

Edward's good eye squinted, then he realised the ladies on the rug were watching him rather than the increasingly closer and louder plane. Edward forced a smile and had to shout above the throbbing and clattering of engines which was now painful on their ears. 'Of course. Handley Page.'

But no one heard him as the bi–plane roared above, over the cliffs and out towards sea. Patrick turned and ran after it, shouting and waving. Georgette called something after him but it was lost. As the sound died with the plane's distance Edward heard Catherine explain, 'It's from Manston. They use the base for training mechanics these days. We don't often see them flying though and few folk like them. They're a reminder of the bombs the Germans dropped on us in seventeen. One of Beatrice's laundry girls was killed. Awful for her family. Still, I think the planes are quite exciting. A few months ago there used to be some joyriding from there, holidaymakers would pay a lot to be taken up, but I think that's stopped now. Shame. I'd like to try.'

Edward took the hip flask William offered and hoped the slight tremble as he raised it to his lips wasn't obvious. He turned away to sip, not confident he would find the right place on his lips this time. William stood next to him and took the flask back when Edward had finished. Georgette shouted to Patrick but he was out of earshot, close to the cliff. 'He's all right,' William said.

'I'll get him,' said Edward, going after the boy. Edward had gone ten or so yards when Evelyn caught up with. He was just taking a cigarette from a pack and offered her one which she refused,

'Of course, you don't. Sorry, forgot,' he said and stopped walking to light the cigarette with his trench lighter but his hands were still unsteady and Evelyn took the lighter to help. He sucked hard on the cigarette, 'You should, you know. Can't beat a good fag,' he said and walked on. Though the breeze was a bit stronger as they neared the cliff he was sweating more and wanted to wipe his forehead before the bead dribbled under his mask, but didn't want to draw any more attention to it. Evelyn called to Patrick as they neared the cliff. The bi–plane was just a dot over the sea and the boy turned back to them.

'There's more ginger ale.' Evelyn called, and the boy ran past them back to the picnic rug. Edward carried on walking and stopped a few yards short of the cliff edge.

'Well, that was exciting wasn't it? I haven't seen one of those since nineteen seventeen. We were always grateful to see our own but I'm not sure you'd catch me up there, not now. It's not a pretty sight if they crash land or have to bail out and then ... well, you know. Not a pretty sight.' Edward looked out to the horizon but asked, 'Do you think that's true, what Catherine said, about that reverend not sleeping?'

'I don't see why not.'

'So if not even a man of God can sleep well ...' he didn't finish the sentence, dragging on the cigarette.

After a couple of minutes Evelyn said. 'Isn't it quite lovely here? Shame the sun is hiding.'

Edward nodded. 'And thank you for preparing the picnic. I haven't been on one since ... I can't remember. With my parents I suppose. Years ago.'

'Where are they?'

'Lincoln. Where I grew up. My father is a solicitor. We rarely went out into the countryside for picnics though. It was mostly farmland nearby and lovely in its own way but not as ... dramatic, as here. Though I probably don't see it as well as I might, what with ... you know.' He gave a vague wave to his face.

'But you do see all right, with the ... real eye?' Evelyn asked.

'Better than the painted one.' Edward tried a joke and Evelyn laughed politely. Edward continued, 'The good one's not very good for long distances, or in the dark, for some reason, but then lots of people have to wear spectacles and they have ... two working eyes. So I've no complaints and it is a lovely view.'

'I probably shouldn't say, but I think this is where Alastair comes.'

'Alastair?'

'Trenter. Alice's husband from the tea shop.'

'Oh, Alastair. Of course. And why wouldn't he? It is beautiful, I imagine, especially with the sun shining.'

'He ...' Evelyn paused, '... he ... is watching, for Curtis.'

'Who's Curtis?'

'Their son.'

'Is he a fisherman?' Edward indicated to the smacks leaving Margate harbour with the tide.

'No, he's in ... was in ... the navy during the war ...'

'And?'

'He didn't come home.'

'Oh.'

'His boat, the *Gurkha*, hit a mine, near Dungeness.'

Edward took a bearing from the sun. 'But that's south from here, he couldn't possibly be looking in the right place.'

'Edward, he's never going to be able to look in the right place,' said Evelyn.

'No, of course not, stupid of me.'

'I suppose he might as well watch here as anywhere and if praying for a miracle then it's as good as anywhere.'

'But he doesn't really think he'll ever come home?'

'I don't suppose so, but if you don't have a place to go, a place to be sure? What do you do?'

'I don't know. Sometimes, I wonder if ... I mean those people who just ... weren't there anymore. What if ... they are ... somewhere?' Edward spoke haltingly.

'Could they be?'

Edward dropped his cigarette and stamped it out. 'No. Of course not. Stupid idea.'

'Please don't mention to Alastair or Alice I told you. Alastair seems not to want anyone to know he's still ... watching.'

'Of course not, our secret. And sometimes there's nothing else a father can do I suppose. Mrs. Trenter must be worried.'

'She's considering asking a medium to help.'

'They say some have found comfort that way,' Edward said but the caution in his voice was obvious.

'My father wouldn't approve either,' said Evelyn,

'but there are those who are desperate.'

'And broken beyond reason, I daresay. Your father might be correct and I may be dubious, but do we have the right to protest? Though of course, if the medium can be proven as a charlatan then I would let William deal with them his way,' Edward said.

'William?'

'He has strong views on such loathsome exploitation, but then I don't know if he has ever lost someone close and known such despair.'

'And you have?' Evelyn asked.

'Not so close as Alastair and Alice, I'm sure.' Edward took another cigarette from his silver case.

'Another, so soon?'

'Sorry nurse Evelyn. But it helps, I have a headache coming. And a sip from William's medicinal hip flask may also help. We should return.'

'Is that what you were drinking a few evenings ago, at The Winter Gardens?' Evelyn asked.

Edward thought for a second before answering, 'No. It was some medicine. I wasn't feeling quite well that Friday.'

'Georgette did say you had a headache.'

'They come and go.' Edward said.

'Do the doctors say they will stop?'

'They don't know.'

'Do the doctors know why?'

'There is some shrapnel, just small pieces, still in … there. I think they may be moving around, trying to escape.' Edward indicated to his head and tried to joke but it wasn't funny.

'Oh. I'm sorry. Can they take it out?' Evelyn asked but Edward was already walking back to the picnic rug and didn't answer.

Georgette was tidying away the picnic while Catherine and Patrick listened to William's stories. Edward raised his hand to his mouth and tilted it, as if pretending to drink, and William passed him the hip flask.

'Is that a good idea Edward?' Evelyn asked.

Edward shrugged and sipped anyway. There was an awkward silence which Patrick broke, asking Edward, 'Please, can I wear your mask?'

'Patrick! What a thing to ask,' Georgette shouted. She leant forward and slapped the back of Patrick's legs. Patrick screamed with the sharp pain. 'I'm sorry Monsieur Thompson,' said Georgette.

The force in Georgette's smack was a shock and Catherine instinctively went to Patrick. 'Georgette!'

Georgette started to speak but stopped before apologising again to Edward and then asking William to make sure Patrick was brought home safe. Then she left, walking briskly back over Hodges Bridge towards Margate. Catherine cuddled Patrick. Edward sipped again from the hip flask. The pain in his head was growing.

'To Major Gillies and Derwent Wood?' said William quietly. It was a question.

The Blue Bench

Evelyn, Calcott hop farms, Sunday 22nd August 1920

Evelyn hadn't realised her father and Alastair corresponded frequently, and in some detail apparently, until she received the letter, on the Wednesday following the picnic.

My dear Evelyn,

I hope you are well. Alastair tells me you are busy both at The Winter Gardens and in the tea shop. He is grateful to you for taking on so much work in the shop in order to give Alice as much rest as possible. I am reminded of Colossians 3:23:

Whatever you do, work heartily, as for the Lord and not for men.

Alastair also tells me, and it is heart–warming to know, you are making new friends. Alastair has written of Miss Blundell, Miss Burton, Mr. Thompson and Mr. Burrslow.

I'm visiting the mission this coming Sunday to check on readiness before the pickers arrive in earnest and to conduct a short Sunday service in the new marquee to see if it is suitable. Is there any possibility you could bring your friends to the mission so I might meet them? Otherwise I shall be moving to the mission two weeks later, on the 4th September, and might meet them sometime soon after. I will be there until October.

In the meantime please know I am missing you and, in

particular, our evening discussions of our day's events over cocoa, but what a lot we shall have to share when we do come together.

All my love and blessings,

Father

PS I enclose a crude map of the location of the mission as I know previously we have relied on the bus and you may not be clear on its whereabouts.

PPS I believe Mr. Tewson will be down for the harvest again, but I will make sure he is aware you are busy with other important work.

Evelyn read the letter again and wondered if her father knew by now that Alastair was no longer attending services and she had yet to join Alice in church on a Sunday. She felt guilty, more so for knowing of Alastair's faith crisis when perhaps her father did not, rather than her own non–attendance at church. That was easily rectified and her father's invitation for the following Sunday was the obvious solution. She read the letter to Catherine that evening, during a quiet time at The Winter Gardens.

'It's nice of your father to write. I especially like the piece about evening discussions of the day's events. It's a bit like ours when walking home from here with Edward and William. Speaking of which, our night time walk home with them has not gone unnoticed. The constable mentioned it to my aunt again. She complimented him on his concern whilst also saying how pleased she was that we had two young men to see us back home safely.'

'So the constable is watching. Perhaps he's jealous? For you?' Evelyn teased.

'Hmm. I think the constable would need to be several years younger and an Inspector at the very least.

But back to your father's letter, why does he want to meet us? We're not children,' Catherine said.

'I know it might not seem it from the tone of his letter but he's a kind man and likes the company of younger people. Anyone younger than himself that is. And it's an excuse to ask me to visit him at the mission and perhaps increase the congregation at the Sunday service there for his trial run of the marquee.'

'Will an extra four matter?'

'Five.'

'Oh I doubt my aunt would go. Her Sundays are reserved for St. John's. She's keen to hear Reverend Railton's sermon and seems to be giving more attention than ever to the church flowers.'

'But we might get Edward and William to go?' Evelyn made it a question.

'I don't know about William. He doesn't strike me as the church type.'

'But he'll go if you do,' said Evelyn.

'What do you mean?'

'I think he has an eye for you,' Evelyn teased.

'Then you haven't seen him look at Georgette. And anyway, much as my aunt has a sense of humour I'm not sure she would approve of a communist in the family.'

'Is he?'

'He talks as one, but doesn't live the life of a working man, so I don't know. Though I have to admit his stories do make me laugh.'

'Then we should invite them to the mission on Sunday.'

'We?'

'Yes, and if they take the car that would be convenient and though we needn't mention the service we could time it to be there as it starts and it would be rude not to attend, wouldn't it?'

'And what's that about Mr. Tewson? It's a rather cryptic comment by your father.'

Evelyn shrugged. 'Nothing important. We walked out together once or twice last year, but he is too old for me, and a widower.'

'Well which was it? Once or twice?'

'Twice. But he is too old. And anyway, after the hop harvest he didn't go back to Spitalfields. I heard he went back to his home, up north somewhere.'

'I think there's more to this than you're saying. A pretty young lady and a rich widower?'

'He certainly isn't rich or he wouldn't be hop picking, would he?'

'Handsome then?'

'I didn't notice and he's too old.'

'Well perhaps I'll see him for myself if we go down to the mission, and anyway, it would be a chance for you to spend a little more time with Edward.'

'I suppose,' Evelyn said, and avoided further discussion by returning to the coat check.

Evelyn watched Catherine while Catherine watched the boy, Patrick, as he watched William. It had been easy to persuade Edward and William that a trip to the hop farms on a sunny Sunday morning was a good idea – fresh air and a little walking exercise and scant mention of the mission as such – and William had been keen to take the Wolseley. He enjoyed driving Edward's car and, even more, enjoyed being watched by Patrick as he drove. It was likely Patrick had not been in a private motor car before and he sat at the back between the two ladies, his expressions alternating between excitement, fear and more than a touch of wonder. Catherine had taken Patrick's cap from his head and pressed it into his lap, telling him to hold it; he gripped so tight his small hands were white. Evelyn had been surprised, though Catherine less so, that Georgette would not be joining them, but William's charm offensive on Georgette's mistress at the guest house had its limits. Catherine had suggested they bring Patrick, a day out would be better than a day stuck on the top floor of the guest house, and Georgette had agreed enthusiastically. William was happy to oblige.

Edward was given charge of both the RAC roadmap and the crude diagram sent by Evelyn's father and directed the forty–five minute drive to the mission, via Herne Bay – not the shortest route but Edward insisted. It was a sunnier day than of recent and it felt to Evelyn perhaps there was still time for summer. A few miles south of Herne Bay they turned left off the Canterbury Road and down an unmade lane. It bumped them along between rows of hop poles, tall enough that the track was darkened by the shadows from the rich green plants climbing to the top. The hop plants were nearly full height and swamped their poles, teeming with leaves though the hops were still a few weeks from ripeness. Two hundred yards on they came to a farmyard with a house and two large barns. Edward consulted Reverend Coughston's hand drawn map and instructed William to follow the track through the farmyard and out the other side. The mission was set in a clearing amongst the hop gardens and consisted of a couple of old huts, made from corrugated iron over a basic timber frame, a marquee which would be used for services and a larger hut for communal cooking.

William parked near the marquee and Patrick was first from the car, climbing over Catherine.

Evelyn was excited, anticipating meeting her father and friends she had made in previous years. Catherine followed Patrick as he went straight to a long rope with a piece of wood tied to the end, hanging as a makeshift swing from a tree in the clearing. There were three older women in the larger of the huts, scrubbing dishes. They looked up on hearing the car and seeing strangers but didn't stop scrubbing. Edward and William followed Evelyn into the marquee, looking for her father. The marquee was covered on three sides but, being of white canvas was light inside and Evelyn went straight to the man tidying a trestle table at the far end. Reverend Coughston put down the heavy wooden cross he was cleaning to open his arms as his daughter went to him and they embraced. Edward and William hung back at the entrance to the marquee. Then Evelyn waved them in, introducing them as they neared,

'Edward, William. My father.'

'Morning sir,' said William, 'we're pleased to meet you.' William spoke for both as usual.

'And I you gentlemen.' Reverend Coughston took a few seconds to look at them both before saying, 'Our paths crossed in Margate briefly and I'm sorry we didn't have a chance to talk.' The men shook hands. 'I'm afraid you've just missed service.'

'Already?' Evelyn asked.

'I wasn't sure you'd be coming and we've only three families here at the moment, they wanted an early start. I'm sorry.'

'No need to apologise on our account sir,' William said.

'No, I expect not,' said Reverend Coughston, with a knowing smile. 'Anyway, you are here now. And here is Miss Burton,' he added as Catherine joined them. 'Thank you for helping my daughter settle in at The Winter Gardens. And who is that?' He pointed to outside the marquee where Patrick swung and span on the rope swing. Evelyn explained and her father nodded approvingly,

'Fresh country air and a swing will do wonders for a young mind and body. Let me show you the mission while you tell me how busy you have been keeping.' He took Evelyn's arm and led her from the marquee. The others followed and as Evelyn had seen all this before she understood the tour was not for her benefit. It didn't take long and, afterwards, they were shown the huts where the hop pickers would stay, in another clearing a hundred yards further on. At the moment just three families were there, readying and cleaning the huts, fixing roofs, preparing the communal kitchen and repairing the baskets and sacks for collecting the hops. Catherine enjoyed chasing after Patrick from hut to hut. Evelyn recognised two of the families, the younger children shouting her name and running to hug her. She dropped to her knees and they hugged.

'The little ones love her. They will miss her this year but I think Alice's needs are more pressing. As it says in Hebrews thirteen sixteen, 'Do not neglect to do good and to share what you have, for such sacrifices are pleasing to God.' Though I too, find I am missing her more than I anticipated. This year's mission will be much harder for me without her.'

'You're embarrassing me,' said Evelyn, above the chattering of the four children around her.

'Oh I think your friends will forgive a father's indulgence and pride. Come now, some refreshment. But let's walk back the long way. The air will be good for us.'

Reverend Coughston led the way into the hop gardens, the tall plants forming maze–like rows, providing shade and channeling a gentle breeze, welcoming in the growing heat of the day. The men walked either side of the reverend while Catherine and Evelyn walked ahead. Patrick and the hop pickers' children played chase and hide–and–seek alongside them and among the hops. Occasionally they would stop and stare, from a safe distance, at Edward, and though Evelyn couldn't hear their whispering it seemed Patrick was able to answer their questions. They walked to the oast house, not yet in use, but just seeing it was enough to bring back to Evelyn the smell of hops and she was momentarily sad not to be spending the summer there. It was a gentle walk in a gentle place, though Catherine's shoes were not suitable for the uneven grass around the hop gardens and she stumbled more than once before taking Evelyn's arm for support.

Back at the mission clearing Evelyn went into the

kitchen hut and boiled a kettle for tea, chatting with the woman there, an old friend from previous years. Evelyn brought the tray outside and passed it to Edward so she could sit alongside them on the rug brought from the car.

'So, gentlemen. Do you like our mission?' asked the reverend.

'Yes sir,' William said. 'But I notice a lack of … everyday items. Like chairs and tables.'

'Ah, the pickers will bring them from London with them. It's almost like moving house for a few weeks. Entire districts will decamp to Kent. It's a most energetic time, isn't it Evelyn?'

'But what about plates and cups and dishes and … all that paraphernalia? Not to mention latrines.'

'Apologies ladies. He still thinks he's in the trenches,' said Edward.

'I see you are a practical man Mr. Burrslow. The pickers are very resourceful, bring what they need, make do for what they can't carry and improvise everything else. Oh, and there is a latrine hut, a little way off and hidden.'

'I expect the mission is more concerned with other needs … spiritual?' Edward said, lisping on the last word.

'Indeed Mr. Thompson. We try. Isn't that so?' The reverend asked the older lady that came from the kitchen hut carrying a bowl of dirty water.

'Oh yes, Father, it can be very trying, but fortunately cleanliness is next to Godliness,' she said, winking at Evelyn, who laughed but was stopped short by the cry of a child in pain. 'Oops, looks like your lad's come a cropper.' The woman said to Catherine, nodding over to the rope swing where Patrick lay on the scar of earth worn into the grass under the tree. The other children stood round, not knowing what to do as Patrick's cry grew louder. Catherine and Evelyn both went to him and between them calmed and soothed him, Catherine holding him and talking gently, Evelyn spitting on her handkerchief and dabbing carefully at the grazes on both Patrick's knees. William soon came to join them, complaining that Edward and the reverend were, 'talking about the healing power of a proper hymn and God working through music, and a lot of other old bull, no offence Evelyn ...'

As Patrick stopped crying William took off his jacket, handed it to Catherine, and challenged the kids to races as he ran into the hop gardens. The children screamed with delight and began the chase.

Catherine folded the jacket over her arm. 'That was a nice feeling, when the woman thought I was Patrick's mother. I've not had much to do with them before, children I mean. Not like you. They love you here, I can see. It must feel good too.'

'It does, but, truth be told, it's not difficult when playing with them or teaching them to read. It's not at all the same as back in Spitalfields where the mothers have to struggle every day just to feed them and clean and keep them safe. It's hard and dark and they've no money and just two rooms and no water. Then it's a different type of caring, of loving.'

'Wouldn't you want that?'

'I suppose so ... I mean, yes, I do, very much. But I'm already twenty six so ... who knows. You?'

'Yes, but I don't know ... if ... there's anyone who ...'

'I know what you mean, it's difficult with so few men our age. They're either taken or not interested or ...'

'... not worthy of us ...' Catherine smiled.

'... or not ...' Evelyn hesitated, '... whole. I think I may soon be too old to meet the right person.' Evelyn had a memory of Mr. Tewson, with whom she had walked out the previous year at the mission. Her thoughts were interrupted.

'I hate to think I might not be a mother though,' said Catherine.

'I'm sure you will be. You're very pretty and great company. I know, what about William? He does look at you. I've seen,' said Evelyn.

'William? He's not … I mean, I'm not …' Catherine looked at William, being chased between the hop poles by the children. '… I think he'd be a good older brother and he seems to like children, especially Patrick, so perhaps a good uncle. Don't you think?'

'Perhaps,' said Evelyn.

'I wonder what he writes in his notebook.'

'Even Edward says he doesn't know. But he seems not to be the romantic type, so poetry seems unlikely, though I'm sure there is something in the way he looks at you,' teased Evelyn.

'Hmmm, you keep saying that but I still think you'll find Georgette is more to his taste. Anyway, who cares. It's lovely here. We should come back when all the pickers are down. We could help for a day.'

'It's more hard work than I'm used to. I'll help in the kitchen, serving tea. Speaking of which, ours will be cold. Norah will be cross with us.'

'Norah?'

'The lady who thought you were Patrick's mother.'

'Oh yes, and let's not dissuade her of that, just for today, do you mind?'

'Of course not.' Evelyn led Catherine back to the rug where her father and Edward sat talking.

'Ah ladies, you must assist. Edward here is trying to help me understand how the musical key for certain hymns lends them more gravitas or levity, as the lyrics require. My ear for music is not educated. Do you think him correct?' He asked both Evelyn and Catherine.

'I imagine so. After all, Mr. Thompson studied at the Royal College of Music.'

'Not for long. Or at least, not long enough,' said Edward.

'Could you go back? To complete your studies?' asked Reverend Coughston.

'I don't think so. I no longer play well enough.'

'I doubt that,' said Evelyn but followed quickly with, 'though of course I'm not a musician.'

'My hands might still be all right but I don't concentrate as well I might.' Edward's voice tailed off as he spoke and he looked up to the hop gardens.

'You've surely sacrificed enough already. You shouldn't also sacrifice the career you might yet enjoy if the Royal College can complete you.'

'Many sacrificed more … everything,' said Edward and there was silence for a few seconds. He looked at the surrounding greenery. 'It is nice here. I especially like the regimented lines of the hop poles. There's a sense of order and calm in them. And a sense of reaching skyward, in the plants.'

The rest of the afternoon was more subdued but no less enjoyable for Evelyn, spending lazy time with her father and friends. William returned from playing with the children, red faced and panting, reaching for the cigarettes from his jacket. Patrick made new friends and though his accent was teased it seemed that play went well until the rope swing broke under the weight of too many of them. William pledged to return with some longer and stronger rope. The Reverend Coughston was good company and as the afternoon progressed so the shadows from the hops lengthened. Edward didn't say much and smoked too much. To Evelyn, there were echoes of tea parties when her mother had been alive and local families had come into their garden. Though the space at the back of the tiny house in Spitalfields was more yard than garden her mother had managed to grow sweet peas and geraniums in tubs and even such a small token to nature was welcome in the otherwise unrelenting smoke and grime. It was her mother who had first suggested the mission to the hop fields but there was never time 'until she had already passed,' as her father said when she reminded him.

By four o'clock Evelyn was feeling guilty at leaving Alice for so long and Edward mentioned he was performing later, so they took their leave reluctantly. Evelyn hugged her father for a long time and promised to come back when he was settled down there for September and the mission was properly underway. Clouds had blown in from the coast and though it was still afternoon the temperature had dropped and the wind over the moving car was fresh. Neither Catherine nor Evelyn had brought driving coats and pulled a blanket over their legs for warmth as they sped along. Patrick sat between them again, quiet with tiredness and fighting sleep, covered by the blanket. Like the journey down to the mission, Edward had wanted to travel via Herne Bay and as they neared the town Edward shouted something to William that Evelyn didn't hear. Rather than take the turn for Margate they went on to the coast. William parked in the same place they had used ten days earlier when stopping in Herne Bay on their way to Whitstable.

'We won't be long ladies, just picking up some cigarettes. Five minutes. You might as well stay here. Catherine, can we get you a pack?'

'Yes please. Black Cats. I finished mine earlier,' said Catherine, fumbling in her bag for a purse.

'It's all right. Pay me later,' Edward said, keen to be away.

Evelyn looked out to the beach. The tide was more in than out but there was still room for the holidaymakers on the sand and out in the wheeled huts. She started to ask Patrick if he wanted to go on the beach but he was asleep. She shared a knowing smile with Catherine and then watched Edward and William as they walked towards the pier.

'Why didn't they wait until we're back in Margate?' she asked herself more than Catherine, who replied anyway,

'I don't know, but it's fortunate as I'm out of fags

myself and would like one before we get home. Aunt Beatrice doesn't mind smoking at home as such but thinks it makes the parlour smell in the morning.'

'It's something to do with that tobacconist Edward was asking after last time we were here.'

'What is?'

'Why they've gone to the pier. I think Edward wants to find the family of one of the men in his platoon. He came from here and I gather he didn't make it home. It seemed to upset Edward.'

'I imagine he must be upset rather a lot then.'

'Catherine. That's cruel.'

'I just meant I expect a lot of his men didn't come home.'

'I suppose. But perhaps he does feel this way about all of them. If so can you imagine how much guilt he must feel? That would be crippling. As if he didn't have enough to cope with.'

'I don't think I could, imagine that is, and wouldn't want to. It's bad enough when family … don't come home.'

Evelyn looked at Catherine before asking, 'Did you? Lose family in the war?'

'Not in the war.' Catherine looked away.

'I'm sorry. It's not my business,' said Evelyn.

Catherine looked back and took her hand. 'That's all right. It's just … not many people know. I don't even really know myself.'

'Know what? You said your mother died when you were nine, before the war. Did something happen to your father?'

'He … didn't come home. But that was long before the war. He worked on the smacks, out of Ramsgate, but one day, in nineteen o two, he didn't come back. They said it must have been a bad storm or a stray wave. The skipper was both good and lucky, many wanted to sail with him, but he wasn't lucky that trip.' Catherine shrugged, almost as if she could shrug away the glistening in her eyes.

'I'm sorry, Catherine. That's awful, especially as you then lost your mother a year later.'

Catherine took back her hand and looked down at Patrick, as if checking he still slept. 'We didn't exactly lose my mother. It's just a bit ... embarrassing.'

Evelyn waited out the pause rather than press and Catherine continued. 'She left me. And I came to live with Aunt Beatrice.' Catherine thought for a moment before. 'Actually, not true. She sent me to live with Aunt Beatrice, then she left. But Beatrice has been as good a mother, better.'

Evelyn started to speak but Catherine interrupted, 'Where are those boys with my cigarettes? Perhaps they'll bring back a stick of rock,' she said, nudging Patrick awake as she spoke, 'that would be nice wouldn't it. Or perhaps a bar of Dairy Milk?'

Patrick stirred but didn't wake.

'If you want to tell me more, about your mother, that would be all right.' Evelyn said. Catherine gave another shrug and Evelyn took the hint. 'He was good today, wasn't he?' She changed subject and nodded down towards Patrick, who rested against Catherine. She pulled the blanket a little higher to his chin, though it was no longer cold with the car stationary. 'You know earlier, when the other children were staring at Edward and whispering about his mask, I asked Patrick what he said and he told them it was because Edward was a special captain during the war and the mask is because he has a magic eye that can see through trenches and he is a hero.'

'I suppose it is a special eye, and he must be a hero. Though he never talks of how he came to be wounded so. You should ask,' said Catherine.

'I don't think he likes to talk about it.'

'He'll tell you one day I expect. You have a way,' Catherine said but did not look at Evelyn, 'a good way.'

Before Evelyn could react William was back. 'No

good I'm afraid. The tobacconist was closed.'

'Again,' added Edward.

'Here, have one of these,' William tossed his pack of cigarettes into the back.

Catherine caught them, 'About time and is there anything left in your hipflask? A girl could do with a drink about now.'

They were back at Margate by five o'clock, plenty of time for Edward to prepare for that evening's performance. Georgette was not at the guest house but as Evelyn was needed to help Alice and Alastair tidy and clean the tea shop it was left to Catherine and William to take Patrick for a fish and chip supper on the front.

Two days later, on the Tuesday, Evelyn received another letter from her father. It was a quiet morning and the postman delivered a half hour or so before Edward and William's usual refreshment time. Aunt Beatrice was in the tea shop, chatting with Alice, asking if Alastair had sold any more paintings and admiring the latest one, hanging in place of the picture Edward had bought. Catherine was in the kitchen, listening to Evelyn read her father's letter.

My dear Evelyn,

It was such a joy to see you yesterday and to meet your new friends.

Miss Burton is a fine young lady and I hope to meet her aunt one day. I think you may find Miss Burton to be heartwarming company and an excellent confidante, should one be needed. Mr. Burrslow seems to be a down to earth fellow and, I expect, a good man to have close by in an emergency. I think perhaps his God–fearing self may need nurturing but fear he may not be open to such.

He was adept at entertaining the children and perhaps this comes from his parents who, Mr. Burrslow told me, were music hall performers. Mr. Thompson is thoughtful and intelligent and carries with dignity the misfortune the war has placed on him, though I fear the mask hides as much spiritual impairment as physical. He is a man of integrity and we should wish, and help, him to be at peace with his sacrifice. I am reminded of Isaiah 26:3:

You keep him in perfect peace whose mind is stayed on you, because he trusts in you.

In any event, I know they are blessed to have you as a friend and I look forward to seeing more of you all when I'm down at the mission on a more regular basis from September.

With much love,

Father

PS Norah misses you, as do the children

Edward, Margate, Friday 27th August 1920

On Wednesday morning Edward and William were in the tea shop, enjoying their now ritualistic mid–morning hot drinks though Edward was still avoiding the coffee. He didn't react on hearing the door open, the newspaper held his attention, but when he heard Catherine's aunt call a welcome to Alice he put on his smile and lowered the paper. Beatrice's greeting was a distraction to all the customers and a few looked up. She scanned the shop as she threaded her way through the tables towards the kitchen door at the back. With her petite frame she moved lightly and with an energy Edward admired. She caught both Edward's and William's eye and waved, mouthing, 'Good morning.' Edward nodded a response. He'd been formally introduced a few days earlier and already liked Beatrice. Somehow, more by attitude than word or action, she had been able to acknowledge his masked appearance with no patronisation, as if it were normal, expected even, whilst still respecting its origins. Alice came from the kitchen to greet her and Beatrice led the way back to Edward and William's table.

'Good morning gentlemen,' Beatrice said again. 'I'm glad to catch you both here, though of course, it's no surprise. I trust you are both well and did you know, you have a mention in the *Isle Of Thanet Gazette*?' The latter question was directed at Edward, who shook his head. 'Unfortunately Mr. Burrslow is not mentioned,' she continued, 'however, Mr. Thompson, you are lauded by the local newspaper's musical arts critic. He, or is it a she?

the name is Hilary Talmet, and the surname sounds
peculiarly foreign and, of course, Hilary could be either a
man or a woman as I understand the Americans believe it
to be a lady's name, which, by the way, means to be of
good cheer, which, in my experience, most Americans are
not, but in any event, Mr. or Mrs. Talmet is most
complimentary of Mr. Thompson's skills at the piano.
Your Mozart interpretations are particularly admired and
he, or she, is looking forward to hearing more. When
Cook has finished with the paper I shall cut out the review
for you, though, of course, you may want to buy a copy for
yourself, which would be the right thing to do as our local
paper is in need of support. Now, Alice, do sit with us, I
need to ask a favour.'

'If the gentlemen don't mind,' said Alice, ignoring
the fact Beatrice was already seated.

'Please. Join us,' said William, 'and, from idle
curiosity, tell me, Mrs. Blundell, was there any mention in
the review of Edward's war ... record?'

'None I recall. Which I would take to be a good
thing as Mr. Thompson's talent at the keys is quite rightly
of primacy. And I seem to recall a review from last year in
which an accomplished tenor was criticised by the same
Hilary Talmet for requiring help in climbing the stairs to
the stage simply because he was missing a leg. For my part
I think it was more than a little harsh as the poor man,
who was a very fine tenor, had not progressed past the
rank of private during the war, and as such, might be
expected to seek as much support and, dare I say it,
sympathy as is deserved, whereas an officer, such as our
Mr. Thompson, might be expected to display a greater
degree of independence under any circumstances, though I
do not say I necessarily agree with that view. What do you
think Alice?'

Alice stifled a laugh. 'I think, Beatrice, a cup of tea
might be a good idea.'

'Of course. With a little sugar as you need to keep

up your strength. Your date draws ever closer. But, let me arrange my own tea and, actually, that's close to the favour I've come to ask.'

'Of course. Please ask.'

'May I take Evelyn's place here, in the tea shop this afternoon?'

'Is that appropriate? A lady of your standing in the community?'

'I should think so.'

'But why?'

'Ah, well, this morning, over breakfast, I overhead one of my guests say they would be going to the cinema to see a new film. *The Tidal Wave*. That happens to be the title of a short story by Ethel Dell, my favourite author, that I have just finished reading and a quick conversation with my guest confirmed this new film, is indeed, taken from the very fine short story.'

Edward and William looked at each other. Alice, looked at Beatrice, waiting, and when no further explanation was forthcoming asked, 'But why should that mean you wish to take Evelyn's place here this afternoon?'

'Because Catherine is insisting on reading that book the American left and I am hoping to convince her Miss Dell's stories are a more fitting read and perhaps seeing the film will act as encouragement for Catherine to borrow the book from me.'

'But still, Beatrice, why do you need to be here in Evelyn's place?

'So Evelyn can accompany Catherine to the cinema this afternoon. A young lady should not go there alone and, besides, I'm sure it would be good also for Evelyn to enjoy the film and, now I think of it, Mr. Thompson and Mr. Burrslow should also go. Are you performing this afternoon Mr. Thompson?'

Edward shook his head.

'Then I'll take Evelyn's place here and you gentlemen shall accompany Evelyn and my niece to the

Cinema de Luxe, on the High Street.'

'Could they not go Thursday? We close on Thursday afternoons.'

'I thought Thursday you could join me at the St. John's Ladies afternoon club. Some of the local ladies meet, to gossip mainly, but that in itself can be entertaining and educational, though I daresay the new reverend may not approve although I understand the Reverend Railton is a man for the twentieth century, and if he's there, I do need to ask him about the church flowers for the coming weekend. Anyway, it will be good for you to relax with some new friends. Besides, I'm looking forward to a busy afternoon here already. It will do me good and I can make sure you are resting properly,' Beatrice said, patting Alice's hand.

Alice, bemused, looked to Edward and William. Both men nodded, neither daring to disagree with Mrs. Blundell.

The Cinema de Luxe was on the High Street, perhaps a quarter mile from the seafront. Evelyn and Catherine were already there when Edward and William arrived. There was no breeze and it was one of the hottest afternoons so far that summer. Edward was pleased to be going inside, hoping it would be cooler – besides, darkness was welcomed. He wasn't excited at the prospect of the film itself, not having heard of it and, from what Beatrice said earlier, it wasn't the type of film he would choose. Not that there was a type he particularly did like, nor was there a type he specifically avoided, he just didn't go to the cinema often. Partly that was because while his good eye was all right, it was not, as William might say, 'pukka', and if the scenes on the screen were ill–lit they could be tiring to watch. But it was also the case neither theatre nor novels seemed to capture his imagination as they had before the war. But Beatrice had asked him and William to accompany her niece and Evelyn and their company was welcomed. So here they were, waiting by the ticket office while William paid entry for all. They sat in the middle of a middle row, having a choice of seats as so few were occupied in the cinema on such a fine day. Edward enjoyed waiting patiently in the dark; smoking and occasionally sipping Old Orkney scotch from the hip flask offered by William. The short newsreel was followed by the main film, *The Tidal Wave*, and Evelyn and Catherine were both engrossed while Edward suspected William dozed. For Edward's part, though the film had not held his attention – a tale of a fisherman's unrequited love for a beautiful young girl who was infatuated by a visiting artist – Edward enjoyed listening to and watching the pianist. There was neither sheet music nor a script for the musician, who watched the screen above to inform his playing. Edward couldn't see the player's hands, prevented by a combination of his good eye's constraints, the darkness and the pianist facing away, but suspected his technique was sound and, from the occasional classic refrains he introduced, Edward surmised he had formal teaching; he wondered how many times he'd played along to this film and if he played the same accompaniment each time.

It was late afternoon but still warm and bright when they left the cinema. Evelyn squinted against the light and Catherine teased that the glassy shine to Evelyn's hazel eyes was due to the tears she had barely contained watching the film. Edward glanced, Evelyn's eyes did sparkle, but he did not stare. He didn't think the film warranted tears but perhaps missed the point. There was time before his evening performance and he would have enjoyed asking Evelyn her opinion, perhaps during a walk up Fort Hill, and on to the place they'd picnic'd a few days earlier, but Evelyn was keen to get back to the tea shop.

'Aunt Beatrice might be tired by now. I should make sure she and Alice are all right.'

Catherine agreed. 'And she'll want to hear about the film. Which, by the way, did seem rather old–fashioned, to me.' She took Evelyn's arm as they started towards the tea shop, adding, 'But Columbine and Rufus did make a handsome couple.'

'I think Columbine was a little ... flighty. What did you think Edward?' Evelyn turned to ask Edward, who walked behind.

'Yes. Flighty. That's perhaps no bad thing and without it I don't suppose the story had much else,' Edward said.

'Oh you men. You're so ... practical,' said Catherine, 'and did you think Columbine pretty?'

'More than passable,' William said, smiling.

'Edward?' Evelyn asked.

'I'm ... I'm not sure. Even my good eye doesn't see well in the dark. But yes, I'm sure she was very attractive.'

'And did you think Rufus handsome then?' asked William.

'Passable,' said Catherine, imitating William.

They strolled down the High Street towards the front and though Evelyn had wanted to get back to the tea shop to relieve Beatrice there didn't seem to Edward to be a rush; the afternoon was warm, the air calm and though Edward's sense of smell was poor he could imagine the almost sulphurous odour of the sea, bringing that curious combination of both fresh and staleness. The atmosphere was heavy and familiar; Edward drifted back to Le Havre, three years earlier, given leave from the Front ahead of the spring offensive at Arras, walking the promenade with Captain Oldsmond, behind the two young women who promised to show them the best cafes and a cheap bar; a slow, easy walk that had gone nowhere. The women had talked quickly in French and giggled, looking behind to the two young Englishmen. They had to know the fresh faces they teased might not survive the next few weeks but it took little more than a smile and an unfulfillable promise

156

to erase the spectre of the Front for an afternoon – a precious afternoon with Camellia – and Edward thanked God. Was Camellia the last young woman who was not a nurse to see his undamaged face? The question brought him back from Le Havre and he was sad to leave but it had been so long since such a memory had touched him he'd forgotten he still held them – they were there for him, somewhere, and that was a comfort. He watched Evelyn and Catherine ahead of him, arm in arm, chatting, alive; echoes of Le Havre.

'... and anyway, such a pretty girl as Columbine would not fall for a fisherman. What do you think Edward?' William disturbed Edward's reverie but before he could answer Evelyn turned to William,

'I'd have thought you'd consider a working man as deserving as any.'

'Of course. But in the few moving pictures I've seen, the young hero has been handsome and has a few bob in his pocket. Like me.' William laughed.

'Except for the money and the handsome part,' Evelyn teased.

'There's not many fishermen round here like that,' said Catherine.

'Ah well, films are mostly romantic nonsense ...' said William.

'Is that why you fell asleep after the newsreel?' said Edward.

'I quite enjoyed that. The Duke Of York inspecting a rifle team? More my style, though I did think the officers looked more than a little ... wet. I doubt many were in France. Speaking of which, I hear some Frog has made a film about the war I'd like to see, Jackuse.'

'He means *J'accuse*,' said Edward.

'That's what I said. J'accuthe,' William exaggerated Edward's lisp, 'and at the end the dead soldiers rise. Now that I'd like to see, though it doesn't make sense.'

'They aren't raised in a biblical sense, it's more they

come back to ... to ...' Edward tried to think of the right word but William said,

'What, to complain? Perhaps about the war? Blimey, if all the dead souls come back from France there'll be a lot of complaining to hear and precious few to listen. But I doubt they'll find their way back.'

'You don't believe in the soul?' Catherine asked William.

'I don't know what I believe anymore, but I'm sure if they could come back, they wouldn't waste their time here.'

'Edward, what do you think?'

Edward shrugged, 'We've seen things happen, in battle, miracles of survival and courage. And men, strong men, claim to have seen angels ...'

'... and devils,' said William.

Edward nodded, '... and I've seen soldiers ... disappear ... so I'm not sure what to think.' His voice drifted away.

'Some think they can talk to the dead,' said Catherine.

'They're bloody liars and charlatans,' said William with a sudden anger that stopped the conversation until Evelyn said,

'Alice wants to try.' She spoke tentatively.

'What? Some ouija board nonsense?' said William.

'I don't know. There's a medium, here, in Margate. She claims to be able to help people like Alice.'

'Don't let my aunt hear Alice has been to a medium. She won't have anything to do with them, especially since her husband died and his sister claimed to have spoken to his spirit and he wanted to change his will and leave the guest house to his siblings, not his widow,' said Catherine.

'But if Alice thinks there is a chance ... that, you know ... her son might ... you know,' Evelyn said vaguely.

'What does Alastair think?' asked Edward.

'I don't know.'

'Your father would be appalled,' Catherine said.

'I know, but what if Alice can be helped? I feel, perhaps, I should go with her, if she needs to. She shouldn't be on her own, in case ...'

'... the thieving fraudster cheats and lies. Which they will,' said William.

'Perhaps. But isn't that more reason to be with her?'

Catherine said, 'Whatever happens, she should not be alone. We should go. Though I'm a little scared already to think of what might happen rather than what might not and we mustn't let either my aunt or your father know. And perhaps a man should accompany us?' She let the question hang.

'Don't look at me,' said William, 'it's all rubbish. Shouldn't be encouraged. I've better things to do.'

There was an awkward silence until Evelyn looked at Edward and said, 'For Alice?'

Edward nodded, though it wasn't really for Alice.

They met mid–morning Friday on the south side of Trinity Square, close to the allotments below Holy Trinity Church. They had been dug for the war effort and gave the square a utilitarian appearance. The three ladies had been nervous, especially Alice. Edward suspected doubly so because of deceiving Alastair and closing the tea shop for a couple of hours, but then Alastair was taking his usual morning walk on the cliffs. There was an air of conspiracy in their meeting. As Alice was deceiving Alastair, so was Catherine deceiving her aunt and Evelyn her father. William had laughed when Edward left the guest house that morning, the laugh he reserved for mocking and to cover the anger Edward knew he would be suppressing; he was still against the visit to a medium and refused to take part. There was nothing auspicious in what now felt to Edward a fool's errand.

Mrs. Capais was watching for them and opened her

front door when they hesitated at the bottom of the steps leading up to it. She watched them climb, not reacting on seeing Edward's mask, and was friendly and welcoming. She said she preferred to entertain only three people at such sessions and Edward thought it a veiled request for him to wait elsewhere, which he ignored. They went through to the dark front parlour and Mrs. Capais initiated some polite conversation while taking their coats and offering seats in the dark parlour.

The silence in the room was such that Edward wanted to stifle the cough in his throat but the instinct was too strong. Though the sound was suppressed, it was still an almost offensive intrusion. Two people looked at him – Evelyn and Catherine – while two kept their gaze to the table in front of them – Alice and Mrs. Capais. Edward shrugged an apology and considered lighting a cigarette but couldn't see an ashtray, though that was no surprise in the near darkness. The heavy curtains were closed and such meagre light as there was crept in past the edges. The house was a narrow terraced property with a basement just below street level and three floors above. It looked out on to the allotments in front of Holy Trinity Church and Edward wondered if the irony of the location was lost on Mrs. Capais. He was sure the church would not bless her business. He looked at Evelyn and she wore as serious an expression as he had ever seen on her – an expression with a hint of self–reproach perhaps? Or fear? Edward tried to catch her eye, wanting to give her a smile of ... of what? Encouragement, comfort? Neither was appropriate, but anyway, she didn't look his way. Mrs. Capais gave a deep sigh and started to speak but stopped after a single, unintelligible word. Catherine gave a hint of a smile and Evelyn was still serious but, to Edward, Alice looked to be afraid and he supposed that was the most sensible feeling for her to hold. It was a shame William wasn't there to break the tension with an inappropriate story – perhaps the one of Captain Hall unloading his Webley revolver into the shadow of his dead dog that wasn't there and wounding his batman sufficiently that the lucky sod spent the rest of the war convalescing in Bedfordshire but Edward was no raconteur, and hadn't been, not even before the war, though he did recall a dinner arranged in the early days of his studies at the Royal College of Music. A pretty young lady, Mary Marant, a fellow student's sister, had listened attentively to his account of leaving his sheet music on the bus and chasing it to the next stop. Mary Marant had laughed at the correct places in the story and been so pretty. She probably still was. But that was a long time ago, and Evelyn was more attractive and taller, he considered, then realised his mind was wandering. He took a deep breath and wondered if he had missed Mrs. Capais do or say something. He looked around the dark parlour in which they were sitting and wished again to light a cigarette. Mrs. Capais was wearing a dark kaftan which draped over her substantial frame and flowed onto the floor. She tilted her head back and made another gutteral, animalistic noise before shutting her eyes and falling forward in her chair.

Edward thought William had been right not to join them, knowing he would not be able to contain his contempt, but how could Edward have refused Evelyn's request? He wished for a cigarette.

Mrs. Capais was slumped over in her chair, emanating odd growling noises. Then she sat up, leaned back, sighed, shook her head and opened her eyes.

'Ah well, nothing yet. I thought there was but it was an old oysterman, died years ago, keeps coming round, but he didn't know any of you so I asked him to leave. He's a nice enough old man but a little too ... familiar ... sometimes, if you know what I mean,' Mrs. Capais said and winked at Catherine, before lighting a small gas lamp on a side table. 'Anyway, I expect someone else will be along soon. Meantime, may I?' She reached over and took each of the lady's hands in turn, examining them and searching their faces, before turning to Edward. She took his hand and held it tight. He was embarrassed it was damp with sweat. Then she studied his face, her dark eyes black in the poor light from the lamp. She let go of his hand and passed him an ashtray. Edward lit a cigarette.

'Bless you all,' she said. 'Such a lot of pain you all carry. Alice, I know there is someone close that has gone away and you would like to know if they are all right. I can't say if we will find out today, but you will find peace in new life soon. Catherine, many are entering and leaving your life but there is a constant, someone older who will always care for you. You are like a daughter to her, I see. And both you and Evelyn are wondering if you will meet husbands and bear children. I see children in both your futures. You are loving and kind and children will love you back, though you may not have discovered or believe that yet.'

Edward thought back to the day at the mission and how the children had followed Evelyn, so naturally.

'And Edward,' Mrs. Capais turned to him, 'how much pain you have felt and seen and how much more you hide.'

Edward sensed, rather than saw, the others watching him.

'But there are those who will help you, given the chance. It will benefit you if ... wait, someone else is here. He or she may take my place and perhaps will bring another, someone you may love, or miss ... yes, someone is here. A guide.'

The gas lamp flickered then was extinguished. Alice gave a quiet gasp of shock, or fear. In the sudden darkness Edward's good eye was all but useless. There was a thudding sound and as Edward's eye acclimatised he saw Mrs. Capais was again slumped forward, her forehead on the table. She spoke, in a deeper voice than before, 'Good morning Mrs. Capais. We have a visitor. A young man. I believe he is here for one of your guests. He is ... reluctant.

I believe he may not want to worry or scare our visitors. I will ask him to come closer.'

Alice, Evelyn and Catherine held hands and Edward could hear their breathing quicken. His own heartbeat was raised though he had neither heard nor seen anything that could not be faked or guessed. He knew the fear of the trenches, so an atmosphere such as this, that he could break simply by challenging, was nothing to him, but still his heart was quicker.

There was a long silence until the unnatural voice coming from Mrs. Capais said, 'The young man might be wearing a uniform. He is very young and knows someone here. Might that be the case?'

Alice shifted in her chair. Edward knew how she grieved for her son, Curtis. He missed others, like Kayst, but not in the same way, nowhere near as deeply, nothing like as painfully or relentlessly, but he missed him, and many like him.

Mrs. Capais went quiet and the silence was unpleasant, then broken by the creaking of a door. She sat up and, barely visible in the dark, reached towards something, still speaking in the deep voice, 'Don't go. Stay. I feel one of our guests is looking for you.'

Alice could no longer hold back and asked with shaking voice, 'What does the young man look like? You say he's in uniform. What type?'

'It's hard to tell. He is ill–lit. Could it be … green, or brown or dark blue?'

'Can you see his face?' Alice asked.

'He is a young man,' the deep voice repeated.

They all were, Edward thought … remembered.

'What colour are his eyes?' Alice asked, speaking more quickly.

'He is too far away for me to see. Ah, now he's a little closer. Yes, it is a military uniform,' said the deep voice from Mrs. Capais.

Edward tried to recall Kayst's eyes. The colour

eluded him but they were bright and alive, always, even when squinting through a peep hole in a trench wall, straining to make sense of the wasteland beyond.

'Can you see his hair? What colour?' Alice was desperate for a connection.

'It is dark, perhaps brown, perhaps black?'

'Oh,' Alice said, with crushing disappointment.

Kayst had black hair. Edward remembered.

'Though it's hard to tell. It could be much lighter. And I see he's not a particularly big man,' said the deep voice.

Kayst was slight of build. Edward remembered.

There was a long pause. The room seemed darker.

'The young man is talking but I can't hear him properly.'

Kayst had liked to talk, to tell stories, Edward recalled and could easily imagine the young man's face in the darkness of the room.

A draught of cold air billowed the curtains away from the window. Alice reached for Evelyn's hand. Edward breathed deeply. His heart beat quicker again. The deep voice said, 'And there, beside him, is something. I can't see properly but could it be an animal? Perhaps a dog, a pet from when he was a child?'

Alice was shaking her head.

'A cat, perhaps?'

'We've not had pets, though Curtis did play with next door's dog, when he was young. Is it not our Curtis?' said Alice, tearfully.

A small flame burst to yellow in the hearth and light flickered across the walls in random patterns. Edward felt cold. He recalled from listening to the men in his platoon chat that Kayst's uncle bred Jack Russell terriers. Edward closed his eye. He could see Kayst laughing as he told stories of ratting on his uncle's smallholding. Kayst had entertained the men. Edward smiled. Even Sergeant Burrslow had laughed and how they could have used a terrier for ratting down in the trenches.

The deep voice said, 'Ah, perhaps not an animal. It may be only a shadow, at the young man's feet. I can't see clearly. But he is coming back to me. He is walking a little lopsided. Does he have a limp, or perhaps has lost a boot?'

'Curtis did lose a shoe, on the beach, one summer,' Alice said, with a touch of desperation while Edward remembered how Kayst favoured his right foot. He had broken a toe jumping down into a trench, and it hadn't healed well. Perhaps he had been better to break the leg badly, perhaps a severe limp may have made for a blighty and he wouldn't have come back to the platoon. Edward remembered. Kayst had been forced to jump when ...

Mrs. Capais still spoke with the deep voice, 'He's calling something to me. Perhaps a name. Does it start with a C?'

'Curtis?' Alice asked, fearfully.

'Or perhaps a K? He is calling,' moaned the deep voice from Mrs. Capais, 'but I can't hear, he is surrounded by noise.'

... Edward was back there. Kayst had been forced to jump when a barrage filled the air ...

'Yes, I think he's telling his name ...'

Edward was back there and the barrage was from nowhere:

'K ...'

There was crash, from somewhere – loud and fast and then gone. Shattering noise. Instant silence. Edward was shocked from his chair but he alone stood, the others were unmoved. Had they not heard the explosion? Why didn't they react? His heart was racing and beads of sweat seeped from his forehead and down behind his mask. He only just resisted the impulse to brush them away. Mrs. Capais opened her eyes to watch Edward who started to speak but no words came. With the flickering light Edward saw the fear in Alice's eyes and the shock in Catherine's, but Evelyn's face was calm, almost stern, as she watched him. Then, before the voice could say more through Mrs. Capais, Evelyn stood and drew back the curtains. Edward breathed again.

In the seconds after Evelyn interrupted, Mrs. Capais slumped back onto the table before breathing slowly and sitting upright but not talking. Evelyn went to stand by Edward while his breathing slowed. As he relaxed his embarrassment grew. Alice held her hands to her cheeks. Catherine lit a cigarette. Eventually Mrs. Capais spoke calmly despite the anger Edward saw in her eyes. 'What happened?' Were we close to a breakthrough? Did a sprit visit? Was it someone you know?' She asked Alice directly, ignoring the standing Edward and Evelyn.

'We should take Alice for some fresh air.' Edward said, pulling from his wallet the pre–agreed fee for Mrs. Capais and leaving it on the table.

'But ... but it may have been Curtis, our Curtis,' said Alice, 'please, try again.'

'Not today Alice, come,' said Evelyn gently, with a hand under her arm to encourage her to stand.

Mrs. Capais saw them to the door and suggested they call back next week.

There was little conversation during the walk back to the tea shop. Alice seemed to blame Evelyn for the interruption and Edward was embarrassed at what he feared must be construed as a lack of control. Catherine smoked.

Two days later, on the Sunday morning, Edward knocked hard on Mrs. Capais's door. On the steps behind him stood William, holding a young man's arm high behind his back in a tight, painful grip. The young man was an accomplice of Mrs. Capais, who, with encouragement from William, had confessed to gathering information on Alice, Catherine and Evelyn ahead of the arranged seance, not to mention operating the paraphernalia of Mrs. Capais's deceit. It had taken William only a day to watch the Capais house, and identify her likely accomplice; a task William relished almost as much as encouraging the truth from him. Edward was ashamed of his behaviour during the seance and his embarrassment was matched only by William's anger. Within half an hour they had secured a letter from Mrs. Capais, addressed to Alice, admitting the fraud. William had wanted to go further and press for charges, or mete out his own immediate justice, but Edward didn't want to put Evelyn and Catherine in the awkward positon of explaining the events to Reverend Coughston or Aunt Beatrice. William told him he was going soft.

The Blue Bench

Evelyn, Margate,
Thursday 2nd September 1920

Evelyn stopped wiping tables on hearing the tapping against the glass of the tea shop's front door – it was just past one on Thursday; early closing. Evelyn unlocked the door to let in Catherine and Beatrice, who was saying to her niece, '... and I do appreciate that the liberal view, to which I myself subscribe, is fair for the worker, and I know they deserve the rest, but I can't help feeling a little sorry for the proprietors, as a half day loss of business is no small thing. What do you think Evelyn?'

'True,' said Evelyn, 'but in Spitalfields the shop girls are generally grateful for the half day, though many miss the lost money, so not all agree. But I think the most important thing is for the factory children at least to have the afternoon off.' Evelyn shut the door behind Beatrice and Catherine.

'You've a kind heart,' Beatrice said.

'She has,' Catherine said, 'and of course, it's important for Alice to take time away from here. I suppose Alastair isn't back yet?'

Evelyn shook her head. Alastair's morning walks were lasting longer each day.

'Ah well, what can we do to help?' Beatrice asked.

'Nearly all done thanks, Aunt,' Evelyn said, calling Beatrice aunt as she had been instructed. 'Alice is upstairs, taking a short rest.'

Alice came down as Evelyn tidied the menus on the tables and Evelyn thought her smile genuinely welcoming though her voice betrayed some nerves.

'Are you sure it's all right for me to come along? I don't worship at St. John's.' Alice asked after the usual pleasantries were covered.

'Of course dear. I know you've been going to Holy Trinity a long time, and will continue to do so, but St. John's is wonderfully friendly and, besides, today we're not even going to the church. The friends of St. Johns' are meeting in one of the lady's houses, on Hawley Square. You will be made very welcome. I'm told our new vicar's wife will be coming along today. Mrs. Railton, Ruby, is a lovely lady, isn't she Catherine?'

Catherine nodded.

'It's not far but we'll go slowly. It's a little uphill.' Beatrice took Alice's arm, guiding her from the tea shop. The two younger ladies walked behind, also arm in arm.

After the previous Friday's experience at the medium's Alice had been distant for a couple of days but on the Monday morning, after Alastair had left for his walk, she thanked Evelyn for, '... looking after me at Mrs. Capais's and not mentioning the episode to Alastair.'

Evelyn had hugged her and said they need never speak of it again, and it was also desirable neither her father, nor Beatrice hear of it, to which Alice had agreed, adding, '... especially as it's highly unlikely the figure seen was Curtis anyway. Highly unlikely.'

It was an odd thing for Alice to say but Evelyn didn't pursue it, wishing she had never gone there and wondering how, if at all, she should speak to Edward about the seance. She had seen him since, at The Winter Gardens, and they had walked home as usual, but nothing was said about Mrs. Capais except an overly casual, almost throwaway remark from Edward that, '... Alice needn't worry, he and William had taken steps to make sure Mrs. Capais did not bother them again.' Edward had then changed the subject. Evelyn wanted to ask what had seemed to distress Edward so at Mrs. Capais's, but was reluctant in case it was embarrassing, for either of them.

Catherine had remarked how proud she was of Evelyn for, '... thinking to take control ...' but Evelyn said she'd simply reacted.

Evelyn had spent a little over a month in Margate and yet here she felt more involved in her own life than ever before. There was more activity and drama in her life back in Spitalfields and, as a reverend's daughter surrounded by poverty, she had seen, heard and been frightened more than many women her age. And always she had tried to act as her father might and to help and aid whenever she could, but now she was a little removed she looked back and felt she had still been an outsider. The hurt and pain of the parishioners' struggles just to feed and shelter their children might weigh heavily on her, but were still not hers, no matter how she tried to alleviate them. But here in Margate, though she could not pretend experiences to be so fundamental, diverse or polarised, she was aware they were happening to and, perhaps, because of her. There was a sense of a beginning she couldn't quite grasp and, in part, didn't want to, in case she returned to Spitalfields before the beginning could lead somewhere.

She squeezed Catherine's arm in hers and enjoyed the returned pressure. Ahead she could hear Alice reiterating her concern that as a worshipper at Holy Trinity rather than St. John's, she might be considered 'disloyal' by attending the St. John's Ladies meeeting. 'What do you think Evelyn?' Alice turned to ask.

'I'm sure the good people of Holy Trinity will not mind at all Alice. And anyway how would they know?'

'If there's one thing at which the ladies of Margate excel, it's gossip,' Alice said.

'Then why not join me in worship at St. John's?' said Beatrice. 'Our church is more ... modest ... but we are sincere and friendly and I think our new vicar will bring new vigour.'

'But what of Alastair?' said Alice quietly.

Evelyn knew Alastair was still not attending Sunday

service. Alice's question was of a more fundamental nature and something in the sincerity of her manner stopped Beatrice from answering.

The rest of the walk to the house on Hawley Square was made in silence. They slowed further to accommodate Alice as she tired.

The Ladies of St. John's invited Alice and Evelyn into the drawing room of a large house overlooking the green square. By half way through the first cup of tea they already felt welcome. While Alice spoke with Mrs. Railton, the new vicar's wife, Beatrice asked Evelyn about the paintings on the wall of the tea shop.

'... I know Alastair has a good reputation so I'm thinking of asking if he'd do a portrait. Does he do portraits? I can't see why he wouldn't as I understand he was nearly accepted into the Royal Academy. Of course I would pay the appropriate rate. Would you ask him, for me?'

Evelyn hesitated before answering. 'I don't know. I haven't seen any portraits.' Evelyn hadn't shared Alice's secret.

'Catherine. What do you think? Would Alastair paint a portrait for me?' Beatrice called Catherine over.

'How would I know, Aunt? I don't know Mr. Trenter at all well. Like Evelyn, I don't think I've seen any portraits.'

'Well I'm sure he could. He's obviously talented and the sunrises are beautiful and though I know the other picture there, of the sinking ship, is not to everyone's taste, I'm told, by Mrs. Grundy, with a cousin in the city who is an architect and who knows a great deal about art, Mrs. Grundy that is, not the architect, though for all I know he may, and, at any rate, far more than me, says it's a very powerful piece, though I'm not sure I understand what that means. But Mrs. Grundy also said it reminded her of a work by Turner, in fact she hinted it was almost a copy, but I'm sure that would be a coincidence. Don't you think?' Beatrice asked, pausing to breathe.

'I've no idea, Aunt,' said Catherine, 'but I'm sure we can find someone to paint your portrait.'

'Why?' asked Beatrice.

'Because you want a portrait,' said Evelyn.

'Not of me. Why would I? No, no no, I want a portrait of you and Catherine. Though of course even Mr. Trenter may struggle to capture such beauty.' Beatrice reached up and gently took Evelyn's face in her hand.

Evelyn flushed slightly.

'We'll ask Alice what she thinks of the idea,' said Beatrice.

Evelyn tried to think of a reason not to ask Alice but had no time before Beatrice was leading both her and Catherine towards the settee where Alice and Mrs. Railton sat, talking easily.

'Alice, I see Mrs. Railton is taking good care of you and your precious cargo.' Beatrice said and stroked Alice's bump as she sat next to her.

'Indeed. And Mrs. Railton was just telling me about her husband's desire to do more for our broken heroes. I was thinking about that disabled veteran we have seen on the front, on a crutch.'

'Do you know where he sleeps?' asked Mrs. Railton.

'No, though I understand the sergeant and constable keep an eye out for him,' said Beatrice.

'I'll ask my husband to do the same. He often walks at night and may come across him. Mr. Railton fears for such veterans and how poorly they are treated.'

'I understand your husband served in France,' said Evelyn.

'As an army chaplain, though I fear serving both God and the army was a difficult balance. Were it not for the men ...' Her voice tailed off. 'Excuse me, I do need a word with the Treasurer and it looks like she may be about to leave.

Mrs. Railton left Alice and Beatrice sitting on the

settee, Evelyn and Catherine standing over them. A maid came through, topping up cups with fresh tea and offering biscuits.

'How did you find Mrs. Railton?' Evelyn asked Alice.

'She is quite lovely. She said her husband felt the pain of the men deeply and the hurt of the families of those who didn't come back just as much,' Alice said.

'Did you tell her about Curtis?' Beatrice asked, more directly than Evelyn considered appropriate, but then Beatrice was able to soften such questions in a manner Evelyn admired.

'No,' said Alice, 'what is one more name?'

'Oh my dear,' said Beatrice, placing a hand on Alice's arm, 'I think you'll find Mrs. Railton and her husband hear each name as keenly as the first. He was awarded the Military Cross you know.'

'She did say Reverend Railton had written to the Dean of Westminster Abbey with a proposal to honour those who died in service and whose graves were not marked.'

'How?' asked Evelyn.

'I believe the proposal is for a grave in Westminster Abbey.'

'A good idea? Do you think?' Evelyn asked tentatively.

'Perhaps. I wonder what Alastair would think.'

Evelyn wondered what Edward might think.

'Speaking of Alastair,' Beatrice said, and Evelyn thought she hoped to lighten the tone, 'would he paint a portrait of our two beautiful young women here? I know he is talented and of course I would pay.'

Evelyn looked to Alice, but before Evelyn could think of a diversion Alice said, 'Oh Beatrice. I wish he would, but ...' Alice looked at Evelyn who nodded encouragement, '... but,' continued Alice, 'Alastair has not painted for a long time.'

'But the paintings in the tea shop?' Catherine asked.

This time Alice nodded at Evelyn who took it as permission to speak, 'Most of the paintings you see in the shop are by Alice.'

Alice looked around the room at the other small groups of ladies talking amongst themselves. Evelyn thought she might be holding her breath.

'Really?' said Beatrice. 'Well I'm not surprised. The sunrises have the touch of a sensitive hand, the hand of someone looking for opportunity in each new day. A women's hand.' Beatrice took a sip of tea before continuing, 'So the question remains but is a little changed. Alice, would you paint Catherine and Evelyn's portrait? I leave it to you as to the pose and background, I'd only ask it's not in that romantic style which puts a mist on the subjects' faces, rendering them inoffensive and appealing but unrecognisable. We must be able to see our young womens' clear skin and fine features and, especially, bright eyes. Don't you think?'

Alice exhaled. 'I do Beatrice. Thank you. I'm not adept at portraits and would prefer not to work in oil, but if you're happy to accept a watercolour I'd be thrilled to take on such a commission.'

Evelyn found she too had been holding her breath and was relieved others now knew Alice's secret. She looked at Catherine who shrugged and smiled, probably not appreciating the heaviness of the load Alice had shared. In Spitalfields, as part of Evelyn's support for her father's ministry, she was party to many of the parishioners' secrets – Mrs. Price's second child not being her husband's, Ivy Hunter's botched abortion at fourteen that almost killed her, even Mr. Kinghill's indiscretions with Mr. Boxall, which had been a shock at first – and there was no denying such secrets were of huge significance, but she hadn't felt their weight as much as Alice's covert painting and Alastair's compliance.

'Though I wouldn't want it to be a secret from

Alastair,' said Alice.

'We'll be guided by you Alice, won't we ladies?' Beatrice gestured to Evelyn and Catherine, who both nodded, 'And meantime, might I suggest sittings take place on Thursday afternoons, at my guest house? As the season ends I'll almost certainly have a room free.'

'I'll need some materials, to make some sketches first. I usually go to Lovelys, in the High Street,' said Alice, thinking aloud. 'I'll pop down there this afternoon on the way home. We should do as much as possible before the baby is here. We need to think about pose, background, attire and light, what do you think Evelyn? Catherine?'

'I think it's a good idea and perhaps an excuse for a new dress,' said Catherine.

Beatrice laughed.

Evelyn was more cautious, 'I'm not sure I'll be the best subject for a portrait.'

'Nonsense, you'll be perfect and Alice will do us proud, I'm sure,' said Catherine and Evelyn was in no position to deny the enthusiasm of the other three women.

Evelyn, Margate,
Sunday 5th September 1920

Part way through her evening shift at The Winter Gardens Evelyn asked Catherine, in the ticket booth, if she'd keep an eye on the coat check desk. Evelyn slipped into the main auditorium. The Booking Manager, impressed by the reception to Edward's playing, had asked him to play a thirty minute slot in the middle of the Sunday evening performances and Evelyn wanted to listen. She thought Edward played well, but then she always did. As Edward left the stage he caught her eye and gave a slight nod she didn't know how to interpret. There was much about Edward she didn't know. She went back through to the foyer where Catherine looked up again from her magazine and smiled – an open smile, easy to construe, and Evelyn smiled back. Catherine's warmth and easy nature was a joy to Evelyn and, partly, a lesson.

The remainder of the shift was uneventful and afterwards Evelyn and Catherine waited on the promenade. The moon was in its last quarter and there was little light, despite the lack of cloud. They waited for Edward and William; there was comfort in the nightly walking home routine – both security and companionship. Another part of the routine was finding the constable waiting half–way down Fort Hill, ready with a formal, 'Good evening,' to let them know he was looking out for the ladies and distrustful of the newcomers, as Edward and William still were.

Edward acknowledged the constable while William muttered something which Evelyn thought wasn't helpful, though she couldn't hear what. Fifty yards on, the constable began his stroll behind them, following back down the hill. The night was quiet and with the tide at almost its lowest there was little sound from the sea. When they'd reached just past the harbour pier entrance and were between streetlights, William, without notice, took Catherine's hand, saying, 'This way. Quick,' and pulled her across the road and into the town. Evelyn and Edward followed instinctively, trotting to keep up, hearing Catherine laugh. They turned into King Street, Evelyn stopping to see the constable start walking more quickly, and then slipped into an alley between shops. William, 'sshh'd ...' and they huddled in darkness, waiting. After a minute they heard footsteps pass the top of the alley, though Evelyn couldn't tell if it was the constable. She didn't know why they'd done it – it was childish, but, oddly, felt the right thing to do. Catherine started to speak but William put his finger to her lips and they waited a further two or three minutes in silence – tense in a way Evelyn hadn't known before; tense with no fear.

William indicated the others should stay there and he went to the top of the alley. Seconds later he was back and waved them to join him.

Catherine laughed, saying, 'You know the constable will go to my aunt in the morning and you two will have some explaining to do.'

'Your aunt is a fine woman,' said William. 'Edward will smooth the way. He has her affection.'

Edward nodded. 'And she mine. Besides, what's to say? The constable simply went a different way.'

'Exactly. So, ladies, now we have lost your escort, would you like to accompany Edward and me to The Compass? I believe we owe you a drink.'

'Oh, I don't think so,' said Catherine.

'No, I'm sure we do. You have been fine company

since we came as strangers to your town and would like to repay you.'

'I think Catherine means it's not a good idea,' said Evelyn, looking at Edward.

'Don't look to me. I didn't know he was going to suggest a drink. But, now he has, it doesn't sound like a bad idea. Just the one?'

'Or the couple. Come on. It's still early,' said William.

'It's not,' said Catherine, 'the Compass will be closed.'

'The landlord has a private lock–in tonight. There's a ragtime club. You'll love it. It'll be just like the lurid stories in that magazine your American guest has been sending over,' William said.

'Except this is Margate, not Manhattan,' said Evelyn.

'And what do you know of Manhattan?' William asked.

'You forget I live in Spitalfields, not so far from the West End. I know someone who saw the Dixieland Jazz band at the Palladium last year. And, by the way, I think you'll find jazz has replaced ragtime.' Evelyn put on an air of exaggerated superiority.

'Thank you Evelyn,' said Catherine, 'and, also by the way, the gentleman who occasionally sends over the *True Story* magazine is not my American, he's just a guest, who may yet return next summer, and pays a good rate for a room.'

'And anyway, *True Story* magazine is a very educational publication,' added Evelyn, laughing.

'Well that's me told,' William said, lighting a cigarette and offering one to Catherine who refused.

'Evelyn's not wrong though, jazz is the thing, not ragtime,' said Edward.

'I know, I also saw the Dixieland band last year, remember? The programme alone cost me thruppence.

You didn't come 'cos you had a headache. But Margate hasn't caught up and ragtime is the next best thing. So, come on, and Edward, you might learn something. I might be able to get you more bookings if you play ragtime and jazz properly.' William started to walk away. He took a hip flask from an inside pocket and drank as he walked.

'Just show me the sheet music and I'll play it,' Edward said to William's back, then turned to the women. 'It might be fun though, shall we?'

'It is late,' said Catherine, 'but as the constable doesn't know where we are ... perhaps just a couple of drinks. Aunt Beatrice is always asleep when I get home anyway.'

'But we're still in our uniforms,' Evelyn protested half–heartedly.

'And very smart they are too,' said Edward.

Catherine took off her cap and indicated to Evelyn she should do the same and they both tried to fluff away the flatness caused by wearing them all evening. Catherine took a small glass jar from her bag, opened it and dabbed a touch of deep red lipstick across her lips before offering it to Evelyn who did likewise.

'That'll have to do,' said Catherine, pulling both Evelyn and Edward after William.

The Compass was but a minute away, off Market Street. There were no lights visible. William led them to the alley at the side. With no hesitation he knocked hard on the door at the end.

'Not his first time,' Evelyn whispered to Catherine. Edward shrugged. Evelyn could hear a piano playing but it was faint and discordant.

The door opened a couple of inches and William stood back so he could be seen. He led through his small party, Edward last. They were in an ill–lit parlour, with precious little more light than outside. In the room's centre was a dining table with a bottle of Johnnie Walker scotch, a Lamb's Navy rum and a tea pot. Three men sat at the table, drinking and smoking – all looked up as the four newcomers entered but, as far as Evelyn could tell, only one noticed Edward's face in the poor light. She grimaced at the smell of stale alcohol and tobacco. There was a door on the far side of the room through which they could now hear the piano more loudly. There was also more light there and Evelyn was grateful they moved through, though the smell was not much better – cigarette smoke clung to the yellowing walls and ceiling. It was the public bar, usually accessed from the street but at this time the doors were locked and heavy curtains covered the windows. Twenty or so drinkers sat at tables while a handful stood at the bar. There were as many women as men. The room was lit by gas wall lamps, giving enough yellow light for the bar's customers to notice the four of them enter and, almost in unison, look their way. Edward's mask could be seen and a few stared and muttered but nothing was said directly to them. Edward stood straight and didn't try to hide his face here – Evelyn made sure to smile at him when she caught his eye.

In a corner was an old upright piano. A heavyset man slouched on the stool with his back to the bar, his fingers dancing lightly in contrast to his size, rattling out a hectic ragtime melody. Evelyn didn't recognise the tune, but then she was rarely, if ever, at a club or music hall where such music played. Nevertheless the energy in the driving rhythm put a bounce in her step and the melody was infectious with humour. The piano was loud enough that the customers' conversations were no more than noise and she had to ask William to repeat his question on what she would like to drink. She copied Catherine in requesting a gin and tonic and followed Edward further into the room to sit at a table. Edward sat with his back to the wall. William soon joined them, carrying a tray with the ladies' drinks, a brandy for Edward and a scotch for himself, complaining as he placed them on the table that, '... the barman hasn't heard of a Sidecar. I told him how to make one and he said they didn't have Cointreau anyway. You know, sometimes I miss the war.' He spoke loudly to be heard above the piano.

Edward laughed and sipped from his glass, 'And the brandy's cheap, but not in a good way.' He took a cigarette from his silver case and offered one to Catherine who accepted.

'Well after I'd bought good gin for the ladies I was a little short of readies and thought you wouldn't mind.'

The piano player stopped, was applauded enthusiastically, and asked for requests. Someone shouted, '*Maple Leaf Rag!*'

'Not again,' shouted someone else.

The pianist started playing.

'Is that *Maple Leaf Rag?*' Evelyn leaned forward to ask Edward.

'No, I don't think so. I have heard it before though, I think it's *Easy Winners*.'

'Are you sure?' asked William, 'It's not exactly your cup of tea.'

'I've heard enough to know what I recognise and it's good, if not quite my thing,' said Edward.

'But you couldn't play it,' said William, still teasing.

Edward looked to the pianist. 'As I said, if he's got the sheet music ... but I'm not going to, so you can stop trying. And, anyway, ragtime is no longer the thing.'

'You keep saying, but here we are, in Margate, after hours drinking, music made for dancing and two beautiful ladies. Jazz can wait,' William said with a smile and they settled in their chairs, listening to the music. Two couples went to the small floorspace by the piano. The men took the ladies in hold and they began to walk in time to the rhythm, occasionally turning and bobbing.

'That's a one–step,' Catherine told Evelyn, leaning over to be heard.

Evelyn nodded, watching the couples enjoy. The drinkers were mostly around her age and quite fashionable; she guessed the after hours ragtime club was not for the pub's usual crowd – perhaps they were the older men hunched over bottles in the first room. The bar was noisy with the piano and loud conversation, just like the pubs back in Spitalfields, but unlike those, here she felt comfortable – though usually when in a pub back home it was with a collecting tin for the church, which wasn't always welcomed, especially if the Sally Army had already been in that night. Here, in The Compass, the drinkers looked to be talking or listening as much as drinking and the young men and women were together in groups or, in a few cases, separate as couples. There were few men who appeared to be on their own or in a group without women. She saw one girl look furtively around the bar before reaching up to kiss the man she stood with and his reaction to pull her close seemed easy and natural. Evelyn flushed a little. Three or four people were looking at Edward, but with curiosity, Evelyn thought, which wasn't a surprise – there were still occasions when she wasn't immune from the stark shock of the mask's lifelessness. It was easy to prepare for it when greeting him after not seeing him for a little while or a day, but sometimes, when she'd forgotten and turned to speak, or listen, to him, it was still unexpected and she feared something may show in her face. She sipped from her gin and tonic as Catherine did the same. Catherine watched the dancers, patting her hand against her leg in time to the music. Edward was watching the pianist, as best he could in the dim light. William lit a cigarette and was looking around the bar, though trying not to appear to do so. A light smile settled in his eyes and Evelyn followed his line of sight to the far end of the bar where a woman stood on her own, smoking and sipping from a tall glass. William caught her eye and called her over.

Georgette wore a straight black dress with a low

waist and shoulder straps to a straight neck line, also low. Her hem was just two or three inches below her knee. She carried a small handbag, held closed by a drawstring. As she neared the table she smiled at Catherine and Evelyn who was suddenly conscious of the uniform she still wore. Thanks to Catherine it was a better fit than Georgette's dress but even so its utilitarian nature was obvious and it hung down to her mid–calf, even when seated.

'There you are. I wondered if you were coming.' Georgette spoke to William first, and then the others around the table, 'Bonsoir all. Enjoying the music?' She talked loudly to be heard. Evelyn nodded her hello and William brought over another chair so Georgette could sit with them. Georgette and William spoke to each other for a minute or two but as the music stopped, so did they.

'Hi Georgette, nice to see you. We didn't know you'd be here. How's Patrick?' Catherine asked.

'He's well thanks.'

'Where is he?'

'He is in our room, at the guest house.' Her accent was stronger than usual.

'Oh, who's loooking after him?'

'No one needs to. He's sleeping,' Georgette said, turning back to William for a cigarette.

They listened to three or more songs, watched the couples dance and were close to finishing their drinks when William indicated another round was needed. Edward fished some coins from a pocket and passed them to William who asked Georgette to help him at the bar. As they left the table the music stopped. Evelyn asked Edward, 'Has William seen much of Georgette, recently?' Evelyn hadn't seen Georgette since the picnic, three weeks earlier.

'We see her most days. She does work and live–in at our lodgings.'

'Evelyn means, has William been walking out with Georgette?' Catherine added.

'Occasionally, I think.'

'He hasn't mentioned it.'

'I wouldn't read too much into it. William is no stranger to walking out with a lady,' Edward said and there was mischief in his voice his face couldn't match.

'And who looks after Patrick? When they go … walking?' asked Catherine.

'I don't know. I suppose he stays in his room.' Edward shrugged his shoulders.

'But he's only six,' said Catherine.

Before Edward could reply William and Georgette returned, drinks in hand, and passed them out. William raised his glass, 'To Major Gillies.'

'And Derwent Wood.' added Edward.

'There it is again. Who are they?' Catherine asked.

'Something to do with Edward's … wounds?' Evelyn asked.

William looked at Edward who said, 'A story for another time.'

Catherine shrugged and raised her glass. Evelyn took a sip from hers. It tasted more of gin than the previous one, but she thought nothing of it, the first drink had already made her a little light–headed, unused as she was to alcohol.

'And ladies,' said Georgette, 'I must say you are both looking very well. Is that a touch of rouge on your cheeks Evelyn?'

'No, I don't use it.'

'Are you sure? Pale is no longer the fashion you know.'

'It's just the sea air,' said Catherine, 'but it does suit her.'

'I think so. Don't you Mr. Thompson?' Georgette said.

Edward looked to Evelyn and though the light was poor and the gas lights reflected in his spectacles, she saw.

'Yes, I do. But I also think you're a little tight,'

185

Edward said to Georgette, who raised her glass in acknowledgement.

The piano player started again and another ragtime melody filled the bar. The couples that had been dancing were back to the tiny dance floor, joined this time by two women who took each other in hold to dance. Evelyn's group settled back to listening, watching and drinking.

After another three or four songs, Evelyn lost count – they were beginning to sound the same – the pianist took another break. Evelyn was grateful. She was lightheaded and the bar was crowded and hot. But with the break in music William went to the bar for another round. Edward went with him, ignoring the looks from those few customers he passed that hadn't already noticed his face. Georgette stayed at the table but edged round to sit next to Evelyn.

'A touch of colour does suit you,' said Georgette, adding before any response, 'I hear you ignored William's advice and went to see a medium. I would have, you know, come with you, if you'd asked. You should have.'

'I beg your pardon?' said Catherine, though her tone suggested otherwise.

'Oh I know there's plenty like William who think it's ... what's your word? ... nonsense, but my Patrick wasn't one.' Georgette took a gulp from her drink.

'Patrick? He's only six. What do you mean?' Evelyn asked.

'Not Patrick. Patrick's papa. Patrick.'

'Oh, so Patrick is named after his father,' said Evelyn.

'Of course. What did you think? Who else would he be named after,' Georgette said with a sudden aggression.

'I'm sorry,' said Evelyn, 'I didn't know his father ...' Evelyn was taken aback at the strength of Georgette's reaction.

'No, and you never thought to ask about him. And you never thought to ask if I might come to the medium.'

'Perhaps we should have but ...' Evelyn was flustered and before she could properly respond Catherine spoke.

'Enough Georgette. You know better than to take that tone, especially with Evelyn.'

The resolve in Catherine's voice was stern but controlled and patient, and seemed to come naturally. Evelyn was grateful.

Georgette emptied her glass in a gulp but put it down gently, saying, almost meekly, 'But I would have come with you, to the medium. Patrick always said he'd try, if something happened, he'd try to get back to me ...' Georgette's voice died away as tears came.

'What's the matter?' Edward said as he sat back at the table.

'Patrick didn't come home,' said Georgette, half–sobbing. She took the fresh glass Edward had brought back for her.

'I thought you said he's in your room,' said Edward.

'Not that Patrick. She means her husband,' said Evelyn.

Georgette started to speak but stopped short.

'I see,' said Edward, 'but, in any event, don't you think you should go home to your son? It's late.' His voice was calm and authoritative and for a second Evelyn thought what a good match he and Catherine might make, but that was upsetting and then the thought was gone as she finished her own drink in preparation for William bringing another.

Georgette either ignored Edward or hadn't heard as she said to him, 'I would have come. To the medium. William told me about it and I know it's not for him but I would have come. My Patrick might have too. Tell me, what happened? William won't say much but he wasn't there. You were. What happened?'

Edward lit a cigarette, before speaking more slowly than usual, 'Nothing happened Georgette. Nothing. You shouldn't go there.' He looked to Evelyn and though the mask made it so hard to read his face she thought he sought some confirmation or approval,

'That's right. It's all ... bullshit,' Evelyn said.

Catherine burst into a laugh, '... bullshit ... you say that word so well, for a vicar's gal.'

Evelyn blushed.

'But it's true, Georgette,' said Catherine. 'Nothing happened and I doubt your Patrick would have turned up and, perhaps, you should be home looking after young Patrick.'

There was an awkward silence until William returned with more full glasses. 'Blimey, you lot look proper miserable. Get these down. What's the matter?'

'Nothing,' Edward said, turning to Catherine, 'So tell me, how's Beatrice? I like her style. We could have done with her in the trenches.'

'We could always have done with women in the trenches.'

'William! That's my aunt your referring to. But I daresay you're right. She's well thanks, and keeps busy, and needn't know about the visit to Mrs. Capais.' She spoke to Edward.

'Absolutely. And I'd rather it was forgotten. There's no talking to those gone. All you can hope for is to not forget.'

'There's memorials enough springing up,' said William.

'My aunt said the new Vicar, Reverend Railton, has written to the Dean of Westminster Abbey, with a suggestion for a different sort of memorial, for those who didn't come back from the war and have no grave to mark them.'

'We don't need any more,' said William.

'Reverend Railton's idea is different. He suggests a grave in which the remains of an unknown soldier are interred. A public place,' said Catherine.'

'Who would bother going if they don't know who's buried there? My Patrick's in France, somewhere, and I do not know where and it makes no difference. He is not here but if I went to Mrs. Capais ...?' Georgette spoke to her glass.

'An unknown soldier?' said Edward, ignoring Georgette.

'According to Aunt Beatrice,' said Catherine. 'Do you think it's a good idea?'

Edward didn't respond. Evelyn watched him, trying to catch his thoughts.

'What about the unknown soldiers who did come back?' William said.

'What do you mean?' Catherine asked.

'Well, there was one poor lad, at Queen's hospital, when Edward was there, came back, at least, most of him did, he was missing a few important bits from his face, but he was also missing his name. He was unknown.'

'I don't understand,' said Evelyn.

'He was wounded and rotting in a shell hole. He had no tags, the shrapnel tore them off, along with ... other bits, and not enough uniform left to say which regiment he was with, though of course it could be narrowed down to one of a couple. But along with his face he'd lost his name, couldn't remember it and they couldn't find anyone to identify him. They reckon all his platoon was gone too. So he was unknown, even to hisself. Poor sod.'

'I don't believe you,' Evelyn said but Edward nodded.

Catherine said, 'As may be, but I don't think that's the type of unknown the Reverend Railton has in mind. More those whose fate and resting place is a mystery.'

'And there's plenty of those,' said Edward. Evelyn was still watching him but he didn't look up.

'Anyway,' Evelyn sought to lighten the mood, 'did we tell you, Aunt Beatrice has commissioned a portrait, of me and Catherine.'

'We are to be captured on canvas,' Catherine said, leaning into Evelyn. 'Two English roses, though, to be fair I believe there is more than a touch of Dutch in the family on my father's side ...'

The pianist began to play again.

'... but a story for another time. Come on Evelyn. We should dance.' Catherine stood and tried to pull Evelyn alongside her.

'No, I don't ... can't.'

'Of course you can. Can't she Edward?'

'I'm sure she can.' He laughed. Catherine tugged Evelyn to her feet, to join the other couples now on the floor, some hesitant and learning, others dancing with confidence and verve. The pianist's fingers danced across the keys as Catherine placed her right hand on Evelyn's waist and took Evelyn's right hand in her left. 'I'll lead. You follow. You'll pick it up,' she said, pulling Evelyn closer to be heard. The tempo was quick but Evelyn soon gathered the steps and their faltering clumsiness became a rhythmic, co–ordinated one–step, with the occasional half–trip by Evelyn.

'Are you a little tight?' Catherine asked as the first song finished.

'I think I am ... a little. It's a bit like Christmas Day, when Mrs. Craver brings round a bottle of claret for Father,' said Evelyn, giggling.

'Then best hold on a bit tighter. Here we go again. Ha, that's funny, we're both a little tight, so we should hold on tighter,' said Catherine, amusing herself, as the pianist began another song, this time slower.

'By the way,' said Evelyn, 'do you think I shouldn't have told them about the portrait. Alice's painting is a bit of a secret.'

'It's all right, you didn't say who the painter is.'

'Didn't I?'

'No.'

'That's all right then. Oh, and thank you.'

'For ...' asked Catherine.

'Not letting Georgette ... bully ... me.'

'I'd never let her. Besides, I do think she should be at home looking after Patrick. Don't you?'

'Yes. I do. I think.'

'I would, if I had a little boy,' said Catherine.

There was key change in the melody and Catherine slipped in a quick turn that almost caught Evelyn by surprise but she reacted well and followed Catherine's lead. Looking over Catherine's shoulder she could see Edward watching them, his familiar awkward smile just noticeable. She smiled back.

After a couple more dances Catherine led Evelyn back to their table where Edward and William applauded more than politely. Edward raised his glass to Evelyn and Catherine, 'Well danced ladies. A joy to watch and you quickly became as one in your movement and rhythm, as if by instinct.'

'I thought so,' said Catherine, 'we were quite ... nifty ... out there.'

'Nifty?' Edward said.

'Yes, as the Americans are saying,' said Catherine.

'Well, I'm not sure about nifty, but you two seem ... matched, and not just on the dance floor,' said Edward.

'Evelyn is a good friend,' Catherine said.

'And, I should say,' added Evelyn, 'Catherine is probably ... no, definitely ... the first proper friend I've had.'

'Good, you are a pair, a slightly drunk pair, but that's all right and there's something appealing in the matching uniforms,' Edward said laughing, 'though I hope in the portrait Beatrice has commissioned you might be wearing something more ... alluring? I hear the fashion in America is for shorter skirts.'

'Mr. Thompson, is the term alluring appropriate?' Evelyn teased.

'I think so,' said Catherine

'And so do I,' said Edward, 'but I should apologise for using it, though perhaps not for thinking of it. I'm afraid I've had a little more to drink than I've been used to for quite a while.'

'That's all right Mr. Thompson.' Evelyn studied his face, perhaps more openly than usual. The light was poor and his mask flickered with yellow but his right eye was clear and bright. 'Do you know, I've not noticed before but your right cheekbone, the real one, is every bit as fine and sharp as your left, if not more so, and it's not made of tin.'

Edward laughed.

Evelyn took a large gulp from her glass then exclaimed, 'Oh my lord, I'm sorry, that's so inappropriate. Forgive me.'

'Yes it is,' said Catherine seriously and Edward laughed harder, his mask being displaced by the facial movement so he had to push the arms of his spectacles behind his ears a little further.

After another song the pianist stopped but, instead of sitting at a stool by the bar as he had previously, he came to their table. He was a big man, sweating from his efforts, and introduced himself as he approached, 'Good evening. I'm Arthur. It's such a pleasure to play for you Mr. Thompson.' He held out his hand, across the table, to Edward. 'I've heard you play at The Winter Gardens. I enjoyed it very much.'

Edward took a deep breath and said, 'The pleasure is mine Arthur. You play very well, it's a joy to hear. William, we should buy Arthur a drink, and perhaps another round for the ladies.'

William stood and held out his hand for the coins Edward gave him.

'Please sit.' Edward invited Arthur.

'I'm afraid I don't have time. We've not long before we need to finish and I just wanted to ... well ... I've already said it, but it bears repeating ... I enjoyed your playing.

Would you like to play tonight?' Arthur indicated to the upright piano. 'I know it's not to your usual standard of instrument, but does very well for ragtime.'

'That's kind Arthur, but the truth is I'm not able to play your music half as well as you and I'm enjoying listening so much and, I should say, learning.'

'Ah, Mr. Thompson, you're very kind, but I think you're being modest.'

'No, really, it's not a style I play well.'

'Hmmm. But I would like to say I've played with Mr. Thompson. Could you be tempted to a duet? I know there's nothing you wouldn't pick up in an instant. Ladies,' Arthur appealed to the others, 'you'd like to hear a duet surely?'

Catherine and Evelyn agreed.

'Well, as long as you promise to lead. I'm sure I'll learn more quickly at your side,' said Edward, standing and following Arthur back to the piano, carrying his chair to put alongside the piano stool. From behind it was comical to see big Arthur almost squeezing Edward to the end of the piano's higher register.

Arthur started to play a simple ragtime melody and Edward joined in cautiously. The few dancing couples back on the floor applauded and resumed their one–steps.

William came back with more glasses and though Evelyn felt it not a good idea, she drank anyway. Before William could sit, a large woman with a red face and a thick neck on top of a square body started clearing glasses from their table and asked William, 'How's your friend this evening? Looks like his headache is gone, though he may have another in the morning, along with a few others.' She nodded to the three seated women.

'Yes. He's much better thanks. And I'm glad you've come over. Is Rolf in?' William made it a tentative question.

'Rolf? Yes, he's up at the bar. Come over in five minutes and I'll introduce you.' The woman stacked the glasses from the table and carried them back to the bar.

'Who's that?' asked Evelyn.

'The landlady, of course,' said Georgette.

'I'd gathered that. I meant, who's ... Rolf?' Evelyn asked, 'and what's that about Edward having a headache?'

'Not that it's your business, but as it happens I hear Rolf came over from Germany during the war, when taken prisoner, and it turned out he used to work in the Junkers factory. So they brought him to work at Manston airfield, and he never went back. It turns out he's a useful man to know. I believe he has cousins working on the London docks,' said William.

'But what about Edward's headache? What does she mean?'

'Oh, you know how they come and go. One time the landlady was able to assist, just a little. Nothing to be excited about. Anyway, excuse me, I need to talk to Rolf.'

The three women were left sitting at the table. Evelyn's head started to spin when she turned to see how Edward was getting on at the piano and she pushed away the drink on the table in front of her. Georgette undid the drawstring on her bag to pull out a pack of cigarettes – Ogden's Robin – there was one left. She looked at the pack with disappointment. Evelyn heard Catherine sigh. Catherine pulled up her dress to take a pack of Black Cats from her stocking top, seeming not to care if anyone noticed.

'Here, join me,' Catherine said, taking out two cigarettes and passing one to Georgette who looked at Evelyn. 'Evie doesn't smoke,' said Catherine.

'Thanks,' Georgette said, putting her own pack back in her bag but stopping to look around the bar. 'Where's William?'

'He's at the end of the bar, talking to that tall man.' Evelyn said. 'Rolf, I suppose.'

'Quick, see these.' Georgette pulled her chair round to sit close to the other women, closer than Evelyn might have wished.

From her bag Georgette took a set of battered postcards, edges curled and torn. 'I found these in William's room. I was cleaning. I don't think he's missed them yet.' She passed them to Catherine who held them between her and Evelyn so they could see together. 'Do not you dare say anything to Will,' Georgette said, taking a matchbook from her bag to light their cigarettes.

The postcards were not easy to see in the poor light but Evelyn's eyes adjusted to the black and white images. 'Oh, she said on seeing the first – a young woman with dark hair sat upright on a chaise longue in an Edwardian parlour. Her hair was piled high on her head and she looked into the mirror she held. She wore only white undergarments and one shoulder strap had fallen, exposing one full breast. She seemed not to notice, concentrating on her reflection. From the hair and undergarment fashion Evelyn guessed the picture was pre–war. 'Oh,' she repeated.

'You found these in William's room?' Catherine asked.

'On his dressing table. I imagine he had been looking through them the evening before, while he ... you know.' Georgette giggled. Catherine nodded.

Evelyn thought about what '... you know,' might mean and then said, 'Oh,' again as she guessed.

Catherine put the card to the back of the pack, to show the next. It was similar, perhaps the same woman with her hair allowed to fall, but this time standing and looking into a large wall mirror. Her reflection was seen in the camera and she looked embarrassed but not cowed. She wore white drawers with a high waist but was bare above and her breasts jutted toward the mirror. Evelyn couldn't remember the last time she'd seen her own in a mirror properly, or if at all, other than fleetingly.

Georgette urged Catherine to move on to the next card, having one eye on William who was still in conversation with the tall man.

In the next picture the woman was naked, standing with one leg on a chair as she rolled up, or down, a white stocking. She looked directly at the camera and Evelyn thought there was more than a touch of contempt in the woman's gaze but the detail was hard to see and Evelyn's attention was drawn from the face to the heavy patch of pubic hair that was such a contrast to the woman's pale skin. Catherine drew on her cigarette and turned to the next card. A different woman, this time with long blonde hair, was standing naked next to a table where two men played cards. Both were dressed in soldier's uniforms – officers – and both held cards. On the table was a pile of coins. The woman, bigger than that in previous cards, looked bored as she watched the game and it was a surprise to Evelyn the display of flesh wasn't a distraction to the men. It was an odd pose.

'Now that lieutenant looks the definition of uninterested, don't you think?' Catherine nudged and asked Evelyn, who had no answer. Of course, back in Spitalfields Evelyn had come across pornography and there was no shortage of prostitutes nor men wanting to take advantage, but the sellers of such pictures in the markets were quick to hide such wares when they saw Evelyn or her father and though she had seen fleeting glimpses this was the first opportunity to ... to what? Study? That didn't seem appropriate and yet there was a fascination which couldn't be denied. She still felt lightheaded, flustered and a little nauseous but reached for the gin and tonic she had not long pushed away. But though the previous pictures had been surprises the next was a shock that brought an instant flush of embarrassment. A naked man stood side on at fireplace, leaning against the mantelpiece. On her knees in front of him was a naked woman, her face close to his erect penis.

'Please, hurry ladies. I don't know how long William will be away,' Georgette said and Evelyn was grateful for the interruption. The picture in front of her was a little repellent, partly mysterious and quite compelling.

Catherine went to the next and silently mouthed, 'Oh dear.' The man from the fireplace was now sitting on a chair and the woman had her back to him but was astride. Though the picture wasn't clear, Evelyn could see he was penetrating her. The woman's head was tilted back and her eyes were closed, her mouth open in a silent, frozen cry – but Evelyn could not tell if it was pleasure or pain. A rush of blood brought tingling to Evelyn's neck and face. She wanted to know more, of the woman, to see more, of the detail, to understand more, of the act.

Evelyn looked away briefly but back again as the next card was shown, two women were topped and tailed on a bed, surrounded by cushions. Both were naked but the picture wasn't clear and before Evelyn could make out the images Georgette said, 'Quick! Give,' and took back the cards, slipping them into to her bag. Evelyn looked at Catherine who was stifling her giggles.

'But nothing you ladies haven't seen or done I expect,' Georgette said and Evelyn thought she was being sarcastic but knew she'd had sufficient to drink that her judgement was unsound. She shrugged her shoulders but the last image was not to be so easily discarded. Catherine controlled her laughter to draw on her cigarette.

'And they were in William's room?' Evelyn asked, wanting to be clear.

'Oh yes, not your Mr. Thompson. He has other ... diversions,' Georgette said and moved her chair away before Evelyn could respond and as William returned. He was pleased with himself but didn't say why.

The music stopped and Evelyn realised she hadn't paid attention to the last few songs and how Edward had been playing. She turned to look and he was still seated at the piano, talking to Arthur, who shuffled the papers on the piano's sheet music stand and then stood to face the bar. Edward moved on to the piano stool and began the opening bars to a gentle melody. A few bars later Arthur sang in a rich tenor ...

'I've seen some beautiful flowers,
Grow in my garden fair,'

... the first lines of a popular song. Evelyn recognised *The Rose Of No Man's Land*, but performed more slowly than usual. Arthur sang well and it was a deep contrast from the uptempo ragtime music played earlier. The pub's customers seemed to take the change in mood as acknowledgement that ragtime club was over and they began to leave as the landlady shouted, 'Time!' and rang a small hand bell. Neither Edward nor Arthur were distracted and the song flowed beautifully. Evelyn looked to the clock behind the bar, it was nearly twelve thirty and, despite the gin induced inhibitions, she felt a sudden guilt; Alice might be awake and waiting for her. Arthur's song came to a close as the remaining customers finished their drinks and Edward stood to shake Arthur's hand.

William took Georgette's hand and half–pulled her over to the piano, 'Lovely song. And now, Edward, while we have you at that piano, you should hear Georgette sing. I've heard her and she's good.'

'Of course,' Georgette said, perhaps with false bravado from the alcohol.

'What have you got?' William took the sheet music from the stand and sifted through until, 'Ah! Exactly the right song,' showed Georgette, who nodded, and placed the chosen music in front of Edward. He nodded in recognition and started to play but Georgette missed the introduction. Edward started again, this time counting Georgette in and, on cue she sang...

'They were summoned from the hillside,
They were called in from the glen,'

Georgette's voice was a clear soprano with a gentle, natural vibrato and little accent. Her tone was sweet and the pitch controlled. The few drinkers left joined in with the chorus ...

'Keep the Home Fires Burning,
While your hearts are yearning,'

... and Evelyn thought she might cry. She looked at Catherine who was watching Georgette. William stood next to her, conducting the remaining drinkers in the chorus. Georgette held the final note easily and Edward led the applause.

Back at the table Catherine said to Evelyn, 'We should have a go, don't you think?' and tried to pull her towards the piano, but even in her half–drunken state Evelyn knew she was not good enough.

'If we can sing *Nearer My God To Thee* perhaps, but otherwise ...'

'Come on,' Catherine implored but Evelyn was not to be moved.

'No, you go on. I've heard you sing. You're good. You don't need me.'

'All right,' said Catherine almost defiantly, stumbling a little on leaving the table. William was talking to Edward, reminding him how he'd told Edward, '... not a week ago, Georgette could sing proper.'

Edward nodded agreement while Georgette beamed.

'Can I sing something?' Catherine asked.

'Everyone is leaving,' said Georgette, pointing to the fast emptying pub. Evelyn came to stand at Catherine's side.

'But I don't see why not,' said William, 'What have we here,' and started sifting through the sheet music again but Catherine bent down to talk into Edward's ear. Evelyn couldn't hear what was said but recognised Edward's introduction and Catherine sang ...

'Oh Danny boy, the pipes, the pipes are calling,
From glen to glen, and down the mountain side,'

... in a warm alto, darker in character than Georgette's soprano. Though not as clear as Georgette's voice, Catherine's seemed to carry more emotion. Edward's playing was sparse and Catherine's voice not loud, inviting the few people left to concentrate their listening. Later Evelyn thought it might have been the combination of song choice and gin rather than the voice itself, but this time she couldn't hold back a tear.

Edward let the final note hang before standing and commenting, 'Georgette, Catherine. It was a pleasure to hear you sing. Thank you.'

'Indeed. It was lovely ladies,' said William and then turned to Edward, 'didn't I tell you,' and then back to Georgette, 'Hackney Empire here we come.'

'Perhaps sooner rather than later,' said a new, deeper voice. Constable Simms had come into the pub. 'Ceinwen!' he called towards the bar, 'time to be closing. It's gone the hour we agreed.'

The landlady apologised as she herded the few remaining customers towards the door. Evelyn felt guilty again, guilty to be worse for drink with the constable present, but he didn't seem too concerned about the pub's lock–in as he asked Ceinwen, '... and let me know when the next one is but perhaps you can finish the music a little earlier,' before he turned to Catherine, 'and Miss Burton, we should also be on our way now and this time we'll walk together.'

Catherine nodded and Evelyn was grateful for the suggestion; the alcohol now brought fatigue as well as confusion. Constable Simms waited by the back door and followed Catherine, Evelyn and Edward outside. William and Georgette were not with them and Evelyn didn't remember seeing them leave, but they were no longer in the pub.

'I'm sorry we've kept these good ladies out so late.' Edward offered his apology as they walked.

'So you should be Mr. Thompson. And perhaps even more sorry for the drink. You have drawn them into an embarrassing positon. And Mrs. Blundell will not thank you for it, and I'm sure the sergeant will not thank me.'

'Beatrice is a very understanding lady. I'm sure she will be ... well ... understanding. Much like your good self.'

'Hmmm. That remains to be seen, and I think that should be Mrs. Blundell to you, not Beatrice. And of course the person you should want to be most understanding is the duty sergeant, and I can assure you he's not renowned for such.' Constable Simms was as calm as he was resolute but Evelyn couldn't help but giggle at Edward being told off.

'I'm sorry. Truly. It won't happen again,' said Edward.

'As we both know Mr. Thompson, deeds and actions are the true measure, not words, so we'll see.'

Evelyn giggled again and nearly tripped as they came to a kerb. Edward was quickly by her side and with Catherine at the other the three walked arm in arm with Constable Simms behind, shepherding.

They walked in and out of the gas street light shadows, Evelyn leaning ever more heavily on her supporters.

The Blue Bench

Edward, Margate,
Monday 6ᵗʰ September 1920

The bed was cold but Edward was warm enough. His head ached a little but it was a general nag, not focused and he doubted one of his episodes was gathering. His legs hurt and he struggled to calm his mind but when he did, for short periods, he sank into the pillow and could relive and enjoy the previous night, playing at The Compass, drinking with Evelyn, until the memory was stolen by a pang of anxiety and breathlessness. His knees and hips ached, deep into the joints. There was no reason to rise for the day ahead, why bother, except it was a beautiful day and why wouldn't he? He felt alone and glad to be so but that was a melancholy thought and his throat was a little sore and his eyes heavy. There were butterflies in his stomach for no purpose and his chest was tight while his guts were a little loose. It might be flu, if he didn't know better – but he did. He struggled to see what the week, the month, the year, could offer and didn't care – a dispiriting sadness. It was an effort to move though the sun called him to the day. His neck ached. He sniffed hard to hold his nose from running. He raised his head. It eased and felt good not to wear the mask. He resisted the urge to scratch the irritation at his cheek and the tight skin there caught a light breeze from the open window. He smiled, knowing there was no chance of catching his own reflection anywhere. The watercolour of the sunrise had replaced the only mirror. It was a good painting, but in truth, didn't hold anywhere near the same power as the dark ship that relentlessly sank, horrific and compelling in equal measure. His mind had no focus but its wandering was not gentle, amusing, distracting – it was disjointed and frightening. A stronger wind blew in, colder and his face felt fresh and clean, revealed, though his body felt old and a low mood cloaked his mind and corrupted his thoughts. He remembered his head hurt and summer was nearly done and he hadn't been home since … since he was someone else. He fought the urge to vomit, knowing how the retching would stretch the tightness where his left cheekbone was no longer. Then he was happy he'd controlled the urge to be sick and then miserable to think that might be the best of the day. There was no reason to do or be and no answer in asking.

Thankfully, fitfully, he dozed.

The bottle of laudanum had run dry four days earlier and he'd used the last of the morphine sulphate tablets three days ago. The alcohol last night had helped ward off the withdrawal but it had never been more than a day or two away.

He dozed until William banged on the door at just past eight thirty, calling him to breakfast.

Despite the previous night's drinking, Georgette showed no sign of a hangover as she brought hot kedgeree to William and toast to Edward. Like Georgette, William looked to be suffering no ill–effects of the lock–in at The Compass and Edward supposed it was only he who found the bright sun flooding into the breakfast room at the guest house painful. They were the only ones there, not having come down for breakfast until gone nine, and Edward had smoked more than he'd eaten. The effort to dress and take breakfast had been heavy. William's encouragement to try the kedgeree – Georgette insisted they used the freshest haddock – was ignored. The toast was dry in Edward's mouth, despite the butter and marmalade, and he struggled to swallow, though that wasn't due to the drink the night before; he'd noticed of late swallowing was sometimes more difficult and wondered if he should visit Major Gillies when back in London. He lit another cigarette, poured another cup of tea, trying to concentrate on the newspaper.

'I see your Blackburn drew with Spurs on Saturday.' Edward spoke slowly.

'Did they? Why do you think they're my Blackburn?'

'Aren't they? You said so …'

'… ah, I remember, but only to rile young Kayst when he insisted on following Everton and Blackburn had just beaten 'em.'

'That was a touch unnecessary, wasn't it?'

'Do you think? He had no reason to follow a team so far from his home.'

'To be fair, it's not as if he could have a home team, coming from Herne Bay.'

'Gillingham? Or there's always Southend.'

'Bit of swim across the estuary on match days though.'

'Fair point. Anyway, what will you do on your day off today?'

'Not a lot. My head hurts and …'

'… those bits of metal shifting about again?' William indicated to Edward's face as he forked more kedgeree onto his plate.

'No, I don't think so, it's more to do with last night's drinking at The Compass. Or …' he hesitated, '… I've run out of … tablets, again. And the laudanum just isn't enough. I could do with a … pick up.'

'Before we came down here didn't you think the sea air might do the trick?'

'Did I? I suppose. And it nearly did, but … after that last episode I'd been keeping … it at bay, just a little each day, until …'

'… all the soluble tablets gone?' William asked.

'Yes.'

'I don't think Major Gillies would be best pleased. It's fair enough if for pain but otherwise …?'

'Well just assume it's for pain then. Major Gillies would understand.'

'Hmmm. That's as may be. Anyways,' William said with growing smugness, 'thankfully for you I managed to catch up with Rolf last night, the Kraut.'

Edward put down his paper. 'And?'

'I've a couple of syringes and some morphia salt in solution.'

'That's … good.' Edward said with a forced casual air.

'I picked them up last night, while you were chatting to the constable. Snotty bugger.'

'He's all right. Just looking out for Catherine and Evelyn.'

'Aren't we all.' William said as Georgette came back into the room to clear one of the other tables.

Edward felt a little brighter, though from the homemade marmalade or considering William's successful transaction with Rolf, he couldn't tell. 'And talking of last night. Did you have a good time Georgette? You sang beautifully.'

'Thank you Monsieur Thompson. I enjoyed it very much.'

'Good, and I did enjoy playing. We should go again.'

'I'll ask Ceinwen about the next ragtime club night,' said William before whispering, 'She's quite a lass, as the Welsh girls tend to be, in my experience.'

'I don't want to know. Anyway, what are you doing today?'

'I've been told Karl Marx has stayed here in Margate

and we're going find out where, it's only minutes from here, isn't it Georgette?'

'I believe so. Patrick told me. Patrick's papa, that is, when he was ... here.' Georgette said as she took away dirty crockery.

'You're not still pretending to be a Marxist are you?' Edward asked William.

'Perhaps.'

'Or is it a socialist? Or a communist? I don't really understand the difference.'

'Few do. Perhaps even the great man himself,' said William.

'And now I don't understand what you mean,' Edward said.

'You're the son of a solicitor from Lincoln, you wouldn't. Would he Georgette?' William shouted through to the kitchen. He turned back to Edward. 'Come with us. Patrick's coming, and then we'll take a wander up to the cliffs. See if we can find some proper bracing air to clear your head.'

Edward had no good reason to refuse and though his head and body still ached he knew returning to bed would make no difference – perhaps the sea air might.

'Patrick's papa said Marx stayed here, before it was Albert Terrace. He wanted a sea view.' Georgette stood on the small triangular green behind the Clock Tower and pointed to the terraced houses. Patrick stood beside Georgette, holding her hand.

'Yes, but which house?' asked William patiently.

'I don't know.' Georgette shrugged. 'Sorry. One close to the sea, he wanted a sea view, though I believe they were all closer to the sea in those days. Fifty years or more? Patrick didn't say.'

Edward looked at William, expecting anger. William looked at young Patrick and rolled his eyes. Patrick copied him.

'Ice cream?' William asked Patrick, who dropped Georgette's hand to take his and they started along Marine Drive towards the harbour. Georgette and Edward walked behind. Though it was early September, the beach was no less crowded than a week earlier and the weather was still warm enough for sea bathing and sand castles, if you could stand cold water. It was gone ten and the tide only an hour from its lowest. The boats in the harbour were already resting on the sand. A steam boat bound for London was leaving the jetty and Patrick pointed to it, '*London Belle*.'

'Are you sure?' William asked.

'He will be sure,' said Georgette, shrugging her shoulders inside her blouse. It was light blue with big wing collars and though it looked new it was perhaps a size too big, but then what did Edward know of women's fashion. They walked on and up Fort Hill and Georgette said something to Edward but his attention was elsewhere and it wasn't until she left him to catch up with William he realised perhaps it was a question to which he should have responded. Though the sea air was refreshing his bones still ached and his mind was weary. Georgette settled into step alongside William, taking his hand. Patrick let go William's other hand and dropped behind to walk beside Edward. As they walked up Fort Hill the breeze strengthened but was always pleasant and, when they reached Fort Crescent, Edward asked, 'What flavour ice cream do you like?'

Patrick shrugged.

Edward pretended to think hard. 'I have a particular favourite but they rarely have it. It's a bit special.'

'What is it?'

'It doesn't matter. They won't have it.'

'Why?'

'Because they're hard to catch.'

'What are?'

'But they are great for ice cream.'

'What are?'

'You'll not believe me,' Edward said.

'I will.'

'No, you won't. People always say that, but they don't.'

'I will.'

'Promise?'

'Promise.'

'And don't tell others.'

'Promise.'

'All right. My favourite ice cream flavour is ... octopus.'

Patrick's eyes widened. 'Really?'

'Absolutely. But don't forget. Our secret, otherwise everyone will try it and there's never enough for everyone.' Edward winked his right eye.

They stopped walking and Patrick looked from Edward's right eye to his left and back, three or four times. Edward resisted looking away. Patrick thought for a moment then said, 'Can your tin eye do that?'

'Not yet. But I'm practicing.'

'Good,' Patrick said. He took Edward's hand and they walked on. After prolonged deliberation Patrick might have said, 'Octopus?' but Edward didn't react; his attention still wandering. The last six year old's hand he'd held had been his brother's, in 1905, 24th May, Empire Day. Their father's office had held a party and invited family. Edward, James and their sister, Amelia, were their parents' pride and joy. Edward was eleven and remembered well the festivities to celebrate the Empire's more benevolent traits. His brother James died just two weeks later, in the typhoid outbreak in Lincoln. He hadn't thought of his brother for a long time and felt a sudden guilt. It was the same guilt he felt when he realised it might be a day or two since he'd thought of his platoon's dead and injured.

And wasn't he the Lucky Lieutenant, even as a child?

James caught typhoid and died – Edward slept in the next room and didn't.

The platoon had been devastated at Vimy Ridge – he was inventing octopus ice cream.

Patrick squeezed his hand and pointed back to the jetty where another steam boat had just landed and said something Edward didn't catch.

They meandered along the cliff top, past the bandstand in the Oval Gardens and across Hodges Bridge to where they'd picnic'd three weeks earlier. A little further on was a tea room and they found a table outside. Edward was grateful to sit. William ordered coffees and tea and a vanilla ice cream for Patrick, who leaned over to Edward and whispered, 'I don't think they have octopus.' Patrick sat back and when he was sure neither Georgette nor William were watching tried to wink. The tea shop was crowded but Edward didn't feel he was being watched and the September sun was low and gently warming. Georgette and William shared a private joke. Patrick finished his ice cream and was looking further down the clifftop to where two boys, around his own age, tried to keep kites high on the breeze flowing onshore. Patrick tried to catch Georgette's attention but she brushed him away. William took out his hip flask and poured a little into both his and Georgette's cups. Edward shook his head, saying, 'Patrick and I are going to have a look at the kites.'

Edward indicated to Patrick he should go with him and they left the tea shop to walk along the clifftop overlooking Palm Bay. Patrick ran ahead as they neared the kites. He stood and watched the two boys for a while, Edward standing a few yards behind. One of the kites floated effortlessly but the other was tumbling along the ground as its flyer ran some thirty yards ahead, pulling the string and hoping to catch the air.

'I think he's running the wrong way.' Edward told Patrick. 'Why don't you see if you can help? Hold the kite and run toward the wind for him. And if it picks up I expect he'll let you fly it a little.'

Patrick thought for a second then ran after the boy. Edward watched the two of them struggle to find the wind. When the kite took flight they cheered and Edward didn't care about the tightening of his face as he laughed. He looked along the cliff and out to sea, taking off his hat to feel the air through his hair. There were people around him on the cliff but none seemed to be aware of him. He breathed deeply and tilted the frame of his spectacles slightly as he turned to the sea. The rush of air under the mask was cool and its freshness a revelation, a delight. The ache and confusion of earlier that morning were forgotten in the rollercoaster of withdrawal. He stood that way for three or four minutes, entranced. There was music in the breeze, where he had heard none for so long, and a refrain he had never heard before played in his mind. He enjoyed it's spontaneity for a short while then repeated it and repeated it in his mind, hoping to take it back with him, desperate to be able to capture it – it had been such a long time since feeling the need to compose – but the shouts of the boys flying the kites brought him back. Both kites had fallen with twisted and tangled strings and the three boys were working through the challenge together. Far out at sea a freighter inched across the horizon. Down on the beach, at the bottom of the cliff, three rows of white beach tents stood to attention, their military bearing tempered by the random confusion of happy beach lovers and bathers. On the grassy clifftop around him were happy groups, strolling, sitting, chatting and laughing; except one man, fifty or sixty yards on. Standing alone, close to the cliff edge, he was a man apart. He wore a dark suit and was hatless, facing the sea. Edward recognised him. The last time he had seen him was in the tea shop, giving instructions to Alice and Evelyn. Edward remembered the conversation with Evelyn on the same cliff, three weeks previously and put his hat back on, walking over to Alastair, offering, 'Cigarette Mr. Trenter?'

Alastair took but a second to recognise him. 'Mr. Thompson? No, thank you.'

'How are you, sir?' Edward asked.

'Well, thank you. And you?'

'Yes, and better for the sunshine and clear air, though today I have missed my morning tea from your shop,' said Edward.

'Oh, you should have asked Alice to prepare a flask.' Alastair responded seriously, missing Edward's attempt at establishing rapport.

Edward hesitated, lit his cigarette, then said, 'Thank you, I'll remember, for next time. Mrs. Trenter is looking well and there's not long before her confinement.'

'Alice is a strong woman.'

'And a new child will bring new blessings.'

'I expect so.'

There was a pause. Edward said, 'It's a fine day and this is a fine spot from which it can be appreciated.'

'One of my favourites, though I prefer it a little quieter.'

'And how has Evelyn settled in at the tea shop?' Edward asked.

'Very well. We have been lucky to have her help this summer. She is a credit to her father.'

'I'm told you and the Reverend Coughston have known each other some time. We met him at the hop field mission, he is a great character and of sharp intellect.'

'I met him at Cambridge and we disagreed about much, but found more to share. He has done great things and many have reason to thank him.'

'And I hear, from Evelyn, the reverend is very proud of your successes and skill at the easel.'

'Ah, then Evelyn and the reverend are being generous. I studied with Henry Tonks you know, and had the Royal Academy accepted me then perhaps, but … no matter.'

'Henry Tonks?' Edward repeated.

'You know the name?'

Edward hesitated. He had met Tonks and though he was a good man the circumstances were not for consideration on a day as fine as this. 'Yes, I have heard of him. I believe he is a distinguished sculptor and artist.'

'Just so. But after studying with him I took over my father's business and hope we are now the best tea shop in Margate.' Alastair's cheerfulness was forced.

'Well, it's certainly the most welcoming and William and I are glad to have found it. And talking of painting, I have one of your sunsets hanging on my wall. Evelyn chose it and it brightens the room.'

Alastair hesitated before replying, 'Oh yes, I remember. It's a ... nice ... piece. But not one of my best I'm afraid.'

'I'm no connoisseur but I do find it ... calming and it's nice to think it was Evelyn's choice.'

'I suppose, but it wouldn't be my choice. Others have more substance.'

'Then perhaps I should buy another, with your advice.'

'Apologies Mr. Thompson, it was not my intention to solicit a sale.'

'And my apologies too, I didn't mean to imply I felt pressure to buy another painting. Though am I correct in saying Mrs. Blundell has commissioned a portrait of Evelyn and Catherine?'

'Mrs. Blundell?'

'Catherine's aunt. Alice's friend.'

'Has she? Commissioned a painting?'

'I thought it was mentioned last night, though, to be honest, and, just between the two of us, I'd drunk more than I'm used to.'

'No, Mrs. Blundell hasn't spoken to me of such a commission. Besides, portraits are not my forte, as the Royal Academy noted,' said Alastair.'

'My apologies, I've misunderstood or made a wrong

assumption.'

The two men stood in awkward silence for half a minute or so until Edward said, 'Anyway, nice to talk sir. I expect I'll see you at the tea shop. The best tea shop in Margate.'

'Thank you Mr. Thompson. Now, if you'll excuse me.'

Edward turned away but took just a few steps before halting, pausing and turning. Alastair had already turned back to the sea.

'Mr. Trenter,' Edward called. Alastair didn't turn or acknowledge his name until Edward was standing back beside him.

'Yes, Mr. Thompson.'

'Your painting of the ship sinking, the men ... suffering. Would you consider that a painting of more substance? It is difficult to look at, and hard to turn away from, but, excuse any impertinence, is it the reason you walk here most days? To watch?'

'To watch?'

'Just in case. Impossible as it may be. But ... to watch for ...'

'What has Alice told you?' Alastair interrupted.

'Nothing. Alice has said nothing, but Evelyn mentioned you came here ... to watch ... for ... Curtis.'

'Young Evelyn has overstepped her position,' Alastair said, staring out to the horizon.

'Evelyn has your well–being, and Alice's, at heart,' Edward said, defensively. 'I understand you come here most days. Is it a comfort?'

'A ... comfort?' Alastair said, his voice breaking with anger. 'What comfort could there ever be? What comfort will we ever find? You know my son did not come home but not what that means, not where that leads us or what has been taken from us or how I would let a wave take my own life from this very cliff if I could change places.' He turned back from the sea to look at Edward. 'Comfort?

No. There is no comfort, but yes I come here. What else should a father do, if not watch for his son? Please, tell me. What else should … could … a father do?' In an instant Alastair's anger was blown and his eyes glistened with tears. 'There are some so weak with desperation they might seek solace in the services of outrageous frauds, masquerading as mediums, but I have nowhere else to watch for Curtis and nowhere to watch over him.'

Edward realised Mr. Trenter was aware of the visit to Mrs. Capais and he wondered how Alice had told him and how he had reacted. But that was not an episode he wished to raise. He dropped his cigarette to the grass and ground it under foot. 'I've no words that will help but I understand a little of what it means to have nowhere to watch over someone, when they've gone. I knew, right from the beginning, not all my men would live, but I always thought if I came home at least I'd bring them with me. I didn't. I'm sorry, for all of us.'

The boys had unravelled the strings and the kites hung on the breeze. Patrick was holding the string to one of them and another boy was shouting instructions to him. Edward returned to the tea room, regretting having spoken to Mr. Trenter. He looked back and Alastair was walking further down the clifftop. The musical refrain Edward had tried to capture just a little earlier returned, but its energy was gone. Edward's thoughts were distracted by Patrick calling for his attention, wanting to show his new kite flying skills. Edward waved an acknowledgement and wondered again about Alastair, who would soon be a parent, again. Would that be the time for Alastair to stop watching for Curtis? Edward hoped so, but then he wasn't a father.

'You all right?' William asked as Edward sat back at the table, next to Georgette. 'Who was that?' he nodded back to along the clifftop.

'Alice's husband, Alastair.'

215

'Really?' William squinted. 'Oh yes. So this is where he walks. He needs to make the most of it. Once the baby comes he'll be run off his feet in the tea shop.'

'I think he is too old to be a papa,' said Georgette.

'How old is he?' asked William.

'How would I know?' Georgette answered. 'He must be near sixty, but the age of his wife is more important. She may be near forty. A ... dangerous age for a first baby.'

'It's not her first.'

'Is it not? Where are the others?'

'He ...' Edward stressed the word, '... didn't last the war.'

Georgette didn't look at him but said, 'Alice will be lucky to have Evelyn around. But then aren't we all?' Her tone was ambiguous. Edward looked to William but he either ignored or hadn't recognised any sarcasm. Edward wanted to tell William more of his conversation with Alastair but without Georgette around. He lit a cigarette as Patrick came back to them, smiling broadly.

'Can I have a kite? Please?' Patrick asked, speaking quickly.

William answered before Georgette could respond, 'Of course. As long as I can have a turn,' William promised, 'and did I ever tell you of the time we used kites in the war? Imagine, six or seven big kites, as tall as a man, in a row, all lifting a man, sitting in a little rope hammock, with his binoculars round his neck.'

'I don't believe you,' said Patrick.

'It's true, isn't it Lieutenant Thompson?' William asked Edward.

'After a fashion,' said Edward. 'The Yanks tried it, but I don't think it worked well. I never saw it myself.'

'I did,' said William, 'and it worked well enough until the Huns sent up a Fokker or two, and the poor Yank had nothing but a revolver. Hardly sporting eh?'

'Another story for another time,' interrupted Edward,

'and I could do with going back to the guest house. My head is beginning to hurt again.'

'I am not surprised, after all we had to drink last night,' said Georgette.

'Perhaps that's it,' Edward said, but knew better. The sun no longer brought him a soothing warmth – it had become uncomfortable and the breeze was no longer offering respite. He indicated to William they should leave and they made their way back along the clifftop, across Hodges Bridge and on towards Margate. Patrick spoke non–stop of flying the kite though Georgette's interest soon dwindled. William and Edward walked behind and Edward slowed down, to increase the gap.

'I'm ashamed to say I may have upset Mr. Trenter.' Edward told William.

'Really? How?'

'You know he comes here watching for his dead son, Curtis?'

'Does he? Why?'

'Because he has nowhere else.'

'I don't understand. What did you say to upset him?'

'I may have implied I do understand, that I feel something similar for our boys, that were lost.'

'Our boys? Like Kayst you mean?'

'Yes. But of course I can't compare that with Trenter's loss.'

'Though of course Kayst's parents can. Talking of which, you never did write them after Kayst … disappeared? To tell them what happened or explain.'

'No.'

'So why worry about him so much now?'

'I don't know, and it could be any of them. But perhaps I would have written if I knew what happened.'

'Edward, you know. You may not have seen, there may not be a grave to see, but you know.'

Edward stopped walking, William stopped a yard ahead. Edward said, 'Trenter knows what happened to his son but he is still here every day, watching. I should have told Trenter about Reverend Railton's idea, for the grave, for the unknown soldier.'

'I shouldn't worry. If it happens he'll hear about it.'

'Do you think if he could visit such a place he might not need to come here, every day, to watch?'

'Coming here every day sounds to me more like an addiction than a grieving.'

'What do we know? We're not fathers.'

'And unlikely to be, at least, knowingly.'

'You still might. But, look at me, who would want a child with me?'

'Come on, cheer up, you're proper maudlin. Forget about Trenter and the likes of Kayst for a while. I know what you need. Time to try the goods I bought from Rolf. Just enough to keep you ticking over nicely.'

Edward said nothing. He felt low, his body ached and he was nauseous. He dabbed a handkerchief to his nose as blowing it would not stop the running. It was the same as he'd felt that morning. Perhaps he should not have come out after all but after breakfast, out in the sun, he had felt good and nearly alive. He had wanted to be there, both on the cliff and in the moment, but now he was low again and wished someone could ease the discomfort, balance his self–hatred. He knew this feeling, had been through it before, in London, and knew if he could last the week the withdrawal effects would cease, but then the shrapnel might move and he'd need the morphia again and the cycle would repeat.

'Come on,' William said, beckoning him to follow. 'You need to try some of Rolf's wares. And don't fear, I've another bottle of syrup of figs.'

Edward wanted to say no, but was ashamed of his conversation with Trenter; he wished for a soft hand on his brow but loathed his own weakness.

William brought the syringe and solution to Edward in his room just before going to lunch. Edward would not be joining him, he preferred an empty stomach for what his afternoon would bring. He ran the syringe under the cold water tap of the small basin in his room and drew half a fluid ounce of morphine solution; he didn't know the concentration and this dose was just to relieve the withdrawal effects. He squeezed out a small air bubble then dipped the needle in a glass of diluted scotch before pushing it into his thigh. Injecting into the muscle rather than vein meant a slower, and lesser, reaction, but his months of treatment at Queen's hospital had fostered an aversion to going into the vein. He drank the diluted scotch, removed his mask and settled on the bed, waiting for his world to settle and be right and wishing there was someone there to share it. As he relaxed, the more he dared to imagine Evelyn in the room with him, holding his hand.

The Blue Bench

Evelyn, Margate,
Thursday 9th September 1920

'Salt, flour and a dozen eggs,' Evelyn repeated back to Alice, pencilling on the small slip of paper that held the rest of the shopping list. Alastair was supposed to have brought the supplies the previous day, but hadn't, and was already out taking his morning exercise, as his daily disappearances were known. Though it was a Thursday and the tea shop would be closed that afternoon, Alice wanted the ingredients ready for the next day. Evelyn took off the apron, left it with Alice and went out the front door, acknowledging Alice's call of, 'Oh, and yeast,' as the door closed behind her.

It was a warm September day and Evelyn wore the simple black dress Alice had given her for working in the tea shop and which Catherine had been able to alter to a far better fit; the dress was now a few inches shorter and the collar smaller. Evelyn was happy to wear it as a day dress, though it didn't match her favourite green cloche hat as well as it might. The grocer's shop where Alastair held an account was a couple of minutes away but on such a nice day Evelyn took the longer route, along the promenade. She turned to the left and the man who had been standing opposite and a few yards down, outside a nondescript terraced house, moved away from the iron railings he had been using for support and began to walk the same direction as her. Though Evelyn was not paying full attention she noticed he had a slight limp and there was something familiar in his gait. But it was not enough to stop her thoughts wandering – that afternoon was to be the first sitting for the portrait Beatrice had commissioned. She was walking slowly, enjoying the sun's warmth and day dreaming about what to wear for the sitting, when her name was called. She bumped into Patrick as he ran toward her,

'Regardez!' He passed to Evelyn a large brown paper bag with wooden struts poking from the top.

'Patrick, hello, that looks … exciting. What is it?' Evelyn smiled at Patrick's happiness. Edward joined them.

'Lieutenant Thompson bought it for me. It is a kite.'

'We haven't put it together yet, and I'm not a lieutenant anymore, remember?' said Edward.

'I should hope it's not been assembled, because it's not a good job if you have,' Evelyn teased.

'I'm afraid I'd not make it in the Royal Flying Corps.'

'Uncle William would,' said Patrick.

'Uncle William?' said Evelyn, looking at Edward, who shrugged.

'And where is Uncle William this morning?' asked Evelyn.

'He's taking mama to see the shells,' said Patrick.

'Down on the beach?' Evelyn looked to Edward.

'To the grotto,' Edward explained, 'there's a cave, and the walls are covered with shells, thousands of them.'

'I know of it, Catherine told me. It's quite an attraction and, some say, romantic.'

'Which would explain why Patrick and I are finding other entertainment,' Edward said. 'We spent some time on the beach, watching the tide go out …'

'… but Lieutenant Thompson doesn't like sand under his mask. It scratches,' Patrick interrupted.

'Well I imagine that would be the case,' Evelyn said.

'And we saw a man, under the jetty … and he had one leg and one arm. Lieutenant Thompson gave him half a crown.'

'The disabled veteran that's been seen around?' Evelyn asked Edward.

'He seems to be getting by but I don't know what he'll do when the season ends,' said Edward.

'I know the Reverend Railton has been trying to arrange some lodgings and a job for him. Perhaps he can stay here.'

'Perhaps,' agreed Edward, unconvincingly. 'Anyway, how are you?'

'Well, thanks. And you? You and William haven't been in for your habitual morning hot drink this week.' Edward's and William's absence had caused some concern – whether simply from an established routine being changed or some other reason she didn't try to fathom.

'It's been a busy couple of days. Did you enjoy the ragtime club at The Compass?'

'Very much. The music was exciting and I've never danced that way. Thank you for taking us.'

'It was our pleasure. But I'm sorry if we got you into trouble with Constable Simms and Mrs. Trenter.'

'No, there's no problem. I think Constable Simms has a soft spot for Catherine and Alice was asleep when I got in. Though I did have a headache in the morning. I don't think I've ever drunk so much in an evening.'

'More apologies are due. I should have known better than to let William keep bringing drinks. I too had more to drink than was good for me. I'm sorry if I overstepped any boundaries.'

'Not at all.' Evelyn had a vague memory of talking about Edward's mask inappropriately. 'In fact, I'm sorry. I think I may have said something offensive.'

'Not that I recall, and I find it hard to believe you would. I had a good time, as good as I can remember for quite a while.'

'And aren't Catherine and Georgette good singers?'

'Very good,' agreed Edward, adding, 'and you're a good dancer.'

Evelyn smiled and shrugged, 'It was good to see you laugh.'

'It was good of you to make me,' Edward said and there was a comfortable silence.

Evelyn had an urge to tell Edward about the pornographic postcards Georgette had shown them, but checked herself after starting, 'Georgette ... also seemed to enjoy herself. I didn't see her and William when we left. Was everything all right?'

'With William? Oh yes, at the end he had some ... business to attend to, with that Kraut, Rolf. You know William, always on the lookout for a deal.'

'What does Rolf do?'

'He ... he's a ... he has a lot of contacts and if there's something you need he can find it for you.'

'And what was William after?'

'I'm not sure ... cheap scotch, fags or ladies' cologne I expect. If William offers you some, you know where he found it. Anyway, we should fix this kite and try it out, shouldn't we Patrick?' Edward patted the boy's shoulder.

'He's been very patient,' said Evelyn, 'and I need to go to the shops. Will you be in for tea tomorrow morning?'

'I hope so, I've missed the ... routine.'

'Me too. Oh, I know, if you're free this afternoon why not pop over to Mrs. Blundell's. Say, one thirty? Catherine and I are having our first sitting for the portrait and I know Beatrice would love to see you.' Evelyn invited Edward on impulse and immediately regretted it – would Alice want Edward to know she was the painter? And there was also Catherine to consider; she might not want Edward there and Evelyn was loathe to upset Catherine – they had become so close. But she did hope Edward would come, adding, 'Beatrice always asks after you.'

'Oh yes, the portrait, you and Catherine. I'm sure I'll have time to come over once William and Georgette are back to look after Patrick. Besides, I think Georgette's mistress is growing tired of her increasing absences and I'm not sure William will be able to placate her much longer. I'm not playing at The Gardens until tea–time and it would be nice to see Mrs. Blundell this afternoon. Right, come on Patrick, let's build this flying machine.' Edward touched his hat by way of saying goodbye.

Evelyn watched Edward and Patrick walk back along the promenade, impressed by how easily Patrick ignored Edward's mask, then changed her mind; Patrick didn't ignore the mask, he accepted it.

A little further on Evelyn saw the man with the slight limp on the promenade, some fifty yards ahead. Again, there was something familiar in his look and manner but she thought little of it as she crossed the road, away from the front, on her way to the grocer's.

At just past one thirty Evelyn and Alice left the tea shop, on their way to Beatrice's guest house. Alice took a detour, needing to pick up some pencils from Lovelys art supplies shop. Evelyn went on alone and it wasn't until reaching the steps leading up to Mrs. Blundell's guest house she felt the presence of the man behind her. He called her name.

She turned, more surprised than threatened, and now recognised the man, 'Oh, Mr. Tewson.' It was he she'd seen earlier.

'Miss Coughston.'

'Mr. Tewson.' Evelyn repeated, as if to convince herself of who stood in front of her. Mr. Tewson wore his working suit and heavy boots and smelt of hops. He had come straight from the farm. 'You have a beard,' she said and, realising it to be an asinine statement, added, 'How are you?'

'Well, thank you. And yourself?' He stood to his full height, matching Evelyn though she stood one step up.

'I'm very well thank you.'

'Good. I'm glad to see you again.'

'It's been a long time, well, obviously, a full year. You look well.'

'You too.'

He hesitated.

'And what brings you to Margate?'

'I was back at the farm, for the harvest, and your father said you were spending a few weeks here. I wanted to … to come and say hello.'

'That's … nice.'

There was an uncomfortable silence. Evelyn found a question to break it. 'How's the hop harvest this year?'

'All right I think. Enough to keep the pickers busy.'

'Good. I'm missing the mission this year.'

'And the mission is missing you, especially the children.'

'I'm hoping to see them all soon.'

'That's good,' said Mr. Tewson then hesitated before asking quickly, 'I wondered, are you busy this afternoon? Could we take a walk?'

'Oh, I'm sorry, I've an appointment.' Evelyn pointed up to the polished front door at the top of the steps as if to explain and wondered why she had apologised.

'Oh. But I need to get back to the farm this evening,' said Mr. Tewson. 'Can you change your arrangements?'

'Not really, but I will be visiting the mission soon.'

'How soon? We could … walk again.' His voice trembled.

'I … I don't know when. I'm sorry, I need to go. I'll see you at the farm.' Evelyn went up a stair.

'When?' Mr. Tewson asked and reached out to hold Evelyn's arm, preventing her from taking the next step.

'Soon.' Evelyn tried to pull her arm free but it was held tight.

'Please, when?' The question was repeated.

Evelyn felt a rising panic. Her heart beat quicker and she wanted to tug herself free and run up the next few steps but was afraid of a stronger reaction from Mr. Tewson. She felt the flush of her cheeks and looked to the front door above her for help but it was closed. She looked down the street.

'Oh, Mr. Thompson, there you are.' She almost shouted on seeing Edward seven or eight houses away. He walked quickly. Mr. Tewson looked to see but didn't release Evelyn's arm until he saw Edward's face under the shadow of his hat.

Evelyn took another step up and Edward moved between her and Mr. Tewson offering a guarded, 'Good morning.'

'Good morning. You are?' Mr. Tewson asked.

Edward took a couple of seconds to look at the older man and said, 'Lieutenant Thompson. You are …?'

'Mr. … Corporal … Tewson.'

'And, Corporal Tewson, what can I do for you?' Edward spoke in his slow fashion.

'Miss Coughston has promised to walk with me and we were just confirming arrangements.' He was embarrassed but defiant.

Edward looked at Evelyn who shook her head almost imperceptibly. Edward nodded and placed a hand on Corporal Tewson's upper arm. 'Miss Coughston has an urgent appointment this afternoon.' He turned Corporal Tewson and ushered him a few yards down the street so that his back was now to Evelyn and Edward could see her over the corporal's shoulder. Edward said, 'I notice you limp. Where's that from?'

'Amiens, eighteen.'

Edward nodded. 'Eighteen? That's bad luck Corporal, you nearly made it all the way through,' and offered him a cigarette,

'Nearly, sir.' He took the fag.

'Anyway, Miss Coughston is unavailable this afternoon. Where have you come from today?'

'The hop farms, near Calcott.'

'Well you should go back there and, next time, you must write in advance to ask Miss Coughston if you should visit, though I think you'll find the answer will be no. But writing is the sensible thing to do, you'll agree.' Edward spoke loudly to ensure Evelyn heard and indicated to her she should go into Mrs. Blundell's guest house.

As Evelyn entered the house Catherine came down the stairs with a loud greeting but Evelyn shushed her and looked through the window at the door's side. Catherine joined her and they squeezed side by side, looking out.

'What's going on?' Catherine asked.

'Edward is out there.'

'I can see that. Why are you whispering?'

'I don't know.'

'Oh, all right then.' Catherine whispered back with a giggle. 'Who's Edward talking to?'

'Mr. Tewson. He came to ask me out walking.'

'Mr. Tewson?' Catherine thought for a moment. 'Oh, Mr. Tewson. You must have made quite an impression on him when you walked out last year.'

'Well I'm not going again.'

'Clearly not,' said Catherine as Edward bade Corporal Tewson farewell and came towards the house. Corporal Tewson limped away.

Evelyn felt a shudder of relief and then a flush of pride at Edward's intervention. She opened the door and offered thanks but Edward raised his hand to indicate it was nothing, 'I can't say if he's a good man or not, but I think he's more embarrassed than anything else. It's been made clear to him not to return uninvited but we'll keep an eye out for him. He looked a bit old for the last show but it turns out he's a regular from way back and even fought in the Boer campaigns.'

'Yes, we'll keep an eye out for you,' added Catherine, 'but what did happen last year?'

Before Evelyn could answer Mrs. Blundell came down the stairs, 'There you are. Come through to the drawing room, I'll ask Cook to bring tea and scones. She found a new recipe that includes honey. I'm not convinced myself but you can taste for yourselves and let me know.

Come.'

Beatrice took Edward's arm and led him through to the large front room, 'Oh, but before tea you must see this.' In the corner of the room, on a sideboard, sat a gramophone with a large red horn. 'It's new, by HMV. Model seven I believe, as if the model number has any meaning for me. The man in the shop assures me it produces a wonderful sound and who better than our Mr. Thompson to judge. Please, choose a recording, I put in a new needle this morning. I'll go and find Cook.' Beatrice showed Edward to a small pile of records.

Beatrice came back as Edward finished winding the mechanism and the opening bars sounded.

'Ah, Chopin. I bought this last week, isn't it lovely? Though my favourite is still *Madame Butterfly*. I shall wear it out before I tire of it. Do you know it, Mr. Thompson?'

'Not enough to play it well but I understand it's very popular.'

'I think Edward's favourite is Rachmaninoff,' said Evelyn.

'I don't believe I have any such recordings, sorry,' Beatrice apologised.

Edward was still standing by the sideboard, sifting through the records.

'Have you made any recordings Mr. Thompson?'

'I'm afraid not. My … musical education was interrupted by the war. But I'm hopeful perhaps one day I might. And I believe The Winter Gardens may yet be the location for some recordings. William intends to speak to the Booking Manager there to see if something can be arranged.'

Evelyn watched Edward. There was an optimism in his voice she had rarely heard. 'And what would you play?' she asked.

'Probably Rachmaninoff. As you say, he is a favourite. Or perhaps Grieg. Though of course one day I might finish my own compositions.'

'You write?' Beatrice asked.

'Not nearly as much or to the quality I should like.'

'Well you must. And what about something more modern, like ... ragtime. I daresay my niece and Evelyn might prefer that.' She raised her eyebrows at the younger women. 'Is that a style of which you approve Mr. Thompson?'

'There's no denying it's popular and I would like to play it better. There is skill in it.'

'Which I'm told you've acquired at The Compass,' Beatrice said mischievously.

'I'm sure Edward can play anything,' Evelyn said, seeking to deflect attention from whatever Beatrice had heard about the ragtime club at The Compass.

'And, now I think of it, you should bring that old piano out of storage. It would fit neatly over there if you get rid of that hideous dresser,' Catherine added, again to change the subject thought Evelyn.

'True, it is hideous, but then it was left to me by my late husband's brother, and, to be frank, though I never liked him I'm in mind of my cousin Neville who once gave away a dining service his sister–in–law left him. He was convinced she never forgave him and haunted the house until he found it in an auction in Bermondsey and bought it back. So, as you say, hideous, but,' Beatrice turned to Edward, 'Mr. Thompson. If there was piano here, would you come and play some ragtime for us?'

'Of course.'

'Good, and then perhaps our two young ladies won't feel the need to stay over–long in public houses where such music is played, unless, of course, I am invited next time.'

'I am to blame Mrs. Blundell, and next time I insist you come along,' said Edward.

'Good. And, with a piano here I could invite the St. John's Ladies over for a musical evening. Would you play?'

'My pleasure and Catherine could sing. She has a

lovely tone and it's an honour to play for her,' Edward said.

'Hmmm, I'm not so easily charmed as my aunt,' said Catherine, 'but, in this instance, I'll take that compliment as sincere. Thank you, and that decides it, Aunt. The dresser must go.'

'Of course. Ah, here's Cook. Mr. Thompson, come and sit next to me.' Beatrice led Edward to the settee in the bay window.

'And we'll take our tea upstairs while we choose our dresses for the portrait.' Catherine took Evelyn's hand and they left Beatrice and Edward discussing the merits of ragtime and if the Royal College of Music should be encouraging the new jazz music.

Catherine showed Evelyn up a flight of stairs explaining, 'Aunt Beatrice has made a room available for all the sittings. Alice says the light is good and Beatrice has rented two easels for her which can stay here. The room won't be let to paying guests until next year now. But we might need to remove or change the furniture. I don't know what Alice has in mind for the background or pose.'

They went into a plain room at the back of the house. It was furnished with a wardrobe, a bed and a small settee. There was a mirror over the settee and in a corner stood two easels, each with a canvas.

'It's one of the cheap rooms,' said Catherine, 'but it's had a good clean.' Catherine sniffed deeply. Evelyn copied her and caught the smell of Catherine's flowery perfume and wondered if she too, should have put on some eau de cologne.

'So,' said Catherine, 'before Alice comes, tell me more about the thing with Tewson.'

'Not much to tell. We walked out twice, in the evenings, at the hop farm. I only went at Father's suggestion. Nothing happened and I certainly didn't mean to give any encouragement after the second time.'

'Hmmm, Mr. Tewson might think otherwise. They're a funny lot, men. Especially if a little older, which he appeared.'

'It's very sad. He'd been a soldier for years and was about to be pensioned out when the war started and he was forced to stay, in the artillery I think. And he nearly got through the war but fell under a field gun, crushing his leg. His wife was nursing him when she caught scarlet fever. She was a lovely lady.'

'That is sad, and then he thought to try for a younger lady?'

'As I say, we only walked out twice and I did feel sorry for him. He struggled to find work because of his leg.'

'Hmmm. Did you hear about that reverend from Bristol who wanted unmarried women to offer themselves in marriage to disabled veterans? The idea was quite well received until the Bishop stepped in. I'm not sure marriage for pity is a good idea, no matter how worthy the old soldier.'

'Or young soldier,' said Evelyn, 'though I'm sure many have married for less worthy motives. If they were wounded in service perhaps they deserve something.'

'A woman as a reward? Sounds medieval.'

'Put like that, I suppose. Anyway, nothing like that was ever going to happen with Mr. Tewson and me.'

'But you walked out with him?'

'Only twice, on the hop farm, last harvest.'

'And …'

'What?'

'Did you kiss?'

'Good grief no. We just held hands, the second time.'

'Well that would explain it. He's totally smitten and I'm not surprised. You have lovely hands.' Catherine spoke seriously and took Evelyn's hands, but her eyes betrayed her mischief.

'Ha, ha,' Evelyn pretended to laugh. 'Anyway, we're not here to talk about Mr. Tewson. I thought we were going to choose dresses for the portrait.'

'And poses.' Catherine threw her arm behind her head and arched her back theatrically, 'They need to be complementary.'

Evelyn watched her. There was energy in her mischief. Her knack of finding fun in simple ways was refreshing. Spitalfields was a different world and though she knew her father didn't intend it to be that way, his earnest desire for an honestly pious approach to everyday living had encouraged a constant self–questioning which could be wearying.

Catherine was looking at herself in the mirror, testing various outlandish poses and asked, 'What do you think?'

'I think Alice is lucky to have you as a subject.'

'And you, of course,' Catherine answered and went to the wardrobe to pull out a number of dresses. 'Now, I've been looking through *Vogue* and, with a bit of cutting here and touch of fixing there, I've made some alterations, updating some old frocks. Here, have a look.' She passed Evelyn a light blue summer dress with short sleeves, a round neck and drop waist. There was little shape to the dress but Catherine was confident it would fit well. 'I know your size.'

Evelyn held it up against herself. It stopped at her knee.

'Fashionably short,' Catherine said confidently.

'Fashionably so,' said Evelyn.

'Try it on,' Catherine said, undressing herself. She wore a light slip and tight fitting bandeau, flattening her breasts. Evelyn thought back to the first night in The Winter Gardens when she had undressed with Catherine in the same room, embarrassed – not as long ago as it seemed.

Evelyn took off the black tea shop dress, conscious of the old fashioned bodice she wore underneath, and pulled on the new dress. It fitted as well as Catherine had promised. Whether due to the colour, style or company Evelyn couldn't say, but when she looked at herself in the mirror she felt as free as ever she had. She looked over to Catherine who was struggling to pull her own dress over her chest.

'It's a bit tight. I think I took it in too much.' Catherine struggled a little more. 'I know what it is. My monthly. I'm always a bit … bigger … up top during my period. Do you find that?'

'I suppose. But not a lot. And oddly the left is more tender than the right,' said Evelyn, surprised to find herself sharing an intimate detail. It was even more surprising not to be embarrassed and a delight to feel part of a friendship that could make it so.

Catherine shuffled and shimmied, pulling the dress down. 'There, done. What do you think?'

'They don't look much bigger,' Evelyn said, looking at Catherine.

'I didn't mean them. I meant the dress. What do you think?'

'Looks … nifty,' said Evelyn.

'Ha, yes, it does. It's a shame I didn't wear it to the ragtime club on Sunday. That was a good night wasn't it?'

'I had a very good time.'

'It was the berries. Would you like to go again?'

'Yes, but perhaps not drink so much next time. I almost threw up when I got in but was desperate not to in case I woke Alastair and Alice.'

'Well let's go to the next one, even if William and Edward don't, and we can wear our new dresses. Do you like it?' Catherine indicated to Evelyn's dress. Evelyn turned to look back into the mirror.

'Very much, but is it a little … short?'

'Not at all. I just hope these are the sort of thing Alice has in mind. Has she said anything to you?'

'No, but I expect she'll have discussed it with

Beatrice.'

'Not that I know of,' said Catherine, 'but I think as long as it looks like us Beatrice will be happy.'

'Perhaps it would be easier to have a photograph?' It occurred to Evelyn.

'Perhaps,' agreed Catherine. She giggled. 'As long as it's not like those Georgette showed us at the ragtime club.'

'Oh. I'd forgotten. Do you think they really were William's?'

'Why not?

'I don't know. They were just so … I don't know what.'

'Do you think you could pose like that?' Catherine asked.

'Which one?' Evelyn asked.

'Any of them.'

There was a pause.

'Oh my god, you're blushing.' Catherine accused Evelyn.

'No I'm not.'

'You are. Which picture are you thinking of?'

'I'm not.'

'Yes you are. Which picture?'

'I'm not. I wouldn't. Imagine what my father would say.'

'I know, it's the one with the man at the fireplace With the woman kneeling and it looks like she's about to … you know.'

'Do you think she did?' Evelyn asked.

'I expect so, she didn't look the shy type.'

'And men like that?'

'I believe so. Have you ever seen a man … naked before?' Catherine asked.

'Not quite like that. There's a man back in Spitalfields who often shows his … you know … to the women, but he keeps his coat on and the women mostly laugh.'

'And you've seen … it?'

'Oh yes, at least three times, but only briefly, I didn't make a point of staring. That would be rude.' Evelyn answered casually. They both laughed.

'What about you? Have you seen … one?' Evelyn asked.

'Er, not so much seen but …'

'You haven't …?'

'Almost. There was a lot of kissing and more than a bit of touching but … it … rather he … didn't seem right.'

'So you didn't.'

'Not quite.'

'What happened, to him?'

'We argued too much and my aunt didn't like him and she was right. But never mind me, what about you and Mr. Tewson?'

'Really, we held hands, that was all. Thankfully, having seen another side to him today.'

'It's lucky Edward was there.'

'Yes,' Evelyn agreed. The shock she'd felt earlier when Mr. Tewson held her arm had quickly been replaced by pleasure at Edward's intervention. She wasn't sure she had done anything to warrant his protection, just as she wasn't sure of deserving her blossoming friendship with Catherine and there was an odd guilt at enjoying both. 'You know his men called him the Lucky Lieutenant?'

'The lieutenant in that postcard Georgette showed didn't look lucky, he seemed rather put out. Perhaps the woman was more interested in the cards.'

'Oh, that lieutenant.' Evelyn remembered the pose.

'I wonder if Edward was luckier, in that way, you know.'

'What way?' Evelyn asked.

'I mean, I wonder if Edward has …'

'Has what?'

'You know.'

'Oh,' Evelyn realised what Catherine meant. 'Well, he

was a soldier, so I expect so. And I suppose the French ladies would be quiet sophisticated.'

'Oh I'm not so sure. I expect such ladies are the same the world over. Though I wonder if the ladies in the last postcard Georgette showed us were French.'

'What ladies?' Evelyn asked.

'In that last postcard, with the two ladies, on the bed. They were … top to tail.' Catherine giggled.

'Oh, I'd forgotten that one as well. But I didn't see it properly. Were they … would they?' Evelyn's question was interrupted by the door opening and Alice came in, carrying some paper and drawing materials.

'Good afternoon ladies, I'm so sorry I'm late. I was talking to Beatrice and Mr. Thompson.' She was a little flustered. 'I didn't know Mr. Thompson would be here. He seemed surprised it was me painting the portrait. He had assumed it would be another local artist, having inadvertently mentioned the portrait to Alastair the other day and Alastair not knowing of it. I will tell Alastair but hoped to keep it to ourselves for a little while. At least until there is something to be shown.'

'Oh, I'm so sorry Alice. I shouldn't have suggested to Edward he visit Mrs. Blundell this afternoon.' Evelyn apologised. 'What did Alastair say about his conversation with Edward?'

'Nothing … yet. Ah well, never mind. We're here now and I'd like to get the preliminary sketches done and the outline finished before baby comes. So we've lots to do. Did you have any thoughts about a suitable pose?' Alice asked.

Evelyn looked to Catherine and they both managed not to laugh.

The Blue Bench

Edward, Herne Bay, Sunday 12th September 1920

It was colder in the car than outside. The rain on the hood was a distraction – not persistent enough to drum a tattoo worthy of listening but occasionally heavy enough to interrupt conversation. The Wolseley was parked on a patch of bare earth on the Beltinge Downs, just off Reculver Road. It was half–way between Herne Bay and Reculver and from the car they could see the grass slope away and then disappear as it dropped to the beach. The tide was coming in, but was a long way from submerging the expanse of dark, wet sands, rocks and pools extending perhaps a mile in each direction. This stretch of beach was empty, adding loneliness to the exposed landscape reaching out seamlessly to the North Sea. To the east the pillars of the groynes marched in single files towards and into the water, relentless in their sacrifice.

Edward turned in the front seat of the car. 'Not a view for Mr. Trenter.' He spoke for Evelyn's benefit more than the others.

'I quite like the rain,' William said, 'or at least, I did, back in France.' He lit a cigarette and passed the pack and lighter to Catherine in the back seat. 'As long as it was heavy enough to keep us in the trench or from the front line.'

'But it stopped, always, and the war started again, mud or no mud,' said Edward.

'True, but we learned to grab what respite we could.'

'Some did. Some just wanted it over and done,' said Edward.

239

'Also true, but no point wishing time away. A soldier's time is rarely his own and what will come to us will come in its own hour. Eh?' William looked at Patrick, who looked at Edward, bemused. Edward shrugged his shoulders and Patrick copied him. William laughed.

It was just nine, early for a Sunday, as Catherine kept reminding them on the drive over. She sipped from the coffee, just poured from a flask, and lit a cigarette, careful to blow the smoke out of the car, away from Patrick. She gave the pack and lighter to Patrick who leaned forward, returning them to William in the front. Patrick sat between Catherine and Evelyn on the back seat. The car was quiet save the rain on the hood and occasional sound of Edward drawing on his cigarette. William began to tell Patrick of the day one of the tunnel entrances had collapsed and they needed volunteers to dig out whoever could be saved …

'… what's a valunter?' Patrick interrupted.

'Someone who offers to do something no one else would want to, and for no reward, and it's usually dangerous,' said William.

'And did you volunteer?' Catherine asked him.

'Of course. It was my duty and coal mining is in my family … besides, they offered an extra tot of rum every day for a week.' William smiled at Patrick.

'And did you save them?' asked Patrick.

'As many as we could, but not as many as deserved it.'

'So your family really are miners then,' said Catherine.

'Yes, and proud of it, though not so much I wanted to join the tunnellers when they asked after I'd dug them out.'

'Oh, because we heard your parents were in music hall,' Catherine said with assumed innocence.

'Did you?'

'Yes, from Evelyn's father,' said Catherine and

240

Evelyn nodded.

Edward spoke, 'William's family would turn their hand to anything to earn a penny, I expect.'

'When times were hard ...' William agreed.

Edward continued, 'But thankfully, that day, digging was in his blood and I didn't mind him being given an extra rum ration for a week. And his skills with a spade will come in handy today, if it stops raining.' He looked through the windscreen out to the sea. The sky was a little lighter. 'I think you two might make a start,' he indicated to William and Patrick, 'and the rest of us will join you in a little while. I need some cigarettes from Herne Bay and the ladies will want to make sure the rain has stopped.'

The idea for the trip had been suggested a few days previously, by Edward, after reading an article in a local guide book. The writer claimed the beaches east of Herne Bay were among the best in the world for fossil hunting.

'... in the world,' William had emphasised when reading the article to Patrick. And though Patrick didn't know what a fossil was, he knew hunting for a shark's tooth had to be exciting. That it would be millions of years old was of interest, but didn't matter much – it being a shark's tooth was enough.

'... in the whole world,' Patrick repeated to his mother and Georgette was happy for him to go with William but the mistress wouldn't give her the Sunday morning off work, except for church.

On the Friday, Edward had told Evelyn of how excited Patrick was to be hunting sharks' teeth and thought she had enjoyed being teased for not at first understanding he meant fossilised. Catherine heard from Evelyn and was happy for an excuse to miss Sunday service, again. Aunt Beatrice acknowledged Patrick was only six and a woman's touch would be useful in the event of a scraped knee or elbow. To that end Beatrice had Cook put together a small package with a bottle of iodine, smelling salts, some cotton wool and three bandages of varying sizes. The package sat in the small hamper alongside two flasks and a selection of scones and cakes. Patrick's excitement had been contagious and William accepted with good grace the teasing for wearing his 'special' dark driving glasses even though it wasn't sunny.

Patrick was first from the car, with his new tin bucket and spade. Edward watched as William followed close behind and they trotted down to the beach. They stopped, where the grass merged unevenly with the sand, to remove their shoes and socks, leaving them behind to walk further out onto the beach. Back in the car, Catherine asked Edward to get her a pack of Black Cats from Herne Bay. Edward pulled his hat down a little and opened the door, saying to Evelyn, 'I'm only going in for some cigarettes and it's ...' he looked westwards towards the pier at Herne Bay, '... at least a mile and half. Will you stay here?'

'It's a bit chilly to be on the beach, but I would like some fresh air and I wouldn't mind seeing the pier again,' Evelyn said.

'Are you sure? It's quite a walk.' Edward climbed down from the Wolseley

'Of course,' said Evelyn, leaving the car.

'Don't be long!' Catherine shouted from the back seat and Edward waved to show he'd heard as Catherine left the car to follow William, stopping at the top of the beach. There was a breeze off the sea and she crossed her arms as she finished her cigarette.

'You don't need cigarettes, do you,' said Evelyn, falling in step alongside Edward.

'A soldier always needs fags,' said Edward. 'A fag, a decent kip, a hot mug or a tot of rum and a ... well, the simple things. And the longer he's been away the simpler the wants. You'd be surprised.'

'Perhaps not. We see a lot in Spitalfields and Father has to accept all. Anyway, you're not a solider anymore.'

'No.'

'Do you wish you were?'

'Sometimes … no, not really. I just wish I'd stopped for a different reason.'

'Surely it's a good reason.' Evelyn gestured hesitantly to her own face. 'You've more than done your bit.'

'Perhaps, but I didn't finish doing my duty. Especially to the men.'

'Do you miss them?'

'I don't know. But I let them down.'

There was silence and Edward was pleased Evelyn didn't try to fill it with platitudes. They walked in a comfortable quiet and then Evelyn said, 'I didn't thank you, for helping when Mr. Tewson became … awkward … last week. I'm sorry, it was a bit embarrassing.'

'Not at all. I'm sure it was just a misunderstanding.'

'But it was fortunate you happened along and saw something wasn't right.'

'Well a good friend told me there are just three reasons for a gentleman to lay a hand on a lady. To help them if they have fallen; to assist in or out of a carriage; to take their arm if they are walking out together. And none of those looked to apply in Mr. Tewson's case.'

'Your friend is wise.'

Edward nodded, 'Yes, he was.' There was, of course, a fourth reason his friend had spoken of but that was trench talk and Edward wasn't about to risk offending Evelyn.

'Was? Did he do something to prove otherwise?'

'No, not at all, he … he's dead.'

'Oh, I'm sorry.'

They walked a few yards in silence.

'Anyway,' Evelyn tried to rescue the mood, 'thank you, for helping. And I wanted you to know Mr. Tewson wasn't … I mean, I hadn't encouraged or …'

'Please, no need to explain. It was nothing. But you shouldn't hesitate to call on me again, in similar circumstance.'

'Thank you.' Evelyn brushed his arm and he couldn't help but think of the fourth reason.

As they neared Herne Bay they came across a few holidaymakers, strolling the downs or digging the beach. Then they were at the promenade. Edward turned to go on to the pier, Evelyn at his side. They passed, and ignored, the newsagent that had been so unhelpful four weeks or so previously and walked through the entrance lodge and out on to the pier. It was busy. They edged past the Sunday morning strollers to find the tobacconist kiosk. A tall man, skinny to the point of looking malnourished, turned away from the customer he'd just served and did a double-take at Edward.

'A pack of Players Navy and ten Black Cats please.' Edward said, sifting through some coins from his pocket. He handed a couple over, saying, 'Also, I'm hoping you can help. I'm looking for the Kaysts. I believe they had a kiosk on the pier. This one perhaps.' Edward stared at the tobacconist, daring him to look away.

'I heard there was a tin mask asking questions,' said the tobacconist, glancing at Evelyn as if seeking some acknowledgement of the poor attempt at humour.

'And?' Edward asked calmly but his good eye was fixed on the taller man and his face turned upward, visible.

'And what?'

'Do you know where the Kaysts are?'

'Who says I bought this from them?'

'Do you know of them or not?'

'It was a fair price. The business was dead. They killed it.'

'I don't care. It's a simple question. Do you know the Kaysts?' Edward stepped a half-yard closer; the tobacconist half a yard back, coughing – a hacking, rough, rasping cough.

'Mustard gas?' Edward asked.

'What's it to you?'

Edward sighed. 'Are you from around here?'

'Close enough. None of your business.' He coughed painfully again.

'Perhaps you knew the Kayst's son? He served too.'

'Serve? Ha, that's the word all right ain't it. Served the country, served the brass, served the bloody officers who put us over the top with pointed pistol … like you.'

'Young Kayst served, like you.'

The tobacconist laughed again, 'Yeah, just like me,' and coughed again. He looked, then spoke, to Evelyn. 'No, I didn't know him but there was a young woman in the family, perhaps his sister. She married an oysterman, over in Whitstable. She needed somewhere to go, when they gave up on this.' He indicated to the kiosk behind him.

Edward breathed slowly, managing his impatience. 'And the oysterman's name?'

'Something like Dougherty or Docherty.'

'Thank you. Keep the change.'

The tobacconist handed over the cartons of cigarettes.

'Oh, and you don't have you any liquorice sticks do you?'

'Who are they for?' Evelyn asked as the tobacconist went to a cupboard at the back of the kiosk.

'Beatrice. When I was there on Wednesday, she mentioned they are her favourites.'

'They are. And so will you be.'

'But perhaps not Alice's. I hadn't realised it was she painting your portrait, but then I saw her at Beatrice's on Thursday … but Alastair didn't seem to be aware when I mentioned the commission to him.'

'I think he's worked it out by now.'

Edward paid for the liquorice and led Evelyn away from the pier.

'So, now we're off to Whitstable, to find Kayst's sister, are we?' Evelyn said.

'Not today.'

'But you will.'

'I expect so.'

Though the rain had stopped, and the grass on the downs was wet, Evelyn stooped to remove her shoes, explaining, 'I know it's cold but it just feels so nice and I prefer it to sand.'

Edward laughed. 'So do I. Sand is … unfriendly.'

'Because …' Evelyn hesitated, '… because you don't want sand behind the mask?' Remembering Patrick's remark from a few days earlier.

'I suppose,' said Edward and then, more seriously, 'The tobacconist was wrong. It's not tin.' He stopped walking as if to let Evelyn see him.

Evelyn looked at him, 'What is it then?'

'It's not tin.' He started walking again, asking, 'How hard is it for people not to show … how shocking it is? How hard is it not to turn away?'

'It's not a shock, not any more,' Evelyn said.

'Really?' Edward stopped walking again. Evelyn walked on a yard then turned.

'No, that's not true. Sometimes it still is, when I forget. I'm sorry,' she said.

'Thank you, for the truth. I've wanted to ask someone for a long time.'

'But it's a shock less and less often.'

'That's something.'

'I'm sorry.'

'Because?' Edward asked, without scepticism.

'Because I don't know what else to be?'

Edward nodded, understanding the reply but thinking that might be the most sorry thing of all.

The sky was a shade lighter as they finished the walk back to the car in silence. The refrain Edward had been toying with the day he'd walked the cliffs and met Mr. Trenter was playing through his mind, unbidden but welcome. It was slower than before and in a minor key now, but no less welcome.

They reached the car. The others weren't there.

In the distance, on the headland, they could see the outline of the twin towers of St. Mary's Church.

'They call those the sister towers,' said Evelyn.

'Do they?'

'According to Catherine. The church used to be further from the seafront but what with the wind and tides it was abandoned as the sea took the land and now it's a ruin.'

'Why sister towers?'

'I don't know. Perhaps because they're like two old spinsters, past their best but dedicated to each other.'

'They don't need to be sisters for that.'

'I suppose not. Anyway, Catherine and I won't ...' Evelyn stopped talking as they heard a woman's cry. It was repeated. They looked to the edge of the downs. From where the car was parked they could see no sand. They had walked the downs both ways, into and out of Herne Bay, and been oblivious to the tide. Edward ran down the slope, towards the water. As he neared the beach, Evelyn close behind him, he could see there was only a narrow strip of sand still visible, the sea was close to swamping the entire shoreline and, though not rough, its relentless roll towards shore was suddenly terrifying.

They heard the cry again.

'Catherine!' Edward called, scanning the beach. She stood a hundred yards or more away, on the last of the sand, shouting at the sea, waves lapping her feet. Edward followed her line of sight. On a sand bank just breaking the water were William and Patrick. Edward couldn't see William's face, it was too far, but he could hear his shouts. Edward ran down the beach to Catherine.

'The tide … they weren't … I wasn't … paying attention, and, oh my God, Patrick!' Catherine was close to panic. Edward took off his shoes and socks, not sure why and with no plan as such, but when he looked up he could see Patrick was on William's shoulders as he waded to shore, occasionally stumbling on something under foot. The water came only to his knees.

William was laughing while Patrick shouted directions, clutching William's neck with one hand and the bucket with the other.

Catherine was shouting, screaming, at Patrick to hold on.

'William won't drop him,' Edward said, picking up his socks and shoes.

William was soon out of the water, complaining it was cold and cursing the cuts and bruises on his feet from the rocks. Patrick, oblivious to any danger, showed his bucket to Catherine, insisting there were at least three fossilised shark teeth. Catherine agreed, expressing relief, not interest.

William appeared not to notice Catherine's fear and near panic, even as the sea lapped over their feet.

'Coffee and a cigarette, that's what we need and, Patrick, I believe there's a Fry's Chocolate Cream in the hamper. Shall we see?' Edward said, leading the way back to the car.

Evelyn was at the beach head. As Edward reached her he removed his hat and pushed back his hair, 'Bugger, I've got sand behind the mask. And the bloody thing will probably rust in this air.'

By the time they were all back at the car Catherine was calm and they sat on a rug, in the lee of the car, finishing the hamper's contents. Patrick's bucket contained some water, sand and a few rocks which Edward agreed could well be fossilised sharks' teeth. Evelyn supported Catherine's assertion they needn't go looking for any more. Patrick frowned and Catherine added, '... at least not today, then.'

William laughed loud as he dried his feet and put back on his socks and shoes, 'Well that was quite exciting. Wait 'til your mother hears.'

'Is that a good idea?' Catherine asked.

'What do you think Patrick?'

Patrick shrugged and Catherine gave him a cuddle.

'And did you get your cigarettes?' William asked Edward who nodded and remembered the Black Cats and liquorice sticks, passing them over to Catherine and explaining the liquorice was for Beatrice.

'And ... anything else?' William prompted, standing to retrieve his hip flask from the car.

Edward shrugged as William sipped.

'We learnt Kayst had a sister who married an oysterman from Whitstable.' Evelyn said, with a hint of triumph.

'Why is Kayst of such interest?' Catherine asked, and looked to Evelyn as if seeking approval for asking.

Edward was silent and William said, 'Perhaps because Edward doesn't think Kayst should have been there. He could have been home, on compassionate leave as his grandfather had died and his mother and father were ill. But the lieutenant didn't grant leave. He couldn't.'

'Couldn't I?'

'No. Of course not. Had he, within a week we'd all have had dead and dying relatives back home.'

'So now you want to tell his parents ...?' Catherine didn't finish the question.

'I don't know. Perhaps it's not that. Perhaps it's because it's just not right he should have disappeared like that. Someone should know. There should be something.'

'What, like … this?' William took one of the small pieces of rock from the bucket, 'An old fossil? Should we all be fossils when we go? Sorted on a museum shelf. I don't think so. We come, we stay a while, we go. Some stay longer than others. Some are remembered longer, but in the end never for long, not really. Simple.'

'William!' Catherine said sharply and nodded towards Patrick but the boy showed no sign of listening. The Fry's Chocolate Cream was a distraction.

'Anyway, next week we'll go to Whitstable to see if we can find his sister,' Evelyn said confidently.

Edward smiled a thank you.

'I expect so,' said William, 'but now,' he reached and took Edward's wrist to see his watch, 'it's time to make a move. I said we'd meet Georgette in The Compass. They like a sing–a–long on a Sunday lunchtime and I told her Edward would play her favourite songs if she'd sing. C'mon.' He stood, not waiting for comment, and began packing the hamper.

The drive back to Margate was mostly in silence, the rain had started again and the battering on the roof, together with the blustery wind, was a challenge to any conversation. Patrick huddled between the women in the back and Edward shrank in his seat, holding his hat. Only William seemed his normal self. They pulled up outside Edward and William's guest house where William raced Patrick through the door, carrying his bucket. Evelyn and Catherine were out of the car ahead of Edward, who remained in his seat, head down.

'Are you coming Edward?' Evelyn asked. 'I expect we'll go to The Compass.'

'I think so,' said Catherine, 'if Georgette's going to sing I think I should have a go too, don't you?' It was said with a smile, just.

Edward stirred in his seat and then climbed slowly

from the car. 'I … I'm sorry ladies. I don't think I'll be able to join you.' The right side of his face was pale and he was hunched, as if against a biting wind, though there was none, just a steady light drizzle.

'What's wrong Edward?' Evelyn asked.

'I think it's … on the move, perhaps.'

'What is?' Catherine asked.

'I think he means the shrapnel.' Evelyn guessed.

Edward nodded, 'I … should be … in … my room,' and spoke haltingly, 'I'm afraid you'll … have to find another … pianist … sorry Catherine.'

'Let me help you to your room,' Evelyn offered.

'No, I'll be all right. I …'

Edward was interrupted by William and Georgette coming from the guest house, Georgette insisting Patrick would be all right on his own up in the attic room.

'If you say so. Now, what will you want to sing down at The Compass?' William asked but was brought up short on seeing Edward, leaning against the car. 'Uh–oh. I see the lieutenant's having a turn.'

'I'll take him inside,' said Evelyn but Edward shook his head.

'Can you still play the piano?' Georgette asked.

'No need to worry, there'll be someone there, and I do want to hear you sing again,' said William. 'You'll be all right, won't you Edward?' Then he whispered, 'There's plenty of Rolf's medicine left, isn't there?'

Edward looked up but said nothing and walked slowly to the guest house. Evelyn started to follow but Catherine touched her arm, 'Shall I come in with you?'

'No … that's all right, you … go on to the pub. Take … Evelyn.' Edward spoke over his shoulder.

Catherine took Evelyn's arm and they followed William and Georgette.

Edward was in his room sitting on the edge of the bed,

when the knocking on the door crashed into his thoughts, even though the rapping was gentle. He had been there ten or fifteen minutes and the intrusion was unwelcome, especially so when he heard Evelyn half–whisper, 'Edward, are you all right?'

He rolled down his shirtsleeve and pushed himself up from the bed, grateful he had not yet removed his mask. He opened the door a little, 'You ... probably shouldn't ... be ... here.' He spoke even more slowly than usual, as if the pain was worse for talking.

'I'm sorry, but I wanted to make sure that you're all right. William told me the room. Are you? All right?' Evelyn pushed on the door and it opened more fully, Edward was in no state to resist. 'Is it the shrapnel?'

Edward nodded, 'But you ... shouldn't ... be here.'

'They don't need me at the pub, though Catherine does want me there if she sings later.'

'I'm sorry ... I can't ... play for them.'

'Don't be silly. You must rest.'

'And you should ... be with your friend. I'll be ... all right ...' Edward sat on the bed, thinking how awkward Evelyn looked, unsure of what to do now she was here.

'If you're sure,' she said. 'Catherine will be missing me in the pub, but I just wanted to make sure ...'

'Please ... go.'

Evelyn started to leave but the glass tube caught her eye and she turned back, asking, 'Where did you get that?' She gestured to the syringe and bottle of morphine solution in the sink.

'William ... knows someone.'

'Have you taken much?'

'You sound ... just like ... the nurses at Queen's.'

'But how much have you taken?'

'It's always a bit ... trial and error, but I hope ... it's enough to take it away. It hurts.'

Evelyn inspected the syringe and phial, then the bottle of laudanum by the tap. 'And this isn't enough.' She replaced the bottle. 'It's all right, we know a lot of men back in Spitalfields that … need it. I've seen them use it. Sometimes Father makes sure there's somewhere safe for them, though he doesn't approve.'

'Do you?'

'Does that matter?'

'Sometimes, it's … the only thing … can help. But it takes a lot … to make … a difference.'

'So you only take it when the pain is bad?'

'Or a very little, every … other day, just to … keep things even. But, just now, I need to be alone. Please, leave. I'd rather you didn't see … and besides, you shouldn't be in my room, without a chaperone, Catherine perhaps,' he laughed quietly, a little more relaxed, and spoke more easily as the morphine took effect. 'Oh, but please don't tell Catherine about …' he gestured to the syringe in the sink, 'I know you two are close and share much but …'

'I do understand,' Evelyn said, and though Edward didn't know what it was she understood her words were comforting. She seemed to be smiling as he showed her from the room. She turned at the door but before she could speak Edward said, 'Thank you, for coming with me earlier, to ask about Kayst. I didn't want anyone to walk with me, at first, but I'm glad you did.' He closed the door behind her and waited, making sure to hear her footsteps on the stairs, before going back to the bed. He knew the next half hour or so would be bearable as the morphine peaked in his system but after that the pain would likely attack with a vengeance. Only the false calm from the morphine was enough to take away the fear of what was to come, for now.

The Blue Bench

Edward, Calcott hop farms, Thursday 16th September 1920

Edward understood the reason for William's bad mood. They had left the guest house early and without breakfast. The Wolseley started first time, startling the quiet morning, rumbling and clattering down the street, rattling windows. William drove, as usual. Edward sat up front and in the back sat their passenger, huddled in William's old trench coat. It was too big but served a purpose; it was mid–September and the morning air carried a chill. William drove slowly through town, speeding up when they reached the outskirts but Edward called, 'Might as well slow down. We don't want to be there too early.'

William shrugged and eased off the accelerator.

Edward looked back to the passenger and shouted, 'All right Tosh?'

The other man looked out from the coat and barely nodded.

Edward tried to light a cigarette taking seven or eight attempts in the buffeting wind before it caught. He settled back in his seat, drawing his own coat around him. This trip, back to the hop farms at Calcott, would not be enjoyable like their previous visit; he didn't know how Reverend Coughston would receive his request.

The previous night, after The Winter Gardens performances had finished, Edward stayed on. He made sure William would walk home Catherine and Evelyn, as usual, and gave both the caretaker and electrician half a crown each to stay later while he practised in the now empty auditorium. Catherine had told him to be careful of the haunting and Edward assured her he wouldn't stray from the auditorium and, besides, he wasn't alone – Bill and Frank were still about, at which point Frank shouted from somewhere, 'Half a crown won't keep me if ... *it* ... turns up again tonight.'

Edward didn't know him well enough to gauge if it was joke, but laughed anyway. Evelyn said she'd stay a bit longer but Catherine didn't want to and Edward insisted they go; he practised better with no distraction. He went up to the stage waving them away and William walked them out.

The chandeliers were out and there were no stage lights – wall lamps provided the only illumination. Edward stood at the piano for a minute or two. He had enjoyed playing earlier that night, but knew he wasn't playing well, never mind close to his best. Perhaps it was a good thing the holiday crowds were thinning as the season neared its end. The episode on Sunday had shaken his confidence, again. The morphine had helped the pain to an extent but he knew each time it was less effective and the dose was increasing; it didn't help that even when not suffering an 'episode' he was maintaining a low level intake. He had missed the Sunday evening performance – partly because of the pain and partly the morphine, but without the pain relief he couldn't have made the auditorium anyway. He'd also missed the Monday performance and Mr. Taylor had expressed disappointment to William. The way William told it, the Bookings Manager was upset because he was an admirer of Edward's playing, not because he felt let down – but Edward had not heard this from Mr. Taylor himself. Anyway, he was as frustrated as Mr. Taylor, he was sure, and wanted an hour with the piano to himself. He sat and adjusted the stool – the pianist with the Municipal Orchestra was much bigger than he – and relaxed into the keys with some scales and arpeggios. Then he tinkered over some Chopin and Bach before focusing on Mozart. Though his head still ached, the pain lessened as his concentration grew. He was waiting for the moment he would stop thinking and no longer feel the keys under his fingers – the moment instinct would both take him over and take him away. It would be a gradual thing and he slipped into Rachmaninoff's piano concerto number three, smiling at a memory of Evelyn telling him he should play it again, at that bar in Whitstable. He closed his eyes and the moments came – for a brief while the music was his to embrace, to command, to set free – effortlessly. And then, nearly halfway through the first movement he found himself slipping away from Rachmaninoff and into the refrain he had imagined on the clifftop at Hodges Bridge and again, when walking with Evelyn into Herne Bay. He didn't try to control or direct the refrain but let it seek its path and, suddenly, the joy was not in the playing but in the creation. It had been a long time.

Before the war, when he'd studied at the Royal College of Music, he had tried composing – they all had – and then, in France, in the early months, scraps of compositions had thrown themselves at him, as random as the bullet or shrapnel that claimed or missed, and there had been some joy in pretending he could still be a musician, still think like a musician, still was a musician. There was both chaos and order in the trenches and a relentless exhaustion that could slip into a trance which might lead who knows where. But by late 1915 the musician was gone and the imaginings of clear and beautiful music were lost – until these last few weeks.

Frank was calling at Edward and theatrically checking a pocket watch. It was the movement rather than the sound which caught Edward's attention and he let his fingers slide to a stop. He checked his old Elgin and took away a few minutes – it was well past midnight – and gathered his belongings to leave, thanking Frank once more for staying on and giving him an extra shilling.

Outside, Edward pulled his coat tight against the breeze off the sea, lit a cigarette and made his way down Fort Hill. It was odd not to be accompanied by William and the ladies, and not to have Constable Simms nod his customary greeting, which served to both comfort and warn. At the bottom of the hill Edward heard voices. They came from the Droit House, where the harbour pier joined the promenade, and Edward recognised the constable's deep tones. Edward turned off the promenade to see. The constable stood just inside the porch of the Droit House, on the bottom step. In the shadow behind him Edward could see another man standing. They were both looking down at something or someone on the steps leading up to the white building.

'Good evening Constable. Can I be of assistance?' Edward asked loudly and a good distance from the constable in order not to be a surprise.

The constable turned. 'Good evening Mr. Thompson. I thought I'd missed you earlier. Everything in order?'

'Yes, thank you. I stayed on to take some practise.'

The constable nodded and Edward felt relieved, as if his explanation needed acceptance.

'Ah, Mr. Thompson,' said the other standing man. Edward couldn't see him clearly in the poor light but there was a confident welcome in the voice. 'It's a pleasure to meet you. I've heard much about you.'

Edward shook the proffered hand and looked to Constable Simms who explained, 'This is Reverend Railton, of St. John's. And I think you already know this man.' The constable stood back a little and Edward could see the huddled form of the disabled veteran they had helped that first day in town and seen on the promenade and beach area since.

'Our paths have crossed,' Edward said, cautiously.

'The reverend found him here …'

'Again …' Reverend Railton interrupted and then spoke to the man on the floor, '… and we seem to be in a circle of trying to help and then finding him back on the street. And, do you know, we still don't know his name. Do you?' he asked Edward.

'No, sorry.'

'I've no wish to take him in,' said Constable Simms, 'but …'

'He can come back to the Rectory,' said Reverend Railton.

'Again,' Constable Simms said.

'Again?' asked Edward.

'He's stayed there a couple of nights over the last few weeks, but leaves in the morning. He says he's looking for work but no one offers any,' said Reverend Railton.

'A cripple. Who's gonna give a cripple a job,' said the disabled man quietly without looking up from his uncomfortable step.

'He can't sleep here. We've had enough complaints about him already. And the begging,' said Constable Simms.

'And you still don't know his name?' Edward asked.

The constable and the reverend shook their heads. The reverend bent down, 'I can provide a bed for a few days but we might be able to help more if we knew your name?'

The disabled veteran shook his head.

'Well I can't have any more begging or sleeping under the jetty.' The constable reached down and started to pull but the man resisted.

'You can hardly expect much help if you don't help yourself.' Edward said, in a voice he hadn't heard himself use for a long while. 'If we can find out a bit more about him can he stay at the Rectory for a few days?' he asked the reverend.

'Of course, and we can try again to find work for

him, again.'

Edward turned back to the veteran, 'But you can't expect a man to let you into his house if you won't even give your name.'

The man said nothing and the constable reached for him again. The man resisted again.

'Here's an offer,' said Edward, 'and it's not for negotiation. If you tell us your name and the reverend gives you a bed for the night, tomorrow we'll go to a hop farm and see if they've a job. It's only temporary, of course, but from there you can get back to London with the rest of the pickers.'

'Ha, a cripple at a hop farm. That'll work. I'm a dab hand at climbing ladders.'

'I'm sure there'll be other work. Tallying, or in the kitchen. And if there isn't, I'll bring you back and pay for a room for you for three nights, while you try again for a job here in Margate. But if you don't find one then you'll go back to London, where there's more chance.'

'And I know people there may be able to assist,' offered Reverend Railton.

The veteran was silent, then said, 'Tosh.'

'What?'

'That's my name. Tosh.'

'I don't believe you,' said Edward. 'My offer is conditional on knowing your name, rank and serial number. Now, sit up!'

The man started to push himself up but slumped back down, saying, 'They call me Tosh.'

The reverend spoke more quietly. 'Tosh is as good a name as any. I'll provide a bed for tonight.'

Edward sighed. 'The reverend is a good man and I don't want to hear you have taken advantage of his hospitality in any way. If you go with him I'll pick you up at o seven hundred hours tomorrow. Else take your chance with the constable.'

Constable Simms nodded, though barely visible in

the dark. 'My cell is unlikely to be as comfy as the reverend's camp bed.'

William, on being woken at six thirty and hearing Edward's story and request, had been less charitable than the reverend and the constable. He begrudgingly followed Edward out to the car.

At St. John's Rectory Tosh was already waiting outside the door. Reverend Railton came out to greet them, thanking Edward, before taking a few seconds to look at him.

'I hear your playing is causing quite a stir Mr. Thompson. My wife has twice seen you at The Winter Gardens and is insisting I come along to hear for myself.'

'Your wife is kind Reverend.'

'You don't want to leave it too long,' said William, 'the season ends soon.'

The reverend smiled and spoke to Edward. 'Meantime, if there is anything I can do for you please come and see me.'

Edward nodded and turned to the veteran, 'Tosh, let's be off,' and ushered him towards the car then turned. 'Excuse me Reverend, but I believe you're promoting the idea of a grave, for those who … didn't come back.'

'And whose remains are lost. Where did you hear that? Oh, I know, my wife is acquainted with Mrs. Blundell.' The reverend smiled. 'Well I have hopes for something like that and have written to the Dean of Westminster. He has brought the idea to the attention of both Lloyd George and the King, though I'm told the King is unsure. What do you think?'

Edward hesitated, then said, 'It might … help. So please, yes, if you can do something,' his voice dropping to a whisper.

The hop farm near Calcott was busy and pickers stopped work briefly to watch as the Wolseley moved through the shadows between the tall, lush plants. William drove to the clearing near the kitchen and the marquee. A group of younger children played on the fraying rope swing hanging from the tree though its bough drooped further and the large knot at the rope's end now scraped the ground. The few women in the kitchen gave them a second glance, but no more than that, and Reverend Coughston came from the marquee church. His welcoming smile was genuine and he called to the kitchen to boil a kettle for tea. Tosh was last out of the car, balancing on one crutch as he pulled his leg behind him. Reverend Coughston acknowledged him with a nod and looked into the car to see who else might be there, before turning to Edward,'

'Evelyn is not with you?'

'No Reverend, I'm sorry, we've come at short notice.'

'Hence the early hours and lack of letter or postcard to let me know.'

Edward heard the hint of recrimination in the tone and apologised. William stood by the car and lit a cigarette before offering one to Tosh. The late summer air was cool and there was dew on those stretches of grass still in shade. Edward took a few deep breaths and followed the reverend to sit at a trestle table just inside the marquee.

'Please, Mr. Burrslow and your acquaintance should join us, and you can tell me what brings you here over a cup of tea.'

'Coffee for me if possible,' called William, ushering Tosh to the marquee. The four men sat and Edward said,

'This is …' but stopped, '… you should introduce yourself,' and nodded to Tosh as he laid his crutch on the floor beside him but Tosh said nothing.

'Tosh,' said William impatiently.

'Nice to meet you, Tosh,' said the reverend.

Tosh still said nothing.

The reverend turned back to Edward, 'Is Evelyn all right?'

'Yes sir. Evelyn's well and ...'

'... and too busy to visit.'

'No ... I mean, I don't know. Evelyn doesn't know we're here. It's been rushed.'

'Not 'alf,' said William.

Tosh sniggered.

'Well, business before pleasure. You can tell me how Evelyn is later, but first, what is it you want?'

'Well sir ...'

The reverend raised his hand, 'Please, not sir. Father will do.'

'Of course. Tosh here is in need of paid employment. He has been ... ' he looked at the disabled veteran and then back to the reverend, '... begging on the streets of Margate and sleeping rough, and though Reverend Railton at St. John's has helped, he needs something that will pay, even if only for a few weeks.'

'Reverend Railton, you say?'

'Yes, do you know him?'

'No, but I have heard of him. Good things, and I believe he was awarded the Military Cross.'

'I don't know but he does seem a good man,' said Edward.

'Indeed, but even so, I'm not sure there's much we can offer a ... let's be frank ... one–legged man.'

'And one armed, Father,' Tosh said before Edward or William could find a more gentle way and showed his prosthetic arm. The reverend nodded thoughtfully.

'I wondered if you might need help with something less physical. Tallying perhaps?' Edward suggested.

'I doubt it. I'd have to speak to the farmers but they use their own people for that side of things, and besides, we've only a few weeks left. Would he know what to do?'

'I'll bet he knows how to clean a kitchen ... or a sh ... latrine,' William said.

They sat in awkward silence save for the women's chatter from the kitchen and the children's laughter from the swing.

'Bollocks,' said William, looking over to the children, 'I was going to bring them some new rope, after it broke last time we were here.'

'Looks like they found some,' said the reverend.

'Looks a bit dodgy to me. I'll see what we've got in the car.' William went back to the Wolseley.

A woman came from the kitchen, carrying a tray of drinks. Edward took the teas from it and told the woman the coffee was for William. She took it over to him. Edward looked to the reverend but he was watching Tosh intently. Tosh reached for one of the teas and the reverend passed him a biscuit on a plate.

'It's not down to me, I'm afraid. The Mission doesn't employ anyone and the farmers' foremen handle all hiring.'

Edward lit a cigarette and suppressed the urge to push the question. Their attention was diverted by William shouting for the children to come over as he pulled a length of rope from the box on the car's running board.

A few of the children came closer and a couple recognised Edward, stopping just outside the marquee where he sat with the reverend and Tosh. Edward realised one or more of the children remembered him and the whispers of, '… tin face …' were audible. Tosh grinned and lifted his trouser leg to show and tap the false leg. A younger child gasped but the older ones were intrigued. One stepped closer. Tosh settled back in his chair.

'Tell me … Tosh, what did you do in the war? Do you have any skills?' The reverend asked.

'I'm as good as any at being shot at, catching shrapnel and bleeding. Honestly, Father, as good as the best, except p'raps for the bleeding part I suppose, 'cos if I'd been a better bleeder I'd have bled to death wouldn't I?'

'Hmmm, can you read and write?'

'I can't write no more. It's the wrong one.' He held up the wooden arm.

The reverend looked to Edward and shook his head almost imperceptibly.

'He can peel potatoes and carry water. Can't you?' Edward said.

'I suppose,' said Tosh.

The reverend left them to go to the kitchen and came back with a young woman who avoided looking at Edward.

'Amy here will show you the chores and we'll find you a place to sleep. You've three days to show you can earn your keep …'

'… or …'

'I'll put you on the train to London,' Edward said.

'Please go with Amy, I need to speak to Mr. Thompson,' said the reverend.

Amy waited while Tosh collected his crutch and bag and led him to the kitchens. When he was out of hearing Reverend Coughston said, 'I doubt it'll work and in any event, we're finished here in a few weeks. What then?'

'I don't know Father, but won't there be more for him back in London, when they all go back, than Margate?'

'Not really. He's one of so many.'

Edward took a wallet purse from an inside pocket and passed the reverend a white fiver.

'For the church, or Tosh's wages?' the reverend asked.

'As you see fit.'

'It's very generous.'

'Thank you for trying to help.'

'You have taken time to bring him here. That's persuasive. But now, tell me, how is Evelyn?'

'She's keeping well and enjoying her work at both the theatre and the tea room. I'm sorry I couldn't arrange to bring her today, though, being a Thursday I expect she'd have been busy anyway. Mrs. Trenter is painting her portrait, together with Catherine's. I believe Thursday is the day for their formal sitting, at Mrs. Blundell's guest house.'

'A portrait? Evelyn? Why?'

Edward hesitated, then, 'Why not? Such a likeness would grace any home, wouldn't it?'

'Proverbs thirty one thirty,' said the reverend. 'Charm is deceitful, and beauty is vain, but a woman who fears the Lord is to be praised.'

'I'm not sure I know what that means Reverend, but I think Mrs. Blundell just wants a picture of two pretty women of whom she's very fond.'

'Of course,' the reverend nodded, 'and ... as you say, why not? I just hope it's not falsely flattering.'

'I don't see how it could be.'

The reverend thought about that for a second or two, then laughed. 'You're right, of course. Evelyn is pretty, like her mother. Though did you say Mrs. Trenter is the artist?'

'Yes.'

'I didn't know she painted. How might that be? After all these years?'

'That she paints?'

'No, that I didn't know.'

Edward shrugged and sipped from his tea. From the corner of his eye he caught the movement of a couple of younger children easing closer, presumably to catch better sight of his mask.

'Does it bother you?' the reverend asked and indicated to the children.

'No. Not so much. Not any more, at least, not the younger ones. As for the others, it's not that I mind being looked at, I understand, it's just I don't want to be able to see them when they look. They can't always hide their own faces and ...'

'Perhaps it would be better if the onlookers were to

wear the mask?'

'Perhaps, or maybe we all should.'

'Mostly we all are, in one form or another.'

'Even you?'

'I try not to, but I'm no saint.'

'And Evelyn? She seems to have no sides.'

'True, At least none I have seen, and she has the same innate goodness as her mother in her core. Though I have to admit I may be biased.'

'I don't think so.'

'I hope not. You know, when she was younger and her mother alive, I was strict, perhaps overly. I thought a reverend's daughter should be beyond reproach, some vain reflection of my own ambition. Why do we expect more from those we love?'

'I don't know. When I was young I thought I might grow to understand human nature, but in France I learnt not to worry about understanding it. It's not possible to change it and the best you can hope for is to recognise it as early as possible and not expect too much.'

The reverend looked thoughtful. 'And what do you expect of Evelyn?'

'Nothing sir. I wouldn't presume. Your daughter has been kind to me but I expect nothing.'

'And I would expect nothing less from my daughter.'

They sat in silence and Edward thought the reverend might be stifling a smile. Edward dropped his cigarette butt on the ground and stamped it out before lighting another and saying, 'I met a Mr. Tewson in Margate a few days ago. He was visiting Evelyn. I believe you may know him.'

'Evelyn told me, in one of her letters, though he had already mentioned he would go to see her. I understand you intervened on Evelyn's behalf?'

Edward shrugged. 'I did, though subsequently I did think perhaps it wasn't my place. Is Mr. Tewson … would he be … suitable? I didn't think so but it's not my place to judge.'

'As much as many others, but then not so much as some. Although they walked out last year, just a few times, I don't believe Evelyn would encourage his affections. But then again, she has not encouraged many, as far as I'm aware.'

'And does Mr. Tewson understand?'

'I don't know. You could ask him.' Reverend Coughston nodded to the far side of the clearing where Mr. Tewson was sitting on the bench at the front of a horse drawn wagon, its flatbed bowing under the weight of heaped sacks of hops.

'I should at least say hello, having spoken in Margate,' Edward said.

'Quite so,' said the reverend, 'and while you do I'll write a brief note for Evelyn you can take back with you.'

Edward nodded and stood to leave the table. He crossed the clearing, a group of young children following a few yards behind. William was standing close to the rope swing, where some older children played, and was smoking and chatting with a young woman. Mr. Tewson saw Edward approach but stayed seated, high on the wagon's driving seat.

'Mr. Tewson, good to see you again. I hope you're well?' Edward said.

Mr. Tewson nodded but said nothing.

'I wanted to ask you a favour,' said Edward.

'If I can.'

'The Reverend Coughston has offered to help another ex–serviceman we've brought today. He's quite disabled but independent enough. I'm just concerned he'll know nobody here and may feel … lost. Would you do me the favour of looking out for him? His name is Tosh and he may appreciate the company of someone else who served.'

Mr. Tewson nodded again.

'Thank you. I'm obliged.'

'Perhaps.' He climbed down from the wagon. 'Is Miss Coughston with you?'

'No, but I did wonder if we should talk of her.'

'Does she have a message?'

'Not through me but …' Edward was stopped by the shriek of an angry woman,

'Bitch! Dirty, lying bitch! Whore! Don't so much as look at my old man again, you cow …'

He turned to see William trying to separate two figures, fighting on the ground. One was the young woman to whom William had been speaking; the other Edward didn't recognise.

'So what did you and the reverend talk about?' William asked as he drove Edward away from the clearing and back through the rows of hop plants.

'I asked him to help Tosh. He'll try but I think we'll be back here in a few days to pick him up.'

'In which case the boot may be on the other foot. We might be asked to take that woman back with us.'

'What the one who started the fight?'

'No, the other one, on the receiving end. The one I'd been talking to.'

'Oh, the one called a whore?'

'Yes.'

'And is she?'

'I don't know. She did seem very friendly and also looks to be a disruptive influence at the farm. Her name's Margaret.'

'Well you seemed to be getting on with her all right.'

'Exactly. And though we didn't set a price she was flirting round the subject, I think.'

'We're not in Le Havre now,' Edward laughed.

'More's the pity. Speaking of which, you haven't seen my postcards have you? I've lost them.'

'No.'

'Odd. I'm usually very careful with such ... art. Anyway, it's been an eventful morning out.'

'Yes, a good morning. And it's still early. I thought we might go over to Whitstable and see if we can find Kayst's sister, the one who married an oysterman. It shouldn't take long. We're half–way there.'

'I suppose we were going sooner or later,' said William.

'And afterwards, as we'll have the afternoon to ourselves, I might see if The Winter Garden's piano is available.'

'You don't need the practise.'

'Not for practise. I'm thinking I'd like ... need ...' Edward was hesitant, '... to write down some ideas I've been hearing.'

'Hearing where?'

Edward tapped his head. 'I'm already thinking about the second movement. It's been a long while but about time, don't you think?'

'Oh, of course, why not. Just don't expect to make much money that way.'

'I don't need much. We earn enough and I have my pension and allowance.'

'You might, but I've only got what we earn and, anyway, your allowance won't go far if you keep giving away fivers to vicars. I saw.' William said, now having to shout above the increased wind noise as the car's speed increased and it bounced along the grass lane.

'Don't worry. I'll look after you.'

'Hmmm. And speaking fivers, I had to fork out a couple of guineas to Rolf for some soluble morphine tablets.'

'Two guineas?'

'Give or take. It's the going rate under the counter. And at least it means you don't need to break into any more pharmacies. And you still have plenty of the morphia solution and syringes left?'

Edward said nothing.

'And if it helps you compose then it's money well spent,' William continued, 'and meantime I've nearly convinced Georgette she's good enough for the stage. She'll need a manager.' William looked away from the track to grin at Edward, not catching the movement between the hop poles ahead, and when he turned back a figure in a dark suit and brown hat was there and the car jumped as the off–side wheel ran him down and the man was gone, under the car, as William stamped on the brake pedal and yanked hard on the lever.

The Blue Bench

Evelyn, Reculver,
Friday 17th September 1920

The convalescent home was in Reculver Road, on the way to the beach where William and Patrick searched for fossils the previous Sunday. Before 1914 the home had offered respite to railway workers but converted during the war to a military hospital. Now, two years later, it was all but empty. Evelyn's stomach had tightened further with each mile closer they'd driven and now here she wanted an excuse to turn back, but, of course there was none. Edward helped her from the car, repeating, 'You don't need to be here.'

'He's right,' said William, 'There's nothing to be done. I don't know why they brought him here. He's well past convalescing.'

'If there was anything that could be done they'd have taken him to a proper hospital,' Edward said.

'I just feel I should … see him,' said Evelyn, making a definite move towards the front door, not wanting to let her doubt show. Edward hesitated. She looked at him. He was looking at the building, a large rambling house with a small dome protruding from the roof. There were rows of windows over three floors and a variety of annexes that looked to have been tacked on indiscriminately. It appeared neither formal enough to have been a hospital nor friendly enough for a convalescent home.

'Well I've seen plenty broken men in such places, including Edward here, so I'll wait outside, thank you.' William lit a cigarette, leaning against the car.

'You don't think, in light of what happened, you

should … come in?' Evelyn asked William.

'I saw enough yesterday. Though I imagine they've put some of him back together and he probably looks better this afternoon, but even so, no thanks.'

Evelyn turned back to the home. She had expected Edward to lead the way in but he was still hesitating. 'Are you all right Edward?'

Edward nodded and walked to the open front door, stepping aside once there to let Evelyn pass through. Just inside was a small reception office. Evelyn tapped on the glass. A young man in a grey uniform opened the door.

'We've come to see Mr. Tewson,' said Evelyn, trying to catch the young man's attention as he stared at Edward's face. Edward stared back, saying,

'He was brought here yesterday, after an automobile accident.'

The young man went back into the office and checked a logbook. 'Are you sure?' he asked.

'Oh yes. The accident was yesterday and though they managed to get a doctor to the farm where it happened, he, the doctor that is, decided there was no point in taking him to any of the local hospitals. He's … he's quite badly …' Evelyn's voice broke as she tried to finish.

'No, I meant, are you sure you want to see him?' said the young man.

Evelyn nodded.

'This way.' He left the office, locking the door behind him, leading the way down a short corridor and up a flight of stairs. 'This place was very busy during the war. We treated all sorts and some of them even got better.' He tried to joke as they walked but Evelyn felt his 'old boy' demeanour forced; he looked too young, but then so did Edward, still.

'These days we've only two wards left open, and we need to close them soon. There's a couple of veterans left convalescing, until we can find somewhere for them to go, oh, and of course now there's Mr. Tewson. Though I don't suppose he'll be here long,' he said when they were at the top of the stairs. Ahead of them was another short corridor with four doors leading from it and a nurse's station. 'This is Nurse Bower. They've come to see Mr. Tewson.'

Evelyn said hello and Edward nodded, again allowing Nurse Bower's gaze to settle on him without turning.

'You've come to see Mr. Tewson? And you are?'

'Friends. Close friends,' said Evelyn.

'We usually only let relatives on the ward.'

'Does he have any relatives here?' Edward asked.

'No.'

'Then we'll have to do, won't we?' Edward said.

'I should ask the doctor.'

'Is it likely any relatives will turn up before he … passes?' Edward said and walked past the desk to look in the first ward.

Nurse Bower followed him, saying, 'I suppose it'll be all right. It's the next one, he's in a room of his own. He's still unconscious.'

'What's that smell?' Evelyn asked as she followed Nurse Bower into the small ward.

'Ether, chloroform, chlorine. We don't use them anymore, there's no further surgery, but this used to be a theatre and the smell is, I don't know, soaked in to everything I suppose. It's quite safe. Here's Mr. Tewson.' Nurse Bower stood to one side as she finished talking and Evelyn gasped quietly and put her hand to her face.

Mr. Tewson lay on the only bed in the room. A window faced south and the light fell evenly. There were clean white sheets pulled to his neck. His face was pale and the top of his head wrapped in a spotless white bandage. His features were serene and he appeared freshly shaved.

Edward pulled two chairs closer to the bed and indicated to Evelyn to sit. Nurse Bower muttered something about fifteen minutes and left them with Mr. Tewson.

'He is breathing, isn't he?' Evelyn asked, trying to see Mr. Tewson's chest rise and fall.

'I suppose so,' said Edward.

'He doesn't look as bad as I feared, after what that young man said downstairs,' Evelyn said. 'Was there a lot of … damage. You saw him.'

'More than you should know,' said Edward.

Part of Evelyn wanted to ask more, perhaps to hear a description, but she knew it wouldn't make any difference. Instead of a question she said, 'It wouldn't have happened if I'd gone walking out with him. He was a good man. I could have made a difference.'

'He may have been a good man, I don't know, but even so, that's not reason enough. You can't walk out with every good man for whom you feel sorry and you've no reason to think it would have made any difference.'

Evelyn took a handkerchief from her purse and wiped the tear at her eye. 'I know it sounds trite, but he does look at peace.'

'Thank you,' said a voice from the doorway, 'I'll take that as a compliment. We tidied him up quite well.' The voice was loud and deep and belonged to a large grey haired man. He wore a light summer suit and offered his hand as he entered the room, introducing himself as, 'Doctor Gardiner.' Evelyn shook his hand but stayed seated. Edward stood. The doctor continued, 'I was here yesterday when they brought him in. Lucky really, as I'm only here a couple of days a week now, and they're quite dull, truth be told.' He stared at Edward's face as he spoke and Evelyn felt embarrassed for Edward, though Edward didn't flinch. Doctor Gardiner continued, 'Though to say it was lucky I was here is a bit of a lie. I couldn't do anything for him other than clean out the broken bits, put a few pieces of skull back together and wrap it up. There's a few bits missing, I wonder what happened to them? Still, he never gained consciousness and I can't think he ever will. Do you know what happened?' The doctor spoke without taking his eyes from Edward's face before pulling up a chair to sit.

'He stepped out in front of a car.'

'You were there?'

'Yes.'

'Driving?'

'No,' Edward gestured to his mask, 'I was in the passenger seat. Mr. Tewson stepped out from between the hop plants. We weren't going fast but could never have stopped in time. He was unlucky. Maybe if he hadn't a bad leg he could have jumped back in time but a front wheel ran him down and he was dragged under the car for quite a way.'

The doctor nodded as if that explained the injuries.

'But why would he? Step in the way?' Evelyn asked and looked at Mr. Tewson's pale face.

'I don't know. I think his hand was raised but I'm not sure, it happened very quickly.'

'So he may have been trying to stop the car?' Doctor Gardiner asked.

'Possibly. I don't know.'

'Did you know him before?'

'Yes, and we spoke earlier yesterday.'

Evelyn looked to Edward. 'You didn't mention. What did you say?'

'I asked him to keep an eye on Tosh, the disabled veteran we'd taken to the hop farm.'

'You didn't talk about me?' Evelyn asked.

Edward hesitated and before he could reply the doctor spoke, 'Hmmm, sounds a little complicated. I'll leave you to it. But may I just say that's excellent work.' He gestured to Edward's face. 'Major Gillies?'

'And Derwent Wood's craftsmanship.'

'Of course. Amazing aren't they? You were lucky to have Gillies. I'm just sorry I never had the chance to work with him. I'm afraid I was one of those sending on the problems rather than coming up with solutions, but then the field hospitals over there were always a bit of a rush job. I know we learned quickly and cleverly how to keep them alive in the field hospitals, just, but were it not for the likes of surgeons like Gillies I might wonder why. Keeping them alive wasn't always the same as giving them back a life. But that looks splendid.'

There was an awkward silence.

'Anyway,' said Gardiner, 'I'm sorry about your friend but I'm back in London for the rest of the week. The nurses will keep him comfortable, but there was so much damage, I don't think it will be long.'

Evelyn watched him go before asking Edward, 'There's that name again. Who was Gillies? It was almost as if that doctor was inspecting your ... your face.'

'I'm sure he was.'

'And you didn't mind.'

'No, nor the orderly and the nurse. They've seen it all before. I enjoy their detachment.'

'So who was Gillies? You've toasted him often enough.'

Edward studied Mr. Tewson's face for a few seconds while Evelyn studied his.

'Do you remember when I told you about the tin nose wards at Wandsworth?'

'You didn't say much.'

'Well before Wandsworth I was at Queens hospital, Sidcup, and Major Gillies was there. He ... tidied up the mess I brought back from France. At Queens he was ... everything, to all of us. Without him we ... I ... I don't know. There were hundreds, thousands of us, I suppose, but there is only one Major Gillies and ... well, he was the major.'

Evelyn looked at Edward's good eye. It was damp and she wished she knew if from a gentle nostalgia for what Major Gillies had given back to him or a deep sadness at what had been taken. She thought of the letter from her father which Edward had brought back the previous day. She still held her handkerchief and wanted to dab at Edward's right eye, under the spectacles, but hesitated. Edward stood and went to the window. 'Well,' she said, 'I don't know if it's the ether or the chloroform, but it's enough to make your eyes smart, isn't it? Reminds me of The London Hospital, Whitechapel. I spent quite a few evenings there last winter after Mrs. Durnell fell under a lorry when chasing after her youngest, who, truth to tell, is a tearaway, but she loves him as a mother does. Anyway, I got used to the smells, especially on days they had to give her lots for the pain, which was odd as the leg had been taken.'

Edward kept his back to Evelyn. 'I can hardly smell anything anymore. After the war I could, for a while, still smell, and didn't mind the ether. It was preferable to gangrene and pus.'

Evelyn thought he might be trying to make a joke and forced a short laugh but Edward continued with an even voice, 'It's nice here, a little nicer than Queens in Sidcup, though I preferred it there. The buildings were … ordered, the wards regular. You felt you'd be there temporarily, if eighteen months is temporary. I preferred that. It was a place of business, not a home. This is … too comfortable, too permanent.'

'Mr. Tewson won't be going home,' Evelyn said and began to cry, more openly than before, and wished Edward might leave the window to stand at her side and perhaps lay a hand on her shoulder, as Catherine might have, were she there.

'It's not your fault and you have behaved entirely properly, I'm sure. Though I'm not surprised Mr. Tewson may have … hoped for more.'

'So you did talk of me with him yesterday?'

'No. But … it was understood.'

'What was?'

Edward looked to be struggling to find the words and turned back to the window. Evelyn thought to wait a little while before repeating the question but after a couple of minutes of awkward silence the nurse came back, carrying a tray. 'Doctor Gardiner said you were to have tea. We've no biscuits left I'm afraid. They're using up all the supplies and we should be out of here in the next few days, though Mr. Tewson might complicate matters a little, if he doesn't … you know …'

She put the tray on the bedside table and as she went to leave Evelyn asked, 'Excuse me, but did Mr. Tewson suffer any pain?'

The nurse looked at the figure in the bed and back to Evelyn, 'Judging by the state of his injuries I'm afraid there must have been, but as soon as he arrived here Doctor Gardiner dispensed morphine and he's been unconscious since.'

Evelyn thanked her and left her chair to pour the tea. She took a cup over to Edward, still at the window. 'Thank God for morphine,' she said as she handed over the cup. Edward took it without speaking. Evelyn returned to her seat.

'The other day,' Edward said after finding the best place on his lips from which to sip from the cup, 'when you came to my room, to see if I was all right …' he hesitated,

'Sunday?' Evelyn prompted.

'Yes, and you saw the syringe?'

'Yes.'

'… I'm sorry. I'm more than a little embarrassed by the situation, and even more so to ask if I said or did anything … inappropriate. I would be ashamed to think so and mortified if I acted in a way to make you think less of me.'

'No, not at all. I'm just sorry you're sometimes in such pain you need to take such a drug.' Evelyn said, wanting to ask what Edward had meant that day about also taking regular smaller amounts but not wanting to explore the topic when he appeared so embarrassed.

'Thank you. And thanks for not telling anyone else. There is at least some comfort in feeling a secret shared with a reverend's daughter is safe,' Edward joked.

'Don't worry, this reverend's daughter has seen much and kept bigger secrets for longer,' offered Evelyn to show she understood.

Edward laughed quietly. For a few seconds Evelyn forgot why they were there, not that she had really known why in the first place, it just felt the right thing to do. The previous evening, when Edward had told her of the accident, she had insisted they come to see him and Edward's arguments against it had seemed half–hearted. Now, looking at the still figure on the bed, she knew it was vain to think that being there made any difference. 'Could William not have stopped?' she asked.

'I don't know. I don't think so. Tewson just stepped out.'

'To halt the car?'

'I don't know.'

'What if he wanted to stop the car, to talk to you, about … I don't know.'

'We'll never know.'

'But if he hadn't come to Margate and you hadn't seen him, then … and if I hadn't walked out him with last year, then …'

'You can't take on any guilt. It isn't down to you and, take it from me, guilt won't achieve, help, or change anything anyway.'

'But he wanted to stop the car?'

'I don't know. It happened very quickly. William and I were talking … and then he was there. Then he was gone, under the car. Perhaps it's just all down to bad luck.' Edward lit a cigarette.

'Did you know his wife died of scarlet fever?'

'No.'

'And she'd only just nursed him back to health after his leg was injured.'

'He was unlucky,' Edward said.

'Do you believe in luck? I don't. Father disapproves of such notions.'

Edward shrugged. 'I was once considered a lucky lieutenant. On my first four commands in the front line I hardly lost a man. They used to joke about wanting to walk close to me over the top. One or two even asked to join my platoon, I was considered that lucky. I didn't pretend to be otherwise, and then I even thought it might be true. But it wasn't. Young Kayst especially thought it was, but it wasn't.'

Evelyn left her chair to join Edward at the window. 'And you have the impudence to chide me for feeling guilty,' she said gently. Edward smiled.

'We were going to pop across to Whitstable yesterday, before ...' Edward looked at Tewson.

'Whitstable? Oh, to find Kayst's sister.'

'Or perhaps his parents I suppose.'

'Why?'

'How old was ... is Tewson? Does he have children?'

'About forty I suppose. No children. Why?'

'Kayst once told me his father had tried to stop him enlisting. He had to sneak way to London and ended up in the Royal Fusiliers.'

'As did you.'

'I had less to travel. I only had to leave the Royal College of Music.' Edward turned back to the window. 'I'm almost composing again. Did you know? No, of course not, I have told only William. I have some ideas but it's been a long while. I could have stayed at the College I suppose, and hoped the war would finish quickly, but it didn't, of course, so not enlisting wouldn't have worked anyway, would it?'

Evelyn shook her head. 'You should go back there.'

'Do you think so?'

'Yes.'

They lapsed into silence and Evelyn wondered what Catherine would think when she told her about this time with Edward and Mr. Tewson.

Nurse Bower came back in to clear the cups and hint they should leave. Edward asked her if she knew who would look after Mr. Tewson if … when … he died but she didn't know and assumed someone would find a relative somewhere, though Edward commented that would only be if someone searched. Evelyn said she had never heard him speak of relatives and Nurse Bower suggested a pauper's grave beckoned, though even that, as Edward said, meant his resting place was marked. Evelyn gave Nurse Bower her address and asked her to write and tell her when Mr. Tewson … when there was more news. She felt even more guilt for having spent so much time there and not given proper consideration to poor Mr. Tewson. She resolved to pray for him that night and to write to her father to ensure the congregation at the hop farm remembered him in their prayers.

The Wolseley was parked outside the front door. Though the September sun was bright and warming it brought no comfort to Evelyn as she followed Edward from the home. William was half–in, half–out of the back seat of the car, rubbing at the leather with a cloth he occasionally dipped in a bucket. Between rubs he chatted to a couple of men in matching blue suits, one on crutches. On reaching them Edward held out his silver case to offer cigarettes, which were taken with a nod of thanks as William introduced them,

'This is Lieutenant Thompson of the Royal London Fusiliers, and this is Evelyn, who is a reverend's daughter so mind yer Ps and Qs.'

The two men saluted but Edward waved their hands

down, saying, 'I no longer hold a commission,' undisturbed by the two men staring at him.

'Private White,' said the man on crutches, 'and this is Corporal Jung. I'm afraid he don't say much, or anything at all, but though his name sounds Kraut, I'm assured by Nurse Bower he comes from Bridlington, though I've only her word for it and I've known her to lie about other things. For instance, she said I wouldn't feel the thermometer when she shoved it up me 'arris but I definitely did. And that was the first time I'd met her.'

Edward laughed while Evelyn blushed.

'I was telling these two gentlemen you're no stranger to the blue suit yourself.' William said to Edward and then to the men, 'Eighteen months in Queens, Sidcup.'

They nodded understandingly.

'Well Jung and me have been here nearly as long but we'll be gone soon. They can't keep this place on just for us two. And I had a sneak at that poor sod they brought in yesterday. He'd stopped bleeding but had the look of a goner about him and I've seen more than a few. He'll be leaving here soon too, in a box. Shame, seeing how he came in such a fine motor car.' He indicated to the Wolseley.

'Too right it's a shame. I'm struggling to get the blood off the leather. We should have been more careful when we brought him in.' William said, leaning back into the car to rub the seat again.

'Or you could have been more careful when driving. You might have seen him and stopped in time,' said Evelyn, coldly.

'Or if he didn't have a gammy leg he might've jumped out the way.' William quipped, without hesitation or remorse.

A surge of anger shook through Evelyn as she stifled tears.

Edward turned to the two men. 'Excuse us

gentlemen. It was good to meet you but we need to leave. Good luck with your next postings.' The man on crutches laughed as he led the other man away. 'Too far William,' said Edward. 'Sometimes you're just an arsehole.'

'Well you know us working classes Lieutenant. No class.'

Evelyn stared at William until he looked away and returned to scrubbing the back seat.

Evelyn forced a smile as Catherine sat behind the steering wheel of the Wolseley and squeezed the horn, jumping at the sudden noise. William, sitting next to her, laughed loudly and turned to Georgette and Patrick in the seat behind, to make sure they too laughed.

It was the afternoon following the visit to see Mr. Tewson in the convalescent home at Reculver. The drive back to Margate had been in silence, even though William, reminded by Edward, had apologised to Evelyn as they set off. They'd taken a light lunch at the Trenters' tea shop. Alastair was terse as usual and Alice was tense – the baby would soon arrive and she was not sleeping well. The atmosphere was awkward following the morning's visit. Evelyn wanted to ask more about the incident with Mr. Tewson and the conversation he and Edward might, or might not, have had. Also, she wanted to understand if the guilt she was feeling was justified, but didn't know how to talk of it. Edward had said nothing except to tell Evelyn his head hurt and he might benefit from a nap before that evening's performance. He had refused Evelyn's suggestion she should walk with him and she didn't press the point. When William left to pick up Catherine for the driving lesson he had promised her, Edward went back to his guest house, leaving Evelyn and Alice being waited on by Alastair. William had returned with Catherine, Georgette and Patrick, now parked outside the tea shop, squeezing the bulb of the brass trumpet horn, laughing as passers–by started with surprise. One or two looked angry at the shock but either William's presence or Patrick's honest pleasure was enough to prevent any unpleasantness.

On recognising Catherine's excitement, Evelyn went outside and listened as William explained the car's controls. There was a confusion of levers, switches, pedals and knobs but Catherine was unfazed, reminding William she had. '… been a bus conductor during the war and they'd shown her how to drive, though admittedly never with passengers on board …'

The motor had an electric starter and fired to life first time. Evelyn couldn't hear William's instructions over the noise but saw Catherine's smile as she turned and waved before releasing the brake and the car moved forward gently. Evelyn wished she was in the car and admired Catherine for insisting on the lesson and not worrying she carried an audience with Georgette and Patrick in the back, but then remembered it had so badly injured Mr. Tewson and wondered how it was she had even been able to take a ride in it that morning. She shook her head to clear the image of William cleaning blood from the back seat, next to where she had sat, and went back inside. Alice poured another cup of tea and told Evelyn how well the preliminary sketches for the portrait of her and Catherine were going, though she changed the subject when Alastair came out from the kitchen.

Catherine's driving lesson took half an hour or so and she came back into the tea shop red faced and a little breathless. She stood just inside the door and watched as William explained the controls to Georgette; it was her turn for a lesson. Patrick was still in the back.

'Georgette's not as confident as you were,' Evelyn said as Catherine joined her at the table in the tea shop, having watched Georgette struggle to follow William's instructions.

'But, to be fair, I've driven before, and buses are

more difficult. Georgette's doing well and I'm sure she'll be enjoying William's attention. Though I'm a bit worried for Patrick in the back.'

'He's probably safer with Georgette driving than William,' said Evelyn, 'after yesterday.'

'Oh, I'm sorry, I should have thought and not gone out with William,' Catherine said.

'That's all right. It looked like fun and why not?'

'And I did think if I could persuade Aunt Beatrice we needed a motor car, then I could drive it and we could take it out some days, if you fancy.'

'Yes, of course, and it's not long before Alice has the baby. I'll still be here for a few weeks after then.'

'Is that all?'

'I'm not sure. But I expect father will want me back home when the mission is closed and he goes back to Spitalfields. Though he did write something strange in a letter Edward brought back yesterday. I haven't read it properly yet, I've been upset by what happened to poor Mr. Tewson, but there was something about me not going home if other opportunities arise.'

'Like what?'

'I'm not sure, but there was a reference to Edward and how a good man might influence a woman's duty. It was a bit vague and he quoted Hebrews thirteen sixteen, again.'

'Evelyn,' said Catherine leaning over the table to touch her hand, 'as if I'll know what that is.'

'It's something like, do good and share, for such sacrifices please God.' Evelyn reached into her handbag to retrieve the letter. As she sat up she jumped, Beatrice was suddenly next to her, saying,

'You always do, my dear. I was so sorry to hear about Mr. Tewson. But was it wise to visit this morning? I'm sure Catherine would have gone with you.'

Catherine nodded, adding, 'Of course. I'm sorry I didn't.'

'I understand you and Mr. Tewson were close?' Beatrice made it a question.

'I don't think so, aunt,' said Catherine.

Evelyn nodded agreement and changed the subject, 'Aunt Beatrice, you should have been here earlier. Catherine drove Edward's car as if born to it. She was wonderful.' The praise was sincere and easy to give.

'Much as I'm sorry to have missed it, it's just as well, else I may have been so impressed my niece would have convinced me we need a motor car of our own and I'd almost certainly say yes and who knows what trouble that might lead to? No, it's unthinkable. Though I'm not surprised. Catherine has a flair for the unexpected, the charming and the enquiring.' Beatrice said straight–faced apart from the slight creasing around her twinkling eyes.

Evelyn found herself looking at Catherine and agreeing.

Catherine smiled, 'Then next lesson with William I'll come and pick you both up and you can experience it for yourself.'

'Oh I don't think so,' said Beatrice. 'I don't mind the trams and the trains but a fast motor car makes my stomach churn. The last time I was taken for a drive, by the late Mr. Upland, I was nearly sick after just a mile or two, though, to be fair, he was trying hard to impress me with the speed of his new motor car. And he'd bought new driving gloves for the occasion. I do think he may have been building up to ask for my hand, not for the first time of course. Though I don't mean it wasn't Mr. Upland's first time, with me at any rate, because it was, or at least would have been had he lived and got around to it and I can't speak as to whether he had previously asked any other lady, despite the rumour spread by Mrs. Martin, but then she also said the pharmacist was diluting the ginger beer he was quietly selling under the counter and when I challenged him he denied it. No, I meant Mr. Upland wasn't the first to ask for my hand after Mr. Blundell died, not that Mr. Upland did ask, in the end. But at any rate, after the drive in his motor car and nearly vomiting I wonder if he may have changed his mind? Ah well, we'll never know. Shame, as he was a handsome man and, I might add, of means.' Beatrice rambled as she sat and made herself comfortable at the table.

Evelyn watched Catherine as she watched her aunt. Catherine smiled affectionately, first at Beatrice and then at Evelyn.

'Well that's Mr. Upland's loss,' Catherine said.

'Which? Dying or not asking for my hand?'

'Both,' said Evelyn.

'You're probably right and now we'll never know if I would have said yes,' said Beatrice, before she leant forward and whispered, 'it would have depended on the extent to which Mr. Upland expected me to carry out the full range of … matrimonial duties. I'm not sure I have the energy after a busy day running the guest house, though perhaps that's the price to pay for companionship?'

Catherine burst out laughing. Evelyn watched her and laughed more gently, still thinking about her father's letter.

The Blue Bench

Edward, Margate,
Monday 20th September 1920

Edward tried to re–imagine the scene. Again. But still he didn't see from where Mr. Tewson had stepped. One second he wasn't there. Then he was. It was the antithesis of Kayst's disappearance. One second Kayst had been there. Then he hadn't. Two seconds. Two very different seconds. Two seconds, three years apart. Two seconds embedded in Edward's thoughts and yet elusive, incomplete and transient. And with Tewson he couldn't say whether his hand was raised to stop the car or not. Why would it be? But why else was Tewson there? Edward had a fleeting and ridiculous notion perhaps they should ask Mrs. Capais to find Mr. Tewson's sprit and ask him. And Edward felt guilty – not for what happened to Tewson but for giving the scene as much time over the last couple of days as he had Kayst's – possibly the more deserving? Though why, he couldn't say. And more deserving of what? His guilt? As if that commodity held any value. Poor Kayst. Poor Tewson. But at least Tewson would have a place to rest. Edward wondered where that might be and who might go there. He thought Evelyn might and that was unnerving. But what if no one went? He turned to William and thought about asking, even though he was never going to be the right person, but he was in deep conversation with Mr. Taylor. Anyway, he'd rather ask Evelyn. Perhaps, as a reverend's daughter, she might know. And if nothing else, wouldn't sneer at the question. Since the incident with Tewson, William had been touchy, quick to anger. If Edward didn't know better he might think it was guilt. But he did know better. It was more likely indignation at the suggestion he may have been at least partly to blame. The police sergeant had questioned them both at length, though there wasn't much to be said and, at some stage in his life, William had learned to draw his battle lines early. Or perhaps William was just irritated by Edward's decision to move into Mrs. Blundell's guest house.

Edward left William and Mr. Taylor talking, just inside the door to the auditorium, and went to sit at the piano on the stage, though he didn't play. He looked out over the empty seats. This was a welcoming place – not as grand as the concert halls in which he'd dreamed he would play, but the acoustics were good and the audiences generous. There were only two weeks left for his contracted services and he would miss this venue. It was mid–morning Monday and Edward was seeking a private moment, concerned such time might become a luxury once he moved into Mrs. Blundell's later that day. But there were others in the auditorium and he recognised Mr. Pine, the young man he had met on his first visit to the Winter Gardens; the young man who would be trialling his new recording technique here and the reason William was talking with Mr. Taylor in the corner. Edward watched Mr. Pine join William and Mr. Taylor's conversation and tried to read their faces but they were a little way away and his good eye wasn't good enough. After a minute or two the three men shook hands and Mr. Pine came over to the stage. He said how much he looked forward to recording Edward's playing that coming Friday, though he didn't climb to the stage or look to catch Edward's eye until he passed up a list of piano pieces saying, 'Please have a look and choose four or five from which you'd like to play extracts.'

Edward took it and had chosen by the time he reached William at the door. Mr. Taylor had already left and William led the way from the building without speaking. Outside both men lit cigarettes, not deterred by the light drizzle. Edward spoke first.

'So Taylor agreed then.'

'Eventually, but he's got the 'ump. He admits you play well but he's still wary 'cos of the times you've been … poorly … and not turned up.'

'I can't blame him.'

'But I mentioned we had a mutual friend in Rolf, and hinted I'd seen the Hennessy in his office. We soon came to an arrangement. They'll be recording on Friday, you'll be up first.'

'And I've already chosen the pieces. A nice mix. I think I've already got the sheet music back in my room, somewhere. Shame they have to be short extracts, just to fit on the records.'

'Same for all. Think yourself lucky you've got a chance.'

'Lucky? Just like the old days eh?' Edward tried to make light of it but William was in no mood. Edward broached the subject they'd avoided all morning. 'Still, at least by moving in to the Blundell guest house I can practise those pieces before recording on Friday. Beatrice is having that piano moved in today.'

William grunted.

Their differences had surfaced on Saturday morning after leaving the police station. The sergeant had requested their presence and on reporting to the police station they'd been put in different rooms. For the next hour and a half the sergeant alternated between them, asking their accounts of the incident involving Mr. Tewson, who had died on Friday, not long after Edward's and Evelyn's visit. The sergeant had asked them to repeat their stories, this time interrupting with questions. Later, they learnt he had been asking them both the same questions and then, when he came back a third time, he was accusatory and challenged their accounts, though, in truth, there wasn't a great deal to say. Afterwards, as he escorted them from the station, the sergeant thanked them for their co–operation but made it clear the matter was not necessarily settled.

William didn't care and Edward saw little reason for concern, other than for Evelyn and, of course, poor Mr. Tewson. William led the way to The Compass, looking forward to a lunchtime drink and some shelter from the September breeze that brought cold rain with the incoming tide. There were few people on the front and even fewer on the narrowing beach. In The Compass William waited for Edward to order a scotch for each of them and a glass of water. They took a seat in a booth, poorly lit from the dirty window at its side. Edward took four tablets of soluble morphine from an inside pocket and dropped them into the glass, swishing it round to encourage the dissolution.

William took a sip from his scotch, toasting, 'Major Gillies.'

Edward raised his glass of water, 'And Rolf,' before emptying it in one.

'Head hurting?' William asked.

'Not especially, that'll be when the syringe is needed.' Edward said, picking up his glass of scotch. They drank without speaking for half a glass before Georgette joined them. William nodded over to Ceinwen at the bar and mouthed half a stout, which Ceinwen brought over. Georgette made herself comfortable. It wasn't until the third sip from her drink Georgette said,

'Oh, you have missed the excitement this morning. After you went and I'd cleared the breakfast room, Catherine and Evelyn came. They asked if you had seen Mr. Trenter. I told them I didn't think so and anyway, why would you? He went out for a walk last night and didn't come home.' She shrugged. Though her words were curt, the French accent softened them.

Edward sat forward, expecting his obvious attention

to elicit more information, but when it didn't he asked, 'And?'

'Pardon?'

'Did they find him?'

'I do not know. They went to look. Mrs. Trenter did not open the tea shop, she was so worried but, of course, she will have her baby soon and should not be out looking for her husband, should she?'

'Where are they looking?'

'Catherine will go towards Westgate and Evelyn to Palm Bay.' Georgette drank from her glass while Edward pushed his away.

'I'd better see if I can be of help. Georgette, it would be useful if you went to make sure Mrs. Blundell is aware, so she can go and sit with Mrs. Trenter.'

Georgette nodded but said nothing, still concentrating on her glass. Edward left them and William said something to his back he didn't catch. Outside the pub, sitting on the kerb, was Patrick. He smiled on hearing his name and seeing Edward and smiled even wider when Edward passed him a tanner, suggesting, 'Ice cream or sweets, as you fancy.'

'Thank you Lieutenant Thompson,' said Patrick, leaving Edward standing outside The Compass.

Edward took half a turn to the right, intending to go back out to the front and then up Fort Hill and on to Palm Bay. But he and William had come down that way earlier and there was nothing to suggest Alastair's presence, though he had to acknowledge they hadn't been looking. But, as Evelyn would almost certainly have gone that way he turned left, away from the front, intending to walk up and round the back of town and come out at Fort Crescent, just because it was a different route which Evelyn probably hadn't covered. He couldn't deny he'd like to find Alastair for her sake as much as Alice's. After a few minutes walking he turned left from Kings Street, up towards Trinity Square. The last time he had been here was to accompany Evelyn, Catherine and Alice to visit the medium, Mrs. Capais. He had a memory of Alastair making a reference to the 'outrageous fraud' of which mediums were guilty, whilst acknowledging people weaker than himself might be tempted when desperate. It had been a barely disguised criticism of Edward's own part in the visit to Mrs. Capais and Edward had been ashamed enough at the time that he offered no defence. He wondered now how desperate Alastair himself had become. He walked around the allotments in front of Trinity Church and stood at the bottom of the steps leading to Mrs. Capais's dark blue front door. He waited there for a minute, trying to remember Alastair's words more clearly. Was it likely he would have stopped here and, even if so, surely not all night? Perhaps not, but Edward was here and the curtain at the window next to the door twitched. As he went up the steps the door opened and Mrs. Capais stared down at him. He tried to read her mood but her expression was flat as she took a long draw on a cigarette. She filled the door frame, looking beyond Edward, up and down the street. Edward guessed she was checking to see if William was there. When Edward reached the top stair she said, 'Yes?' There was no move to invite him inside. Edward stared at her but could see she was not to be intimidated.

'I'm looking for Alastair Trenter. Have you seen him?'

'Trenter? Why would I? Especially after you set your bully on us?' She made reference to William.

'I don't know but this is a place for people who are … searching. And so is he.'

'Searching? You mean desperate. Like you.'

'Yes, perhaps, a little,' said Edward, after hesitation.

'Ha. A little? Saw or felt something you didn't count on, as I recall. Not so different or special. Any of you.'

Edward didn't know what she meant or to whom she referred, but her stance seemed to soften a little as he acknowledged, '... seems to me most of the special ones didn't come back. I don't know if Mr. Trenter is desperate but I do know he's swamped with despair. Did he come here, as a last resort?'

Mrs. Capais took another long draw from the cigarette. 'As a last resort? You think flattery will help?' she said sarcastically. 'Was his old lady here as a last resort too? Perhaps if she knew how to comfort him he wouldn't have to look elsewhere.'

'Your sort of comfort is a lie.'

'Ah, but to lie with someone is often the best type of comfort. Perhaps you should ask your friend Alastair what type of comfort he tried.'

Edward's anger rose. The right side of his face flushed while the left tingled under the mask – a rare feeling – but he took a breath and a step back, 'So Mr. Trenter is here.' Now he was out from under the house's porch the rain settled on his hat and shoulders.

'Was. All night as it happens. Did Mrs. Trenter miss him?'

The spite in her voice was almost chilling and Edward wished for a second he could free his anger, but breathed again, trying to release the knot in his stomach. 'You're disgusting. Where is he now?'

'Ha. I don't know. Last I saw he was heading to the church,' she nodded towards Holy Trinity on the square behind Edward, '... to beg forgiveness I expect. Now bugger off.' Mrs. Capais sneered and before Edward could unleash the vitriol he felt towards her she turned and went in to the house.

'Odious, malicious, hateful hag,' he said to the door but didn't feel better for it. For a second he was sorry William wasn't with him, though he understood it was vindictive enjoyment which led Mrs. Capais to admit Alastair had been there at all. Or perhaps he hadn't. Perhaps she was simply a liar. Would Alastair really have spent the night there? It was hard to believe.

Edward went over to Holy Trinity church. It stood proud but was protective, not imposing, its square tower tall and strong but not oppressive. He walked in through the door under the west tower, grateful to be out of the rain, though it was not warmer inside.

Holy Trinity had two floors of pews. The ground floor was arranged as expected but the upper floor was made of two long balconies, each stretching the length of the nave with tiered seating rising to the outer walls. The front of the balconies stopped at the main supporting pillars, leaving a wide expanse of space above the ground floor pews open to the ceiling. There were many spaces where a man might sit and be unseen. Edward walked the length of the nave, checking the pews on both sides but didn't see Alastair until he turned to retrace his steps – he sat in a shadow behind a pillar. Edward went to him. Alastair would have heard and seen him but chose not to leave his seat. Edward sat beside him. Alastair looked away but not before Edward saw he had been crying. Edward had no prepared words and they sat in silence for a few minutes.

'You should go home to Mrs. Trenter. Don't you think?' Edward said, almost a whisper. Alastair didn't reply. Edward settled a little further back in the chair and felt a calmness wash away the anger from the engagement with Mrs. Capais. He looked up to the altar then stifled a short laugh as he realised it was the morphine solution he had drunk in the pub beginning to affect him, rather than some divine peace.

Alastair looked at him.

Edward shrugged, 'Mrs. Capais said you'd be here, asking for forgiveness. That's not my business but I imagine Alice is a worried lady and in her condition that's to be avoided. Also, Evelyn is out looking for you and it's raining. I should go and tell her you've been found. Would you also like me to tell Alice you're safe?'

Mr. Trenter nodded but said nothing.

Edward stood to leave but, before turning away, asked, 'So what did you hope to gain from visiting Mrs. Capais?'

Mr. Trenter looked up at him. 'You know. You've been there.'

Edward couldn't disagree. 'True, but I didn't go on to spend the night.'

'Spend the night? She said … and you take Mrs. Capais at her word? Alice told me, eventually, about her visit to the fraud.'

'But you still went?'

'It was a lapse in judgement. It won't happen again. I won't let it.'

'Poor judgement perhaps, but at the very least shouldn't Alice know? And if you weren't there all night. where were you?'

'Not that I'm obliged to explain, but, it so happens I was here.'

'And it helped?'

'It was better than being lied to by that … woman. She said Curtis had never wanted to be in the navy, should never have been on the *Gurkha* that day. But she was wrong. That is how I know she lied. He wanted to be there. He volunteered as soon as he was of age and was proud to be there. And I was proud of him.'

'And still should be.'

'Of course. But that makes it harder, not easier.'

'Yes, but there's no shame in feeling that. The only shame would be in not sharing with Alice.'

Mr. Trenter stood to be face to face with Edward, 'And you believe that would help do you?' he asked almost as an accusation. 'So who do you share with?'

Edward simply shrugged, the morphine induced serenity negating the emotional threat behind the question.

Edward left the church, heading towards Fort Crescent.

He allowed himself some pride at having guessed right about Alastair Trenter and, in a lightheaded state, was looking forward to finding and telling Evelyn. As he began the walk towards Hodges Bridge and the clifftops the refrains he had been imagining in the last week or so filtered through to his consciousness. He was but a hundred yards or so further on when his name was called. Evelyn came toward him, anxious both in appearance and voice,

'Did Georgette find you?' She called when near enough not to shout.

'In The Compass.'

'And you know about …'

'Alastair?' Edward interrupted. 'It's all right. I found him and told him to go home, not ten minutes ago.'

'Thank God. Where was he? Is he all right?'

Edward, despite his relaxed mood, gave it some thought before answering, 'Holy Trinity church. He'd been there all night. He seems all right. Certainly not harmed.'

'Oh, I'd never thought to try the church. He isn't, or at least wasn't … anyway it doesn't matter. You found him. What made you go there?'

'Blind luck. Lucky Lieutenant, remember?'

Evelyn looked blank.

'Never mind, you're cold. Let's go to The Compass and get you a warming drink.' Edward nearly put his arm around her. The rain had stopped but it was evident Evelyn had been searching for some time. Though she wore a coat it was damp, probably through to her dress below, and her green cloche hat drooped over her ears. Her shoes were dirtied with both mud and sand and she looked pale and tired, all the more so as the excitement at hearing Alastair had been found waned.

'No, I'd better go and find Catherine. She might still be looking for Alastair. Let's go to Mrs. Blundell's first, in case she's already back there.'

Edward found himself walking alongside Evelyn,

more quickly than he might prefer, back down Fort Hill.

'Where were you this morning?' asked Evelyn. 'Catherine and I popped round to the guest house to see if you could help with the search but Georgette said you'd already gone out.'

'We were called early to ... oh, I'm sorry, you probably don't know. Mr. Tewson died ...'

Evelyn stopped walking and turned to him, speechless.

'... yesterday,' continued Edward. 'William and I were asked to the police station this morning, to give statements.'

'Yesterday? After we saw him ...'

'Yes.'

'Oh. I didn't know ... I thought I might visit him again, before ...'

'I'm sorry.'

'No, there's no need. It's not as if ... well, you know.'

'Of course.'

The rain started again.

'I'm sorry.' Edward repeated, and he was, though it made no difference.

'Who will ... look after the details?'

'I don't know.'

'Should I?'

'Let's think about that later. First let's find Catherine.' Edward spoke with firm kindness.

'Yes, of course,' Evelyn said and started walking again as the rain continued. 'You know,' she said, 'I've been all the way to Hodges Bridge and past, looking for Mr. Trenter. And I can't deny, I was scared of not finding him and having to tell Alice, but more scared, terrified, of coming across him ... you know ...'

'... at the foot of the cliff?'

Evelyn nodded and Edward saw her tears. She gave a nervous laugh, 'It's been a traumatic day.'

Edward wondered if he'd the right to hold her and if it would comfort.

By the time they reached Mrs. Blundell's the heavy rain had returned and soaked Evelyn's limp hat and Edward's light jacket. They went straight to the drawing room where Catherine was already waiting and stood to hug Evelyn as she entered, explaining she had come back via the tea shop and Alastair was home. Evelyn became tearful again and muttered, 'but Mr. Tewson is dead.' Catherine held her more tightly.

'Well it's been quite a day,' said Mrs. Blundell, who had been standing by the unlit fire, 'and quite a miserable one, with the rain. But even more miserable for Mr. Tewson. Catherine dear, why don't you take Evelyn upstairs and find some dry clothes while I arrange for tea. And then later I'll pop over to see Mrs. Trenter to see if she is all right. Of course I could telephone her if only they had the equipment installed. Ours was put in last week, in the study, and I'm keen to make use, though I'm hoping Catherine will be here to answer should it ring, I understand she has become quite adept at using them at The Winter Gardens and I hear most of the hotels have them. Does the house you're staying in have one Mr. Thompson?

'Not that I know of. Though it would be useful. I'm sure William would like one, especially for business.'

'Well I expect it will soon. Now, make yourself comfortable and I'll have tea sent in. Put on a recording if you wish.' Beatrice gestured to the gramophone.

Edward removed his damp jacket and sat on the edge of the settee. He was looking around the drawing room when Beatrice returned. 'It's a little different isn't it, Mr. Thompson?' she indicated to the room in general.

'I think so, though I've only been twice before and my memory isn't ... well it doesn't work as well as it once did.'

'The dresser is gone. I've had it put in storage and asked politely, through prayer, for Lincoln to forgive me.'

'Lincoln?'

'My late husband's brother, younger by some margin. His parents had cousins in America and were enamoured of the president's aspirations and were most upset when he was assassinated, or so I was told. Anyway, when Lincoln died the dresser passed to my late husband, who wasn't named after a president, or a prime minister, unless there was a prime minister called Spencer, hideous as it was, the dresser that is, not a prime minister, nor my husband who was a rather handsome man.'

'Actually, I believe there was once a prime minister named Spencer.'

'Really?'

'I think so. Spencer Perceval, and the name sticks with me as I believe he, too, was assassinated. Shot. Many years before Lincoln.'

'No! Are you sure? Well, why was I never told? My dear Spencer, named for a dead prime minister. Well at least his parents were consistent I suppose. I wonder if he knew.'

Edward suppressed a laugh, enjoying Mrs. Blundell's company, as usual. Before he could ask more about Spencer Blundell the door was opened by Catherine, leading Evelyn.

They had both changed clothes and now wore similar dresses; round necks, straight bodices to low waists and pleated skirts. Long heavy beaded necklaces draped almost to their waists and the skirts stopped just below the knee, shorter than typical daywear.

'Who knew what, Aunt?' Catherine asked.

'Did my dear Spencer know he was named for an assassinated politician? I'm not sure he would have approved,' Beatrice said, then turned to Edward. 'Was he Tory, do you know?'

'I believe so.'

'Well that might help. Though I myself remain staunchly apolitical on the grounds it doesn't help to declare such interests too deeply to the St. John's ladies. I believe some of them may be leaning towards socialism, though in its most benign form, so I'm told.'

'Dear Aunt, what are you talking of?'

'We were discussing the dresser, now back in storage.'

'Thank goodness,' said Catherine, 'and the best news is we can now bring in the piano. Edward can entertain us while we pose for Alice's painting. We'll be only upstairs and I'm sure would hear him play.'

'Would we, Edward?' Evelyn asked.

Her cheeks were pale, probably still from the cold rain thought Edward, and perhaps all the paler against the dark cloth of the dress, but her hazel eyes were warm. 'Of course,' Edward said. 'I'd play something especially loud to make sure. Though, perhaps not this week. I need to find a piano somewhere to practise before next Friday.'

'Why Friday?' Evelyn asked.

'I'm hoping to record, at The Winter Gardens,' Edward said, and his face lapsed into an instinctive, ill–prepared smile he knew would be askew, but couldn't help.

'Well that's exciting,' said Catherine, 'does it mean we will have a recording for the gramophone?'

'And what will you play?' asked Beatrice.

'I don't know yet, and it may come to naught. I'll find out on Monday, and even then I don't know if it will be available for gramophones. It may be only a trial for some new recording equipment. But still, I should practise, in case William can persuade the Booking Manager there.'

'Then why not practise here?' Catherine said, asking her aunt more than Edward. 'The piano will arrive on Monday.'

Before Edward could say otherwise Beatrice was agreeing. 'Why of course, and the last of our summer guests is leaving tomorrow. You'll have the drawing room to yourself. It's a splendid idea, though I hope the quality of the piano won't be an embarrassment. It was left to me by one of Spencer's aunts, who I never did meet despite …'

'Aunt …' interrupted Catherine, 'Edward is thinking about the idea.'

'Which makes sense to me,' added Evelyn.

Cook arrived with a tray of tea.

'And I'm sure Cook won't mind if Mr. Thompson stays for lunch on those days he practises.'

'No, Mrs. Blundell. When all the guests have gone it wouldn't do not to keep busy.'

'There, you see?' Beatrice asked Edward, who wasn't sure if Cook was being sarcastic. 'What do you think?'

'I think,' said Catherine, 'we should allow Edward time to think about it and let us know. In any event the piano will be here on Monday.'

Edward nodded to Catherine and sipped on the hot tea. The ladies chatted and it seemed the distressing events of Alastair's disappearance and Mr. Tewson's death had passed especially as Catherine went on to discuss fashion and explain to Aunt Beatrice she had made both the dresses she and Evelyn wore. They were designed for the portrait Alice was painting and did Beatrice think they were a little short? Beatrice wasn't sure. Edward thought not but didn't say so.

After another pot of tea and much conversation that Edward enjoyed, though he rarely joined, Evelyn said she should go back to the tea shop. She went upstairs to change back into her own clothes, now nearly dry, though the hat had not retained its shape well and draped lifelessly. Edward thanked Beatrice for both her hospitality and the offer of piano practise. He followed Evelyn down the steps from the front door and they walked the first few yards together, until reaching the junction where they would part; Evelyn for the tea shop, Edward back to The Compass to see if William was still there.

'Perhaps I'll pop down to the tea shop tomorrow,' said Edward, 'to see if Alastair and Alice are all right. Though I suspect Alastair may be embarrassed by events. With Alice due so soon he needs to be there.'

'Why don't I see what the mood there is like and I'll come over to your guest house in the morning if I think it's a good idea.'

'Meantime, are you all right? What with Alastair and … Mr. Tewson?'

'Yes, I think so, though Mr. Tewson's death is distressing and I do worry about the funeral details. Should I do something? Should the mission at the hop farm?'

'That's a better idea. Perhaps you should write to your father. It would be good to think Mr. Tewson is properly looked after and has a place to lie, to rest. And please, do not think there is anything you could have done to prevent the accident.'

'That's kind of you to say but without knowing for sure it was an accident I can't help but think there may have been something. Yes, I'll write to father, he may have another view. Meantime, you should think about Catherine's idea to practise at Beatrice's. You're not sure are you?'

Edward stalled for a second or two. Could half a face still be so easy to read? 'No, in truth, I'm not sure.'

'But especially with the potential recording coming up … why not?'

Edward hesitated, 'Well, ideally, I'd like a place I could also use to compose. I have some ideas, at last, and I think I'd like to capture them properly. Somewhere like the studios at the Royal College …'

'It's obvious how much the College meant to you but …' Evelyn let the words fade.

'I've been thinking, if I had something to play them, something ... worthy ... though it would take months to prepare, but the ideas are there, sometimes.' He looked at Evelyn and let her look back.

'So you need time. But what about The Winter Gardens?'

'The contract is only for another couple of weeks. William is already contacting other venues, looking for the next work. He'll find something. He always does.'

'Why?'

'Why what?'

'Why another contract? Why not take the autumn and winter to compose?' There was excitement in Evelyn's voice. 'And 'I'm sure you could even move in to Beatrice's, and be there, with a piano, for whenever you need it.'

'I ... I ... suppose ...'

'I could ask Beatrice for you.'

'No,' Edward said, 'if I think it's a good idea, I'll ask.'

'It is a good idea. And don't talk to William, just tell him,' Evelyn said, resting a hand on his forearm before saying her goodbyes and leaving him to walk slowly back towards The Compass, thinking about Evelyn's idea and wondering for how long after Alice's baby was born Evelyn would remain in Margate.

Patrick was back outside the pub. Edward saluted as he passed him. Patrick returned the salute.

William and Georgette were still in the booth. William acknowledged him by raising his glass and asking, 'You've been gone some time. Did you find the old boy?'

'Yes, in church, and he's gone home.' Edward turned to Georgette, 'Did you know Patrick is still outside?'

'I should hope so.'

'And it's been raining.'

'Has it?'

'Shouldn't you go and see if he's all right?' Edward

went to the bar, returning with two glasses of scotch. Georgette wasn't there.

'Georgette taking Patrick home?' Edward asked, sitting opposite William.

'I expect so.'

'Good. Poor lad looked cold out there.'

'I expect. So anyway, old Trenter was at church.'

'He was. All night so he said.' Edward considered mentioning the conversation with Mrs. Capais but could guess the animosity that would build in William. He changed the subject, 'Any luck with our next contract?'

'No, not yet. I've written to a handful of promoters and four or five venues direct. Something will turn up, especially if I can tell them you're a recorded artiste. I'll talk to Taylor again on Monday.'

'Good, though ... maybe ... I'm thinking about taking some time, to try composing. I've a few ideas that could work.'

William nodded. 'I'm sure we could find something which doesn't have you playing every evening. You'll have plenty of time.'

'No, I'm thinking I need to do it properly, or not at all. I'm thinking of staying here, at Mrs. Blundell's. She'll have spare rooms and there's a piano.'

'So you want me to see what Taylor has going on during the autumn then? Not much I shouldn't think.'

'No, I'll concentrate on composing. Not performing.'

'Oh,' William toyed with his glass. 'Still trying to get back into that stuffed up college? For what? And what do you do for money meantime? Play the ragtime club here once a month? And, more to the point, what do I do? Is there a room for me at dear Beatrice's too?'

'I don't know. I haven't asked. But I thought you might prefer staying where we are anyway, what with Georgette already living there. I'd pay for the room.'

'You do know I negotiated a cheaper rate for taking

two rooms? And you reckon your pension, what's that? seventeen shillings a week, and allowance from mama and papa will cover all this, do you? You do remember I wasn't lucky enough to get wounded for a pension, don't you?'

Edward leant forward and spoke quietly, causing William to also lean forward to hear. 'Don't be an arsehole. If I tell you I'll cover it, it's covered.'

'And you think I haven't seen this coming? Bollocks to you. Georgette's got the voice for music hall, and the looks and the front and she's French, all the boys like a Frenchie. We've already decided I'll manage her and yes, while I'm sorting out her bookings, you can bloody well pay my rent.' William emptied his glass and pushed it hard across the table. It fell towards Edward's lap. He caught it and placed it back on the table, repeating,

'Arsehole.'

William gave his best smirk, 'It's not as if that bloody college gives a shit about you anyway.'

'It's not as if I've asked though is it?' said Edward, standing and leaving before William could respond.

On the Sunday, Edward went to see Mrs. Blundell to ask if he might take a room for the next six months, offering to pay a summer rate even though the season was finished, together with a premium for use of the piano in the drawing room. Beatrice was in quick agreement. Edward moved into the guest house on the Monday, directly after William had arranged for Edward to be part of the recording session that coming Friday. By four o'clock Monday afternoon Edward was practising Rachmaninoff's *Prelude in G–flat major, Opus 23 no.10.*

The Blue Bench

Edward, Margate,
Thursday 23rd September 1920

The upright piano stood against the wall, where Mrs. Blundell's late husband's brother's hideous dresser had once failed to grace the room. The piano was a Chappell and the dark wood didn't suit the lightness of the drawing room but Edward was grateful for it. The tone was acceptable, the tuning good enough and Edward had thanked Mrs. Blundell by having a large bouquet of pale yellow roses sent down from Covent Garden. They sat in a dark blue glass vase on the table to the side of the settee in the window bay. Edward sipped on his after–lunch cup of tea, provided by Cook, and fiddled again with the stool. The mechanism didn't work properly but Edward was not complaining. He was alone in the drawing room, apart from the stuffed ferret in a glass case. The ferret had been brought out of storage along with the piano – Edward didn't ask why – and sat on the piano's lid, unperturbed apart from an occasional wobble when particular chords and notes were played in the lower register. Next to the glass case was Edward's briefcase and on top a handwritten list:

Grieg – *Papillion*
Grieg – *Little Bird*
Grieg – *To Spring*
Rachmaninoff – *Prelude in G flat major, Op.23 no.10*
Rachmaninoff – *Prelude in C sharp minor Op.3 No.2*

… the pieces he would be playing for the recording,

tomorrow. He had practised for over six hours the previous day and two already this morning, enjoying the solitude of the task. Catherine and Mrs. Blundell had 'popped' in, separately, to see him on a couple of occasions each and Mrs. Blundell knocked again as he finished *To Spring*. She entered without needing invitation.

'Edward, I thought you might like to know Evelyn and Alice are here,' they walked in behind her, 'for today's portrait sitting.'

Edward stood up from the piano to welcome them.

'Edward, how are you settling in?' Evelyn asked.

'Very well thank you. Mrs. Blundell is an excellent hostess. The facilities are perfect and I enjoy playing to an audience.' Edward indicated to the ferret, looking out from its glass prison.

Alice stepped over to Edward and held out a hand, 'Thank you for persuading Alastair to come home on Saturday.'

'It was no trouble, Mrs. Trenter. There was no persuading necessary.' Edward didn't know if Alastair had told Alice about his visit to Mrs. Capais.

'Well it didn't occur to me he'd be at Holy Trinity. Of late he has ... not been a frequent visitor. Perhaps with the autumn looming he will find more solace there than keeping lookout from the cliffs.'

'I'm glad all is well,' said Edward without knowing if that was the case but hoping to deflect the conversation. 'And how are you? The baby will soon be here.'

Alice rubbed her heavy pregnancy. 'I do hope so. Though that will slow down the portrait work. But the sooner baby is here the sooner we can organise our lives to suit.'

'And the portrait can wait, Alice,' said Mrs. Blundell, 'while the baby won't. I know you've been coming here in the evenings to work on it as well but I think best to come only on Thursdays from now on.'

'Well, the preliminary sketches are finished and the

first drawings already on the canvas, ready for paint, so I'm hopeful it will be finished in the autumn. Meantime, there is something I wanted to show Mr. Thompson. Something I have been working on to practise my rather average portrait skills.' Alice blushed a little, though it may have been the sun's warmth through the bay window.

Edward nodded vaguely and didn't appreciate Alice's movement towards the door was an invitation to follow her until Evelyn moved. She indicated Edward should follow, shrugging to show she didn't know why either.

Alice led the way upstairs to the room being used for the portrait painting. She moved slowly, pulling on the handrail. On reaching the landing Beatrice went on to the floor above, explaining, 'I'll tell Catherine you're here.'

Evelyn and Edward followed Alice into the bedroom. There were no curtains at the windows and the light was brighter than down in the drawing room. Two easels stood at one end of the room, at the window's side. The easels were both covered and between them stood a small table, crowded with Alice's painting materials and tools. On the other side of the room were a chaise longue and a small table with two dining room chairs. On the table was a chess set, game in process. Alice took the cover from one easel and placed it over the other, saying, 'A little while ago Evelyn mentioned you might need a portrait from which to print posters, for the theatres you play. I wasn't sure I had the right. No one has seen it and now I'm embarrassed in case you think it presumptuous but … might this be of use?'

'We thought it was just a practise easel,' said Evelyn stepping further into the room, then turning back to Edward, 'We haven't seen any of Alice's work yet. She's been very secretive.'

'It's not finished … I spent a couple of evenings each week on it and it needs a lot more work … I'm sorry it's not quite right.'

From the door Edward couldn't see the front of the easel and stayed there as Evelyn went to Alice's side. He watched Evelyn as she looked at the painting. He thought the surprise on her face was more joy than shock or horror, but didn't move. Evelyn looked from the picture to Edward and back to the picture, then back to Edward, nodding and smiling encouragement. 'It's a fine picture Alice,' said Evelyn, indicating Edward should come to the easel.

Edward hesitated and thought to buy some time by lighting a cigarette but wouldn't want a trembling hand to reveal him. 'I'm not sure ... I mean, why would anyone want to ... unless it's a profile, right side of course.' He forced a laugh but Evelyn waved him forward and he trusted her. As he reached the easel both Evelyn and Alice stood back, Evelyn placing a hand on his shoulder as he turned to look.

The portrait was head and shoulders. Edward wore a black dinner jacket and bow tie. His face was turned a little to the left, but not so much that his mask was hidden, both eyes were visible. Soft light came from a sunrise over open sea, on the picture's right. Edward studied himself. Usually, when catching his reflection, he could see only the bloodless mask's deathlike stare. He supposed originally the eye and skin colours had matched but now the mask's cheek was dulled and the eye flat. But in the painting his eyes were the same darker grey and the cheeks alive and, in the sunrise, adopted a light golden tint. It was clear the left side was a mask but it seemed part of his face, rather than lying on the surface. And where the real mask hinted at some visage of horror beneath, the mask in the picture was no longer hiding something unspeakable, but a part of the whole. And the hint of smile was easy and natural.

'You did this from memory?'

'I've seen you often enough, together with some imagination. But do remember it's a long way from being finished. I brightened the mask a little as I expect the colours may have dulled?' Alice made it a question.

'I expect so, I don't remember. It's kind of you to … flatter me so, but I don't look like that.'

'Yes, when you smile,' Evelyn said.

'You're kind too, but I did shave looking into a mirror this morning.'

'Mr. Thompson, can I ask, where was the mask made?' said Alice.

'After they'd done all they could at Sidcup, which was a very great deal, I went to the third London hospital at Wandsworth. Mr. Francis Derwent Wood ran the tin nose shop. A great man.'

'I know of him. He is well regarded in artistic circles,' Alice said.

'He made a cast and then fashioned thin copper to shape before painting.' Edward spoke without emotion, hoping Evelyn wouldn't see the effort it took not to let himself be taken back to that time.

'Well the paint is enameled but has lost some of its lustre and there is a chip or two,' Alice said in the formal manner of a craftsperson examining a piece of art. 'The eyebrow is very clever.'

'Slivers of tin–foil I believe,' said Edward. He turned. 'And they used a picture I had taken, on the day I went to join my regiment, to help with the likeness.' A sudden rush of nostalgia was disabling and he took an awkward stumble backwards. 'It is a fine picture Mrs. Trenter and I thank you for your trouble, but … I should go.' As he turned away Catherine came into the room. 'And you'll be wanting to carry on with Evelyn and Catherine's portrait. And I need more practise before tomorrow.'

Edward, Margate, Friday 24th September 1920

The auditorium at The Winter Gardens was busy with Mr. Pine's technicians moving chairs, running wires, cables and hoses and preparing a makeshift cubicle to surround the recording equipment. Edward stood next to William, near the curtained cubicle, his thoughts running over the pieces he would play. The musicians from the Municipal Orchestra, who would be recorded later, milled at the back of the auditorium or outside, enjoying the late September sun. William took his hip flask and sipped before offering it to Edward, who refused.

'Please yourself,' said William. 'It's not the good stuff. I had to give Taylor another bottle of Hennessy this morning. That's one thing you're going to miss staying at Blundell's, a ready supply of decent spirits.'

'What about the other ... supplies?'

'Don't worry, you may have abandoned me but I'll keep in touch with Rolf for you. Do you need any more at the moment?'

Edward thought for a few seconds, calculating. 'No, I'm all right for a few weeks. The soluble tablets keep things on an even keel and I only need the solution if the head's bad, and it's been all right for the last week or so.'

'Well, you just let me know. Old Burrslow is still around to help. Besides, if today goes well I can claim you to be a recording artist and get on to HMV.'

'And if someone from the Royal College hears the recording perhaps they might invite me back,' Edward said with suppressed enthusiasm.

'Hmmm, and that,' William said.

'But not until the spring. I need some time to compose and,' Edward hesitated, 'I still want to find Kayst's parents. We need to go back to Whitstable and look for his sister.'

Edward and William hadn't spoken much since he'd moved into Mrs. Blundell's guest house but William seemed more amenable.

'Kayst? Still? For what? Doesn't matter. Do me a favour later. Play down at The Compass, for Georgette, tonight, after finishing here. I've convinced Ceinwen to give her a proper turn. She needs the practise if I'm going to take her to the London stages.' William didn't wait for an answer before catching the arm of Mr. Pine who was passing. 'Will it be much longer before you need Mr. Thompson?'

'We're nearly done. The set up's a bit ... complicated,' he said, hassled and with a touch of condescension.

'Is this booth curtained so the recording instruments aren't disturbed?' William tried to make a better connection with the younger man.

'Not really, it's more to stop anyone seeing our new diaphragm. Now, if you'll excuse me.' Mr. Pine went away to instruct another technician in the placing of the sound receiving horns. For Edward's recording there were two large ones under the piano's open lid with a third a yard and half away, but still on the stage. The three horns were attached to rubber tubes which were fed into one end of a copper joint with a single tube leading from there and behind the curtains into the booth where the recording equipment was hidden.

Mr. Pine was back in ten minutes, instructing, 'Now, Mr. Thompson, we're ready for you. I expect you'd like to warm up for a minute and then, when you're ready, let me know and we'll start a recording, using the order we discussed earlier,' he tapped the piece of paper in his hand,

'and don't forget, fortissimo, fortissimo, fortissimo, even in the quiet passages, which I know is against your instincts, but is necessary, and can be the difference between a concert and recording pianist, so they tell me. Anyway, good luck.'

Edward shook the outstretched hand, thinking Mr. Pine seemed more nervous than he and wishing he had been told about the 'fortissimo' requirement before he'd practised so diligently at Mrs. Blundell's. He looked up to the balcony to see Evelyn and Catherine wave encouragement. Evelyn mouthed, 'Good luck,' and he smiled back, but he didn't need luck, he was the 'Lucky Lieutenant' wasn't he?

By eleven thirty all five short pieces had been recorded. Edward was pleased with Grieg's *Papillion* and Rachmaninoff's *Prelude in C sharp minor* but felt there were errors in the other pieces. The Municipal Orchestra's pianist came up to him afterwards and was complimentary, so he supposed it must have been acceptable despite the problems of fortissimo, fortissimo, fortissimo. He was disappointed there was no opportunity to hear the recordings but the technicians had much to do, changing the horns' positions for the orchestra. William led him away, meeting Catherine and Evelyn on the promenade and inviting both of them down to The Compass that evening – Georgette would be singing. But Evelyn was anxious to return to the tea shop and did not expect to be going out later. On Tuesday she had handed in her notice to The Winter Gardens. Alice had not been well and needed far more rest; fortunately Alastair had reduced the length of his morning walks. Catherine also doubted she would come to The Compass. She would be working, as usual.

Back at Mrs. Blundell's, Edward stopped outside the room Alice was using as a studio. There was temptation to enter and view the picture of Evelyn and Catherine, but it was more than deflected by the fear his own portrait might be uncovered. He went to his room. He was tired from the morning's concentration but satisfied he had played passably and dissolved four tablets of morphine in the last of the brandy he'd brought with him. He downed it in one and took off his mask before lying on his bed to rest.

Evelyn, Margate,
Saturday 25th September 1920

The day after recording at The Winter Gardens, Evelyn was bored. Alastair went out early, Evelyn assumed up to Hodges Bridge, but was back within the hour. He made a tray of tea with two cups and took it to Alice but said barely a word to Evelyn – still, she thought his shorter absence an improvement over the hours he'd previously spent away.

Evelyn took payment from a leaving customer, cleaned the empty tables, again, then sat in the window watching the grey sky. She read, again, the letter she had received from her father that morning. He was planning to return to the parish in Spitalfields two weeks hence. Most of the pickers would have left by then and the mission could be closed down. But he wasn't expecting Evelyn back until after the baby had arrived and Alice was settled. Even then, her father wrote, if she had good reason to stay, or if others needed her, he would understand. She wondered what he might have in mind. It was all well and good if she could help Alice or there was 'other good reason', but she had given notice to The Winter Gardens and her savings wouldn't last long. She looked around the tea shop again. With the summer trade all but finished she supposed Alastair would reduce shop hours, making it even less likely he might pay wages and she would be a burden when it came to food and bills.

It was a pleasant surprise when Edward came in at close to eleven. He sat next to her, at his customary table, interrupting her maudlin thoughts.

'I didn't expect to see you today, first time this week. Tea?' Evelyn asked.

'It's been a busy week, what with moving in to Mrs. Blundell's and the recording and all. Has William been in yet?'

'No, Though that's no surprise. No Edward, no William. Have you two fallen out?'

'A little. He's annoyed I'm taking up your idea and want a break before the next season's work. I can see his point, no contract means no commission for him, but I'm hoping this autumn and winter to complete at least one composition. He's resourceful, he'll get by.'

Evelyn nodded and started to speak but William came in, throwing his hat on the table, 'And a coffee for me please, Evelyn,' as if nothing was different.

From the kitchen Evelyn couldn't be certain but the two men seemed to be getting on all right; there were no cross words, they sat mostly in silence, as they usually had. She took the drinks through, with a plate of biscuits.

'Digestives?' said William, 'on the house?'

'Don't tell Alastair. He's in a better mood these last few days, but not that good. Alice is looking tired and worried though. Not long now before the baby comes.' There were no other customers in the shop and Evelyn sat back at the table. 'How did Georgette get on at The Compass last night?'

'Very well,' said William, 'she just needs her confidence building and I'll get her into theatres. Catherine too, if she wants,' he added with mischief.

'She's good enough,' Evelyn said defensively.

'Perhaps, but would she want to leave Margate? She has deep roots here, seems to me.'

'And what about Georgette then?'

'Nothing to hold her back.'

'Patrick?'

'He's a good lad, he'll fit in wherever. In fact, I'm thinking if Edward can teach him to play a couple of simple tunes on the piano, we'd have a great mother and son act. What d'ya say Edward, when can ...' William was interrupted by a call from the kitchen, a shout of panic from Alastair. He came through into the tea shop,

'Evelyn, you must go to Alice. She is having pains. Two in the last half hour and the last was terrible. She wants to send for that woman ... Sharrock.'

'Of course, if you'd like Mrs. Sharrock we'll ...'

'It's what Alice wants,' interrupted Alastair. 'I don't see why we shouldn't go to hospital. What if she needs chloroform or morphine? Why have the baby at home?'

'Most still do, Alastair,' said Evelyn, 'but I'm sure if Alice has ... difficulties we can take her to the cottage hospital, it's close. I daresay Edward would let us use his motor car. Meantime, if Alice would like Mrs. Sharrock then I understand.' Evelyn had seen her share of childbirth back in Spitalfields and stood, giving her most comforting smile, 'We'd thought there was still a week or two. Ah well, two in half hour is good, but a long way to go. Here, pour a tea,' she gestured to the pot on the table, 'and I'll go and see to Alice. Have a seat.'

Alastair's voice rose in anger, 'Don't patronise me.'

'I'm sorry. I didn't mean ...'

'Perhaps when you've given birth you can presume to lecture me, but that doesn't seem likely, so I'll thank you not to ...'

'Mr. Trenter!' Edward almost shouted and left the table to stand by Evelyn. She could see Edward had other words on his lips but they wouldn't come. She looked at Alastair but couldn't read his face: anger, fear, embarrassment?

'That's going a bit far don't you think old boy?' William said, standing and taking a pace towards Alastair. 'You need to calm down.' There was a threat in his voice and Alastair started to speak but stopped and let William usher him to sit at the table.

'I'll fetch Mrs. Sharrock,' said Edward.

'Perhaps best I do it.' William said. 'Unless you know her?' he asked Edward, who shook his head.

Evelyn watched the men in slow motion, Alastair's harsh words replaying over the scene, until Edward touched her arm, 'Perhaps you should see to Alice. William will find Mrs. Sharrock, if that's what Alice wants.'

'Yes, of course,' said Evelyn. 'She's one of the Ladies of St. John's and has had eight children. And I believe six of them survived. She'll be a good person to have here.'

'Then William can go to Mrs. Blundell's, no doubt she'll know where to find Mrs. Sharrock,' said Edward.

'For a finder's fee. Oh, and I assume this puts paid to the Whitstable trip you wanted this afternoon,' William said, then sipped a couple of times from his coffee.

Edward nodded to William, 'Another time,' then to Evelyn, 'come.'

Evelyn let him guide her out to the kitchen where he told her, 'Mrs. Trenter is very lucky to have you here. Alastair is an ass and can be ignored for the moment. If we need to take Alice to hospital we will.'

Evelyn nodded, trying to stifle a tear, though whether caused simply by the shock of Alastair's outburst or the possible truth of it, she couldn't say. A cry from upstairs returned her to the now and she left Edward in the kitchen.

The next few hours were no surprise to Evelyn. As a reverend's daughter in Spitalfields she had often been called to comfort a mother–to–be in the early stages of birth or waited downstairs with the husband when birth was near and one or more of the older mothers from the tenements would attend. Then, with the newborn's first cries, she'd boil water and gather rags and mops for cleaning. She was no stranger to the realities of childbirth; no stranger to the pain, deformities and fatalities, mother or child, that might come with birth. Of course she knew of many successful deliveries, but also understood the risks. She was worried for Alice, but would not show it and though she could excuse Alastair's tense disposition she could not forgive his accusation; it kept returning to her. She couldn't remember the first birth she attended but supposed it was after her mother had died and was no longer around to carry out the duties of a reverend's wife; if, indeed, it was a duty. If she were daughter of a reverend to a wealthy parish in Berkshire or Surrey would it still be expected? Perhaps it was simply what her mother would have done anyway, and now, sitting next to Alice's bed, offering words of encouragement but little practical comfort during the infrequent contractions, she wished her mother was here.

At around mid–day Alice dozed and Evelyn went to her room for her copy of *Great Expectations*. On the way she heard the tea shop door open and the voices of William and a woman she assumed to be Mrs. Sharrock. Evelyn joined them, welcoming Mrs. Sharrock and leading her upstairs. Alastair went to the front door and turned the sign to show closed. There was little conversation and Alastair's agitation was almost an irritation. Within half an hour William had finished his tea, scribbled some notes in his pocketbook and declared he was bored. He left to take Patrick up to the jetty to watch the steamers. There was a scream from upstairs and Evelyn saw Alastair flinch.

Alice's contractions came more frequently as the afternoon wore on. Evelyn saw Alastair's anxiety and Edward's discomfort increase with each cry of pain.

Come late afternoon Edward took a wander around the tea shop, looking at the pictures. Evelyn watched. He turned back to the table, his right hand eyebrow cocked in self–

questioning, and called across the shop, 'Mr. Trenter. I see now how close you and Mrs. Trenter are in style. It's remarkable, not that I claim any expertise in art. But your sunrises here are almost identical to one I saw on Thursday, at Mrs. Blundell's, that Alice painted.'

Alastair looked up from his lap, eyes wide with anger and brushed past Edward and out to the kitchen without speaking.

'Oh,' said Edward, 'that was the wrong thing to say. I thought by now he would know of the portraits.'

'He does, or at least the one of Catherine and me, since you mentioned it on the clifftop that day. Though he's never been happy about it.' Evelyn went to stand by Edward.

'I'm sorry, I should have thought.'

'But it's probably not that so much as ... these.' She indicated to the walls. 'They were painted by Alice. I don't think Alastair has painted for some time. Since ...' Evelyn pointed to the dark, foreboding picture of the sinking ship.

'The sunrises aren't all Alastair's?' Edward went to the picture of the sinking ship.

Evelyn shook her head, watching Edward's face, watching his good eye and mouth, and there was a flicker of understanding, then amusement until it matched the left eye's coldness. With no warning and a sharp, sudden movement Edward ripped the sinking ship from the wall. It crashed to a table and then to the floor. The violence in the action was shocking and Evelyn took a step back, in fear. Edward looked to her. She saw the tense rage in his body dissipate as he looked away, shamed, and pulled a white note from his wallet. He dropped it on the nearest table before taking up the now damaged picture and making for the door, turning to say, 'Tell Trenter if he needs somewhere to look for his son he should look to Alice's hope, up here on the walls.'

Evelyn cleared up the mess from the bowl of sugar knocked to the floor and sat for a while to look at the new space on the wall. She was ashamed for being fearful of Edward's anger and wanted to go after him, but couldn't with Alice upstairs, and anyway, oddly, she now felt some anger at Edward for leaving her here. She wondered what Catherine might do in such circumstances, decided she'd light a cigarette and shrug her shoulders, but Evelyn didn't smoke, so she went upstairs to see if Mrs. Sharrock needed a break.

Mrs. Sharrock came and went three times during the evening. Evelyn rarely left Alice's side and Alastair hovered close by, not knowing how to be of best use. Evelyn gave him the five pounds Edward had left for the ship painting, without telling him of Edward's anger – Alastair had enough of his own when he saw the empty space on the wall.

When it came to the last hour and the final delivery Mrs. Sharrock was remarkable with her calm instruction and confident handling while Evelyn hoped her own gentle encouragement played a part. Alice was adamant the hospital was not necessary. It had occurred to Evelyn that Edward had access to morphine, but it might be difficult to explain and, besides, how would they know the right dose. At just gone eleven, after some twelve hours of labour, Evelyn watched Isabella come safely into the world. With thanks to God she cried with Alice at the wonder.

Evelyn took paper and pen down to the shop, to write to her father in time for the next day's post. She was tired but began writing though the light from the street lamp was poor. She stood to go back to the kitchen for a candle when the sharp rap on the door startled her. She recognised Catherine's silhouette.

'I know it's late but when I came home from work

Aunt Beatrice insisted I come round to find out what's happening. Of course I wasn't going to bother, I mean who wants to see a new born baby,' she smiled, 'if indeed there is one yet?'

'Isabella, nearly an hour ago.'

'Hmmm, the name's a little old fashioned?'

'After Alastair's mother.'

'And mother and baby doing well, as they say?'

'Very well, though we're not sure about father.' There was a croak in Evelyn's voice.

'Perhaps I'll not pop up tonight then,' said Catherine.

Evelyn nodded. 'Best not. It's been a … difficult day … for all,' she said, trying not to cry again but Alastair's comments on Evelyn not being a mother and his criticism of Edward taking the painting were fresh. She wondered if she should tell Catherine but it seemed Catherine didn't need to know as she hugged her tightly.

Evelyn, Margate,
Thursday 30th September 1920

Evelyn spent most of her days following Isabella's birth serving in the tea shop. Alastair remained upstairs with Alice and the baby. This wasn't what she had anticipated when agreeing to be of help. At odd times during the day Alastair would come down and suggest she spend half an hour upstairs while he manned the shop and these were precious times. Isabella was a beautiful baby, of course, but also good–natured and fed well. Alice was a natural mother and the lessons learned with Curtis, all those years ago, came back to her easily. On occasion Alice even compared Isabella to Curtis as a new born and with as much pride in both as sorrow that Curtis was not there.

In the evenings the three of them ate together but when it came time to put Isabella down for the night, or at least a couple of hours until the next feed, Alastair would insist Alice take over; Evelyn found herself an outsider. She began retreating to her own bedroom earlier and earlier, sometimes considering going out – perhaps to see Catherine and Edward or even William and Georgette if they were down The Compass – but didn't want to be away in case Alice needed her. She wrote another letter to her father which offered no real insight into events other than to confirm all was well, and finished *Great Expectations*, but by Thursday was wondering about the coming weeks. When she was with Alice she thought they'd found a new bond, perhaps in part because of her role in the confinement. But at other times she felt an intruder and Alastair's pointed criticism of her for letting

329

Edward take the ship painting was hurtful. The late September air was chilly in the evenings and Margate's summer excitement was fading with the sombre autumn.

Mid–morning Thursday, with only two customers in the shop, Alastair returned from a short trip for provisions accompanied by Beatrice and Catherine. It appeared to Evelyn that Alastair wasn't listening, but that didn't dissuade Beatrice who was explaining, '... and Mrs. Sharrock said Isabella is as beautiful a baby as she'd ever seen, apart from her own, but then, of course, any mother would say that, though to be honest, having seen her children I'm not sure her standards are particularly high, but I'm sure Isabella is a gorgeous little thing and Catherine and I are desperate to meet her. It's been nearly a week. So we thought we'd pop by and you could ask Alice if she and Isabella are ready to receive?' Beatrice made the last statement a question.

'I'll see,' said Alastair, handing the bread and sugar to Evelyn. While they waited Catherine showed Evelyn the shawl she had crocheted.

Alastair returned to invite Beatrice and Catherine upstairs but within twenty minutes they were back in the tea shop, gushing about Isabella. Beatrice interrupted her own monologue, on why a second cousin twice removed had, quite rightly, refused to name her baby Isabella despite her husband's wishes, on the basis he had a previously failed engagement with a young woman of that same name, when she realised Evelyn was now on her own; the customers having left. 'I suppose it's to be expected.' She looked around. 'I detest this time of year, when the guest house is all but empty. Thank goodness Mr. Thompson is with us, though I confess I hadn't realised the composing would be quite as time consuming, or repetitive. He's a persistent young man. Still, a small price to pay for a little culture. And perhaps when it's a famous piece of music we may find a little credit passed our way. The history books may show two of Margate's most lovely young women were the inspiration.' Beatrice indicated to Evelyn and Catherine.

'And the irrepressible, sophisticated Mrs. Blundell,' said Evelyn.

'Yes, why not?' Beatrice said laughing. 'And why haven't we seen so much of you this last week? I know babies are demanding but Mr. Trenter is here too, though not appreciably excited. Still, perhaps that's just his way.'

'Perhaps,' said Evelyn. 'Actually, it's not been as busy as I'd hoped. Most of the day I'm here,' she gestured to the shop, 'and at night, between Alastair and Alice there's not much left for me to do. I just feel I need …'

'… to be here for Mrs. Trenter. Of course dear. But do you need to be here for the nights? And it seems to me, though you must say otherwise if you disagree, Mr. Trenter is not the most welcoming of hosts.'

Evelyn didn't reply.

'I know,' said Catherine, 'I should take you out this afternoon, it's early closing.'

Beatrice nodded as she passed Evelyn on the way through to the back of the shop, saying, 'Good idea and I'll tell Mr. Trenter I'll spend an hour with Alice this afternoon myself so he too can take a break. Oh, and there's a room for you at ours any time you need a break,'

'There's no use refusing, pop upstairs and change,' urged Catherine, 'I'll stay here just in case there's a last minute customer.'

'So, what shall we do?' Catherine took Evelyn's arm as they left the shop. 'We should visit the Shell Grotto, you haven't seen it and it's just a shilling. It's only ten minutes on and will get us out of the rain that'll soon be here.' Catherine nodded up to the grey sky.

Evelyn hesitated, a shilling was still a shilling, but Catherine's enthusiasm was hard to deny and they were there before she could think of good reason not to.

331

They turned into Grotto Hill. The entrance to the Grotto was on the right, a small building marked with a sign proclaiming the mystical wonder of over four million shells. Evelyn joked that counting them must have been the worst job in the world. Just inside the door she could see a turnstile and then a further entrance with darkness beyond.

'Beyond that inner door there are a few steps down into the grotto. It's amazing, I think, and no one knows how they got there, or why.' Catherine said, leading the way. But before they entered a man came running out, clumsily as he was holding his face, blood on his chin and spattered on his shirt. Evelyn screamed. He stumbled, pushing Evelyn to the ground, before finding a fence to lean against, bent half–double and spitting blood.

Catherine helped Evelyn stand and she limped to the side of the road, initially more embarrassed than hurt, though her ankle was soon painful. She brushed down her coat, trying to calm her shaking hands, but her legs buckled. Catherine put an arm around her waist struggling to keep her upright and eased her down to sit on a low brick wall in front of a house. Evelyn put her head low, taking deep breaths, while Catherine started to berate the bleeding man. It must be a comical scene, thought Evelyn, a man and a woman injured and an angry woman between them, and, though she knew it was ridiculous, felt suddenly ashamed perhaps a bystander might think she was the cause of the violence. Her ears were ringing and she wondered if she'd hit her head on falling but felt no pain there. She called to Catherine and steadied herself with more deep breaths before standing uneasily.

It started to rain. Catherine came to her and though Evelyn couldn't make out the words, the shock and worry in Catherine's face was clear. Over Catherine's shoulder Evelyn could see the bleeding man slump to the ground. Then a woman came and bent down to the man, shouting, almost screaming, with anger. Catherine turned at the noise and she and Evelyn looked on as the woman lashed out with an open palm, striking the back of the bleeding man's head. The man cried out and the woman stood back, satisfied. It was Georgette.

Evelyn heard a deep voice calling Georgette's name. Before she could place it she saw the caller: William – he emerged from the Shell Grotto's entrance with Patrick alongside, holding hands.

'Georgie girl! I think he's had enough. We should leave. I think the ticket man is telephoning the constable,' said William.

Georgette took a last look at the bleeding man and seemed to hesitate but was distracted by Patrick calling, 'Maman.'

Both Georgette and William saw Catherine and Evelyn. Georgette was still but William came over, his usual grin implying nothing amiss, 'Good afternoon ladies. Not a good one for a stroll though. How are you both?'

Evelyn pulled away from Catherine to stand tall, composing herself to ask, 'What on earth's going on?' while Catherine turned to Georgette, saying,

'And what do you think you're doing, in front of Patrick?'

'What?' William said, feigning innocence. 'Just a minor disagreement eh, old chap.' He put on his exaggerated posh accent, indicating towards the bleeding man. 'Still we should go. Good day ladies.' William tipped an imaginary hat and went to walk away, ushering Georgette and Patrick, but when a few yards down the road he was stopped by the bleeding man's indistinct call,

'... still a bastard, nothing changes that ...'

Evelyn held her breath as William took half a turn, then forced a laugh and left.

Rain started. Evelyn tried to take a step towards the bleeding man but the sharp stabbing in her ankle made her gasp. Catherine went to help her but she nodded towards the bleeding man, 'Is he all right?'

The bleeding man looked up, still trying to stem the scarlet dripping from his nose and mouth. Catherine asked if he needed help but he ignored her, managed to stand up and shuffled away.

'We should get you home,' said Catherine. Evelyn nodded, taking Catherine's arm and leaning into her to keep the weight from her ankle.

Evelyn hobbled up the stairs to Beatrice's guest house with Catherine's help. As they pushed through the heavy front door and into the polished hallway they heard fragments of music – Edward was composing. The women were wet and cold from the rain and Evelyn was desperate to sit and examine her ankle. Catherine knocked on the drawing room door and they went in without waiting for an answer. Edward was sitting at the piano, facing away from the room, alternately playing a few notes then either scribbling on a notepad on the piano's lid or jotting notes on the musical score in front of him. The stuffed ferret watched. Catherine called Edward's name but he didn't hear, engrossed in his music. Evelyn let herself down in the armchair and the movement, just to his right, caught his attention.

'I'm sorry Edward, we don't mean to disturb but ...'

'We've had a bit of a mishap.' Catherine finished the sentence and took Edward's silence as a request to continue, telling the events at the Shell Grotto.

As she finished, Edward apologised, 'I'm sorry I wasn't there. We had planned to go to Whitstable today, but then Georgette decided to take Patrick to the Grotto. William asked if I wanted to join them but I need to work, though I've not achieved a great deal and perhaps some air would have been a better idea.' He rubbed his right temple and Evelyn saw him flinch, in pain. 'And you think William hit the man?'

'I've no doubt,' said Catherine,

'And, for good measure, Georgette slapped him,' added Evelyn then winced as she moved in her chair and her ankle hurt.

'You sit there, I'll get a cold towel to use as a compress.' Catherine said, leaving the room.

'I'm sorry we've interrupted.' Evelyn said, trying to find a comfortable position for her ankle.

'That's all right. That looks painful. It may already be swelling.'

Evelyn looked down at her leg. Her dress came down to mid–calf and her ankles were exposed. It was the fashion and quite usual, except knowing a man was explicitly looking was not usual, at least for her. 'How is your work coming along?'

'In truth I'm not getting much done today, my head is … not good this morning.'

'Is it … moving? The shrapnel, I mean.'

'Maybe. I don't know, nor do the doctors. They have fantastic machines now, they take pictures of the inside, so they know something's still in there. But is it moving about? I don't know, perhaps it just feels that way. It's probably imagination.'

'Have you taken … anything to help with the pain?'

Edward hesitated before replying, 'Only my usual tablets, the soluble morphine'

'Not the morphia solution injection?'

'Not yet. Too much would … cloud my thoughts and my fingers and I must work on this.' He gestured back to the piano.

'Must?'

Edward shrugged. 'But speaking of pain, your ankle hurts. Would you want to try … a tablet or two?'

Evelyn was suddenly ashamed to have her turned ankle compared to anything Edward was suffering, but before she could respond Catherine was back in the room. She had a small bowl of cold water and a flannelette cloth, telling Evelyn to 'take off her shoes.' She dipped the cloth in the water and held it to Evelyn's ankle. Evelyn flinched at the sharp pain and coldness but welcomed the relief that followed as the cold water numbed the area. Catherine knelt and pressed the cloth around the reddening skin, offering more comfort with, 'And Cook will be in with cocoa.'

'You need to speak to William,' Evelyn said to Edward. 'He needs to curb his temper, don't you think?'

'I'll find out more about what happened. He may have been provoked.'

'Hmmm, well I suspect he didn't need much provocation, and as for Georgette, and in front of Patrick too,' said Catherine, but before she could say more the doorbell rang. Evelyn took over pressing the wet towel to her ankle while Catherine went to the hall. She was back in seconds, 'Edward, it's Georgette, asking for you. William's been arrested.'

Catherine showed Georgette and Patrick into the room as Cook brought the cocoa. Neither visitor wore a coat. They were soaked through; the rain had worsened. Evelyn stopped pressing the towel on her ankle to sit upright. Georgette looked around the room, holding Patrick's hand, but Evelyn thought her not cowed in any way.

'I understand there's been a disturbance,' Edward said, breaking the silence.

'Will asked me to come here. He wants you to see him, at the police station.'

'Why?'

'I don't know. To … speak for him?'

'He's been arrested?'

'I suppose.'

'What for?'

'A man insulted me and Patrick. Will didn't care for it.'

'And?'

'Will put him straight.'

'I can imagine.'

'It wasn't for me. It's not right for Patrick to hear what the man said.'

'But it's all right for him to see William beat someone? Not to mention seeing you slap someone's head?' Evelyn asked. Georgette's face flashed with anger and she started to respond but caught herself and addressed Edward,

'William stood for me, as a friend should, and now he's asked if you'll go down the station, as a friend should.' Georgette started to cry.

Edward stood from the piano and went to the bay window, watching the rain trickling down the glass. Evelyn struggled to stand and hobbled to his side, whispering, 'I know you and William have fallen out a little, but look who he turns to when in trouble?'

Edward shrugged and rubbed his temple.

'Are you well enough to go to the station? Shall I come?' Evelyn asked.

Edward looked at her ankle, then into her face. She saw his good eye was bloodshot – a sign of whatever caused him such pain?

'No, I'll not be long and if I've not returned by tea time ask Beatrice to come and find me. I expect she'll carry more sway with the sergeant than anyone.' He tried to make a joke and left.

'I'm sorry about your foot,' said Georgette as Evelyn limped back to the armchair. There was an awkward silence, broken by Patrick coughing. Catherine went to him,

'In any event we should get you out of these clothes. Come with me, we'll find something upstairs that will fit. You too Georgette, you'll catch your death.'

'Thank you. William will be grateful too,' said Georgette and Evelyn thought it genuine but couldn't be sure.

Catherine took Patrick's hand, 'Well William can

337

make it up with another driving lesson,' and led them upstairs.

Evelyn's injury was sore but not so painful that she suspected any real damage. While Catherine was looking after Georgette and Patrick she soaked the towel in cold water again, squeezed it out over the bowl as best she could and draped it over her ankle. Cook came back in with an extra two cocoas, noted Edward was no longer there and tutted at the waste of his untouched mug.

The others were soon back down, Georgette in one of Catherine's dresses and Patrick wrapped in the smallest dressing gown Catherine could find, an old one of Beatrice's, though it still swamped him. Catherine rolled up the sleeves for him and sat him on the settee in the window bay to give him his mug of cocoa. Georgette stood by the mantelpiece while Catherine pulled a deck of cards from a drawer in the side table and asked Patrick if he knew how to play 'snap'. He turned away from the stuffed ferret, nodding and Catherine dealt the cards.

Evelyn looked at Georgette and could see she had been crying. She indicated to Georgette she should come and sit in the chair next to her.

'Do you want to tell me more about what happened?' Evelyn asked.

'You are a reverend's daughter, aren't you?' Georgette said, with just a hint of smile. Evelyn looked at her. Georgette was a pretty woman with even features, straight teeth and slim figure. She could see why William seemed taken with her.

Evelyn shrugged. 'We all have a cross to bear.' She smiled back.

'I am sorry about your foot.'

'Never mind. I'm more interested to hear why a grown man was running from you.'

'William, not me. I've never seen him angry like

that. I know I was angry too and should not have hit him, at least not in front of Patrick. But William was … beside himself with rage.'

'Frightening?'

'Yes, but the man should not have said as he did.'

'I can't imagine what he could say to make William so furious.' Evelyn said, though it did occur to her it might be nice to have a man fight for you, even so literally.

'The man knew Patrick's father. They were in the same regiment and they were together when I met Patrick.'

Evelyn looked confused.

'Patrick's father was with the Royal West Kent, Lord knows why. He was as Irish as they can be, but such a handsome man, with such a way. And why he came here on leave, in late thirteen, I'll never know. But I'm glad he did, though he didn't stay long, just long enough to …' she looked over to young Patrick, 'then he was back to France.'

'And?'

'Didn't come back. He died at Mons, in the summer of fourteen, though I never found out until October, when I wrote to his family.'

'I'm sorry. We thought you met him in France.'

'No, I was working for a family here when the war started. Teaching French to the children. Until I … met Patrick. And of course it is sad, but I don't suppose I can say I knew him. Perhaps I'm more sad for the life I'm imagining we might have had. Oh, and for Patrick never meeting him.'

Evelyn started to ask if she meant the old or young Patrick, but of course, that was irrelevant. Instead she asked, 'But you receive a widow's pension?'

Georgette laughed sarcastically, 'You know I'd almost forgotten Patrick and I weren't married, until that stupid man turned up today, and reminded everyone. I don't think Patrick understood the names I was being called, but one day he will and the names they'll call him if they find out.'

'Who?'

'Everyone. So forgive me if I'm not offended by William's actions today. He's better than most.' Georgette's eyes were wet with tears.

Edward returned mid–afternoon with William behind joking he'd, '… been surprised until afterwards, when Constable Simms confessed to being his regimental heavyweight boxing champion back in fourteen,' with reference to the purple swelling closing his left eye.

'And now you know a bit of what it's like to only see through one eye,' added Edward, more thoughtfully than humorously.

In the drawing room Patrick was fascinated to see William's injuries, enough to take him away from the jigsaw puzzle Catherine was helping him with – a picture of a British destroyer hunting down a U–Boat. Georgette was less impressed by the wounds. As well as the bruised cheek and eye socket William's right arm was in a makeshift sling, the result of breaking a couple of fingers on Constable Simms' truncheon. Georgette began railing against Constable Simms but William calmed her with a shrug, saying, 'I should have gone easily, but better a beating than bail and a court hearing.'

William apologised to Edward for not taking him to Whitstable that day and promised they'd go soon, then took Georgette and Patrick back to their guest house.

Evelyn sat next to Catherine on the settee, toying with the jigsaw pieces, placing none of them and saying little until Beatrice came back from the tea shop and Catherine had to relay the day's events. Beatrice wasn't surprised Georgette hadn't married Patrick's father – at least one of the ladies at St. John's knew Georgette's mistress – but as she said,

'Bad wars make for bad choices so perhaps in good times we should practise some charity.'

Evelyn wondered if this implied there was such a thing as a good war.

Edward excused himself, going up to his room, and Evelyn thought his good eye more bloodshot than earlier. She started to ask as he went from the room but he stopped her when half out the door with a gesture to his head. She gave what comfort she could with a nod.

'And I think I'll ask Cook to make a cake, for Isabella and Alice. She's such a beautiful little thing, Isabella, I mean, not Alice, though of course she is lovely too and can be so proud of herself, don't you think?' Beatrice said as she left the room without waiting for an answer.

'Well, what a day, I'm quite exhausted. How's your ankle?' Catherine asked, pouring two glasses of sherry.

'Not so bad thanks but yes, what a day.'

'Do you think Edward will speak to William about his temper?'

'I expect so, though he was defending Georgette …'

'And she, in a way, was protecting Patrick,' said Catherine.

'It doesn't do to insult a child when the mother can hear …'

'And as an unmarried mother I expect Georgette has not had an easy time raising Patrick, though I don't always see her as maternal.'

'Yes, it's a hard life for an unmarried mother,' Evelyn said.

'Though Aunt Beatrice coped, and well,' said Catherine.

'I expect you were a model child,' Evelyn teased. 'Why did Beatrice have no children of her own?'

Catherine hesitated before saying, 'She has hinted, in the past, of losing a child when she was much younger, but speaks of it rarely, the only subject in the world on which she won't readily talk, so I haven't pressed the matter. Perhaps one day.'

'How awful for her … but then she did have you, from a young age.'

Catherine nodded and looked serious. 'Would you be sad if you never had children?'

'I expect so, but I don't think about it much. It's not easy to find the right husband.'

'But easy enough to find a father, I expect,' said Catherine.

They shared an uncomfortable silence and then Evelyn picked the book from the table at her side: *The Rainbow*. 'Are you reading this?' she asked.

'Yes, I'll lend you it soon as I finish. I'm nearly done.'

'I thought that was banned?'

'It is, but our American guest sent it over. You can buy it over there.'

'And you still claim there was nothing between you and him. He just enjoys sending you presents.'

'Nothing, honestly. And I'd tell you if there was. He's just a good writing friend. Last week Aunt Beatrice received a selection of gramophone records, the latest jazz recordings, but some were cracked during the journey. Edward was more upset than Beatrice, to tell the truth.'

'Hmmm,' Evelyn said. 'Well I think *The Rainbow* is an … interesting choice of present for a man to send a lady. I've heard a little about it.'

'It's not that shocking, and certainly no more so than those postcards Georgette showed us.'

Evelyn raised her hand to her mouth as she remembered some of the images. 'I wonder if William realised they were missing. He'd be angry at Georgette,' she said, almost as a way of changing the subject.

'Oh I'm sure a man like William would miss them. As for being angry at Georgette? I'm not sure. They seem quite close these days, though that didn't stop him being a little … familiar … with me, a few days ago.'

'What do you mean?'

'When he came to find Beatrice and ask after Mrs. Sharrock, as I showed him to the door he was, it's hard to explain, just a little too familiar in the way he thanked me, and asked if he might buy me a drink down The Compass one evening.'

'Innocent enough?' Evelyn made it a question.

Catherine raised an eyebrow theatrically.

'You're right,' said Evelyn, 'innocent isn't a word to describe him. So you be careful. Mind you, it is nice to be asked,' and she laughed.

'True. And though he's not my type, he can be fun and he's teaching me to drive. Sometimes Edward is a little serious, don't you find?'

Evelyn thought about Edward's use of morphine. 'Sometimes he has a great deal of pain still.'

'I suppose, but he can be a little, obsessive, like with this Herne Bay and Whitstable search thing. Who's it for?'

'The parents of one of his men. Kayst, I believe.'

'Well it seems a bit odd to me.' There was criticism in Catherine's tone.

'It's because he … he …' Evelyn stumbled for words, '… you shouldn't be harsh. He's … Edward,' said Evelyn.

'I don't know what that means, but I'm sorry,' said Catherine.

As it was nearly five p.m. Evelyn said her goodbyes and went back to the tea shop, borrowing one of Cook's walking sticks. She was looking forward to seeing Isabella and Alice, surprised at how even such a short time away was time enough to miss the baby. The front door to the shop was locked, Evelyn went round to the back alley and in through the yard. Alastair was sitting at the back of the kitchen, reading a newspaper. He looked up as Evelyn came through. She asked how the day had been but Alastair was non–committal and didn't ask about the stick she was using to keep weight off her sore ankle. Before she could go upstairs to see Alice, he asked,

'Did you think a fiver was all the painting was worth?'

'I'm sorry?'

'I've been thinking about it, the painting your Mr. Thompson paid five pounds for? Did you, did he, think that's all it was worth?'

Evelyn paused at the door to the upstairs, trying to connect with Alastair's words, 'Ah, the sinking ship?'

Evelyn had given the money to Alastair explaining only that Edward had wanted the painting. At the time Alastair had been indifferent, though of course Isabella had only just been born.

'A fiver?' Alastair repeated.

'I thought that was about the right price, I didn't know. I'm sure Edward would pay more if you want.' Evelyn remembered Edward's mood on learning about the paintings.

'I don't want money.' Alastair said, going through to the tea shop and standing at the space on the wall where the picture had hung. 'I need to make sure we never forget. Are you so stupid you don't know that yet?'

Evelyn was still in the kitchen and the anger in his voice made her fear – it was an anger which had been building since Isabella's birth.

The rain had stopped, the sky had cleared and it was a pleasant late September evening when Evelyn climbed the stairs to Beatrice's guest house awkwardly, stick in one hand, bags in the other. The door was locked. Evelyn rang the bell. Catherine came to answer the door and there was no hesitation in her welcome or insistence that she stay.

Edward, Margate, Friday 1st October 1920

Edward had never known settled home life as an adult. As a child, in Lincoln, he had a charmed upbringing – at least, when he allowed himself to look back, it now seemed that way – as long as he didn't dwell on his younger brother's death, back in 1905. Even after – soon after – James succumbed to typhoid, the house ran smoothly. His father's work hours were regular, as was the decent income from his office as a solicitor, and his mother's love and attention was not always constrained by the mores of the day. He had enjoyed being a day boarder at school and summer holidays were long and easy. Cricket without James was not so much fun, but a sister, Amelia, could often be persuaded to stand in, though she was no bowler. The hired help gave his mother no reason to complain and his father never hit him, even when he shut Plum the dog in the larder and Plum discovered the biscuit barrel. Edward had been addicted to his piano lessons and loved Mrs. Harding, his teacher, but when he moved on to Mr. Price understood that it was right; Mr. Price was far more demanding but better able to help him realise his potential.

Then, when he won a place at the Royal College of Music, there was no pressure to follow in his father's footsteps and his family could afford to send him. Though the College wasn't home there was some routine and a purpose. He was there for two happy years before the war started and he joined the Royal Fusiliers, London Regiment, assuming his father would be proud, though he couldn't say for sure. In the army he found a different type

345

of routine and purpose, though it never felt the right place for him and he always thought himself an outsider. But he received more friendship than he felt able to give and it was for that he was grateful and owed them, all of them. After the war, in the hospitals and convalescent homes, there was a different, even deeper, camaraderie and the most rigorous of routines, none of it domestic, all designed to control and heal. And now, here in Beatrice's house, he was cossetted by a domesticity he considered undeserved and which seemed to place an obligation on him, though he couldn't quite grasp what it was.

He had been at Mrs. Blundell's nearly two weeks when the Friday for his last performance at The Winter Gardens was due. As usual he had arrived early and Mr. Taylor asked him into the office where he presented Edward with a bottle of Hennessy. It was a sincere, if not sentimental, presentation during which Mr. Taylor found a way to criticise Edward's missed performances due to occasional ill–health as well as praise his talent. He was complimentary about Edward's performance on the day of the recording, a view he gained when subsequent recordings by the Municipal Orchestra had been less successful due to mistakes. Mr. Taylor then invited Edward back for a longer season in the new year and even hinted he might consider taking over as Edward's manager if Mr. Burrslow should be found wanting. Edward thanked him for the Cognac and was non–committal on all other topics; he doubted he'd be back the following summer but it was too early to rule out anything. Despite the row between William and Edward, William had been looking for new contracts for Edward in the spring, having accepted Edward's need to spend the autumn and winter composing in Margate – though why it had to be Margate was a question William raised at every opportunity.

Evelyn, now staying in Beatrice's guest house, went to watch Edward's last performance at The Winter Gardens, sneaking in without paying, thanks to caretaker

Bill. It was, she said, his finest yet and he thanked her for the kindness, though he knew he was merely satisfactory. Though not a full house the audience was appreciative and some of the musicians in the Municipal Orchestra, whom he'd come to know a little in the dressing room, said they'd be sorry to see him go. And that was as good a recommendation as he could want. Afterwards he walked home with Evelyn and Catherine, and the cold wind from the sea whistled with low melancholy. Evelyn limped with the pain from her ankle injury, sustained outside the Shell Grotto just the day before.

'I wrote to my father today,' Evelyn said, and Edward thought it was for the sake of something to say. 'I needed to tell him the change of address.'

'Did you tell him why?' asked Catherine.

'No. Father and Alastair are such old friends and I wouldn't want that to suffer on my account. Besides, I'm still working in the tea shop during the day and seeing Alice and Isabella as much as I can. It's only the nights when Alastair doesn't want me there.'

'Though the tea shop will close for the winter soon, won't it?' Edward asked, 'What will you do then?'

Evelyn shrugged. Catherine took her arm, trying to help Evelyn's limp, saying, 'I'm sure Aunt Beatrice will keep you busy. She's thinking of buying another guest house or perhaps a hotel and I might give up work at The Winter Gardens to run it. I'm bound to need help.'

'Won't that be expensive? Has Mrs. Blundell the money?' Evelyn asked.

'My aunt is loaded. Her husband was a rich man and she fought tooth and nail when his cousins came out of the closet looking for their share. I wouldn't bet against Beatrice in an argument. As well as the guest house, laundry and grocers there's a pile of cash in the bank and some stocks in American companies which I think are doing all right. At least so our American guest assures us in his letters.'

'The same American gentleman who sent over your copy of *The Rainbow*?' teased Evelyn.

'All entirely innocent.'

'So you keep saying.'

'I'm not sure I see you as a mistress of a guest house.' Edward said.

'I think Catherine would be marvellous,' Evelyn offered.

'It's just that, well, most of the landladies I've come across, and that's quite a few on my travels, have been .a bit more ... formidable, physically,' said Edward, then more tentatively, '... your aunt is an exception and you are much like her.'

'Well I shall take that as a compliment,' said Catherine, 'and we'll give you a discount on a top floor room.'

'Will it have a baby grand? If so, send me the bill now. I'll move in and compose my masterpiece.'

'Not on the top floor, we couldn't get it up there. You may have to settle for the basement.'

'I could live with that. And talking of music, shall we go past The Compass tonight? William has Georgette doing a turn.'

Catherine seemed reluctant but Evelyn said, 'It's on the way', and led them from The Parade towards the pub.

The Compass appeared closed but they could hear the muffled piano and singing as they approached. Edward assumed Ceinwen, the landlady, had arranged another lock–in which meant going to the back door, using the side–alley which was darker than even the ill–lit street. As they turned into the alley they could make out the grey outline of a man pressed up against the wall, all but unseen in the dark. He turned and snarled at them, startling Evelyn and Catherine. They stopped. Edward tensed, not in fear but in readiness, such was the man's manner. But though the man was looking their way he seemed not to see them and as Edward's eye adjusted to the poor light he saw he wasn't pressed up against the wall, but against a woman, her skirts hitched up around her waist and her face to the wall as the man took her roughly from behind. The man grunted something, and the woman, not seeing Edward and the ladies said, 'Oh yes, and again, and again, c'mon, harder, harder … and …'

She stopped talking on hearing Catherine's, 'Oh,' and turned to see her audience. She smiled and shrugged and began rocking back into the man faster. He reacted, matching her rhythm and came in seconds, groaning. Edward took a step forward, to place himself between the scene and the ladies. The woman against the wall continued to look at him and Edward thought he recognised her, but it was a fleeting memory before he turned to usher Evelyn and Catherine back out of the alley.

They stopped outside the pub's closed front doors and Edward apologised. Catherine seemed flustered, but amused, while Evelyn was calm, saying it was '… like a normal Friday night back in Spitalfields, when the men have been paid,' but Edward thought the calmness unnatural. They stood for a few seconds and Edward tried to think of something to say that would put them at ease but had no witty comment.

'I think I've seen that woman before,' he said.

Evelyn's quizzical look made him realise he should explain about the fight between the two women at the hop farm a couple of weeks earlier, but the muffled piano playing stopped and they could hear Georgette's voice from inside the pub as she started to sing, unaccompanied and slow …

'Rock a bye your baby with a Dixie melody,'

'One of William's favourites, by an American,' whispered Edward, though no one in the pub could possibly hear him.

'Al Jolson,' added Catherine, 'Beatrice has a

349

recording at home.'

'Don't tell me, the American guest sent it. The generous American who was nothing but a paying guest,' said Evelyn.

'He enjoyed his stay, and what are you suggesting,' said Catherine, with mock indignation.

They listened without speaking for half a minute or so and Edward nodded, thinking there was something in Georgette's voice, though it was hard to hear properly outside. Catherine started to say something but the man they had seen with the woman came from the alley, turned toward them and stumbled past, oblivious to their presence either earlier or now, nearly blind drunk.

'I wonder where the woman is?' Catherine said, looking at Edward.

'I hope the man paid her. She's probably back in the pub, looking for the next customer,' said Evelyn, 'if she's like the ... ladies back in Spitalfields.'

Edward nodded.

'If my father was here he'd want to go in and see if he can help her,' continued Evelyn.

'Do you think we should? Edward?' Catherine asked him.

'No, I doubt she wants to be saved, and I'm feeling a little tired.' Edward stopped talking and listened to Georgette. The pianist was now accompanying her, Edward assumed it to be Arthur, with a simple arrangement as Georgette sang ...

'Weep no more, my lady,
Sing that song again for me,'

... 'I'm tired too,' said Catherine, perhaps another night,' and she started to walk on, Edward and Evelyn close behind.

Edward, Margate, Tuesday 5th October 1920

Breakfast at Mrs. Blundell's was a more formal meal than at Edward's previous guest house and serving finished a little earlier. Edward settled into a routine of walking to the seafront to buy *The Times* rather than ask for delivery. The weather was turning, there were few holidaymakers left, and the newspaper vendor was accustomed to Edward's mask. The cooler air was refreshing and he sometimes went on to the harbour pier. Though he had been at the resort for two months he'd not spent time watching and listening to the sea, but now, perhaps self–indulgently, he enjoyed sitting at the end of the pier, by the lighthouse, allowing his mind to wander. The low tide left a handful of smacks on the mud, their lopsided leaning so clumsy compared to their grace when afloat. Looking back towards the town he could see the top of Holy Trinity church tower, bringing a dignity and strength to the resort he was only just appreciating. The contrast between the raw sea and wind and the ordered civility onshore was almost a battle between forces of nature and man, a battle to inspire his composing.

Usually, after the morning walk, he'd return to the guest house, Cook would bring him tea and he'd shut himself in the drawing room with the piano. Evelyn would already be at the tea shop and Catherine and Mrs. Blundell would remain absent from the room until lunchtime. In the afternoon he would continue composing and in the evening sit with Evelyn and Mrs. Blundell, playing cards or chatting, especially with Evelyn.

On the Tuesday morning after the last performance at The Winter Gardens, as he stood at the end of the harbour pier, William found him.

'Evelyn said you'd be here. I've just come from the tea shop. It's very quiet.'

Edward nodded, a little irritated his newly acquired morning routine was disturbed.

William's hand was still bandaged and his face marked and bruised following his arrest the previous week. 'You seem a little more, relaxed, these days.'

'Do I?' Edward said, lighting a cigarette and passing the silver case to William, who took one.

'I think so. So does Evelyn.'

'Well, that's good isn't it?'

'What, you're more relaxed or Evelyn thinks so?'

'Both, I suppose.'

'True. Anyway, I thought I'd better make sure we're still on for Thursday.'

'Thursday?'

'We're going to Whitstable, to find that oysterman who might know Kayst's family. Aren't we?'

'Oh, yes, of course.'

'Good, only I can't drive with one hand. This,' he lifted his right hand, 'isn't working proper.'

'So we can't go.'

'Unless someone else drives. I thought Catherine might do it. She's had a few goes and picked it up no trouble.'

'I'll ask her, later,' said Edward.

'Good. Meantime, thought you might like to know I've had a few responses and reckon there'll be no trouble sorting out a booking, come the spring.'

'Good, thank you.'

'And, I've heard from Mr. Taylor that those recordings from The Winter Gardens might make it into HMV's next catalogue, so we can charge a bit more, what with you being a recording artist now.'

'Fame at last eh?'

'At last. Oh, and I also thought you might be interested to know, Tosh is back in town. He turned up a few days ago and has been hanging round The Compass. And he's not alone. The ...'

'... let me guess. The woman from the hop farm is here. The one you were talking to last time we were there and she was in a fight, with another woman.'

'That's the one. Looks like her and Tosh teamed up at the hop farm.'

'I saw her the other night, outside The Compass, plying her trade. That other woman was right, she's definitely a lady of the night.'

'Yep, but a girl's gotta earn a crust somehow and they say she learned her craft in one of your blue–light houses, in France.'

'They were never 'my' blue–light houses.'

'What? Even in Le Havre? You sure you never ...' He let the question hang. Edward didn't rise to the teasing. William continued, 'So, what do you want to do about Tosh?'

'I need to think about it. But if you see him, it wouldn't harm to mention I'm not pleased and he needs to keep himself out of trouble.'

William raised his hand again, 'I'm not in full form, so to speak, but I'm sure I can still ... be persuasive, if you want.'

'No, just a gentle warning while I think of what to do. I might go and see the Reverend Railton first.'

'As you wish.'

'How's Georgette? And Patrick?'

'All right. I think the boy should be going to school but Georgette's too busy to sort it out.'

'Too busy?'

'The landlady at the guest house is a mean old cow. Georgette does everything, though it's a bit better now there's only me and one other paying guest these days. So you're not in her good books.' William chuckled.

'Who, Georgette's?'

'No, the landlady. She's not happy at losing your rent, not happy at all.'

'If only she had a piano. And how's Georgette's singing?'

'All right. She can hold a tune and she's getting better with an audience, if the regulars down The Compass can be called that.'

'Good. I heard her from outside the pub the other night. She sounded much more confident.'

'We'll break the West End yet.'

'And, speaking of The Compass, is your friend Rolf still about?'

'I haven't seen him in weeks. Why?'

Edward hesitated.

'Oh,' William said, 'you haven't run out already? I didn't think your head had been bad lately.'

'No, I've not run out. I've plenty of the solution left and a good few needles. But I've not so many of the tablets.'

'Then you must have been knocking them back.'

Edward didn't respond.

'I'll ask around. See if Rolf's about.' William said, walking away but turning as he remembered, 'Oh, by the way, when I spoke to Evelyn and Alice this morning she said Alice has asked if we can get the portraits, easel and materials from Beatrice's to the tea shop. She wants to finish it off but only has odd moments, looking after Isabella.'

Edward hesitated, wondering if Alice had meant both portraits or just the ladies. As far as he knew, William didn't know about Edward's. Since Isabella's birth Alice had not worked on the paintings and that room was considered out of bounds to all, not even Mrs. Blundell went in. 'Paintings?' Edward asked, stressing the plural.

'Of course. She wants to finish yours as well.'

William said adding, in answer to Edward's silence, 'What? You didn't think I knew about that? Though, to be fair, it was only mentioned this morning. Sounds like a good idea, as long as it can be used for printing posters. So, all along, it was Alice not Alastair. Who'd have guessed?'

Edward shrugged, surprised Alice seemed to have shared what he'd considered to be two confidences. He wondered about Alastair. 'Of course,' Edward said, 'we'll have them sent round.'

William nodded a goodbye and walked back down the harbour pier.

Edward stayed to finish his cigarette.

That afternoon Edward struggled at the piano. He had gone back to the second movement and had the core refrains but couldn't find the right mood in the arrangement and was doubting the choice of key. He wanted to match the feeling he'd had on the clifftop, all those weeks ago, when the music had come to him. But the memory was elusive and he was disturbed by an irritation under his mask, concerned perhaps the sea air of late may have accelerated some corrosion. He heard the front door close, which was also an irritation, and then the knock at the drawing room's door – yet another. He checked his watch before forcing a cheery, 'Come in,' knowing it was likely to be Evelyn back from the tea shop. It was. She entered, still limping slightly, and matched his cheery greeting, and asked how 'it' was going.

'Ponderous today,' said Edward, turning away from the piano.'

'Perhaps you need a break?'

'Perhaps, and, as it happens, I was planning a trip out on Thursday, to Whitstable.'

'Whitstable?' said Evelyn.

'Why not?'

'It's just that, well, you haven't mentioned your

friend Kayst much lately.'

'He was not my friend,' snapped Edward, immediately regretful.

'Oh, of course not, sorry.'

Edward sighed, 'No, I'm sorry. I just meant I never knew him any more than the next man.'

'And yet Whitstable?'

Edward turned back to piano and played a few runs before asking, 'Do you think Catherine would drive to Whitstable? William is still injured but he's confident Catherine can drive. It was his suggestion. He'd come along too, and so would you … I hope.'

'I'll ask her.'

Edward, Margate, Wednesday 6th October 1920

On the Wednesday evening it was Beatrice's turn to host the Ladies of St. John's. When Edward had returned from his morning walk Catherine had caught him, wanting first to confirm she was happy, excited even, to drive over to Whitstable the following day, as long as, of course, William felt she was up to it. And, secondly, as the Ladies of St. John's would be at the house that evening, Beatrice hoped Edward might play for them, not for long, but perhaps a piece or two. Edward, of course, said he was, 'Very happy to.'

'In which case, would you mind accompanying me on a couple of songs? I have taken time off work to help Beatrice this evening,' Catherine asked, as Beatrice came down the stairs, saying,

'Oh yes please, Mr. Thompson. I'd so much like Catherine to provide some entertainment and, after all, she does have a lovely voice, does she not? And, though Mrs. Dunbar won't be there tonight, her father is ill, I believe, though a half bottle of scotch a day will have that effect on you, nevertheless, it would be … nice for it to get back to Mrs. Dunbar that Catherine sang with you, and sang well, which she will, notwithstanding Mrs. Dunbar's own daughter is appearing in the Canterbury Amateur Dramatic production of *Theodore and Co*, in the role of Sapphire, and though she is beautiful, she does not compare with the lovely Julia James, nor, I'm sure you'll agree with our own dear Catherine or Evelyn. Though as you've never seen her you'll have to take my word for it. So is it agreed?'

Edward looked at Catherine who smiled and nodded. Edward said, 'Yes, of course,' unsure of what he'd agreed to.

'You see dear,' Mrs. Blundell spoke to Catherine. 'Now you must excuse me, I need to help Cook in the kitchen. There's much to prepare for the ladies' visit this evening.'

Catherine ushered Edward back into the drawing room, following him in, explaining, 'I'd like to sing three songs. Will that be all right?'

Edward nodded, part bemused, part pleased his inclusion could be so easily contrived, but also part irritated this was a composing day lost. In the drawing room Catherine went to the gramophone and put on one of the records recently received from the American guest, saying, she'd quite like to sing it for the Ladies of St. John's. Edward recognised the song sung in a rich tenor: *Rock A Bye Your Baby*.

'I've written out the words,' Catherine said, showing the paper to Edward, 'but don't have the music.'

She sounded apologetic. Her brown eyes seemed larger and even darker than usual. 'What do you think?' she asked, looking at him. His good eye held hers, something he had become accustomed to with Evelyn but less so with Catherine.

'Please?' said Catherine, 'I think the Ladies of St. John's should hear something a little more … modern, don't you?'

Edward laughed, 'I think you know I couldn't possibly refuse. I'm sure I'll pick it up from the recording your aunt has, though we may have to change the key.'

They spent the rest of the day practising the songs Catherine wanted to sing – *Danny Boy* and *Abide With Me* as well as *Rock A Bye Your Baby* – and Catherine helped Edward choose two piano pieces he should play – some Chopin and, he couldn't resist, some Rachmaninoff, despite Catherine's reservations.

Shortly after dinner, but before the St. John's Ladies began to arrive, Edward excused himself and went to his room. He had a slight headache and, up in his room, used the last of the soluble morphine tablets. His room was on the top floor, with its own bathroom, more modern than at the last guest house. He suspected he occupied the best room but hadn't seen any others, and certainly not Catherine's or Evelyn's. Nor had he returned to the room on the first floor being used for the portraits. Alice had asked for them to be taken to the tea shop but that was yet to be arranged. Passing the door every day on the way to and from the ground floor, he was tempted to look at the portraits, but Evelyn said they'd all promised to resist and he felt bound by her sincerity. He locked his room door, took off his mask, bathed the area beneath that was the source of the growing irritation and sat unmasked for twenty minutes before hearing the first of the St. John's Ladies arrive. He wiped the inside of the mask clean, noting the small pock mark where there was some corrosion, causing the irritation, and dabbed some carbolated Vaseline on the mark. He put the mask back on, straightened it with a reluctant look in the mirror, lit a cigarette, drew heavily and went downstairs.

The evening went well, as far as he could tell, though of course he had little experience of such occasions. As a child his mother had been socially active but, at that age, it was easy to be petted and adored simply for being that age. Here, at Mrs. Blundell's, the St. John Ladies were kind and attentive with no condescension and none indicated any shock at his appearance – though, of course, they were all aware of him by now and he suspected Mrs. Blundell would have been clear in her instructions on how to behave. The drawing room had been extended by pulling back shutters to the back parlour and Mrs. Blundell guided him through the gathering with introductions he couldn't possibly remember and a talent for small talk that removed any pressure to be witty or erudite on his part. A couple of sherries worked with the morphine he'd taken to settle him into a warm and care–forgotten mood. The Ladies of St. John's were lovely, but none more than Evelyn and Catherine who he sought out after a decent spell of circulating. They stood together, in the bay window, behind the settee and both smiled as he approached; smiles of welcome and, he fancied, a little pride. He suppressed any sceptical thoughts at how ill–deserved even a little pride would be.

'It's busy,' Edward said.

'Beatrice is thrilled with the turnout, though of course it's all because of you. You are quite the celebrity and it helps you have such a talent,' said Catherine.

'I think it's more likely they have heard you are going to sing, and that would be enough to swell any crowd,' said Edward, sipping from the glass of scotch Cook had brought him.

'Goodness, listen to you two, your own best audience,' said Evelyn, 'I think it's about time you stopped talking and started entertaining, don't you?'

Edward looked over to Mrs. Blundell, across the room, and caught her eye. He nodded to the piano and Mrs. Blundell looked at the mantelpiece clock before returning the nod.

With no introduction Edward played the Chopin piece, quietly at first while capturing the ladies' attention, and then more loudly, but never to overpower the occasion. Then, without waiting for applause, he played the Rachmaninoff, but always with control. The piano faced the wall and with the left side of his face not facing into the room, he was not distracted. He played well, he thought, then remembered, on finishing, the morphine, sherry and scotch, so probably he had not played so well, just thought he had. But the Ladies seemed pleased, especially Beatrice. Then Catherine sang *Rock A Bye Your Baby*, causing much conversation and, perhaps, a little consternation but Catherine seemed not to care and anyway, her heart–breaking renditions of *Danny Boy* and *Abide With Me* were to guarantee forgiveness for any impetuosity caused by the American song. There were murmured calls to repeat *Danny Boy* and to refuse would have been churlish.

The Ladies had been well entertained and Mrs. Blundell knew they felt so, though the applause was polite. Edward nodded toward Catherine as a sign she had sung well. Mrs. Blundell came to her and wiped unashamedly at a tear as she hugged her niece then laid a gentle hand on Edward's shoulder before turning to mingle with her guests. He stood, to be next to Catherine, saying, 'Your aunt is very proud of you, and rightly so.'

'Thank you.'

'How long have you lived with her?'

'She took me in when I was nine.'

'Your own parents …?' Edward let the question hang.

'Father died when the boat he was working on went down and a year later my mother … left.'

'Oh, I'm sorry, it's none of my business.'

'You're wondering why she left, so did I, for a long time, but not anymore. And Beatrice has been more than good enough to call my mother.'

'Well, your aunt is a remarkable woman,' Edward watched Beatrice move among the Ladies with a smile or a word of encouragement, completely at ease and easing others. 'Perhaps you should.'

'Should what?'

'Call her mother. You're lucky to have each other.'

'We are. And she's shown me what a woman can do, if they've a mind. She married young, to an older man and when he died it would have been easy to find another suitor, but she was left well provided for and her independence was not for sale.'

'All the more reason to call her mother, if she has no children of her own. Would she have had? If her husband was younger?' Edward was aware the question bordered on unacceptably personal, but the tablets and the scotch were still having effect.

'I think she may have lost a baby, many years ago, but it's not spoken of and, meantime, there's not a child born to the St. John's Ladies she hasn't spoiled.'

'And what of you? You're very good with children, I've seen you with Patrick.'

'Me? And children? I need to find a husband first. And even then, much as I might want a child, can I let go of what Beatrice has shown me is possible?'

'You want the best of both worlds?'

'Well it is nineteen twenty Edward,' she said but Edward thought the humour forced. They stood in silence for a minute, watching the room, until Catherine said, 'She thinks a great deal of you,' indicating to Evelyn who was talking to Mrs. Railton and her husband, the reverend, who had joined the occasion.

'And I her. And you,' said Edward. 'This summer has been ... revitalising. And I'm trying to compose again.'

'Yes, but I think Evelyn thinks a very great deal of you.' Catherine emphasised the 'very'.

Edward said nothing but took his glass of scotch from the piano lid and drank deeply. Catherine watched him.

'Evelyn has a kind soul,' Edward said.

'And a pretty face.'

'Of course, but mine is not so ... pretty. I wouldn't, couldn't, presume ... I couldn't imagine anyone ... let alone ask ...' Edward stumbled over the words and drank again.

'Well, sweeter even than Evelyn's face is her heart,' Catherine said, smiling at Evelyn across the room as she caught her eye, 'which is why she's the best friend I've had, and also why she ... we ... are a little concerned about the trip to Whitstable tomorrow. We're happy to go, I'm excited to be driving that far, but ...'

'It's simply to try and fulfil a promise I made to myself. A duty.'

'Duty? Or obsession?'

Edward looked at Catherine. Her face carried that smile which both challenged and empathised. He nodded and smiled, but the sudden movement of those muscles remaining on his left side pushed skin against the mark on the inside of the mask and he winced. Catherine's smile turned to a frown.

'It's nothing. I need to speak to the reverend.'

Edward went across the room, pleased but embarrassed at the warm smiles and acknowledgements. Reverend Railton held out a hand as he neared, 'Mr. Thompson, apologies. I missed most of your performance, but from what I heard, the reports are true, you play remarkably. And, dare I say,' he spoke to Catherine, just behind Edward, 'you sing beautifully. But you've still yet to join our choir. After tonight I think you'll find yourself in increased demand.'

'Thank you Reverend,' said Catherine, 'perhaps in the spring, I'm rather busy at the moment.'

'Hmmm, well that's playing a straight bat, wouldn't you say Mr. Thompson?'

'I think Catherine is not to be persuaded against her wishes,' agreed Edward.

'Indeed. Now ladies, would you excuse Mr. Thompson and me. I need just a quick word.'

Edward found himself ushered out of the drawing room and outdoors to the steps leading to the front door. Edward was grateful for the fresh air, lighting a cigarette to draw from between sips of the scotch he still carried. Reverend Railton held a large glass of sherry from which he sipped infrequently.

'Mr. Thompson,'

'Please, call me Edward.'

'Of course. Edward. I'm told Tosh, the man for whom you arranged a job at a hop farm, is back.'

'So I hear. I'm afraid I wasn't much help after all.'

'Perhaps not so much as you'd like, but I think putting him on the next train back to London will only move the problem, not solve it.'

Edward nodded.

'So perhaps we need a more … sustainable solution, for Tosh and others. I'm thinking of trying to raise money to start a mission, somewhere in Kent, for men like Tosh.'

'Good luck with that Reverend, I see little evidence of Lloyd George's charity extending this far.'

'Then the community should offer its own charity.'

'Fine words Reverend. But many people are still too swamped with grief for their own losses to find spirit to help the destitute and wounded. Some will feel that at least they came back.'

'Hard words Edward. But I understand. Last time we spoke I believe I mentioned I'd written to the Dean of Westminster about a grave, for those who didn't return. I thought you might like to know the King has been persuaded. There will be a grave in Westminster Abbey. The body will be interred on Armistice Day, when the new Cenotaph will also be revealed.'

'A grave?'

'Yes. Remains will be brought over. I don't know the details yet, but the warrior will be unknown and unknowable.'

Edward sipped long from his scotch.

Edward, Whitstable, Thursday 7th October 1920

The trip to Whitstable was going well enough until they reached the outskirts of Herne Bay and passed the top of Reculver Road. The last time they had been this way, Catherine excepted, was to visit Mr. Tewson, just before he died. But Catherine was not to know and continued chattering nervously as she drove, talking her way through the controls and levers and pedals and asking William, in the front passenger seat beside her, if she was doing all right. Though nothing was said when reaching Reculver Road, Edward thought it might be playing on Evelyn's mind, if not William's. Edward caught her eye and smiled, hoping she would realise it meant he understood. Evelyn returned the smile then looked away. Catherine was a model of talkative nervous concentration as she drove on, asking William to clarify directions, not trusting herself to follow the sign post. The weather was poor and Edward regretted buying the convertible rather than hard roof, but in the showroom, in the sunshine, the soft top had been an easy choice. He and Evelyn sat in the back, both with blankets covering laps and legs, Evelyn in a new heavy coat that Catherine insisted she accept as a gift – Evelyn insisted it was only borrowed for the trip. William, up front, seemed impervious to the cold and wore his favourite tinted driving spectacles, despite the lack of sunshine. Catherine was wrapped in her own new driving coat with a woollen scarf tied around her head and another wrapped around her neck. Edward's mood, already dampened by lack of morphine tablets, worsened when the front off–side tyre was punctured, scaring Catherine as the steering became too heavy for her and she panicked on the brakes. Then William and Edward took half an hour to change the wheel, William not helping much due to his injured hand. It began to rain. When they were ready to go again, there was an argument between William and Catherine over who should drive which Edward finished by supporting Catherine's assertion if she, 'didn't get straight back in the saddle, so to speak, she might not want to ever again,' and besides, William still couldn't see properly out of his bruised eye, let alone tinted spectacles. So Catherine drove them slowly through Herne Bay, then Tankerton. They passed the Thanet Royal hotel, Edward remarking he 'hoped they were looking after the Bechstein,' and were soon into Whitstable, parking close to the quays. It had more of a feel of a working harbour than holiday resort, though the poor weather didn't help. The tide was on its way out but still high enough to float the boats, though few men worked either the crafts or the dock side. The ladies stayed in the car, Edward apologising this was not turning into the pleasant day out he'd hoped, while he and William went to the harbour. With no plan other than to ask around, they approached a man standing on the quayside and asked after an oysterman named Dougherty or Docherty. The short, direct answer, pointed them further westwards to where rows of small boats were lined high up on the beach. There were more men working here but the first three didn't even bother to acknowledge the question. Edward wondered if his mask and manner were the cause, but the fourth recognised the name and William's more cheery manner gained confirmation that Docherty had indeed married a girl from Herne Bay. A half pack of Woodbine elicited further information; Docherty lived locally and the price of a pint bought directions, though the house number wasn't known.

Catherine, still determined to drive, turned the car into Albert Street and parked half way down the first row of terraced houses on the left. Edward stepped from the car but William called him back, 'So the plan is to …?'

'Knock on doors until …' said Edward.

'Hmmm, is that the best plan a lieutenant can come up with? Even the Lucky Lieutenant? You don't think the …' William gestured to his face, 'might be … awkward, in the case of ladies answering the door?'

Edward looked at Evelyn who said, unconvincingly, 'I don't think so.'

'I know,' said Catherine, 'let Evelyn and I try a couple of doors first,' leaving the car, ending further discussion.

Evelyn joined her and it took only three doors to learn the Dochertys' house number.

'See, I told you he was lucky,' said William.

Edward felt a surge of excitement and insisted he should be the one to knock at the door. Ten minutes later he was back, disappointed at no answer and being shouted at by a neighbour the Dochertys had travelled to Canterbury for the day.

The journey back to Margate was mostly in silence and Edward's head began to hurt.

Edward spent the next day in his room, in pain, despite two injections of the morphia solution. In the evening Evelyn knocked on his door but, against his inclination, he didn't let her in.

The Blue Bench

Evelyn, Margate, Friday 8th October 1920

It had been a concern to Evelyn that Edward didn't open the door to his room when she knocked. But neither had he asked her to go away. She didn't know what to read into that, and, as Catherine pointed out, it was just as well she hadn't been invited in as a young lady in a man's room was often misinterpreted, easily and, on occasion, wilfully.

'But is that always a bad thing?' Evelyn asked. They sat on the settee in Catherine's room, an hour or so after the knock on Edward's door.

'You're only saying that because you're tipsy,' said Catherine, topping up her sherry glass. 'Now, tell me again, what did Edward say through the door?'

'Something like, thank you but I'd like to rest, except it was a bit slurred.'

'A bit like you now then,' teased Catherine and Evelyn had to agree. She was lightheaded and relaxed and the concern over Edward having been in his room all day was fading.

'And you're sure Edward said 'like to rest', not 'have to' or 'need to'?'

'No.'

'No what?'

'I'm not sure. Does it matter?'

'Of course,' said Catherine, 'though I'm not sure how.'

Evelyn had waited all day before giving in and knocking on Edward's door, knowing he was in pain. She'd hoped to offer some peace, but suspected Edward was looking for that in the morphia solution, a secret she hadn't mentioned to Catherine. After Edward's muffled response through the door she'd gone to Catherine's room and there must have been something maudlin in her manner as Catherine invited her in and opened a bottle of sherry.

After a pause, to drink, Evelyn muttered, 'I don't like to see Edward in pain.'

'Of course not,' agreed Catherine, 'but what can you do?'

Evelyn drank some more. 'Oh, by the way, William was in the tea shop earlier and Alice asked him if he'd bring over the portraits, so she can finish them off at home. Edward was going to make the arrangements but …'

'Why didn't Alice ask us?'

'We're not meant to see ours yet …' Evelyn said.

'But they're only a few doors away …'

'We promised not to look.'

'You are the perfect reverend's daughter. No wonder Edward is smitten.'

'No he's not.'

'And I don't blame him.'

'And I don't believe you.'

'But do you want to?' asked Catherine.

Evelyn tried to think of the right answer but her thoughts were muddled by Beatrice's good sherry and they drifted into silence, broken a few minutes later by Catherine's almost whispered singing, 'Rock a bye my baby with a …'

'… isn't it 'your baby', not 'my',' interrupted Evelyn, lazily,

'Is it? I prefer 'my'.'

'As you wish. Oh, and I meant to say, you sing it better than Georgette did, that time we stood outside The Compass, listening. You sing it … better.'

'Thank you, but then I did have Edward as an

accomplish … acclompan … playing for me. Imagine that, someone as talented as Edward, playing for me.'

'Imagine that,' Evelyn repeated.

'Speaking of that night, outside the pub, do you think that woman was willing?'

'What? The woman against the wall?' Evelyn asked.

'Yes, her. Did she enjoy it?'

'I don't know. I suppose it's for the money but some do enjoy, they tell me, back in Spitalfields, though they could be teasing me, 'cos I'm a reverend's daughter, but I don't mind. In a way it means they're looking after me. Sort of.'

'I don't understand.'

'I'm not sure I do.'

'Would you, do you think?'

'What, for money? Of course not.'

'I mean, enjoy it,' said Catherine

'Against a wall? It didn't look comfortable. I'm thinking more of soft beds and clean sheets.' Evelyn giggled.

'But in the heat of the moment?'

'Perhaps …'

'And what do you think Edward meant? When he said something about knowing the woman?' Catherine asked, topping up both hers and Evelyn's sherry glasses.

'Did he say he knew her? Or recognise her?'

'I don't know, something like that. But what if he … knew … her?' Catherine stressed the 'knew'.

'As in … paid her, for …?'

Catherine nodded.

'No, he's a gentlemen, an officer.'

'You think they don't pay? Remember those postcards Georgette showed? They looked like gentlemen and officers too.'

'No. Edward's a real gentleman.'

'Hmmm, but even a gentleman has … needs, as Beatrice would say.'

Evelyn nodded, thoughtful.

Half an hour later they were both sleeping on the settee. A further hour later the night was cold and they moved into Catherine's bed, warm and safe under the winter sheets.

The next day, Saturday, Evelyn woke before Catherine and was careful not to disturb her as she left. She was even more careful not to make a noise going upstairs to her own room, on the same floor as Edward's, especially when she passed his door.

Evelyn and Catherine ate a late breakfast, prepared by themselves as Beatrice had given Cook the weekend off to visit family in Canterbury. After coffee, William and Georgette came to collect the pictures, easels and Alice's tools and materials.

In the afternoon Evelyn went to help out in the tea shop while Catherine went with Beatrice to take a look at another guest house for sale. At the tea shop Alice was her usual welcoming self, Isabella was her usual adorable self and Alastair was terse with all except Isabella. He spoke little to Evelyn but did ask if Edward had hung the picture of the sinking ship in his room; Evelyn didn't know.

Evelyn, Margate, Sunday 10th October 1920

Catherine drove Edward's Wolseley to Herne Bay on Sunday. William was in the passenger seat, still nursing his hand. Evelyn and Patrick were in the back. The Reverend Coughston was returning to London that day, via Herne Bay, and Evelyn had arranged to meet him at the Clock Tower on the front. Evelyn apologised for being late as he stood from a bench and kissed her cheek, saying, 'No need, it has been a lovely morning.' He gestured to the clear autumn sky. 'And the breeze is refreshing. It's been relaxing to sit here and turn my thoughts from the mission. It's been such a busy time, and a happy time, but I need to go home to my flock.' He stepped back from Evelyn to shake William and Catherine's hands and tousle Patrick's hair. 'And Mr. Thompson?' he asked.

'He's not well, Father,' said Evelyn.

'Pity, and I had a little news for him. Never mind. How are you?' He hugged Evelyn again.

'Me and Patrick are going up to the downs, see if we can get this kite flying again,' said William.

When they'd gone Reverend Coughston asked, 'Where's the boy's mother?'

'Working,' said Evelyn.

'Again,' added Catherine, then shouted after William, 'Don't be long,' holding up the hamper she had prepared earlier.

'Is Mr. Burrslow injured? I see his hand is bandaged.' Reverend Coughston said.

'He punched a policeman's truncheon,' said

373

Catherine, 'but seems to be getting over it.'

'Hmmm, I suspect he's not one to be easily slowed or affected. Does he ever mention Mr. Tewson?'

'No,' said Evelyn. She felt guilty for not speaking to her father of the events of the day Mr. Tewson died and how it must have upset the hop farm.

'Thank you for visiting Mr. Tewson in hospital,' he said to Evelyn. She started to say thanks were not due, but didn't want to open the subject.

'Let's sit on the front, we've an hour before your train.'

They strolled in comfortable silence to an empty bench and the ladies sat either side of Reverend Coughston. Catherine lit a cigarette. They chatted easily and Evelyn was careful not to mention the day of Alastair's disappearance and subsequent moods, even when it became clear her father knew it was Mrs. Trenter painting the portraits. Evelyn was more concerned her father might criticise her vanity but he said he was looking forward to seeing it, which might be soon as Alastair had asked him to preside over Isabella's baptism.

Catherine poured them hot tea from a Thermos flask and as Reverend Coughston sipped Evelyn asked, 'And what's the news for Edward?'

'Yes, Edward. How is he?'

'Not well,' said Evelyn.

'I know, you said earlier. But how is he likely to be? In the months and years to come?'

'I don't understand what you mean,' said Evelyn.

'I'm sorry, I don't mean to be abstruse.'

'And what's the news you have for him?'

'Nothing exciting, but I thought he'd want to know the crippled veteran, Tosh, he brought to the hop farm, left us a couple of weeks ago. I don't know where he went. I don't think I was able to help him much, or perhaps even at all. Would you tell Edward I'm sorry? The man, Tosh, just left one day, with no warning or goodbye.'

'He came back to Margate, with a woman,' said Catherine.

'Ah, so that's where she went. One of the young women disappeared at the same time as Tosh. They had been together quite a lot before, so we wondered if they'd left together. Back to Margate? You know she was a ...' he seemed to be looking for the right word.

'... working girl ... of the night?' offered Catherine.

'Nicely put, thank you. And you say Edward knows. So you only need impart the second piece of news to him. I've written to The Reverend Plense and asked him to pass on the letter.'

'Who's Reverend Plense?' asked Evelyn.

'A colleague. We studied together at Cambridge. Edward asked if he would pass on a letter.'

'To?'

'Edward hasn't mentioned the letter?' he asked.

Evelyn looked at Catherine who shook her head.

'No,' said Evelyn.

'Reverend Plense has connections with the Royal College of Music. I don't know the contents of Edward's letter but he has indicated a sadness in not having completed his studies there. Anyway, as he didn't mention it to you perhaps you shouldn't either. And anyway, more about you. Is it busy at the tea shop?'

'No and I did think I might be needed more to help with Isabella, but Alice and Alastair seem settled well enough.'

'So you could come back to Spitalfields with me?'

Catherine leant forward, making sure to catch Evelyn's eye.

'I suppose,' Evelyn said.

'Or you could stay in Margate a little longer. Perhaps go back to work at The Winter Gardens?' Catherine made it a question.

'I will need to work soon,' said Evelyn.

'Or find a husband? A young man of means? Not that

I'm suggesting a marriage for money,' said Reverend Coughston, 'and in the meantime, perhaps stay here, if it's not Alice that needs some help I'm sure there are others.'

Evelyn, Margate,
Wednesday 13th October 1920

Though Evelyn's room was on the top floor she could hear Edward composing at the piano in the drawing room. It was mid–morning and she sat in her room, reading *Dracula*. Catherine had given her two books: Bram Stoker's *Dracula* and Lawrence's *The Rainbow*. Evelyn had struggled with *The Rainbow* and given up a third of the way in to try *Dracula*. Outside was a dreary scene but her room was warm and Cook had brought her morning tea and homemade biscuits; Evelyn flattering Cook by claiming that though she'd been there only a couple of weeks her skirts were already tighter. Cook said that was no bad thing with the winter approaching. Evelyn settled back to read, occasionally distracted by Edward's piano and even then pleased she could hear it. Since the weekend Edward had been feeling a little better every day and was back to playing. Though he had been quiet over breakfast at least he was there and, when Catherine and Beatrice went out, to look at yet another guest house up for sale, Evelyn was able to ask how he was. The pain relief had left him drowsy but he hadn't taken any since Monday and the pain was subsiding. Evelyn had told him how well he'd done to go without the morphine for a couple of days and he'd smiled, saying this was the easy bit, he wouldn't feel the withdrawal for another day or so. But he needed to take as little as possible so his mind was clear for his music. His mask was slightly askew and she only just stopped herself from correcting it. Then he invited Evelyn to join him as he resumed his morning routine of walking down to the harbour pier. Though chilly, the air was clear and she came back refreshed. Edward went to the drawing room and the piano, Evelyn to her room where she'd nearly finished the third chapter of her book when she heard a harsh knock on the door. Edward was still playing, perhaps ignoring the door, perhaps not hearing it, so Evelyn went down. Now there were no holiday guests staying in the guest house, the front was kept locked. As Evelyn came down the stairs she could see a woman standing on the other side of the door. She wore a white dress with lace collars and a long, heavy woollen cardigan, tied loosely at the waist. Her dark grey beret was too big. Evelyn opened the door, thinking the quality of the cardigan was good, but not matched by her scuffed and worn shoes.

Evelyn greeted the woman formally.

'Good morning,' the woman repeated.

'Can I help you?'

'I don't think so. I'd like to see the lieutenant, or tin–face, as I believe he's known. I expect that'll be 'im making a racket.' She gestured towards the drawing room where the piano played. The words the woman used took a few seconds to register with Evelyn but as she started to question her the woman pushed past into the hall.

'Excuse me, where are you going?' Evelyn moved to stand between the woman and the drawing room, 'And a bit more respect is expected.'

'Of course it is, but then what's expected and what's given ain't always the same, eh?' The woman smiled coldly and Evelyn had a fleeting hint of having seen this woman before but couldn't hold on to it as the woman reached behind Evelyn to knock loudly on the door, 'There, more respectful?' she said, pushing past Evelyn and into the room.

Edward stopped playing and turned with a half–smile that disappeared as the woman entered, Evelyn just behind, apologising, 'Sorry Edward, this woman has ... insisted on seeing you.'

'Morning Lieutenant. Nice playing. You wanna keep at it, you might be quite good one day.' The woman said and her words and tone were hard for Evelyn to read, but it was uncomfortable. 'Hang on a tick,' the woman turned back to Evelyn, 'I know of you. You're the girl old Tewson took a shine too, ain'tcha. That didn't end well did it?'

Evelyn looked to the woman, then Edward who said, 'It's all right Evelyn, this … lady is from the hop farm, and has been known to frequent The Compass, I believe.'

Evelyn's glimmer of recognition became clear – it was the woman from the alley; the woman who had been up against the wall. 'What can we do for you?' Evelyn asked, moving to stand next to Edward, though she really wanted to ask what the woman meant by her reference to Mr. Tewson.

'What can you do? Very little I suspect. But a cup of tea might be nice.'

'No, I don't think so,' said Edward. 'Why are you here?'

'Shame. Ah well, perhaps next time. Meanwhile, Tosh has asked me to tell you he'd be honoured if you would pop round to see him, this morning, though I doubt he'll be offering tea, so you might want to take your own refreshment.'

'Tosh?' Evelyn asked.

'The cripple,' said Edward.

'Cripple?' said the woman. 'Harsh word from a tin face.'

'What does he want?' asked Evelyn.

'I don't know. He just gave me the message and said not to come back until much later. He don't generally have a lot to say 'bout anything.'

'Why Edward?'

'I don't know. Any chance of tea?'

'No,' said Edward, 'where is he?'

'Tosh? Athelstan Road. There's an empty house

opposite the depository. We've been … availing … ourselves of the basement facilities.'

'Thank you,' said Edward, 'you can go now.'

'What? Not even a shilling for the trouble?'

Edward gave her a florin and Evelyn showed her out.

Evelyn asked Cook for directions to Athelstan Road and walked there with Edward, mostly in silence.

Pettman's Depository was at the bottom of Athelstan Road. Opposite was a row of semi–detached houses, four storeys including basements.

'She mentioned a basement,' said Evelyn. Edward nodded, stopping outside a house displaying a 'To Let' sign. From the pavement it was possible to see the basement door and window. The curtains were closed but the door was ajar. Edward went down the stairs and knocked hard but there was no response. He pushed the door open a little, calling again. No response. He pushed the door further and stepped across the threshold into an empty dark parlour. There was a small table holding a used tea set and a threadbare settee. Edward called again. No response. A faint smell caught Evelyn's senses, but she couldn't place it. Edward went on into a short corridor with a closed door to the left and a small kitchen ahead, the door open. Edward went there first but it was empty. Evelyn shrugged and turned back to the door off the corridor that was closed. She knocked, calling, 'Hello?' The smell came to her again but she still couldn't place it.

Edward went to the door, knocking harder and calling more loudly. The door moved under pressure. He went in, Evelyn close behind. It was a bedroom. The bed was off to one side, unseen behind the door as it opened. It was not until he was in the room that Edward pulled up suddenly short and turned to stop Evelyn coming further. Too late. She saw the bed and the figure on it. It was a mere second before Edward was standing in her way, but in that second she saw the figure sitting up against the bed head. A pale face above a bloodied, mangled throat, the wall behind a kaleidoscope of red and brown, the blood seeping down the white vest on the torso. The eyes open and staring; only for a second did she see, but they stared.

Edward held Evelyn's shoulders and backed her through the doorway and into the corridor. Over his shoulder she could see a small dressing table; a prosthetic lower arm lay on the top, neatly placed. Evelyn was breathing fast and shaking and the smell was stronger to her, 'Fireworks,' she muttered.

Edward led Evelyn by her hand back out to street level. She felt faint and forced slower, deeper breaths.

'I'm sorry,' said Edward, 'I should have assumed something was wrong. And I didn't … couldn't … smell the gun, as you did. I'm sorry.' He lit a cigarette.

'What do you think happened?'

'I don't know. You should go to the police and bring them here. I'll stay to make sure no one else goes in. Are you all right to go?'

'Yes, of course. It's not the first body I've seen.' Which was true, but the others had been lying in far more peace.

It was mid–afternoon by the time the police finished talking to Evelyn and Edward, who suggested they go home via The Compass; no one would begrudge them a brandy or two. Few people were in the pub. William sat in the corner, sipping a pint, smoking and reading the *Daily Herald*. He waved them over to join him. Edward went to the bar first. As Evelyn sat next to William he smiled and waggled the newspaper.

'The revolution has started. The miners are striking. Today.' He slipped his hip flask from a pocket and poured a large measure of a spirit into his pint glass. 'Who knows where it'll lead.'

Evelyn didn't answer. She was weary and drained and, for a moment, angry at William that he didn't know about the morning's events. 'Tosh is dead,' she said quietly.

'Say again?'

'Tosh is dead.'

'Oh. I thought I hadn't seen much of him.'

Evelyn looked at him, frowning.

Edward joined them. 'Did you tell him? About Tosh?'

'Yes.'

'That's a shame. Still, he wasn't having the best of times, was he? What happened?'

'It looks like he shot himself, with a service revolver. This morning,' Edward explained.

'A service revolver? I wonder where he got that. He didn't look the officer type to me. Perhaps he was in the machine gun corps. How'd you find out?'

'We found the body,' Evelyn said slowly, with growing anger for William's disdain.

'Oh, that's ... upsetting.'

Evelyn sipped from her gin and tonic, Edward from his scotch.

'I should have known.' Edward said, and though Evelyn didn't understand if he meant knowing about Tosh's intentions or finding the body, she realised it was likely to be both.

'Have you seen the woman who came back from the hop farm with Tosh?' Evelyn asked.

William nodded, 'Margaret. She was in earlier. Then she left, with a ... new friend. But I expect she'll be back soon. She's a busy girl.'

After twenty minutes the woman hadn't returned to the pub and Evelyn just wanted to go home, despite William offering to buy them another drink and saying, 'Besides, Georgette will be here soon, when she finishes work.'

Evelyn shook her head and left, Edward going with her. Outside, standing close to the entrance of the pub's side alley, was the woman.

'Should have thought to look there,' said Edward, leading Evelyn over.

The woman looked at them and asked, 'Did you find him?'

'What?' Evelyn asked, incredulous.

'Tosh? Did the good lieutenant find him?'

'Did you know?'

'What?'

'What he'd done. Did you know? Did you do something to try and stop it?'

'What are you on about?'

'Oh my Lord,' exclaimed Evelyn, 'or did you help him? And then send us to find him, rather than … my God, you're repulsive.'

'Steady on. I may be a … working girl, but you're a stuck up bitch.' The woman's face was contorted with anger and she took a step towards Evelyn. Edward moved between the two women, saying,

'I don't think she knows.'

'Know what?' said the woman.

'Tosh is dead. Shot himself.'

The woman's face softened, then she took a deep breath, 'Bollocks. When?'

'It must have been just after he asked you to get me.'

'Bollocks,' she repeated, 'and I suppose the local bill know?'

Evelyn nodded.

'So I better not go back there then. And I got clothes there. Bollocks. I'll have to find somewhere else. What a selfish sod.'

'Selfish?' said Evelyn. 'Don't you care how unhappy he must have been?'

'Unhappy? They all are dear. Tewson, Tosh, 'im,'

she nodded at Edward, 'all of 'em. Ain't you got that yet?'
She walked away, leaving Edward and Evelyn to watch.

Evelyn, Margate,
Thursday 14th October 1920

Dear Father,

I'm sorry I haven't written for a few days but it's been a busy time, though the autumn, in general, seems to be weighing heavily on the town. But perhaps that's just in contrast to its summer life.

I'm also sorry to write with sad news. You will remember the disabled veteran, Tosh, who both Edward and yourself tried to help. Unfortunately he was found dead yesterday morning. It appears he shot himself and death was instant. We had no contact with him leading up to yesterday and have no idea of his state of mind, though we can guess he was as unhappy as we could possibly imagine and more. Edward has taken the death badly, with hardly a word to say since. Last night, in an effort to cheer us up, Mrs. Blundell insisted on a visit to the cinema, at her expense – she is a kind hearted lady and hates to see any sadness – Catherine and I were treated to Hobson's Choice but Edward did not join us.

I'll write again in the next day or two, with more usual and, I hope, happier news, but I thought you should know about Tosh.

I hope all is well in the parish and back to normal and will see you soon, I expect – there is little work for me in the tea shop and Alice and Alastair are coping admirably.

Your ever loving daughter,

Evelyn

Evelyn read the letter back to herself, unsure of why she hadn't mentioned Edward's and her own role in finding Tosh. Of course she didn't want her father to worry about her but she was loathe to keep such an event secret from him. Besides, he was a practical man and would provide sound advice as well as comfort. She knew the next time they were together she would tell him but saw little to be gained in causing undue concern before then.

The previous day, on returning to Mrs. Blundell's, Evelyn had explained all to Catherine and Beatrice. Their patience and gentle prompting as the story unfolded was calming. Evelyn understated the events, not wanting to upset either woman but Catherine's distress, for Evelyn, was clear and though Evelyn didn't want Catherine to feel so, there was comfort in thinking someone else understood.

Edward had been there for the telling. He'd said little, nodding where emphasis was needed and offering occasional clarification, but he didn't elaborate on the scene or speculate on the reasons.

Beatrice was nearly as quiet as Edward but when it seemed as much of the tale as necessary for one evening had been told, she insisted on the cinema trip. Catherine insisted she and Evelyn change into clothes more suited to an evening out. Edward insisted he needed to catch up on some work as he'd lost the day already.

Beatrice took the ladies, including Cook, to see *Hobson's Choice*, showing again at The Parade Cinema, up on Fort Hill.

The cinema hadn't provided the diversion for Evelyn that Beatrice would have hoped.

Back at the guest house she had said her goodnights and gone to her room but as she passed Edward's door he opened it, speaking quietly, 'Evening. Are you all right?' Behind him, the room was ill–lit and the door was opened just enough that she could see the outline of the right side of his head.

'Fine, thank you,' Evelyn said.

'Good. Did you enjoy the film?'

'Yes … but not as much as I'd like Beatrice to believe.'

'Of course.'

'Of course?'

'I mean, you would …' Edward hesitated, '… it doesn't matter. I just wanted to say I'm sorry about today. I should have gone alone. I should never have let you into the room. I should have seen it in advance. I should have done better by Tosh, I should …'

Evelyn interrupted, 'That's an awful lot of things to think you should have done.' She emphasised 'should'. 'My father says sometimes we'd do better to replace 'should' with 'could'. It doesn't stop you taking responsibility for something, but can help to remind us we're not perfect and means we might get it right next time, rather than being stuck in what can't be changed.'

'Hmmm. Perhaps I'll try that, but meantime, and most of all, I should have asked how you're feeling … and what you're thinking, about it.'

'I'm trying not to think about it, at least for a day or two. Which I know is cowardly but …'

'No, it's not. You're not … I'm just … sorry.'

'I know. It's all right,' Evelyn said and moved a step closer.

Edward bowed his head, saying, 'Good night as he backed into his room.'

Evelyn sat in her room for ten or twenty minutes, reading neither the copy of *Vogue* Catherine had given her, nor the *Dracula* novel, nor her bible. Not reading the latter was shaming as she knew her father would have found a verse or two to help explain how she should feel about Tosh.

Then she laughed, for thinking how she 'should' not 'could' feel, and went down to see if Catherine was still awake. She was and they sat in easy silence for a while until she fell asleep on the settee. In the morning she awoke to find Catherine had given her a pillow and covered her with blankets.

Edward, Whitstable, Friday 15th October 1920

Early Thursday evening, the day after Tosh's suicide, Edward went to William's guest house. The front door was closed and Edward had to knock hard and repeatedly before Georgette came. She wore an apron over her dress and soft cotton gloves.

'Bonsoir Edward.'

'Bonsoir Georgette. Busy?' Edward asked.

'It is hard to believe? No guests, apart from William, and no bookings until Christmas, but still she wants the silver polished every week. It is not even good silver and if I polish any more it will be tin.' Georgette complained. Edward smiled and followed her in.

'Will is up in his room. A ... sieste ... before he goes to the pub,' Georgette gestured upstairs. 'Oh, I heard about that cripple. Shocking for Evelyn to find him. Is she all right?'

Edward stopped at the bottom of the stairs. He had still to understand Georgette but her concern for Evelyn seemed genuine.

'And with that business of the man run over ... well, it has been a ... summer terrible for her,' said Georgette.

'Tewson.'

'Tewson?'

'The man that was run over.'

'Oh yes, anyway, they say these things go in threes, so poor Evelyn must be worried.' Georgette smiled.

Edward supposed she was trying a joke but noticed

she had avoided commenting that it was William who had run down Tewson.

'I'm sure Evelyn's not superstitious.'

'Of course not. Anyway, look who's coming down.'

'Any chance of a cuppa?' William asked, walking down the stairs. Patrick was at his side.

'Yes. You know where is the kitchen.' Georgette said, taking Patrick's hand and leaving the men to wander into the front parlour.

'You've got your feet right under the table here.' Edward said.

'Oh yes,' said William. 'I'm the only guest and the old shrew that owns this place needs to keep Georgette on while I'm here.'

'Happy families?' Edward made it a question.

'As happy as some and happier than most I've seen. And all without a ring.'

'And the neighbours?'

'Who cares about them?'

They sat in armchairs on opposite sides of the room.

'So, what brings you to our humble abode? What can I do for you?' William asked.

'I thought I'd drop in next month's rent.' Edward took five white notes from his wallet and put them on the table next to his chair, 'Though I expect you're not sleeping in your own room often.' He made a weak joke.

'You'd be surprised,' said William. 'Much as I like the young lad, having him in the same room does dampen one's … ardour. Anyway, you'll be pleased to know I'm lining up two or three theatre options for you, for the spring. And I'm hoping to find work for Georgette alongside.'

'Good,' said Edward, though not with enthusiasm.

'You needn't have brought the cash for a week or two. Anything else on your mind? How's your head been?'

'I did wonder if you'd seen Rolf about.'

'I've not seen him for a while. You may have to break in to the pharmacy again.' William joked but Edward didn't laugh. 'I hear there are a few people looking for Rolf, including Constable Simms. What about the laudanum?' William asked.

'I can pick that up easy enough from the pharmacies but it's too diluted.'

'I'll ask around again. Otherwise, I need to go to London for a day or two soon, I'll find some tablets and solution then.'

'London? What for?'

'Turns out my old man's at death's door. Might snuff it any moment.'

'In London? I thought your family was from the north.'

'Did you? Some of them are. Speaking of snuffing it, do you think that woman Tosh brought back with him knew?'

'What?' said Edward, 'His plans to top himself? I don't know.'

'Do you reckon he had that service pistol all along?'

'I suppose. There were plenty of ways he could have got hold of it, the mud was littered with those who had no further use for their weapons and were in no condition to refuse,' Edward said.

'You don't think he was an officer then?'

'Maybe. Doesn't matter now, does it? We still don't know who he was.'

Georgette brought in a tray of tea, 'Who are you talking of?'

'That bloke who shot himself. Tosh,' said William.

'We don't know who he was,' Edward added.

'He was Tosh,' said Georgette, 'What more do you need to know?'

'She could be right,' said William, lighting a cigarette. Georgette poured tea.

Edward sipped carefully and they sat in silence until

Edward said, 'Anyway, I need a favour. Are you all right to drive now?' Edward pointed at William's hand which was no longer bandaged.

'I can manage.'

'We need to go back to Whitstable, to see if Kayst's sister is there.'

William hesitated. 'Talk about dogs and bones. Do we have to?'

Edward was silent.

'All right, one more time. But if we don't find her then …'

'I know. Enough's enough.'

'Evelyn already thinks you're … obsessed.'

'Evelyn said that?'

'Not as such, at least, not to me. But I heard her talking to Catherine, the other day, when we took those pictures over to the tea shop. Which, I might add, are very good. You look quite the hero and the ladies look, well, quite the ladies.'

'You've seen them? I thought Alice didn't want them seen until finished.'

'And you think that would stop us taking a peek?' William laughed.

'I suppose not. Anyway, I need to go. Pick me up tomorrow, nine?'

'As long as on the way we stop off at that posh hotel, the one that didn't want you to play in their bar.'

Edward nodded, 'Why?'

'I need to talk to the manager, face to face. I called him on the telephone, looking to get Georgette a couple of evenings singing there. It would be good for her and you'll never guess who their pianist is?'

Edward shook his head.

'Arthur, from The Compass.'

'You've already spoken to the manager there?'

'The old woman that owns this place had a telephone put in. But I want to see him, before we take

Georgette.'

'Well, nine tomorrow then,' Edward said, standing to walk to the door. He stopped and turned, 'Sorry about your father.'

Patrick ran in, brushing past Edward, carrying a jigsaw.

William took the box from Patrick, opening it to tip out the pieces and kneeling on the rug, beside Patrick. William looked up at Edward, 'My old man? It happens, sooner or later. At least for him it was later.'

They stopped at the Thanet Royal hotel on the way into Whitstable. Edward stayed in the car, at William's suggestion and it was only a short wait until he was back, happy he'd arranged an audition for Georgette, saying, '… and if Arthur's not around that day, you'll play for her, won't you?'

It was just a quick drive from there into the town and Albert Street. There were no other cars in the road. They parked outside the Dochertys' house, William remarking for the fourth time he hoped someone would be in and reminding Edward if not, there would be no further searching.

The door was opened on the third knock. A man stood in the darkness of the hall.

'We're looking for the Dochertys,' William said.

'I know,' the man said, stepping into the doorway and watching Edward's face. Edward watched back. He was a big man, but not intimidating and, were there to be trouble, Edward was confident in William's abilities. The man was older than Edward had expected, though there was no reason for his expectation.

'You know?' William said.

'People like to talk.'

'True,' said Edward. 'And you are Mr. Docherty?'

The man nodded. He did not appear wary. His face

was creased from squinting into the weather and the lines collapsing into his eyes nearly hid the tiredness Edward saw there.

'I'm looking for Mrs. Docherty. I believe her maiden name was Kayst and I want to find her parents.'

'Maiden name? No. That's not the case.'

'Oh, I was led to believe she was the sister of Joseph Kayst.'

'No. Why are you looking for her?'

Edward looked at William. 'He, Kayst, was in our platoon and I just wanted … thought … I should … tell his parents.'

'Tell them what?'

'I … we … were there when he … wasn't.'

'You know he died, over there?' The man asked, confused.

William spoke. 'Yes, we know. We were there.'

'And that's what you want to tell the parents?'

'I suppose,' said Edward, '… and the sister.'

'I don't think there is a sister,' the man said.

'We're going round in circles,' said William. 'If there's no sister then who is Mrs. Docherty?'

'Kayst's wife,' said the man.

'Wife?'

'At least, until he died, of course.'

'And then she married you?' Edward asked.

'Why do you care?' the man said, but with weary resignation, not anger.

William looked at Edward, 'And you thought you knew the men?'

Mrs. Blundell sat on the edge of the armchair, listening intently, occasionally checking her understanding and nodding when Edward caught her eye. 'And you never knew he'd married?' she asked.

'No. He was home on leave in early seventeen. Just

seventeen years old himself.'

'Why on earth did he marry so young?' Catherine asked.

'He wasn't alone in that. But must have had his parents' consent.'

'Poor boy,' said Catherine. 'And when he didn't come back she thought she'd marry again?'

'Except Docherty said they never did. Lily would have lost her widow's pension had she married, so they just pretended, for the sake of appearances, and she called herself Docherty.'

'And now?'

'Docherty said he sent her away. He's a lot older and a good man. Says she was never happy and told her to start again. She left him ...'

'... leaving him to look the town fool I expect. Poor man,' said Beatrice.

Edward nodded. 'Lily's own parents died years ago and the last he heard Lily was going to work with Kayst's family. After the boy died his parents gave up the tobacconist and scraped by until finding work in service.'

'Where?'

'St. Peter's, near Broadstairs. He didn't know the address but thought they were in service to the Palmers.'

Catherine looked at Beatrice, who nodded, 'Well I daresay, if it's the case they're in service, then the Palmers may well have some standing, though these days it's hard to tell, and if they attend church at St. Peter's, then someone at St. John's may know someone who will know someone who knows them.'

The Blue Bench

Evelyn, Margate, Sunday 17th October 1920

The longcase clock on the landing tocked and creaked, the volume seeming to increase as Evelyn opened the door to leave Catherine's room, hoping not to wake her. It was close to midnight.

The previous evening had been a party of sorts. Beatrice had announced the purchase of another guest house, on Fort Crescent, overlooking The Winter Gardens and the sea beyond. Evelyn knew the news was coming but to hear Beatrice chatter so joyously about her plans was to share the excitement. Cook had spent the evening with them and a bottle of sherry hadn't gone as far as expected. But Evelyn had missed Edward; William had coaxed him into playing for Georgette down at The Compass. William was determined to help Georgette build her experience and, perhaps, a career. Catherine had been dismissive when she learned where Edward was, but Evelyn reminded her he considered Catherine's rendition of *Danny Boy* the better. And when Evelyn expressed disappointment that Edward had chosen William's company over theirs that evening, Catherine reminded her that if not for Evelyn, Edward would not be staying at Beatrice's and composing again.

Cook went to bed first, then Beatrice. Evelyn and Catherine made cocoa and took it up to Catherine's room where they talked until Catherine fell asleep on the settee. Evelyn covered her and crept out. As she passed the clock, the front door was opened and Edward came in. Evelyn crept up to her room, not wanting to be seen, but not understanding why.

The Sunday service at St. John's was not as enjoyable as usual for Evelyn, which she put down to the previous late night, rather than hymn or sermon choice. They filed past Reverend Railton and out into the autumn sunshine where Catherine and Beatrice chatted with the other worshippers. Evelyn excused herself, needing to go on to the tea shop.

These days the shop was rarely busy. Evelyn and Alice had a routine of sorts whereby Evelyn would sit and cuddle Isabella, just over three weeks old, for half an hour or so, while Alice would take a little time for herself. Then they'd chat until it was time for Evelyn to take over from Alastair in the tea shop. If Isabella was sleeping then Alice would often continue work on the portraits, assuring Evelyn they were 'coming along nicely' though not allowing her to see. But this Sunday the tea shop was closed. Evelyn went in through the back door, from the alley, calling out for Alice as she went upstairs. She found her in the nursery, feeding Isabella while sitting in an upright chair next to the bassinet. The nursery walls were pale blue and covered with exotic birds and colourful butterflies painted by Alastair, copied from an old zoology text book.

'Where's Alastair?' Evelyn asked.

'Oh, he went out for a walk. It's all right, he won't be long. He never is these days,' Alice said, looking down at Isabella, 'thanks to this one.'

'Is he back to how he was before … Curtis went?'

'Sometimes, for a day or two, but then, no, and … not today. It was his birthday yesterday.'

'Alastair?'

'Curtis.'

'Oh, I'm sorry I didn't know. How old would he have been?'

'Twenty one.'

'So he was just ...' Evelyn thought about the years but didn't know the date his ship had been sunk.

'... seventeen when the *Gurkha* went down. Seventeen.' Alice looked up from Isabella, eyes damp with tears.

'Poor Curtis,' said Evelyn.

'Poor Alastair,' said Alice, 'which is why you mustn't take it personally.'

'What do you mean?'

'Alastair has asked me to tell you we won't need your help in the tea shop anymore.'

'Oh,' Evelyn shrugged, 'that's all right. I'm not surprised. It's very quiet. I'm sure Alastair can cope.' She didn't mention that as she wasn't being paid she would soon have been looking for another job anyway. 'But I have enjoyed it, and hope I've been of use.'

'Oh Evelyn, of course. It's been lovely to have you here and we'll still want to see you every day,' Alice said, indicating to Isabella.

'For as long as I'm in Margate,' Evelyn agreed, smiling, 'and, while I'm here anyway, is there anything I can do today?'

Isabella stopped sucking and Alice took the opportunity to move her to her other side.

'There is a favour Alastair would ask of you, if he was here.'

'Of course.'

'He ... he thinks the portrait of Mr. Thompson is complete and asks if you would take it back to Mrs. Blundell's.'

'Oh. It's finished?'

'I haven't done any more on it since it came here, but yes, I suppose Alastair is right. After all, one can always do more with a painting and learning how to stop is also a skill, I'm told. Though there's still much to be done on your portrait.'

'Then I'll take Edward's back. I'm sure he will want

to compensate you. I expect he'll use it to prepare some posters and will insist on paying for your time and skill.'

'No, not necessary, especially as it's not quite … as I'd wish. It's downstairs, in the tea shop, covered and ready to go. Besides, there's another favour.' Alice nodded towards the dressing table. There was a white five pound note on the top. 'Would you give that back to Mr. Thompson and ask him to return the picture of the ship.'

Evelyn took a step towards the dressing table then stopped. 'I think it would be much better for Alastair to ask Edward himself. Don't you?'

Alice looked embarrassed. Evelyn pulled up a chair to sit by her side, putting her little finger in one of Isabella's hands and smiling as the tiny hand squeezed around it. They spoke no further of the ship painting and when Evelyn left, before Alastair returned, the fiver was still on the table but she carried Edward's portrait back to Beatrice's, carefully covered.

As Evelyn came through the front door she heard Edward at the piano in the drawing room. A little of what he played was by now familiar and she smiled at the recognition – not so much that the refrain was familiar, more so it was pleasing to recognise Edward's composition. She considered showing Edward the painting but there was no break in his playing and she didn't want to disturb him. She took the portrait to the room Alice had been using as a studio and placed it on the settee, leaning against the backrest. Then she went down to the kitchen. She had missed Sunday roast but Cook offered dripping on toast. Beatrice and Catherine were not yet returned from looking over the guest house Beatrice had bought. The kitchen was warm and welcoming, and Evelyn sat chatting with Cook, who had some reservations of the future, 'what with Mrs. Blundell buying another guest house,' but Evelyn assured her it meant Beatrice would need Cook's counsel more than ever.

Evelyn took a cup of cocoa up to her room and settled on her bed to read. She had finished *Dracula* and started *Far From The Madding Crowd*. After a while she dozed and didn't hear Beatrice and Catherine return.

They dined together as usual – cold meat and vegetables left over from lunch. They had lapsed into informal arrangements for dinner, not bothering to change and Edward wearing his day suit as usual. Beatrice spoke passionately of her plans for the new guest house, turning it into a proper hotel. With modernisation there would be nine bedrooms, five with their own bathrooms, electric lighting throughout and the kitchen would be big enough to provide evening meals as well as breakfast. Catherine interjected with details of colour schemes and furniture and their enthusiasm was infectious. Cook brought them jam sponge for afters and when she had left Evelyn suggested Beatrice might, '… involve Cook in the planning of the new kitchen,' which Beatrice agreed was a thoughtful and useful idea. After dinner they were entertained by Edward's playing, though he politely, but firmly, refused to play any of his new compositions. Evelyn thought Edward quite cheery and, between songs, he mentioned William had received a letter from HMV, stating they would be including four of his recordings in the coming year's catalogue. Mrs. Blundell insisted on opening a bottle of red she had been saving for a special occasion, despite Edward's modesty, and the toast was to Edward's success – at which point Beatrice added, 'and I don't know why we've not spoken of it before but Catherine will take charge of the new guest house,' as she beamed at her niece and made a further toast. Catherine made Edward promise to still play for them when he'd become famous. Evelyn was thrilled for Catherine, who said she'd be giving notice to The Winter Gardens the next day.

Evelyn hadn't mentioned the return of Edward's

portrait, for reasons she wasn't sure of, but told herself they centred on making sure Edward was the first to know and see it.

Beatrice went to bed, leaving Edward and the ladies to chat and finish the bottle of red. They sat in silence for a few seconds before Catherine said, 'And I want you to help me,' resting a hand on Evelyn's arm, 'in the new house. There's so much to do, I need help.'

Evelyn smiled, tipsy. 'Of course. I haven't got to go back to London yet. Even though I'm not needed in the tea shop any longer.'

'Well that's good. I meant you should stay here, with us, not return to Spitalfields and we can work together.'

'Oh, I hadn't thought of that.'

'Well you must, mustn't she Edward?' said Catherine lighting a cigarette.

'Of course.' Edward nodded, then winced in pain. Evelyn noticed but before she could ask, Catherine said,

'And we'll have the best run guest house in Margate.'

'To the guest house,' Edward said, raising his glass.

They drank the toast, finishing the wine, and Catherine took a bottle of sherry from the drinks cabinet. Three glasses later Evelyn helped a happily drunk Catherine upstairs. Edward remained in the drawing room, finishing a glass of scotch and cigarette.

Evelyn was back in a few minutes and sat on the settee next to Edward. 'Oh, I forgot to tell you. Alice said Alastair wants to buy back the picture of the sinking ship. She tried to give me a fiver for it.'

'Then Alastair should come and ask for it himself.'

'That's what I told her,' said Evelyn.

'Though, to be fair, I didn't ask him the price before taking it from the wall.'

'Well I think a fiver was a fair price.'

'So do I, though, again to be fair, I know nothing

about art.'

'And perhaps if Alastair wants it back it's because he thinks it's worth far more?'

'In which case,' said Edward, 'tell him the price is now ten pounds.'

Evelyn laughed, 'I think that's a conversation you should have with him.'

'You're right. And he can have it, it's under the bed, but with the proviso he doesn't display the damn thing in the tea shop. In fact, I'll give it to him and pay another fiver to keep it out of there.'

Evelyn laughed again. 'Oh, and something else. I've brought back the painting of you done by Alice. Alastair said it's finished, though I don't know it's much different from when you saw it.'

'Oh, and how much is it?'

'She didn't say.'

'I should pay for Alice's time and the materials and if it's to be used for posters then Alice should be properly recompensed.'

'I suppose.'

'Another conversation with Alastair perhaps. I'll go and see him in the morning. Though, to be honest, I'm not sure a poster of this,' he gestured to his face, 'is a good idea at all.'

'Have you forgotten how good it is?'

Edward looked at her but said nothing.

'Do you want to see it?' Evelyn asked.

Edward hesitated, 'Now?'

'It's only upstairs.'

'It'll be there in the morning. It's getting late, and I'd like to take this off. There's something on the inside, irritating.' Edward gestured to his mask. It was the first time Evelyn could recall such a relaxed reference.

'Is there anything I can do?'

'No,' Edward said quickly, 'thank you. And I've had enough to drink, so I should go up.'

'Me too,' said Evelyn.

Edward waited for her to leave the room before turning off the gas lights and following. On the dimly lit first floor landing Evelyn turned, intending to say goodnight but instead, 'Are you sure you don't want to see the portrait?'

Edward hesitated but Evelyn had already opened the door to the room. He followed her in. Evelyn lit the gas lamp, complaining, '... about time Beatrice brought this place up to date, never mind the new house.'

She turned and beckoned Edward further into the room. Evelyn uncovered the painting on the settee. The dim light picked out the reds and golds of the sunset behind Edward's head. The detail in the face was difficult to make out, hiding any contrast between the masked cheek and the other. Edward picked it up and held it towards the lamp. Pin pricks of white paint in the painting's eyes glinted, bringing them to life; it was the face of a young man, a man with an ambition to live. The colour of the mask matched the other cheek and, though it was still clearly a false cheek and eye, it didn't appear unnatural; the two halves were Edward.

'It's far too flattering,' said Edward.

'I don't think so.' Evelyn stood just behind him. 'It ... it looks like ... who you are and you're ... real. And it's a little bit ... heroic?' Evelyn turned the comment into a question, fearing Edward would be offended. Edward turned.

'You're kind and I wish I was deserving.' He smiled, sadly.

Evelyn started to speak but Edward interrupted,

'... but the real mask is fading and chipped, looking tired, like me perhaps.'

'Nonsense. I know, why don't we ask Alice to touch it up, so it would be like the painting? It could be like new and we can sort out whatever it is on the inside that's rubbing.' Evelyn had a sudden rush of enthusiasm and

404

took a step towards Edward with hand raised, as if to touch the mask. Edward recoiled,

'No, I don't think so,' he put up a hand, 'I couldn't be without it, for even a day.'

'I'm sorry, I didn't mean to ... I just thought ... well, perhaps it's something to think about. And I'm sure it could be arranged so it's collected and brought back and you needn't ... you know ... be seen without it.'

'Dear Evelyn, always looking to make things better.'

'Of course. I'll say no more, but please think about it.'

Edward nodded and turned back to the painting.

Evelyn stood close behind him.

'So, you'll be staying here then, in Margate I mean, to help Catherine,' said Edward.

'For a little while, but eventually I'll need to find a job.'

'You could work for me.'

'Can you afford it? And what would I do?'

'You'd ... help, like you do.'

Evelyn placed a hand on Edward's shoulder. His back was still towards her. He didn't turn. She said, 'And anyway, how long will you be here. What if the College invite you back? That's what you want, isn't it? That's why you asked Father to pass on your letter to Reverend Plense, isn't it?'

Edward smiled. 'To be honest, I'm not sure I want to go back, but I'd like to think they feel I'd be worthy, though I can't see why they would, unless I can show them why, with my compositions. So, in any event, I won't be going until it's finished ... and I've still to find Kayst's parents.'

'Of course. You can't let that go.' Evelyn said, with a hint of reproach she hadn't intended, 'but after that, you could compose anywhere.'

'I like it here, despite, because of, the distractions. But regardless, if I did go and you stayed, there'd be

Catherine for you to look after. You'd find it hard to leave her.'

Evelyn took her hand from Edward's shoulder. 'What do you mean?'

'You two have become so close, Catherine would miss you terribly if you went back to London.'

Evelyn went quiet. It was true to say she and Catherine enjoyed a closeness she hadn't known with anyone else. It would be hard to forego that but what if there was another kind of intimacy she could share?

'Anyway,' said Edward, 'it will be irrelevant soon, if this bloody lump of shrapnel keeps shifting.' He tried to make a joke.

'What do you mean?'

'I don't know, just sooner or later I suppose it will … you know.'

'Not funny Edward. And …' She was interrupted by the sound of retching from a room down the hall.

'Catherine,' said Edward, placing the picture back on the settee.

'Yes.'

'She's had a lot to drink. You should make sure she doesn't choke.'

Evelyn left, reluctantly. Edward followed.

In Catherine's room Evelyn held back Catherine's hair as she vomited into a porcelain bowl then dampened a cloth for Catherine's forehead. Catherine mumbled 'thank yous' and apologies and not wanting to be seen like this.

Evelyn thought of Edward's comments about her and Catherine and if they hinted he was envious in some way. Then she was a little ashamed to hope perhaps he was and then guilty and sad for what that might mean to Catherine. Then she thought about the shrapnel in Edward's head and held back tears as Catherine vomited again.

Edward, Margate, Tuesday 19th October 1920

Margate jetty stretched nearly a quarter mile into the North Sea. It was mid–morning and the tide was low, exposing the rocks and mud under the first third of the jetty. The clouds were dark and the wind blustery. Beatrice, Catherine and Evelyn walked in a line, arm in arm, Beatrice in the middle. Edward walked a yard or two behind, carrying Beatrice's overnight bag.

'The sea looks quite rough, are you sure you'll be all right?' Catherine asked Beatrice.

'Of course dear. I've never been sea sick. Not once. Not even during the trip across to Calais in nineteen twelve when the captain was so worried about the swell he made us all stand outside in the rain, on the deck near the lifeboats and the Navigator was being sick into the wind and onto my cousin Francine's shoes. Though, as they say, it's an ill wind blows no good as after apologising and vomiting some more he went on to insist on buying her new shoes and asking her to dinner. They married less than a year later and had a baby within another. And I can't blame the captain as it was only a few weeks since the *Titanic* had gone down and it can hardly be denied our little ferry was unlikely to be a superior ship to that immense liner. Anyway, I'm sure today's steamer is more stable than that tiny ferry to Calais.'

Beatrice indicated to the hexagonal extension at the end of the jetty where the steamer, *London Belle*, was moored, waiting for passengers.

'It's a shame young Patrick isn't here,' said

407

Catherine, 'he'd have loved to get this close to the steamers.'

'Perhaps you could bring him tomorrow, if you'll be meeting me on return?' Beatrice suggested.

'Will you be all right on your own for the night, in London? I could've come with you,' said Evelyn.

'I'll be all right. Once I've met the solicitors, signed the papers and the new guest house is ours I'll pop down to the Strand for dinner at The Savoy and take a room there. It'll be a nice treat and make a change, never mind the extravagance, and much as I enjoy Cook's fare it will be exciting to see the latest menus in London and perhaps pick up an idea or two for the restaurant in the new business.'

'Then you must go to the Lyons Corner House in Piccadilly. It's my favourite tea shop and I always go there when I'm in the West End,' said Evelyn.

'I shall tell them you sent me,' Beatrice teased.

As they neared the ticket offices and embarkation points Beatrice turned to take her bag from Edward, saying, 'And you'll look after these two while I'm away, won't you?'

But Edward was not paying attention and Beatrice had to repeat the request before Edward realised, saying, 'Of course, Mrs. Blundell.'

Beatrice hugged the ladies goodbye. At the top of the gangplank she passed her bag to a crew member who, though surprised, took it onto the steamer and then went back to ensure Beatrice boarded with no mishap. Catherine and Evelyn moved to the side of the jetty from where they would be able to wave as the steamer departed. Edward excused himself and went to the ticket office. He returned a few minutes later as *London Belle* pulled away from the jetty and out to sea, a hundred yards or so before turning west, towards London. The ladies found a bench from where they could watch and wave until Beatrice was a tiny figure on the ship's aft deck. Edward sat next to them, lighting a cigarette and forgetting to offer one to Catherine until she exaggerated a cough. They sat for a while, the wind at their back, and watched a steamer approaching from London.

Catherine said something about the smell of the sea and Evelyn might have said something about Edward no longer having a sense of smell but he didn't pay attention to Catherine's question. He realised he had been expected to answer to something when Catherine went on to say,

'Are you all right Edward? You seem distracted this morning. And did you need something from the ticket office? Not planning a trip without us, surely?'

'I'm sorry, I was thinking about what Mrs. Blundell said, over breakfast.'

Earlier Beatrice had spoken, with some pride, of how the Ladies of St. John's had been able to use their contacts to find out a little more of Kayst's wife. As luck would have it, she said, Kayst had married his wife in St. John's at Herne Bay and, having the same name, the two churches had a connection. It was true Kayst had married young, just seventeen, and to a slightly older woman, but the shock was the bride had been pregnant. Just seven months after the wedding she gave birth to a boy. Of course it was possible, said Beatrice, '... the baby was two months premature, but in her experience, though it was, of course, entirely second hand, a baby weighing the best part of seven pounds was unlikely to be two months early. And, of course, it would explain why the parents might so easily give consent for their seventeen year old to marry. Despite the likelihood of pre–marital nuptials,' as Beatrice put it, 'the vicar at St. John's in Herne Bay was a compassionate man as the baby was baptised there. Edward.'

Over breakfast, when Beatrice had said the name, Edward thought she was just making sure she had his attention and it was Evelyn who asked Beatrice to repeat herself and confirm. The baby's name was Edward.

Now, sitting on the bench on the jetty, Edward said,

'I don't understand why Docherty didn't mention a child? As far as we know he told the truth about everything else.'

'Perhaps the boy was adopted, or looked after by the grandparents,' said Catherine.

'Or died?' added Evelyn. 'But if so, how horrible for her to lose a husband and child in the space of months.'

'And how did we not know? How could we share a trench and not know,' said Edward.

'And for the boy to have your name,' said Evelyn.

'There's nothing to be read into that,' said Edward.

'Nevertheless, it would have been nice …'

'… to know,' agreed Edward.

They sat for a few moments, Edward still deep in thought, until he said, 'I bought return tickets for the steamer to Hastings. I thought Mr. Trenter might find a use for it.'

'Alastair? Why?' said Evelyn.

'It goes past Dungeness. It must pass close to where his son's ship, the *Gurkha*, went down. I thought it might help? For him to see the place?' Edward finished the statement as a question, as if suddenly aware, on saying it out loud, how crass it sounded. The silence from Catherine and Evelyn confirmed how insensitive they thought the idea. 'A poor notion?' Edward said.

'I'm afraid so, Edward, especially considering the situation regarding the picture of the ship sinking. Have you taken it back yet?' Evelyn asked.

'No. But I should.'

'Should or could?' said Evelyn.

'Probably should, in this case.'

'I've an idea,' said Evelyn. 'Why don't you give the painting and steamer tickets to Reverend Railton and see what he thinks. It might be easier all round if he talks to Alastair.'

'And I do need to talk to Reverend Railton about Tosh's funeral,' said Edward. 'I'll go up to St. John's. Will you join me?'

'Catherine wants to take me to see the new guest house. There's much to think about.'

'Of course,' said Edward, standing. But as he did so a gust of wind rushed underneath his homburg and he felt it rise from his head. He grabbed to hold it down but his thumb caught the arm of his spectacles, dislodging the mask. A yard or two ahead of him were two young girls. They were startled at the sudden movement in front of them and then the shocking sight of Edward's face with dislodged mask and skewed eyes as he scrabbled to replace it. One of the girls screamed and her mother, some yards behind, rushed to be with her. By then Edward's mask was properly arranged but the girls' reactions were still to recoil. Evelyn was quickly up from the bench and to Edward's side but the woman with the girls was already shouting at Edward – a garbled stream of insults, including 'monster'. Edward stood still and hunched, embarrassed and exposed, and though he was sorry if the young girls had seen him, he was hopeful neither Evelyn nor Catherine had. He took a few deep breaths and stood to his full height. Evelyn muttered something he didn't catch and took his left arm. Catherine took his right and they walked him back down the jetty, setting a casual pace.

'They should have painted that bloody bench blue,' said Edward, hoping to be amusing but, with no explanation, realised it made no sense to Evelyn or Catherine.

They walked back down the jetty, parting when they reached The Parade, Edward towards St. John's and the ladies the other way, up to the new guest house. Edward walked along the seafront before crossing the road to King Street. As he did so a woman fell into step beside him, on his right. It was a short while before Edward, distracted by his thoughts, realised it was no coincidence. He turned to see who it was as the woman said, 'Good morning Lieutenant. How are you this not so fine morning?' It was Margaret, the woman who had come back from the hop farm with Tosh. Edward didn't break stride.

'I'm well, thank you. And you?'

'Well aren't you polite. And I know you don't care but seeing as you asked, I've been better. It's getting a bit cold to be sleeping under the Scenic Railway in Dreamland.'

Edward stopped walking. 'I imagine so. What do you want?'

'More to the point. Is there anything you want?' She moved a little closer to him. Despite his inclination he didn't step back. He took a florin from his pocket but before he could offer it she said,

'A florin a fuck? Is that the going rate do you think? I'd hoped to be worth more. A florin don't seem much from a lieutenant that I hear owns a hotel, is pandered to by at least three women and whose batman serves him like the war ain't done. A florin?'

'You mis …' Edward started but stopped and gathered himself, '… you're wrong but I'm not obliged to explain anything to you. What do you want?' He replaced the coin in his pocket and resumed walking.

'By the way, I'm Margaret,' she said, catching him up.

'I know.'

'Tosh didn't like you. Thought you was a right stuck up arsehole.'

'I'm not surprised.'

'But I like you.'

'I doubt that.'

'And I reckon your man servant, William, likes me.'

'He's not … never mind. What do you want?'

Margaret stopped. So did Edward.

'If I thought you cared I might bother to tell you, but … bollocks.' Then she turned and walked quickly back from where she'd come. Edward watched her, thinking about what she'd said about him being pandered to and irritated to realise to an outsider that might seem to be the case. He walked on to St. John's more slowly, a headache beginning to nag.

'You look troubled,' said Reverend Railton after the initial greetings.

Edward and the reverend sat in the kitchen of St. John's vicarage. The door out to the back garden was open and though cold air was blown in, the oven in the small range was in use and the heat more than compensated.

'I'm sorry Father. It's been a … troubling day already.'

'No need to apologise to me. Tea or coffee?'

Edward hesitated.

'Something stronger. A drop of rum?' asked the reverend.

'If you'll join me.'

'For a small one. I'm meeting some parishioners later and it wouldn't do to smell of spirits.' Reverend Railton smiled and took a bottle and glasses from the dresser. He half filled two small tumblers. 'And what can I do for you?' He sat opposite Edward at the kitchen table, moving aside a pile of letters and newspapers.

'It's a small matter Father. Some advice,' Edward said, pausing to take a careful sip of rum before explaining about the steamer tickets for Hastings and the dilemma of whether to pass them to Alastair Trenter or not.

Reverend Railton thought for half a minute before saying, 'I don't know Mr. Trenter and wouldn't like to guess at his reaction: caring or callous? Cathartic or trivialising? But my instinct would be not to. Being close to the waters that engulfed his son but with no prospect of recovery might be most … upsetting.'

Edward nodded. 'I can see that. But I wondered if it might settle his search. Much like your notion of a grave for an unknown warrior.'

'Perhaps, but I think it would need to be Mr.

Trenter's idea to take the steamer. Consider mentioning it to Mrs. Trenter so she could make the suggestion at an opportune moment. I expect Mrs. Trenter will be adept at making it appear to be Mr. Trenter's thought. In my experience most ladies are.' The reverend smiled.

'To make it his choice,' said Edward, 'as with your unknown soldier's grave. It will be there for all, if they choose to visit.' Edward thought of Alastair's ship painting, lying face down on the floor under his bed back at Mrs. Blundell's; it was never really for sale and to hide or discard it should be Alastair's decision.

'Absolutely.'

'And there will be a body?'

'Yes. It will be a grave, not a monument.'

'That would be an honour, wouldn't it? To be that soldier,' Edward said quietly.

'Yes, but no more than anyone who gave their life in service.'

'So who will the soldier be?'

'I don't know. No one will, now or ever.'

'Then how …?'

'Unidentified remains will be lifted from the major battle sites and one chosen at random. The chooser will not know from which battle the remains have come. And they will be brought to London, to be interred in Westminster Abbey.'

Edward finished the rum. 'A soldier's remains.'

'More accurately, a warrior's. It is possible the body will be that of an airman or marine, but yes, for anyone that has lost someone whose remains have not been recovered and buried, it's possible the unidentified body is that person. They won't know, of course, and it's unlikely, but possible. I believe there is also a preference for the warrior to have been killed in the early part of the war.'

Edward could not help but think of Kayst – one second close by, the next simply gone. 'One soldier's grave and a national tribute.'

'The unique potential to be both personal, for a small number of mourners it will be their loved one, and yet still a place for anyone who grieves.' Reverend Railton poured another rum for Edward, though Edward noticed the reverend's own remained untouched. Edward took his cigarette case and lighter from a pocket, showing them to the reverend by way of asking permission to smoke. The reverend nodded then looked at his watch. 'I'd like to talk more, but perhaps another time? I don't want to be late for the Parish Council. You might be interested to know Tosh's funeral is on the agenda. Or, more precisely, the question of who should pay for it. There's been a great deal of debate already. To be honest, far more debate than the small cost warrants.'

'He was drawing a disability pension, wasn't he?'

'We don't know. There was little money in his purse when he died. And we don't know his name to find out more, or if anyone else might contribute. For all we know he may not even have been disabled in the war.'

Edward thought back to that first day in Margate and the altercation in the tobacconist. He could taste the damp in Tosh's uniform, and, though a tunic proved nothing, he said, 'We should assume so and you should send the bill to me, but no need to tell others.'

'That's generous, but not the reason I mentioned it.'

'That's all right Reverend. I insist.' Edward said, lighting a cigarette and draining his rum. He stood. 'Thank you for your advice about Mr. Trenter.'

'My pleasure.'

'There is one other thing. The woman who came back from the hop farm with Tosh, Margaret, is ... in need of help. Do you know of a place nearby where she might find it? I should mention she is ... has been known ... to offer her ... services, for money. I believe she's sleeping out and winter is coming.'

Reverend Railton finally took a small sip from his rum. 'I'm not sure, but the St. John's Ladies might know.

I'll ask my wife. Meantime, you might talk to Mrs. Blundell.'

'I did think of that but … in light of the woman's … activities?'

'Oh I think you'll find there's little the Ladies of St. John's have not seen or heard about and none more so than Mrs. Blundell. If nothing else the war has been a great leveller and eye–opener for many.'

Edward shook the reverend's hand, reminded him of the offer regarding Tosh's funeral, and left. The weather had worsened, along with the pain in Edward's head. He hurried back to the guest house.

Edward didn't notice his car parked outside the Blundell guest house until he was at the front door, searching his pockets for the key. William opened the door before he could find it.

'And here he is,' said William, turning to the people in the hall behind him. Georgette was nearest, with Evelyn next and Catherine at the rear, holding Patrick's hand. William and Georgette were wearing heavy coats and gloves. 'We're just off.'

'To?'

'Wandsworth. My old man pegged it. I got a letter this morning. His lady friend was too mean to send a telegraph.'

'Sorry to hear that. Not unexpected though?' Edward asked.

'No. And he nearly made sixty. The funeral's tomorrow and I suppose I should go. All right to take the car?' said William, though it was clear he had already planned to.

'Yes. And we'll see you …?'

'Friday or Saturday. If we can make it, we'll be at Isabella's baptism.'

'All right, and here's …' Edward took two white

notes from his wallet and lowered his voice, '... something for flowers, for the funeral, and ... if you find some ... morphine, solution and tablets, this should cover it.'

William led Georgette down the steps to the pavement and opened the car door for her. Edward watched them drive away and joined the others in the hall. Patrick looked close to tears. Catherine still held his hand and bent down to tell him, 'It's all right, maman will be back in a few days. I know, let's go and see if Cook has made scones this morning.' Catherine led Patrick through to the back and down to the kitchen.

'Poor William, it's good of you to let him use the car,' said Evelyn following Edward through to the drawing room.

'I don't think he's seen his father since ... I don't know when. In truth I doubt he's upset. It's probably more an excuse to take Georgette away for a few days and show her London. Though I'm surprised her mistress didn't object.'

'Georgette said her mistress was also away, up in London for some reason. Let's hope they don't bump into each other.'

'It's a big place. Do you miss it?'

'Sometimes, but not enough to go back yet.'

'Good. And it's good of you and Catherine to look after Patrick.'

'William's idea, though Catherine was keen and I'm glad to be of help.'

'As your father might say,' said Edward and hoped Evelyn realised it was meant as a compliment. 'Oh, and thinking of reverends, I spoke to Reverend Railton about the idea for steamer tickets, for Alastair so he might go past Dungeness. Like you, he was dubious. He suggested we see what Alice thinks and perhaps even encourage her to suggest it, if she thinks it the right thing.'

Evelyn laughed, 'When you say 'we', you mean me.'

Edward smiled back.

There was a comfortable pause before Evelyn said, 'I'll think about it, and now I expect you'll want to get some work done.' She indicated to the piano.

'I should,' said Edward, 'but, to tell the truth, it's been a ...' he remembered the conversation with Reverend Railton, '... troubling morning and my head is ... a little painful. But I do need to crack on ...' he took off his coat and sat at the piano, 'if I'm to ...'

'... go back to the College,' interrupted Evelyn, 'You know they'd be lucky to have you.'

'You're kind but ...' Edward shrugged and winced, as if the movement hurt.

'Do you need more morphine? Is that why you gave William two fivers?'

Edward hesitated, 'No, it was for some flowers, for the funeral.'

'Hmmm, that's a lot of flowers for a man you didn't know.'

Edward smiled, 'Well, perhaps some of it will go towards ... you know. You're very perceptive.'

'How much have you been taking?'

Edward hesitated. Now he thought of it, he'd injected daily since Saturday, even though his headaches hadn't been overly painful. It had been over a week since the tablets had finished and after a few days with nothing he'd found a small daily injected dose kept any withdrawal at bay. And, of course, if needed to fight real pain, he could always take an increased dose. And this afternoon might be one of those times; he could feel the pressure building in his head.

He shrugged, hoping Evelyn wouldn't press for an answer but her silence was prompt enough. 'Probably more than I should, in truth, but ...'

Evelyn nodded and Edward hoped she understood.

'But aren't you concerned it will affect your composing?' Evelyn asked.

'A little,' Edward said, 'but, if you'll excuse me, I

just need to wash under the mask. There's an irritation there. Perhaps some salt water blown in during this morning's debacle on the jetty. And I feel my headache worsening.'

Evelyn stepped a little closer. 'Can I help?'

'That is kind,' said Edward, 'but you know, I wouldn't want you to see ...' As Edward spoke, the pain in his left temple seemed to lurch to his forehead and a sledgehammer crashed into the back of his skull. He barely had time to exclaim an unintelligible moan before his vision went black, a sudden dizziness shook him, his legs buckled and he was unconscious.

When Edward came to he was lying on the settee in the drawing room. The light was low but he couldn't say whether from time of day, closed curtains or failing vision. His head thumped and there was a stabbing pain in his wrist. The pain added to his confusion but as his thoughts cleared he reached to his face; his mask was in place but there was a cold flannel on his forehead. He was flat on his back, looking at the ceiling. Turning his head, even slowly, hurt. He looked around the room. Evelyn, Catherine and Patrick were sitting on the other chairs, watching him. Evelyn came over to him.

'What happened?' He took the flannel from his head.

'You fainted.'

'No, a ... a lady may faint, but a man passes out.' He tried to joke but even talking was painful. 'For how long was I unconscious?'

'Just a minute or two. We haven't even called the doctor yet,' said Catherine. Patrick left her side to join Evelyn, standing over him.

'Was my ... did my mask move? Did you ...'

'No, everything stayed in place but you fell heavily. I called for Catherine and we lifted you onto the settee.'

Edward nodded his appreciation and, slowly, pushed himself up into a sitting position, avoiding putting weight through his right wrist. Patrick watched. Catherine brought a small tumbler with brandy. Edward sipped but gagged as the liquid hit the back of his throat and spat it back into the glass, trying to apologise as he did so, embarrassment burning the right side of his face. 'Please, don't let the boy see this,' he muttered. Catherine led Patrick from the room.

'Is the shrapnel moving? Do you need some morphine for the pain?' Evelyn asked. Edward nodded and managed to stand, leaning on the arm of the settee.

It took two or three minutes for Edward to climb the stairs to his room, with Evelyn's assistance. His right wrist was beginning to swell and throb and he feared it was sprained, but the pain was nothing to that in his head.

His room was cold, the window facing out onto the garden was open. Evelyn went to close it but Edward asked it be left, the fresh air was welcomed. There was a small sofa in the room and Edward sat; he would have preferred to lie down but didn't feel it appropriate with Evelyn in the room. Evelyn stood over him for a short time before spending the next few minutes tidying the room, though there was little to be tidied. Edward watched her, both pleased she was there but ashamed she should see him this way. But the hammer in his skull would not abate and it was an effort to murmur, 'Syringe.'

In the cupboard above the sink Evelyn found the box with a syringe, needles and the morphia solution. She washed the needle using scotch, set it in the syringe and took it to Edward, together with the bottle of morphia solution. 'I don't know the dose.'

Edward rolled up his right sleeve, wincing at the movement of the wrist.

'How much?' asked Evelyn.

'A tablespoon,' said Edward.

'I understand some use a vein.' Evelyn said.

Edward shook his head. 'Top of arm. Not as effective but will do,' and turned to offer his arm. Evelyn prepared the solution, took one of her own small handkerchiefs and soaked it in scotch before rubbing a small patch on Edward's arm, Edward nodding encouragement. Evelyn picked up the syringe but hesitated.

'It's all right. It doesn't sting much,' said Edward.

'It's not that. It's just … I don't know if it's … the right thing to do.'

'Nor do I, and …' Edward took the syringe and injected himself, '… I understand.'

He rolled his sleeve back down and asked Evelyn if she'd soak a flannel in cold water to wrap round his wrist. She did so and sat beside him to place the flannel.

'Thank you,' Edward said quietly. The morphine already beginning to relax him – he hoped the dosage would be sufficient. From the garden, through the open window, he could hear Catherine playing with Patrick. 'My father loved cricket. Mother didn't like me to play, because of my hands, but when she was out, and the sun was high, we played and my father was … a good man. Like yours.'

Evelyn nodded.

'When I passed out, are you sure my mask didn't move?'

'I'm sure,' said Evelyn, 'but, now you mention it, would you let me take the mask to Alice while you sleep? Just to show her and ask if she thinks she could brighten the paintwork and perhaps cover the small chips? I'm sure she'd do a wonderful repair. And I'd also see if she has any tools which might be used to repair whatever it is on the back that is irritating.' Evelyn put a hand toward his face but before she could touch the mask his left hand circled her wrist, stopping her.

'No. Thank you, but no. Besides, what would I wear while Alice is carrying out repairs? I can't stay in my room for days, I need to be composing. I'm already losing time.

And thank you. I'm glad you're here. And I'm sorry about Tewson, and Tosh. It's not how I would … normally … not what's right …' He pushed Evelyn's hand away gently, his right eye staring unashamedly into the deep hazel of Evelyn's.

'You're rambling Edward.'

'I'm sorry.'

'You should sleep. I should go.'

'Please, a few minutes.'

From the garden he heard Catherine laughing and Patrick shouting joyfully. Here, in his room, he heard Evelyn breathing beside him. He tried to fight the morphine in order to enjoy Evelyn's company but as the solution took away the pain so it brought sleep.

Evelyn, Margate, Wednesday 20th October 1920

Evelyn was still making time to visit Alice and Isabella, though not quite daily, and, often, Catherine accompanied her. Isabella was nearly a month old and almost into a routine, though of course, as Alice told Evelyn, any routine was always temporary. As Isabella grew and changed a new routine was established, just in time for her to change again. The three ladies sat in the tea shop, Catherine holding Isabella, with Patrick sitting beside her, while Alastair served refreshments. The tea shop was now closed and Alastair was spending less and less time out walking, partly due to the weather but mostly due to Isabella.

The ladies chatted, though Evelyn was distracted, watching the others but still pondering the previous day's events. She hadn't seen Edward since he'd injected and he had stayed in his room – nearly a full day now. Evelyn was glad she had been able to help Edward with the medication but regretted not also administering the injection. It seemed a sign of weakness. If she accepted responsibility for preparing the syringe then any moral argument against delivery was hypocritical and based on a squeamishness with which she hadn't associated herself. Of course she was no nurse, let alone doctor, but if you can't administer medication to someone in need, a friend, a close friend, a … she stopped the thought – grateful for Catherine drawing her into the conversation with Alice.

'… and I know how excited Evelyn is to be godmother.'

'And for Father to officiate is another gift,' added

Evelyn.

They were discussing plans for Isabella's baptism, that coming Friday in Holy Trinity church. On visiting Alice that day, Evelyn had been concerned that the issue of the painting of the sinking ship was not resolved – Edward had not spoken to Alastair or returned the picture. But nothing was said and Alice, in Alastair's presence, had told Evelyn to invite Edward, William and Georgette to the baptism. William and Georgette were still in London and unlikely to be there but Catherine asked if it would also be possible for another guest to attend.

That morning Mrs. Blundell had received a letter from America. Mrs. Blundell finished her porridge and sorted the mail, as was her morning routine, commenting on the letter without opening it, then setting it to one side. Catherine waited patiently until the bills and letters had been read and Beatrice pretended to have forgotten about the more interesting letter. Evelyn watched as Catherine casually mentioned it, knowing it was expected. Beatrice pretended to be surprised to have forgotten it and eventually it was opened. It was from Eugene Portman, the American who had stayed at the guest house for a couple of weeks in June. He was returning to England, on his way to France where his family had business interests, and wondered if he'd be able to stay with them again. He was coming in to Southampton on the *Mauretania*, landing on Thursday 21st. He apologised for the short notice, hoping the letter would arrive before he did, though he couldn't be sure. His ongoing journey would be from Dover, on the Saturday evening, so he hoped Mrs. Blundell would be able to accommodate him for two nights, but if not he was sure he'd find other accommodation locally and didn't want to put her to any trouble.

'Doesn't the *Mauretania* stop at France before Southampton anyway?' asked Catherine, 'Cherbourg I believe.'

'I think so,' said Beatrice, 'but Mr. Portman must have enjoyed Margate's fine air.'

'And he must have money, to keep toing and froing the Atlantic,' said Evelyn.

'It's less than a week's voyage, these days,' Catherine countered. 'Mr. Portman can have the back room on the first floor, I'll make it up ready.'

'And I'll tell Cook we have another guest,' said Beatrice.

Since breakfast Catherine had said little more about Mr. Portman and it hadn't occurred to Evelyn he might be invited to attend Isabella's baptism, but Alice was happy for another, nearly as happy as Catherine, thought Evelyn. The conversation turned to what they would wear to the baptism and Alice went upstairs to collect the baby's gown, proudly announcing it had been made for their 'dear Curtis, twenty one years ago' – cream silk with a lace fringe and collar. It was beautiful and touching.

Evelyn looked around the tea shop before asking, 'Will Alastair be all right?'

'It will be difficult, of course, but we should look to the future, should we not?' Alice asked uncertainly.

'Of course,' said Evelyn, thinking of Edward's idea for the steamer tickets for Alastair, to pass Dungeness. To her, it seemed less of a good idea than ever and she said nothing of it.

The Blue Bench

Evelyn, Margate,
Thursday 21st October 1920

Edward came out of his room on Thursday afternoon, coaxed in part by Evelyn, and though he looked tired he assured her his head was much better, though his right wrist was sore. Cook took him to the kitchen and fashioned a sling from a large piece of clean muslin cloth. Edward wore it reluctantly.

Eugene Portman arrived later that evening. He was dishevelled, from so much travelling Evelyn presumed, but was, he said, '... thrilled to be back, even for such a short time, and pleased to meet Catherine's new friends.' He greeted Edward with no discernible reaction to the mask, and didn't lower his gaze except to point at Edward's sling and ask after the cause. Edward managed to answer without reference to passing out. Eugene's open and excited manner put Evelyn in mind of a puppy, though his frame and appearance marked him out as probably older than her by some ten years. From his greeting, Evelyn realised Catherine must have been writing to him regularly and knew enough about them already to avoid mundane questions.

Cook had some boiled ham left over and prepared a supper bordering on lavish – evidently Cook liked Eugene too, especially when he insisted she call him by his first name, as he had back in June. The evening was relaxed and the only embarrassment arose when Eugene went to his bag, explaining, 'After being made to feel so welcome back in June I couldn't return empty–handed. And so, from Margate New Jersey to Margate England ...'

For Beatrice there was a thick woollen shawl and some Al Jolson recordings. There were two books for Evelyn: *The Awakening* and *The Portrait Of A Lady* – both of which Eugene had been assured were considered important American novels. And there was a bottle of Old Orkney scotch for Edward, who remarked, 'I see you've given this some thought, for which I am grateful, and will think of some way to repay.'

'Not necessary,' said Eugene. 'To tell the truth I'm embarrassed to say I was also bringing over a bottle of Jim Beam bourbon which I thought you might like, but drank it on the boat. Which is a shame as I think you'd like the bourbon. If we have time I'd like to find somewhere we could have a glass.'

'Then I'll insist on buying the first and second rounds,' said Edward.

'We have a deal,' said Eugene. His eastern American accent was strong and Evelyn thought his sentiment honest.

'Good. And this is for you,' Eugene handed a small parcel to Catherine. Inside was a pencil case sized box covered in velvet. The stiff lid was spring loaded. Within was a delicate silver necklace with a single dark blue stone hanging just half an inch below.

'Oh Mr. Portman. It's beautiful. Such a clear stone. But I simply couldn't accept such a … lovely gift.' Catherine handed it back to Eugene, who laughed.

'I knew it. That's all right. I understand. I guessed you may say that, which is why it's paste, not a stone, but, I hope, beautiful nonetheless. And, who knows, perhaps next time I visit you'll be able to accept the real thing. There's a sapphire waiting to replace it. But until then, here,' he passed the necklace to Beatrice, 'Mrs. Blundell, you're a wise lady. I propose you should keep hold of this until such time as you feel your niece should accept it, or send it back.'

'It's beautiful. Is it really only paste?' Beatrice asked,

taking the necklace from the box and holding it under the light from the gas lamp on the wall.

'Catherine can look after this instead.' He handed Catherine a pocket knife. 'It's for young Patrick, but, not having children, I don't know if it's appropriate yet. I'll leave it with you to decide.'

'You could give it to him yourself,' said Catherine, 'he's staying with us for a few days.'

'Excellent, though I will still be guided by you as to whether it's appropriate,' said Eugene. 'And, before I forget, something for Cook.' He took a last parcel from his bag and left the room, without needing to excuse himself.

'They have such different ways, the Americans, don't you find?' said Beatrice. 'But quite endearing.'

'Very charming,' said Evelyn, looking over to catch Catherine's eye.

'He's certainly trying very hard,' said Edward, 'but why shouldn't he, in such company?' He indicated to Catherine and Beatrice.

'Of course I can't possibly keep it. Glass or not, the chain is silver.' Catherine said, referring to the box Beatrice now toyed with.

'Edward, did you meet many Americans in France?' asked Beatrice.

Edward shook his head. 'My time there was finished before they turned up, but William said they were a Godsend and, once you settle into their manners, they're as good as any.'

'Oh, thinking of France and, as one does, such things, I forgot the Reverend Railton's good lady asked me to let you know, Edward, the funeral for that poor man will be next Friday, the twenty ninth. Ten o'clock at St. John's. Poor man.'

'Which poor man, Aunt?' Catherine asked.

'The one who shot himself. Oh, Evelyn. I'm sorry. I didn't think. You oughtn't be reminded of such a thing, having found the … man. I should have thought. I'm sorry,'

'Not at all, Beatrice,' Evelyn said, 'it can't be undone and it's not for me to pity myself. It's that poor man who we should think of.'

'Of course, but still … oh, and also, Edward, I was speaking the other day to Mrs. Newton, one of the St. John's ladies, who I believe once lived near St. Peter's, near Broadstairs, and I happened to ask if she knew of the Palmers, from that area, and she said she had heard of them, a well to do family and I mentioned it would be useful to know their address as we had a mutual acquaintance and I would like to send a card this Christmas. Mrs. Newton said she'd find their address for me. I hope that's useful?' Beatrice looked to Edward.

'The Palmers?' asked Catherine.

'Where the Kaysts may now be in service,' said Evelyn, concerned that the subject refused to die and then ashamed to have thought in those terms. She watched Edward for his reaction.

'Thank you Mrs. Blundell. To know the address would be helpful.'

Evelyn tried to catch his eye but he looked down, studying the bottle of scotch he still held. Before she could ask or say anything Cook was in the room, proudly showing the new set of kitchen knives given to her by Eugene, who stood behind, smiling almost as much as Cook.

The knives were handed round for inspection and Beatrice was especially complimentary. Cook left the room, keen to try her new blades. Eugene sat next to Catherine, on the settee in the bay window, while Beatrice provided him with convoluted details of the summer's events in Margate, culminating in the invitation to Isabella's baptism, the next day, which Eugene was thrilled to hear.

'Speaking of which,' Edward said, rising, 'I must apologise and take my leave for an early night. Thank you very much for the scotch, Mr. Portman.' Mr. Portman stood and went to shake Edward's hand, but it was still in its sling and there was an awkward moment which Eugene dispersed by laughing loudly and apologising while adding, 'And I was hoping to hear you play. I'm told you are the berries,' and looking to Catherine for an approving nod.

'An exaggeration, I'm afraid, but I am sorry not to be able to play this evening.'

'Then perhaps next time.'

'It would be my pleasure. Good night.'

Evelyn stood and saw him to the door, hoping for a chance to ask if he was feeling all right but there was no other conversation in the room and to do so might be considered forward in company.

The Blue Bench

Evelyn, Margate, Friday 22nd October 1920

The vibrant colours in the stained glass at the east end of Holy Trinity confused the images. It was difficult for Evelyn to interpret the figures and story, but, with the morning sun streaming through, it was no less glorious. The small group gathered around the font at the west end of the church, just inside the door. Evelyn held Isabella in the cream silk christening gown. Evelyn's father, Reverend Coughston, was behind the font. He spoke of the meaning and importance of the baptism and how it was their duty to give Isabella a Christian upbringing and to see her happy and safe. Evelyn wondered what Mr. Portman would make of that, as he might never meet Isabella again, but he was nodding to her father's address and seemed fully at ease. Beatrice stood between him and Catherine, who held Patrick's hand. Edward, in his Sunday suit, eschewing the sling for the occasion, stood apart. Closer to Evelyn stood Alice and Alastair, sharing a pride that was palpable. Reverend Coughston was still talking as Isabella began to stir from her sleep. The small moan was enough to prompt him into shortening his speech. He took Isabella and collected a few drops of chrism from the font into a silver chalice. The chrism was dribbled over her forehead.

'And so we welcome Isabella Rose Trenter to the church. I baptise you in the name of the Father, the Son and the Holy Spirit, amen.'

The group repeated, 'Amen,' and the reverend gave the baby back to Evelyn who in turn passed her to Alice.

433

Mrs. Sharrock, who had been standing off to one side, came over to see Isabella and handed Alice a small parcel. Alice thanked Mrs. Sharrock and placed it with the other gifts on a nearby pew. Evelyn heard Eugene apologise, to no one in particular, that he hadn't known to bring a present and Evelyn saw how Catherine smiled at him.

Reverend Coughston pecked Evelyn on the cheek and then went around the group, shaking hands as if for a job well done. He reached Alastair last and hugged him like a brother.

They left the church through the west door, blinking in the bright October sunshine, walking back down the hill towards King Street. On their left were the allotments, untended and barren at this time of year. Beyond them, on the other side of Trinity Square, was the terrace of houses including Mrs. Capais's. Evelyn had hardly thought of that episode for weeks, and didn't want to now, hoping that her father would never find out. He was ahead, with Alastair. They slowed as Edward joined them until Evelyn was just a step behind and easily within hearing.

'… Mr. Trenter,' said Edward, 'firstly, thank you for inviting me today. It has been a pleasure and may I wish Isabella a long and happy future.'

'Thank you Mr. Thompson,' Alastair answered, formally and with no suspicion, as far as Evelyn could tell.

'I also wanted to apologise for presuming to buy that painting without your knowledge. It was … rude. I'm sorry.'

Alastair's pace slowed. 'Does that mean you will return the painting?'

'If that's your wish,' said Edward.

'We're talking of the drowning ship painting?' asked Reverend Coughston. Alastair nodded.

'And I'm happy to return it, no refund necessary, I acted thoughtlessly and I do hope you can accept my apology.' Edward looked to Reverend Coughston and Evelyn thought him seeking support. 'However, I'd be so bold as to ask one favour in return.'

'I'm not sure you're in a position to ask favours,' said Alastair.

'Should you not hear me out first? My apology is sincere,' said Edward.

'That seems fair,' offered the reverend.

Alastair nodded.

Edward continued. 'The painting shouldn't be displayed in such a place that Isabella sees it until she is old enough to understand.'

'You mean understand what happened to her brother?'

'No, I mean understand how hard it has been for you and Alice. To know she had a brother who is a hero will be easy for her, but to understand what it meant to you and Alice to lose him is not for a child to feel.'

Alastair started to speak but the reverend interrupted, '… I think those words wise, my dear friend. And this young man knows something of loss.'

'And perhaps one other thing,' said Edward. 'Should you consider … feel … it might help to see where Curtis's ship lies, then it would be my honour to help arrange it. Should you think it would help.'

Alastair nodded slowly but said nothing. He started to walk on and Edward moved to be next to him but the reverend took his arm, saying, 'He needs time to think.'

Edward nodded, then said, 'By the way, Tosh's funeral will be next Friday, at St. John's. You'll be welcome.'

'Tosh? Oh yes, Tosh. No. Thank you for mentioning but I fear I've buried enough old soldiers and much prefer a baptism these days.'

'I understand.'

'I imagine you do.'

Evelyn took the step forward to move between

them, taking an arm each side. They strolled back towards Mrs. Blundell's, Patrick running ahead, Catherine behind with Eugene, shouting at Patrick to take care. Alice, Beatrice and Mrs. Sharrock took turns in pushing Isabella's pram.

Evelyn and her father went back to the tea shop with Alice and Alastair while Eugene insisted on being taken to a pub by Catherine. Edward joined them. He told Evelyn he hoped to see her at the pub later and said his goodbyes to the reverend, who would be returning to London by train that afternoon. After a filling lunch the reverend went for a short walk on the seafront with Alastair, leaving Alice and Evelyn to replay the morning's baptism and share hopes for Isabella. Then Evelyn walked her father to the station, intrigued by his parting comment, 'Mr. Thompson is a man of thought, manners and humility. A man whose fate should not be determined by the war.'

Evelyn joined the others in The Compass, by which time they were four rounds in. She was self–conscious at having to enter the pub alone and quick to find and sit with them. William and Georgette were back from their trip to London and Eugene was looking a little uncomfortable as William was half way through a story in which, '… Edward was on the toilet, well, not really a toilet, more a plank of wood with a hole in it over a ditch, when his batman opens the door and passes him a dispatch from HQ. The batman stands there waiting for orders, all the platoon can see the lieutenant studying the dispatch. Then he folds it carefully in two and wipes his arse with it. The boys pissed themselves laughing.'

'Will!' Georgette scolded.

'Oops, sorry for the language ladies. But we never found out what was in the dispatch.'

'Orders to have you court martialled for shameless exaggeration, as I recall,' Edward said, shaking his head, then turning to Evelyn, 'Glad you made it. I'll get you a drink.' Edward went to the bar. When he returned William was telling another story, for Eugene's benefit, it seemed, of how Edward had come by his nickname of Lucky Lieutenant and how on one trudge up to the line in the dark fog they got lost but only the Lucky Lieutenant could lead his platoon to stumble into an abandoned German trench which was more comfortable than their own, so they stayed the night and sent back a messenger in the morning to say they'd captured it.'

'As I say,' Edward said, handing over Evelyn's gin and tonic, 'should have been court martialled for exaggeration.'

Eugene laughed and started to ask a question but was interrupted by a fracas at the bar. There, at one end, was Margaret, arguing with Ceinwen, the pub's landlady. Evelyn hadn't seen her since the day of finding Tosh's body and her instinct was to avoid looking her way but as her argument with the landlady faded, Margaret came over to the table.

'Good afternoon all. What a merry group. May I join you?'

There was silence.

Evelyn thought Margaret might be drunk.

'No?' continued Margaret, 'what about you, Lieutenant, have you thought any more about our last … conversation. The offer stands.' She laid a hand on his shoulder. Evelyn watched Edward as he shrugged off the contact. He sighed and began to speak but before anything was said Ceinwen, the landlady, was at Margaret's side, grabbing her arm and dragging her from the bar, apologising to Evelyn's group as she did so.

Eugene watched, then turned to Catherine. 'Well I'd heard the English pub was a place for both great conversation and melodrama. And I'm not disappointed.'

The group laughed politely. Evelyn wondered what Margaret had meant by her 'offer'.

'And where else in the world might you be propositioned in the middle of the day by a ...' William started but stopped, looked at Georgette, who glared at him. '... lady of dubious morals,' William finished. Georgette left the table, following Margaret out of the pub.

Eugene looked to Catherine for an explanation. 'Is she a ...'

Catherine blushed slightly and nodded.

'Oh yes.' William answered Eugene's question. 'Of course we met quite a few of them over in France. Or should I say, the officers more than the men. There was one place in Le Havre in particular, do you remember Lieutenant? The blue–light house down by the harbour? Reserved for officers they were. Me and the lads weren't allowed in. We had our own ... houses. If you were minded for that sort of thing. Some of the lads were so young they'd never ... well, let's just say some thought it was the only chance they'd ever get, and they were often right.'

There was no humour in William's story and the group's silence was uncomfortable.

'We were wrong, about Kayst, you know.' Edward said, cryptically.

'What do you mean?' William asked.

'Not only was he married, he had a son. So maybe he'd known more than most of us.'

'No, really? Well bugger me. Who'd have thought he had it in him? How'd he find time?'

Edward shook his head. 'I've been trying to work out the dates and I think there was a time he had some sick leave just a couple of months after rest leave, but I can't be sure.'

'Well, here's to young Kayst.' William raised his glass in a toast. The others joined him, though clearly not sure why.

'And now, you must excuse us,' said Eugene. 'It was nice to meet you,' he indicated to William, 'but there's a two o'clock showing at the cinema for *Pollyanna*.'

'An American film.' Catherine added.

'I know the story, though I've not read it. You'll enjoy it, I'm sure,' said Evelyn.

Eugene stood. 'I'm leaving tomorrow, so may not get to meet you again. Thank you for introducing me to the English pub.' He reached over to shake hands with William.

'I'll see you later,' Catherine said to Evelyn. 'Tell Aunt Beatrice we won't be late.'

Evelyn smiled and nodded.

'And you and Georgette should be picking up Patrick from my aunt, don't you think?' Catherine spoke to William, who shrugged.

In a few minutes it was just Evelyn and Edward left in the pub. Edward offered another drink but Evelyn shook her head.

'Is it a little awkward? To be in a public house, just us two?' asked Edward.

'I'm not sure my father would approve of being in a pub at this time of day, but I'm only having the one,' she raised her glass, 'and as Catherine might say, it is nineteen twenty. And she is going to the cinema with an American, on her own, so …'

'What do you think of Mr. Portman?' Edward asked.

'He seems nice, if a little forward. What do you think?'

'He's good company but that's easy when you know he'll only be around for a couple of days. He's charming but I can't say I like or trust him yet, and suspect we'll never know him better to judge. I don't know if that's for the best or not.'

'Well that must be painful,' Evelyn said.

'What must?'

'Sitting on the fence like that.'

Edward laughed.

'Well I think he and Catherine seem well matched. Though he is quite presumptuous, bringing presents,' said Evelyn.

Edward shrugged.

'Anyway, how was William's father's funeral? He seemed all right.'

'He didn't attend. He didn't say much but I gather he argued with his father's lady friend, over arrangements or something, and left before the funeral. It's today apparently.'

'Oh, that's a shame. Do you think I should see if he's all right?'

'Dear Evelyn, always hoping to make it all right. He'll be fine. I daresay any dispute was at least in part due to William's approach.'

Evelyn nodded, then asked in a lowered voice, 'And did he bring back any morphia solution? And needles. Might you need new ones soon?'

'You see, dear Evelyn, always thinking about what might make things better.' Edward said but didn't answer the question directly.

Evelyn sipped her drink. Sometimes Edward used the term 'dear Evelyn' like an aunt or older sister might.

'Margaret seemed rather agitated,' said Evelyn, hoping Edward might say something about her comment 'the offer stands.'

'Yes, a troubled lady.'

'Did you meet many … troubled ladies … over in France?'

'They didn't seem as troubled as Margaret. And speaking of which, do you think the Ladies of St. John's would be able to help her? I believe she's sleeping out and winter is coming.' Edward said, again not answering Evelyn's question.

'You should mention it to Beatrice,' said Evelyn.

'Yes, I've been meaning to, but keep forgetting. Sometimes I just …' he waved a hand loosely at his head then winced at the pain in his wrist, '… see I even forgot about my hand. So could you remind me, to ask Beatrice, for Margaret?'

'Of course. When you were in France, did you think Kayst was one of those young men William talked of? One of those who would look out for a … lady … fearing he might never …'

'I don't know. It appears I hardly knew him at all.'

'But what did you mean, about him knowing more than most of you?'

'Only that we assumed he was too young to have lived and his chance was taken from him. Perhaps he lived more than we knew. He was a husband and a father and many of us didn't know what that meant and many never will. It seems Kayst was something of an enigma.'

Back at Beatrice's, Evelyn sat in the drawing room, pretending to read but thinking through what Edward had said about Kayst. She was irritated he had been evasive about the 'ladies of France', and then annoyed with herself for considering it was any of her business. Edward sat at the piano, occasionally playing a few notes with his left hand but, with his right hand back in a sling, cut a sorry figure. He went to his room early. Catherine and Eugene were in the back parlour, playing cards and their laughter was audible. Beatrice had gone out to visit a friend. Evelyn waited up for her, flicking through the books Eugene had brought her.

The Blue Bench

Evelyn, Margate, Saturday 23rd October 1920

Eugene left soon after breakfast on Saturday, promising to return soon. Beatrice arranged a cab to take him to the Margate Sands station, from where he could travel to Dover via Canterbury. Edward and Evelyn waited at the top of the steps down to street level, while Beatrice and Catherine went down with Eugene. He shook Beatrice's hand warmly and pecked Catherine on her cheek, though Evelyn couldn't tell if it was readily offered or not. A subdued Catherine spent the morning in her room while an equally subdued Edward spent the morning tinkering aimlessly at the piano, his morning walk down to the harbour having lapsed from his routine.

By mid–morning the piano had still hardly been touched and Edward's constant smoking made the drawing room smell stale. Evelyn suggested they take a walk, for some fresh air, but Edward was reluctant, as if desperate not to miss some burst of inspiration.

'Have you taken any … medicine today?'

Edward nodded and Evelyn wondered what dose. The second post arrived and Evelyn collected it from the hall, bringing it back to the drawing room.

'Anything for me?' Edward asked.

'From the Royal College of Music you mean?' Evelyn said, hoping to make a light–hearted tease.

'I suppose, mind you, at this rate I'll have nothing finished to show them I should be there,' admitted

443

Edward, indicating to the piano before forcing a smile, 'but you know what they say, no news is good news.'

Evelyn nodded, sorting out the post and taking Catherine's up to her room. She knocked on the door and waited for Catherine to call her in. Catherine was sitting on the settee. Evelyn handed her the post and sat beside her.

'I'm sorry Eugene had to go.' Evelyn said.

'Me too.'

'You like him, a lot, don't you?'

'Yes, of course. He looks to be the sort of man a woman might get on with well enough to marry. A man to provide for, and look after, his family well. But I doubt I love him, and certainly not enough to follow him back to America,' said Catherine, tears welling, 'and who knows when he'll be back, or if at all. Sometimes it's better to make the most, and the best, of what we have here, isn't it? After all, he only came here the first time because he lives in a town with the same name.' The tears flowed freely and she leant into Evelyn who put an arm around her and pulled her tight, hugging close.

'Are you going to keep the necklace?' Evelyn asked.

'I don't know.'

'I don't see how you can return it.'

Catherine's tears subsided and she pulled away from Evelyn, asking, 'Do you like Eugene? Only you didn't join us in the back parlour last night.'

'I could hear you talking and laughing, I didn't want to intrude.' Evelyn said but, in truth, wondered if part of the reason she hadn't joined them was envy. Was she partly pleased Eugene wasn't staying longer? Then she was ashamed to think such a way, 'But I do like him, though, as Edward might say, we don't know him properly yet.'

'And does Edward know how you feel about him?'

'What do you mean?'

Catherine said nothing.

'I don't know,' Evelyn continued, 'I mean I don't know how I feel about him.'

'Hmmmm, and how does he feel about you?'

'I don't know. He seems to be in so much pain sometimes, I don't know if he has space to feel anything else.'

'Apart from his music and finding that Kayst family?'

'I don't know.'

'Well, between us there's an awful lot we don't know. Just as well we've each other.'

'Well if I was Eugene I'd sweep you off to France and take you back to America.'

Catherine dabbed at her eyes.

'I know,' said Evelyn, 'let's go and see Alice. Isabella will cheer both of us and I've a suspicion Alice may be close to finishing the portraits. And I want to ask if she'll consider touching up Edward's mask, if I can get him to agree.'

'Dear Evelyn, you're our very own Pollyanna. But sometimes it's a lot more complicated.'

The Blue Bench

Edward, Margate, Thursday 28th October 1920

Edward's right wrist was improved by the Thursday and he was spending more time at the piano but with little progress. Despite, or because of, injecting morphine daily, his headaches were a constant nag, though only sometimes progressing to a full blown episode driving him to his bed and a larger dose. He was smoking too much and exercising too little, to the extent even Beatrice mentioned, '… and despite the weather a young man should be walking daily, and leaving his cigarette case behind, just occasionally …'

Edward thanked her for her concern and she shrugged before remembering, 'Oh, and one of the ladies gave me the address for the Palmers, in St. Peter's. I've written it somewhere, I'll expect you'll be wanting it.'

'It would be useful Mrs. Blundell, thank you.' Edward ignored the biscuit and instead lit a cigarette to go with the tea she had brought.

Georgette opened the door to the guest house and welcomed Edward with a casual sweep of her hand. 'Come through.' She led him to the front drawing room where Patrick and William were putting together a toy glider.

'Look what Uncle William brought back from London.' Patrick said excitedly, beckoning Edward into the room. 'It is a Warneford,' said Patrick. 'And he won a Victoria Cross.'

'Do you know, I've heard of him,' said Edward,

gently handling the wooden frame and light cloth.

'But we won't be able to fly it for a while, will we Patrick?' William asked, prompting the boy to explain,

'It is too big for indoors and it is too windy outdoors,' Patrick looked to William before continuing, 'it will be across the channel and over Germany if we're not careful. We don't want to start another war now, do we?' Patrick's French accent carried a hint of William.

William smiled and pointed to the arm chair. 'Make yourself comfortable. Haven't seen you for a few days. All well?'

'Not so bad. You?'

'We're coping. Aren't we?' William said to Georgette as she sat next to him.

'Good,' said Edward. 'We didn't get a chance to talk at the pub. Did you square things off with your father's lady friend?'

'Not in a way that suits her. But it doesn't matter. He's in the ground now, the money will soon be in the bank and she'll be out on the street.' It was a matter–of–fact statement.

'So a successful trip back to town.'

'Yes, and, even more importantly,' he tapped Georgette's leg, 'we have a contract for a short season at Wimbledon theatre. Starting in December.'

'That's not going to work William, I told you, I'm here, writing until the spring. Though, to be honest, I'm not getting much done.' Edward rubbed his right wrist.

'When I said 'we', I didn't mean you,' said William. 'Georgette has a part in their pantomime. The New Wimbledon one is highly regarded.'

'Oh, I'm sorry, I thought … no matter. Congratulations Georgette. Will you be singing?'

'The details haven't been agreed, but I'm sure once they hear her …' William patted her leg again.

'Of course,' said Edward. 'You've a lovely voice.' He turned to William. 'So you'll be leaving us then?'

'Afraid so. But I'm still looking for something for you, for after the spring, in London, and you'll come and join us, won't you?'

'I expect so.'

'Good,' said Georgette, 'I may need a pianist.'

Edward smiled. 'Meantime, it's a good job Catherine has learnt to drive. Talking of which, I need someone to take me to St. Peter's. I've the address of the place where Kayst's parents might be working.'

'And widow?'

'Perhaps. I'd like to go early next week, and if Catherine can't make it, I'm assuming you can drive.'

William shrugged.

'Who's Kayst?' a new voice asked – a woman's.

Edward looked to the door.

'Margaret's been staying with us.' William explained.

Edward nodded. His inclination was to ask why but as she had been claiming to sleep outdoors it didn't seem appropriate to question.

'You all right Lieutenant?' You look a bit peaky,' said Margaret.

'Maggie's right. You do look tired. Do you need some … medicine?' William asked.

Edward shrugged, playing down the question, but in truth it was part of the reason for visiting. In the pub, after the baptism, William had said he'd brought back some morphia solution and a fresh syringe and needles. And, back at Beatrice's, Edward was running low. 'It might help. By the way, no change from those two fivers I suppose.'

'Funeral wreaths are expensive in London and I wouldn't want my old man to think I'm tight.'

'You didn't go to the funeral.'

'But I had to send flowers, didn't I? Anyway, your medicine is up in your old room. Margaret's been sleeping there.'

Edward checked his watch and deducted seven minutes, the old Elgin was running faster than ever. 'I

449

should be getting along. I'll go and get it.'

'It's in the drawer of the bedside table,' said William.

Edward stood and went to the door. Margaret moved from his way but followed him out, saying,

'No, I moved it. I'll show you.' She walked up the stairs behind him.

Evelyn, Margate,
Thursday 28ᵗʰ October 1920

On the Monday after Eugene left, Evelyn went back to Spitalfields for a few days. If she was to spend the winter and spring in Margate she would need more, and warmer, clothes. Moreover, there were some personal items she wanted, to make her room feel more homely, especially photographs of her mother. It was also a chance to make sure her father was all right and catch up with friends in the parish. She returned to Margate on Thursday morning, bringing her father; he had changed his mind about attending Tosh's funeral, planned for the next day. She took her father to the tea shop, where, as expected, he was invited to stay. Evelyn and Alice had caught up with a little gossip and then Evelyn went back to Beatrice's with her luggage, arranging to meet her father later.

Catherine was out but Beatrice was in, happy to see Evelyn safely returned, as heartfelt as ever. She was sorting through the morning's post – bookings for next summer were beginning to arrive – and there was a rare letter for Edward. Beatrice put it to one side, explaining that Edward had popped round to see William. Evelyn, with idle curiosity, picked it up. The reverse showed a return address for the Royal College of Music. Evelyn felt a small surge of excitement, was it an acceptance for Edward? Then trepidation, what if it was and he was soon to leave them? Or, surely worse, what if it was rejection? But Evelyn couldn't believe the last would be true. With a haste she knew was uncharacteristic she decided to take the letter to Edward at William's guest house and, if the

451

news was bad for Edward she would at least know and … and what? A bridge to cross if and when, but in any event better to be there rather than have him read bad news alone in his room.

'I'll take it round to him, he might be there a while yet,' she felt obliged to explain to Beatrice.

It was less than ten minutes to William and Georgette's guest house, covered especially quickly with the growing cold of late October. She hoped the weather might improve before Tosh's funeral the next day; she had stood by her father's side at too many winter graves. The grey clouds began to drizzle and she pulled her winter hat lower, it was dark brown with a heavier felt and much stiffer and wider brim than her favourite cloche.

She was half–way up the steps from the street to the front door of William's guest house when, through the door's window, she saw Margaret coming down the inside stairs, carrying a painting of a sunrise. Margaret stopped at the bottom and turned to speak to the man on the stairs behind her, carrying a small cardboard box: Edward.

Evelyn's heart missed a beat. She stopped, turned and was back to street level before she had thought.

Edward, Margate, Friday 29ᵗʰ October 1920

The only person crying was Margaret. The others stood in sombre silence, looking down at the coffin in the open grave. Edward knew the degree of grief expressed was not necessarily a measure of the loss felt, but, in this case, it was likely Margaret would miss Tosh more than the other mourners. He thought he heard one or two comment that the coffin looked expensive but he would not be so crass as to take any pride or credit in that. He didn't know Tosh, hadn't known him and, had he lived, would probably never have come to know him. And he couldn't even be certain Tosh had fought in the war. For all he knew his disablement may have come from falling under a tram or a mine accident or a paper mill guillotine or a ... he stopped himself. His mind was wandering. The Reverend Railton was telling the little he knew of Tosh. The other mourners seemed to be paying attention, except Margaret who wept loudly between sips from William's hip flask.

Across the grave from him stood Evelyn and Catherine. Edward tried to catch their eye, perhaps to give a comforting nod, especially to Evelyn as he feared the circumstances and horror of the manner in which she saw Tosh's body might be distressing her; she had been distant since returning from Spitalfields with her father. Beatrice was also on the other side, standing with three other ladies from St. John's, all dressed in shades of grey, rather than black. The Reverend Coughston and William stood on the same side as Edward but Georgette had not come. Reverend Railton stood at the head of the grave, conducting the interment. Margaret wailed again. Beatrice went to stand next to her, placing a hand on her arm, perhaps hoping to steady her, though Beatrice appeared almost childlike in stature next to Margaret, who was close to the grave's edge. Edward wondered who would have to go and get her if she fell in. Hadn't that nearly happened once in France? When old Soaps was being buried alongside his mate Angus, and Mancini, the brave Italian who'd somehow ended up in his platoon, slipped on the mud and would have crashed through the tatty coffins if not for Kayst grabbing him, and the lads had laughed despite the Padre's chiding. That was not a bad send off. Edward found himself smiling and looked to William, but it was all right, unless someone was watching him closely it was hard to tell. Reverend Railton was still talking and Margaret was now only occasionally sobbing.

At least the sun was shining. Tosh couldn't have had better weather for it, considering it was nearly November.

Reverend Railton stopped to pick up a handful of dirt and dropped it on to the coffin, with some closing words, before leaving the small group around the grave and removing himself some twenty yards from the scene. The Reverend Coughston joined him. Beatrice spent a minute with Margaret, looking down into the grave, before leading her away. Catherine and Evelyn joined them as they said goodbye to Reverend Railton. Edward went to catch them up but William caught his arm, offering him the hip flask, saying, 'To Major Gillies.'

Edward took it. I'm surprised there's any left, seeing how much Margaret knocked back. But yes,' he took a sip, 'to Gillies and Derwent Wood and Tosh.'

They both took another look down at the coffin.

'So,' William said, turning away, 'where's the lunch going to be?'

'No food or drink, I'm afraid. Not enough mourners to warrant it. But if you fancy a pint I'm in the chair.' Edward lit a cigarette and offered one to William, who accepted.

'Maybe, but just the one then I better get back. I expect Margaret will be there soon and I need to make sure she and Georgette don't … clash. Especially seeing how drunk Margaret is.'

'How long will she stay there?' Edward asked.

'We think the old lady that owns the place will be back from London before Christmas, and anyway, Georgette and me are moving back there soon, for the panto season. So Margaret might have to be out in a few weeks.'

'I'll ask Beatrice if there's anything they can do.'

'I wouldn't worry. Margaret will always find a way to get by and a place to put her head down.'

Edward shrugged and went to join those talking to the Reverend Railton, who included Evelyn, but Evelyn took Catherine's arm and led her away as Edward approached. She had hardly spoken to him since yesterday afternoon when she gave him the letter from the Royal College of Music, received earlier that day. Evelyn hadn't waited for him to open it and tell her its contents. Was that out of respect for the privacy of mail? She hadn't mentioned it at dinner or in the evening and had gone to bed early. Perhaps she was upset by the manner of Tosh's death, or, he remembered, perhaps Tewson's; in those respects it had been a distressing summer for her and he decided to ask her later if those were the reasons for her distance, these last two days.

Beatrice was now leading Margaret away from Reverend Railton. As Edward neared, Margaret caught his attention with an exaggerated sob. Edward nodded but didn't stop; he had no words of real comfort for her.

Edward and William were left with the two reverends. They stood in the doorway to St. John's church, chatting.

'Thank you Reverend Railton, for conducting the

service,' Edward said.

'I'm sorry we never knew his proper name.'

'I have a feeling Margaret knows more than she has told,' said Edward, looking at William, who shrugged.

'I understand you covered the cost of the funeral,' said Reverend Coughston.

'It's appreciated,' said Reverend Railton, 'though not strictly necessary. There's a chance he wasn't even a soldier. And we need to think about what to put on the headstone.'

'Without a real name he's a candidate for your unknown soldier's grave,' said Edward.

'In a way,' said Reverend Railton.

Edward drew on his cigarette then asked, 'You did say you'll have a soldier in the grave, didn't you.' He made it a statement rather than a question.

'Or an airman or marine. We'll never know but yes, there will be a body. It's a grave, not a monument. In just a few days unidentified remains will be disinterred from unmarked graves from the battlefields of Flanders and France. One will be chosen and delivered aboard HMS *Verdun* from Boulogne to Dover.'

'From which campaigns?'

Reverend Railton took a couple of seconds to recall, then said, 'Ypres, Arras, Aisne and the Somme.'

'A good spread Reverend,' Edward acknowledged.

'We lost a lot of men at Arras, in seventeen,' said William.

'Like Kayst,' added Edward. 'And just one will be chosen?'

'Yes, and it will be unknown. We are resolute in that. Brigadier General Wyatt will choose one from the four.'

'So it could easily be the remains from Arras,' said Edward.

'Absolutely,' confirmed Reverend Railton, 'but just as easily not.'

'And the interment?' Reverend Coughston asked.

'At Westminster Abbey, on the eleventh. There will be a procession through London for the coffin of the unknown soldier and the King will unveil the new Cenotaph. After that the coffin will be interred, in soil brought over from France with the remains,' Reverend Railton said, 'speaking of which, gentlemen, excuse me as I'm travelling to London this afternoon, to meet with Lord Curzon to confirm the final details.'

The reverend shook their hands, thanking them again for attending Tosh's interment.

As he walked away William said he'd not be joining Edward for a drink after all as Georgette would be expecting him, leaving Edward and the Reverend Coughston.

'You seem distracted, Mr. Thompson. Are you dwelling on Tosh's interment?'

'Apologies, I was thinking about the reverend's unknown soldier. It is a notion of ...'

'... immense compassion and sincerity?' Reverend Coughston filled Edward's hesitation.

'Indeed, and more. But I'm being rude. What are your plans Reverend?'

'I return to London this evening so I'm lunching with Evelyn at the Fort Lodge Hotel. It's extravagant, I know, but I see her so little these days and she'll be spending all her time here for the next few months ...' he let the words fade away but edged a little closer to Edward before saying, 'Walk with me a little Mr. Thompson. I'd like to take some sea air before lunch.'

They walked down the hill to the seafront and on to Marine Drive. The sky was clear and the sun bright, if not warming; the sea breeze was beyond refreshing but neither man complained. The irritation under Edward's mask was sore and he had a compulsion to lift it from the skin and let the air sweep his face clean, but resisted. They stood to look out onto to the beach where the wind blew in a heavily rolling tide.

'I shall miss Evelyn, these next few months,' said Reverend Coughston, 'but it's not right she should spend more time with her old father than others her own age, especially when those others have become so … close to her. Do you think?' he asked Edward.

Edward nodded, unsure if he understood the question. 'If Evelyn returned to London I expect Mrs. Blundell and Catherine would miss her greatly. And so would I,' said Edward. 'Your daughter has been a great support to me this summer.'

'She is so like her mother. And does much for others. But it would be a comfort to me if I could be sure others were returning her support and care.'

Edward nodded, more to encourage the reverend than imply he understood where the conversation was leading.

'Of course I would very much like to know she is provided for by a husband who would respect, and love her.'

'Naturally, and I've not met a young lady more deserving,' said Edward.

'But finding the right person is not easy. It needs to be someone like, well, perhaps like you?'

Edward waited a few seconds to let the implication settle or for the reverend to continue, but he didn't.

'Has Evelyn said anything to suggest that?' said Edward.

'Not directly. But I know how high is the regard in which she holds you.' Again, the reverend's words lacked clarity.

Edward felt the flush under his mask. 'I hold Evelyn in similar regard.' They stopped walking. The reverend held Edward's gaze. 'To be frank, Reverend, I doubt I would remain here in Margate if not for your daughter. This summer has been both enlightening and exciting, in large part due to Evelyn. And I can't imagine not being close to her, but I could not, would not, expect her to feel the same for me.' Edward removed his hat, ensuring the reference to his wounds was obvious. 'She is a beautiful young lady, while I …'

'Don't you think you do Evelyn a disservice if you think her judgement is based on appearance? I'm close to being offended you might think so.'

'It's not only that, sir. Along with my facial … wounds … there are other things to consider.'

'You are a whole man, are you not?'

Edward wasn't sure what the reverend meant. 'Yes, well apart from my face and a toe. But I'm unlikely to keep good health. My head is … not right and sometimes the pain is … I just mean I wouldn't want Evelyn's pity and I believe there's a good chance I will need a nurse, not a wife, and Evelyn deserves better. Though the loss is mine.'

Reverend Coughston looked away, thoughtful.

'And I'd be grateful, sir, if you didn't talk of this to Evelyn,' said Edward.

'Mr. Thompson, I understand and will say nothing. But I fear it may be a conversation you will have to initiate with Evelyn at some stage. And, for my part, you seem a compassionate and honourable man, which may be as much a father can hope for his daughter.'

'What about love?'

'Ah, part of the trinity.'

'The trinity?'

'Not the holy one, the matrimonial one. Love, respect, trust. I cannot speak for the love, but it seems to me that you and Evelyn already hold the other two for each other. The third I suspect, but only you will know. But, as you wish, I'll say no more to Evelyn until you have given it more thought.'

'I'm not sure I could give it more than I already have.'

'Then perhaps the time is to think less and act?' said the reverend.

Edward let the reverend walk away from him, replaying the reverend's words and finding no small pride and excitement in the possibility Evelyn had strong feelings for him, but also distressed at the truth that any love might soon descend into pity and resentment as his health failed.

Edward's mind was cluttered and his head hurt but he didn't want to go back to Mrs. Blundell's yet, though he couldn't say why. With nowhere else to go and the clouds beginning to hide the sun, he found himself at Georgette and William's guest house. William invited him in, notebook and pencil in hand. 'Still writing your notes I see. When might I read the masterpiece?' Edward asked, but it wasn't as amusing as he hoped. William shrugged and slipped the book into his pocket.

'Anyway, how is Margaret?' Edward asked, following William into the drawing room.

'Upstairs sleeping, I expect.'

'What made you think it a good idea to let her drink so much this morning?'

'I was hoping for a bit more entertainment. Perhaps something to shock the good Ladies of St. John's, but Beatrice and her friends seem nigh on unflappable.'

'And where's Patrick?' Edward asked, following William into the drawing room.

'Georgette took him to see the school today. He's still there.'

'It's about time, wouldn't you say?'

'Not my boy, not my business.'

'Hmmm, but what about when you move up to London, for the panto?'

'I suppose he'll have to find a school there.'

'Is that why Georgette didn't come with you to the funeral this morning?'

'Non,' said Georgette, entering the room and having

heard the question. 'I did not know Tosh and I have no time for another dead soldier. If he even was a soldier.'

There was an awkward silence until Edward asked William, 'So what did you think about the reverend saying they're bringing remains from Arras?'

'I think he said might be from Arras, but just as easily might not. And, even if it is, the odds on it being one of our boys are long, very long, to say the least.'

'Ah, this unknown soldier idea again?' Georgette said. 'Let sleeping dogs lie. Look at Patrick's father, he didn't come back but I don't go on about it.'

'Though, to be fair, there is a grave with his name over it, near Mons, ain't it?' said William.

'So what. What makes you think I'd go there? We were not even married.'

Edward looked at William. 'Be that as it may, I like the reverend's idea, and with remains from Arras ...'

'... you don't know that Edward. It could be anyone,' said William.

'Exactly, it could be. And thanks to Beatrice I know the address where Kayst's parents may be working. We can go there next week.'

'No,' said William, 'I've changed my mind. I'm not going. Enough's enough. You should forget about it. No more chasing ghosts. And anyway, what are you going to tell them?'

Edward shrugged.

'Shouldn't you go and bring Patrick home?' William said to Georgette.

'He knows the way,' she said.

'No, best you go get him,' William said and Georgette recognised the tone as well as Edward did.

Georgette left them.

William leant forward, talking quietly.

'Look, Edward, go back to the Blundell's, sit at the piano and play and compose or do whatever you need to do to find a way back to that bloody Royal College of

461

Music. Isn't that where you should be? At least until …
you know …' he gestured vaguely to Edward's head.
'Failing that, I kept back some of the morphia solution and
a syringe. You look like you need a … rest. If you want
you can use the office in the back. I'll make sure you're not
disturbed. Never fear, your sergeant knows his Lucky
Lieutenant, eh?'

That afternoon Edward was back at the piano, trying to
ignore the growing headache and the stabbing twinges
from his right wrist, still not fully recovered from the
sprain a little over a week ago. Evelyn had not returned
from lunch with her father and Catherine and Beatrice
were staying away from the drawing room. He had felt
some small pride at not succumbing to William's offer and
then some shame that all he had not done was something
most people managed not to do every day – and anyway,
should his headache worsen he had a stock of morphia in
his room.

By late afternoon he had retired upstairs.

Evelyn, Margate, Monday 1ˢᵗ November 1920

Catherine looked up from writing in the small book resting in her lap. 'When the front porter is busy with another guest the doorman takes the luggage.' Evelyn nodded and sipped from her coffee. Catherine added another note to the book.

'It's like watching William with his notebook. You'll fill that in no time,' said Evelyn.

'And the senior receptionist wears a suit rather than a uniform.'

'But we won't have one, will we?' Evelyn said with a hint of criticism she hadn't intended. Catherine lit a cigarette and carried on writing.

They had been sitting in the lobby of the Thanet Royal hotel for over an hour. The previous day, Sunday, Beatrice had suggested they spend some time at the Thanet Royal to gain ideas for their new guest house and Catherine had jumped at the chance. Evelyn had commented it seemed extravagant but, in truth, was happy to be away for a couple of days. Since seeing Edward and Margaret accompany each other down the stairs at William and Georgette's guest house on the Thursday she had struggled to forget the image and, worse, struggled to find any context for it other than within Margaret's statement in the pub that 'the offer stands'. The thought Edward and Margaret had … well, it was unthinkable. Not because he simply couldn't have, though of course she hoped not, but because just thinking of them together, like that, was simply, unthinkable. And when later that day she had given

Edward the letter from the Royal College of Music, he had offered no indication of its contents. What did that signify? She hadn't asked, he hadn't volunteered. And the atmosphere at Tosh's funeral and over the weekend had been awkward, or, she felt awkward, or had Edward acted it? She didn't know. And Tosh's funeral had reminded her of how she saw the bloodied body but, oddly more affecting, was also a reminder of Mr. Tewson's accident and seeing him lie clean and white and dying in the convalescent home. Not to mention Margaret's comment about him having taken a shine to Evelyn and it not 'ending well'. Was she to blame? Was Margaret right?

So, although she considered a stay in the Thanet Royal extravagant, the chance to be away was welcomed; a chance to clear her thoughts, except they were no clearer. The image of Edward and Margaret descending the staircase was there, again, and again. And now she felt guilty at not giving due attention to Catherine's enthusiasm.

'And they have a telephone in the lobby for guests to use.' Catherine made yet another note. She sat in an armchair opposite Evelyn, a marble topped coffee table between them. Catherine wore a new black dress, hemmed just above the knee, and black, laced ankle boots with a small heel. She looked relaxed and comfortable, confident and pretty – so suited to these opulent surroundings and always with a beguiling smile.

'What's the matter Evelyn?' Catherine asked, putting down her pencil and notebook.

'I'm sorry, I was thinking about Edward.' Evelyn had been considering if and how to ask Catherine's thoughts on the possibility of Edward and Margaret having been together. Perhaps this was the chance but before it could be taken Catherine said,

'I'm not surprised. This obsession with the Kaysts isn't good for him, is it? And now there's this unknown warrior grave thing as well.'

Evelyn shook her head, though they were the least of her worries.

'And I understand your concerns, of course I do. And I know it's hard but sometimes you have to let Edward find his own way. Like this thing with the composing and the music college. There are some things you can't make right or easy for him. Besides, isn't composing meant to be difficult and a certain amount of suffering expected?'

Evelyn nodded.

'And I do understand you worry about his headaches, of course, but aside from a cooling flannel I'm not sure there's much to be done.'

Evelyn shrugged.

'And anyway, this is our chance to spend some time together and to think about our new venture. I know it's not going to be as big as this,' she looked around, 'but we will make it as good as it can be. I don't want it to be another guest house. It can be a hotel. Much as I admire what Beatrice has achieved I think we should aim a little higher, don't you?' She leant forward and squeezed Evelyn's hand. 'For instance, I saw Edward brought back the sunrise painting he bought from Alice. I was thinking, we could commission some paintings from Alice for our lobby, and, maybe, even put the portrait of us two behind the reception desk.'

'We haven't seen it yet.'

'It'll be great. Of course.'

'Yes, of course,' Evelyn said sincerely. That they didn't have a lobby or reception desk yet was not a barrier for Catherine and her energy was both charming and attractive.

'And speaking of which, I believe Beatrice is receiving the finished portrait from Alice while we're away, but if so, pretend it's a surprise when you see it. I don't think I was meant to overhear,' said Catherine and Evelyn agreed.

Catherine wrote a list in her book. Evelyn watched her, and enjoyed watching, even, or especially, when Catherine looked up, caught her looking and smiled.

They spent the rest of the morning in the lobby, watching, before lunching in the conservatory restaurant. Evelyn thought the sandwiches not as good as those served in her favourite Lyons Corner House, which she always visited …

'… when you go to the West End. I know,' said Catherine, 'so you can decide on the lunches for our new hotel.'

Then they strolled the grounds, which didn't take long. Having worked up a thirst they went back to the lobby for tea and sat reading; *Far From The Madding Crowd* for Evelyn and *Bleak House* for Catherine, at Evelyn's insistence, though Catherine felt it far too complicated for a relaxing read and switched to a copy of *Tit–Bits* magazine.

They retired to their rooms late afternoon to dress for dinner. Catherine had taken the dresses she had made for their portrait and added lace detailing to the neckline and sashes of differing colour and width. They were both stylish and discreet and, on Catherine's dress, the sash colour matched the dark blue glass in the necklace she wore; the necklace given her by Eugene.

Dinner consisted of oysters, from Whitstable, naturally, followed by steak and kidney pie with apple pie for dessert. Afterwards they went through to the Moonlight Bar. Neither had been there since the day two and half months earlier when Edward had played the beautiful Bechstein and drawn a crowd. There were a few customers at the bar but the seats at the tables dotted around the room were mostly empty. It was dimly lit by electric wall lights, appearing frozen in ice behind large square cut glass shades. The mirrored walls bounced back what little light there was but served more to confuse than illuminate. Catherine and Evelyn took a table just inside the door, inspecting the list of cocktails in the tall menu. A waiter was soon at their side. They hesitated with so much choice until Catherine ordered two Sidecars, remembering William's disappointment they weren't available at The Compass.

As the drinks arrived so did music and they looked over to the corner, filled by the Bechstein.

'Isn't that Arthur, from The Compass?' said Evelyn.

Catherine nodded. It was easy to recognise Arthur's big frame though the poor light hid his face and he didn't seem to loom over the grand piano as he had the smaller upright in the pub.

They didn't recognise the music but it was pleasant enough for listening and to not require comment until a figure walked from near the bar to stand by Arthur. With no introduction, other than the first few bars of a song, Georgette began to sing but it wasn't until she sang the chorus ...

'After you've gone and left me cryin'
After you've gone there's no denyin','

... that Catherine remembered the song and nodded at Evelyn, as if to emphasise how good it was. The bar was noisy and the piano loud, such that Georgette's voice wasn't as clear as it could have been, but still it was a rendition with heartfelt sentiment.

Evelyn watched Catherine as she listened and, when the song finished to minimal, polite applause, Catherine said, 'It deserved a better reception than that, didn't it?'

Evelyn agreed, adding, 'I wonder how long Georgette has been singing here with Arthur. I had no idea.'

'I expect William is behind it,' said Catherine, scanning the room and, as Georgette started a new song, saw William at the far end of the bar.

'Shall we go and say hello?'

'Let's listen a little longer first.'

As the fifth or sixth song finished, so nearly were their drinks but as Catherine went to catch the waiter's eye another round of cocktails was delivered. The waiter pointed back to the bar and William, walking over to join them, tumbler of scotch in hand.

'Good evening ladies. Lovely to see you here. Always good to have friendly faces in the audience. What do you think?' He indicated back to the piano.

'Georgette's singing well, and some new songs,' said Evelyn.

'She's been working hard. And she's down here three times a week now.'

'Together with Arthur, I see,' said Evelyn.

'He's not as good as Edward, of course, but Edward has other things on his mind, as well as composing serious music.'

Evelyn thought there more than a hint of sarcasm in the last comment. 'Does Edward know?'

'Of course. I gave him first refusal but ... oh, hang on, this is my favourite,' William said and joined them by sitting at the table as Georgette began a new song. They listened for a minute or two then William asked, 'And what brings you two here? Had you heard Georgette was appearing?'

'No,' said Catherine, 'we're looking for ideas for our new hotel.'

'Ah yes, I'd heard. Congratulations. I'm sure it'll be a success.'

The song finished to muted applause and Georgette came over to join them. Both Evelyn and Catherine complimented Georgette on her singing and William insisted they have another round of drinks before he had to drive Georgette and Arthur back to Margate.

'What do you think Georgette meant, when she said she

wasn't surprised Edward wasn't with us? And if he was, then all we'd need is Margaret for a full house?' asked Evelyn when they were left alone at their table.

'I don't know. I suppose she's just used to seeing us together. And Edward is busy, trying to compose. Though he hasn't seemed himself lately,' said Catherine. 'Did you find out what's in that letter from the Royal College of Music?'

'He didn't say.'

'Then we should ask,' said Catherine. 'Perhaps that's why he's been a little ... distant.'

'Or ...' Evelyn hesitated, 'or it might have something to do with Margaret.'

'What do you mean?' Catherine asked.

Evelyn took a sip to finish her cocktail. 'I saw them, together, last Thursday, at William and Georgette's'

'What do you mean, saw them together?'

'Edward and Margaret. They came down the stairs, together. They didn't see me.'

'Side by side?'

'No. Margaret in front, carrying a picture and Edward behind, carrying a small box.'

'Oh, so hardly together then.'

'I suppose not but ... considering her ... profession ...'

'Profession? What do you mean ... oh, that. But surely Edward wouldn't,' said Catherine.

'Once or twice William has mentioned the blue–light houses, over in France, where ...' Evelyn hesitated.

'... where ...?'

'... the officers met with the French ... ladies. The places used by officers were called blue–light houses. William teased Edward about them.'

'But that doesn't mean Edward and Margaret ... you know,' said Catherine.

'No. And I can't believe he would.'

'Nor I,' said Evelyn, with some confidence, but then

with less, '… though it's hard to know what they're thinking, or feeling, isn't it?'

'Who? Men? I suppose so.'

'What about you and Eugene? Do you miss him?' Evelyn indicated the necklace hanging against Catherine's pale skin.

'Of course, but I'm not sure we'd ever have … and I suppose I should send this back, but that doesn't mean I don't miss his company. And I'm sure you'd miss Edward if he went away.'

Evelyn thought about Edward's desire to go back to the Royal College and then about his wounds, was it possible they might take him first? She forced a smile, 'Well, it's a good job we've each other.'

Catherine finished her drink. The bar was emptying and they joined those leaving, passing through the lobby and on to the lift. Both inner and outer gated doors were open and they went through. The man in uniform pulled them shut and asked for the floor number. They were only a floor up and could easily have walked but the lift was a novelty, though once on the lobby for their floor they agreed it was a noisy extravagance their own hotel could do without.

Their rooms were next to each other, both facing out to the garden at the back of the hotel. They came to Catherine's first. Evelyn waited while Catherine fished in her small handbag for the key. Catherine found it but before unlocking the door, turned to Evelyn.

'Are you all right? About Edward and Margaret I mean. I'm not saying anything happened, I don't think Edward would, but are you all right, and not thinking about it. Not that you should, or shouldn't, except, either way, I want you to be all right, about thinking about it, or not, that is.'

'I'm not sure what any of that means. You sound like Beatrice.' Evelyn smiled.

'I'm sorry, I just don't want you to be upset.'

'It's all right. I'm just a little confused, but knowing I've a friend who cares is a huge help. Thank you.' Evelyn placed a hand on Catherine's forearm.

'We do need to look after each other.'

Evelyn nodded.

'It's not late and I've a small bottle of sherry in my room. Nightcap?' Catherine unlocked her door and took a step inside.

'Why not,' Evelyn said, following Catherine through.

Catherine took the sherry from her case, two glasses from the bathroom and poured generous measures. They sat next to each other on the bed, their drinks on the side table. Catherine turned to look at Evelyn, asking, 'So it would bother you if you thought Edward had visited a blue–light house, in France?'

'I suppose so.'

'But a soldier, a man, would have … needs.' Catherine laughed lightly, 'What a stupid way to put it.'

'So do women. Don't they?' said Evelyn.

Catherine nodded.

'You once told me you nearly …' Evelyn didn't finish the sentence.

'Not really. We kissed and … and … touched. And it was … exciting, but he wasn't the right person, for me.'

'Was it Eugene?'

'Good Lord no. Eugene and I only held hands and touched cheeks.'

'Well I've not even kissed, properly. Pecking cousins on the cheek doesn't count, does it?' Evelyn laughed.

'No,' said Catherine, 'so perhaps you should spend more time with Edward?'

'Perhaps.' Evelyn shifted on the bed and the two women were now facing each other, 'though I'm not sure I'd know what to do.'

'There's nothing to it,' said Catherine, 'kissing, I mean.'

'Really?'

'You just do what feels right.'

'And it is as exciting as they say?'

'More, with someone who cares.'

'I would like to … one day.'

'You will.'

The electric light hanging from the centre of the ceiling was surrounded by coloured translucent glass. Catherine's face was towards the light, though the effect was to make her brown eyes shine with darkness, rather than illuminate. As Catherine shifted her position the occasional glint flashed from the dark blue glass on the necklace she wore, the necklace Eugene had given her.

'I think Eugene cares for you. Don't you?'

'Of course, why wouldn't he? Though I would have preferred a real sapphire,' Catherine said, laughing to show it was a joke but Evelyn wondered if it hid some sadness and reached to cradle the blue glass. Catherine raised her chin as if in invitation and Evelyn's fingers brushed the smooth skin at Catherine's neck.

'Beautiful,' said Evelyn and Catherine's lavender perfume was a gentle enticement. With no intent or thought, Evelyn moved forward just a fraction. There was a flush of fear and then a rush of excitement as Catherine edged toward her. With an instinct she had never known, Evelyn leaned further and rested her lips on Catherine's. For a second she thought Catherine might pull away but Catherine reacted, increasing the pressure but parting her mouth slightly to gently move her tongue across Evelyn's lips. Evelyn felt, rather than heard, herself moan quietly and pulled away a little so she could speak. 'I'm sorry, I don't know why I did that.'

'And I've no idea why I responded like that.'

They were still close.

'Perhaps we're a bit squiffy, from the cocktails?'

'Perhaps, but …' Catherine kissed Evelyn again.

Evelyn's was initially encouraging, then stopped,

asking, 'Is this a good idea?'

'I don't know. It doesn't feel like a bad idea, does it?' said Catherine.

'I'm a reverend's daughter, after all,' said Evelyn with mock sincerity.

'Aren't they the worst?' teased Catherine, kissing Evelyn again and embracing her. Evelyn didn't know what to do next and Catherine's hesitation suggested the same for her. They pulled apart with matching embarrassed smiles.

'I'm sorry. I don't know why I did that,' said Catherine.

'Haven't we already had this conversation, but the other way around?' Evelyn asked.

Catherine shrugged, laughing.

'I've never thought I'd … you know, with a girl,' said Evelyn.

'Me neither. And I don't want you not to be a friend …'

'… but …'

'I know …' Catherine pulled Evelyn towards her.

With no plan or consideration Evelyn found herself lying next to Catherine on the bed and though she couldn't explain the need, she accepted the hand Catherine extended, holding it tightly in hers.

They edged to each other slowly, relaxed each other's inhibitions and touched each other gently, until there couldn't possibly be any shame and physical love was inevitable.

'Are you not sleeping well?' Catherine asked. It was the early hours of the morning and they were lying close, finding warmth in each other.

'I'm sorry. Did I wake you?' asked Evelyn.

'That's all right, it's a good time and a nice place to wake. What are you thinking about?'

Evelyn hesitated. 'I don't know. Not a lot.'

'Really?'

'Partly I was remembering those postcards Georgette showed us, in the pub. The French ladies.'

'I remember.'

'And the two women together, it seemed a little … posed.'

'I expect it was.'

'Nothing like … you know, it really is.'

'That's good.'

'But …' Evelyn hesitated again before continuing, 'it's … confusing. You're so beautiful and this was, is, natural, isn't it? But what of Edward?'

'I don't know if this is right for me or not, but it felt right tonight, didn't it?'

'Yes. What does it mean?' Evelyn asked.

'Does it need to mean something?'

'I don't know.'

'Nor do I. But I think that's all right, it doesn't have to and it doesn't need to change anything and I'm not sorry,' said Catherine with more than a hint of defiance.

'Nor am I.'

'Good.'

They closed arms around each other and enjoyed the new quiet.

Later, come mid–morning, Evelyn put her underwear and dress back on, found her key and left Catherine's room for her own. She ruffled the bedclothes, just in case the maid should come to clean and tidy, then went back to Catherine's room. Catherine was still in bed, sleeping. Evelyn took off her dress but left on her chemise, and slipped under the covers. Though she didn't touch Catherine, the warmth and smell was intoxicating. She listened to Catherine breathing, watched her beauty and enjoyed the fearfulness of what it meant to be there. There was no guilt for her actions, she was sure she loved Catherine as much, if not more, than many women did when lying with a man, and there was a feeling of having changed and learned. Their actions had not been planned and there were no ulterior motives. And now, this morning, she wanted to live this moment, though that meant suppressing a nagging guilt she may have betrayed Edward, regardless of what may have occurred between him and Margaret.

The Blue Bench

Edward, Margate, Tuesday 2nd November 1920

Edward was pleased that Evelyn had gone away for a few days. After Tosh's funeral there had been tension in the house, the source of which he couldn't pin–point. He couldn't even be sure he wasn't imagining it, just as he sometimes wondered if he'd imagined the conversation with Reverend Coughston – had the reverend really all but offered his daughter's hand in marriage? Surely Evelyn would know if so. Was that the source of the tension?

On the Tuesday, with Evelyn and Catherine still at the Thanet Royal hotel, Edward made the mistake of mentioning the conversation with Reverend Coughston to William.

Edward had woken late and missed breakfast, which he put down to misjudging the morphia solution dosage the previous night, but forced himself to go for a walk, to try and revive the habit of going down to the harbour for the air and the exercise. It was a cold November morning but he eschewed his heavy coat, hoping for the strengthening sea wind to refresh and invigorate. A mistake. It was uncomfortably cold. He pulled his homburg lower and his jacket collar higher but still determined to reach the end of the harbour pier.

Edward lit a cigarette, thinking of the letter from the Royal College of Music and trying to read between the lines. Lost in thought, the small voice calling, 'Lieutenant, Lieutenant,' didn't attract his attention until Patrick was almost upon him. The bright young face, red from the wind and running, was a welcome distraction.

'It's a brave ace flies on such a blustery day.' Edward said, referring to the toy plane Patrick carried.

'My mother says they were the bravest of the brave, in the war,' said Patrick.

'Most stupid of the stupid, more like,' William said quietly as he joined them, not wanting Patrick to hear.

'That may well be true,' said Edward, to Patrick, 'but first they would be careful not to have their precious flying machine damaged.'

'Exactly what I told him. But he's a stubborn young man and insisted. So we're on our way to the cliffs.'

'Well good luck on your mission. And in the meantime, best hold tight to that, in case the wind catches it full.'

'But don't forget to let go if it takes off with you.' William laughed, picking Patrick up and holding him high, as he giggled with delight.

William put Patrick down and took the cigarette offered by Edward. They moved a little closer to the lighthouse as William lit the cigarette. Patrick ran twenty yards or so back down the pier and then back to the men, testing the toy plane against the wind.

'It'll break,' said Edward.

'I've told 'im. But sometimes they have to find out themselves,' said William.

'Or else the wind really will carry him away, then you'll have some explaining for Georgette.'

William looked at Edward and started to speak but stopped and drew on his cigarette before asking, 'Anyway, how're you? Finished that concerto yet?'

Edward shrugged. 'It's slow.'

'Of course it is. It's going to be a great piece of work. You can't hurry that.'

As well as Edward knew William, there were times he still couldn't be sure of his sarcasm.

'Perhaps you should have taken a few days off. Like Evelyn and Catherine. We saw them up at the Thanet

Royal hotel yesterday.'

'They're looking for inspiration for the new hotel.'

'And finding it in the bar and each other's company if you ask me.'

It was a cryptic comment and Edward looked at William, waiting for more but all he said was, 'I was there with Georgette. She's singing in the bar a few times a week until we move back to London. She's doing well, but, to be honest, I'm worried how she'll handle bigger venues and audiences. Still, it's what she wants …'

'And you?'

'With you stuck here I need some act to hawk round. I'd rather be working the concert circuit than the music halls but I take it you are still staying here, for the foreseeable?'

'For the foreseeable. And you're still off to London in a few weeks.'

'I'll be popping down now and again but you may need to find your own supply of tablets and morphia.'

'I'll be off it soon,' said Edward.

'Of course, until the next time those shards of metal move about a bit.'

Edward shrugged.

'Another reason for coming with me back to town. I'm sure we can find you somewhere for you to write and … suffer.'

Edward looked at him.

'For your art, I mean, of course,' William said.

'I like it here. It's … inspiring.' Edward indicated to the air and the sea but knew he was not convincing and, in truth, he'd struggled to write anything of quality in the last couple of weeks. 'And once this is fixed,' he held up his hand, though the wrist was all but healed, 'I'll have the concerto finished by spring. Besides, living at Mrs. Blundell's has … advantages.'

'A soft bed, a full belly, a piano … not hard to find elsewhere. We could even paint the piano's bench blue for you.'

Edward said nothing.

'Ah,' said William, 'but three ladies to dote on you? Perhaps not so easy to find. I imagine Beatrice is especially attentive. A very attractive woman for one of her age, if a little … petite for my taste.'

Edward remained silent.

'And then, of course, there's Evelyn.'

Edward looked up from his cigarette.

William continued, 'Of course, Evelyn. Always wants to do the right thing and she's a pretty one, sure enough, but have you looked in the mirror lately?'

After a long pause Edward said, 'Her father has suggested I might … suggest marriage to Evelyn.'

William raised an eyebrow with exaggeration. 'Did he? Well I'd suggest you need to think if it's fair on Evelyn. If it's the fucking you need then I'm sure we can come to an arrangement with Margaret. Georgette's trying to organise something with our guest house owner so Margaret can stay there over the winter and look after it. Perhaps you could move back there and be … looked after.'

'There is no fu … it's not about being looked after. And I owe you no explanation.'

'Oh, so you think you might love Evelyn? That would be even more unfair, on her.'

'That's not your business and you need …' Edward's voice was raised in a quick temper but he caught himself. He feared there was much truth in William's view that marriage would not be fair on Evelyn. 'I know she's better than I deserve but …'

'Deserve? Bollocks. No one gets what they deserve, be it good or bad. Anyway, my Lucky Lieutenant,' said William, almost laughing, 'living with Evelyn may not give the advantage you think, regardless of what the good reverend might say.'

'What do you mean?'

William shook his head, 'I don't know, just, perhaps the reverend doesn't know his daughter as well as he thinks.'

Edward waited.

'Yes, Evelyn is fond of you, anyone can see, but marriage? Ask yourself, is she a woman in love?'

Edward went quiet; it was so often the question on his mind.

'Anyway, other matters,' said Edward, 'Now I know where the Kayst's are working I'll need you to drive me there. Tomorrow?'

'No. I don't think so. And I've already said so.'

'Thursday then.'

'No, I'm not for driving you there. Enough's enough. Let it go. I'm fed up with the wild goose chase. They may not even be there.'

'We won't know until we go.'

'And so what if they are. You've nothing to say to them, not really.'

'They need to know their son was a hero.'

'They were all bleedin' heroes.'

Edward hesitated. 'But Kayst was my fault.'

William shook his head, but Edward thought more in pity than disagreement. 'Bollocks. I ain't going. You need to go? Take the tram.'

'Catherine will drive me.'

'She knows where to get the car from.'

'You won't be needing it in London anyway.'

'It might be difficult getting your ... medicinal supplies ... back to you without a car. The train's ... inconvenient.'

'I told you, I'll be off it soon.'

'Of course. Anyway, me and Patrick are going.' William waved Patrick to come back to him, shouting, 'What say we find a place for a nice hot cocoa before we brave the wind?'

Patrick said goodbye to Edward with his customary

politeness. Edward watched them go and huddled a little closer to the lighthouse. He pulled his collar a little higher still and tried to light another cigarette.

Edward, Margate, Wednesday 3rd November 1920

The next day, Wednesday, Beatrice came down the stairs calling something Edward couldn't quite hear but which, nevertheless, was a distraction. Sadly it wasn't a distraction from composing; there had been precious little of that. He sat at the piano, hunched over the keys, feeling guilty for achieving so little. Though it was mid–morning the drawing room was dark, with no light inside and a gloomy November day outside. He heard Beatrice call something again, but it didn't sound like his name and besides, Beatrice had, of late, not disturbed him in the drawing room. Beatrice called yet again, this time from the hall, and Edward heard the names – Catherine and Evelyn – followed shortly by the front door being shut heavily. Evelyn and Catherine were home. He sat upright, readying to go and greet them, but before he could stand Beatrice led them in, calling over her shoulder for Cook to put on the kettle. He smiled broadly without thinking, ignoring the twinge of pain under the mask. Beatrice was excited and talking, asking questions and answering them herself, keen to share, keen to understand, thrilled to have them home. Edward listened, feeling part of the conversation without needing to contribute.

Catherine went through the ideas in her notebook, laughing off Evelyn's interruptions and explanations of Catherine's obsessive note taking. Cook brought tea and shortbread and joined them for the refreshments before she took Catherine down to the kitchen to hear more about the menus at Thanet Royal. Beatrice spent a few minutes asking Evelyn more questions then left to join Catherine and Cook before they, '… decide to take black pudding off next season's breakfast menu …'

'You look well,' Edward said, to break the silence.

'Thank you. It was nice to see somewhere new, though, of course, Whitstable is hardly Paris or New York.'

'Then perhaps we should arrange a trip, to one or the other.'

'Or both. For the opening nights of your concerto.' Evelyn nodded to the piano. 'Is it coming along?'

Edward shrugged. 'I need some inspiration,' he thought of what Reverend Coughston had said, 'so I'm very glad you're back.' He paused but there was no reaction. 'You stayed longer than expected?' He made it a question.

'There was a lot to see and think about. And how has your head been? Have you had to take much … medicine?'

Edward shrugged again.

'And did we miss anything? I know it's only been a few days but …'

'Nothing I noticed. Beatrice has been more quiet than usual. I think she missed you both more than she'd anticipated. Reverend Railton came round. He needed to talk to your aunt about the flowers for the church and while here gave me more detail on the plans for the grave for the unknown soldier. And the papers are talking of it. There will be a ballot for tickets to attend at Whitehall. The chosen remains will arrive in Dover in just a few days, on the tenth, and then travel by train to London. I would like to see.'

'The remains?'

'The coffin. Wouldn't you?'

Evelyn paused before, 'Yes, I think so.'

'Perhaps we will. Oh, and I've just remembered, Alice finished your portrait, or at least, it's back here.'

'I think perhaps that's meant to be a surprise.'

'Oh, I'm sorry. Can you pretend I didn't say?'

'Of course. How does it look?'

'Well I don't know for sure Alice finished it. I haven't seen it and Alice hasn't spoken to me. She may have spoken to Beatrice.'

'You haven't looked? Where is it?'

'In the room where she painted.'

'Next to your own portrait then?'

'I suppose.'

Edward watched her, wanting to say more, or even a little, about the conversation he'd had with her father.

'Then we should see it. I'll get Catherine. She had this crazy idea we should hang it behind the reception desk, in the new hotel.'

'You should.'

'You haven't seen it and anyway, we won't have a reception desk.' Evelyn laughed. 'And for all you know it may be in the new style of these modern artists we're hearing about. We may look like we're wearing boxes on our heads or our faces are made of a jigsaw.' Evelyn stopped and raised a hand to her mouth. 'Oh, my goodness, I'm sorry, that was an unforgiveable thing to say.'

'No, it's all right. It might be taken to mean you sometimes forget about this ...' he indicated to his mask, 'and that's good, isn't it? In any event I'm sure the portrait will be ... quite charming and it's a good idea to have it on display. And it wouldn't harm Alice's career either.'

Evelyn's smile faded. 'Catherine also had the idea we should commission Alice to produce paintings for all the rooms in the hotel, perhaps starting with her sunrises. You like your sunrise painting well enough, don't you? It is back here now, isn't it?'

'Yes. I know little of art but it brightens the room.'

Evelyn nodded. 'And did you have any trouble bringing it back?'

She looked away from Edward and though the question was innocuous enough he sensed the sudden tension in her voice.

'No. It's light enough a child could carry.'

'Oh, it's only that I heard you had help … bringing it from your room.'

'No, I don't think so.'

'From … Margaret?'

The right side of Edward forehead frowned. 'Did I? Oh, yes, she carried it down the stairs. I was holding … ' he hesitated, ashamed as always of the contents, '… another box.'

'Margaret brought it from your old room, with you?'

'Yes.'

'Margaret?'

'Yes,' repeated Edward, recognising that the question seemed important to Evelyn, though not understanding why. Before he could ask, Catherine and Beatrice returned.

'… well of course,' Beatrice was saying, 'Cook will be a little reticent, but you'll see. Put the ideas forward as questions and say you need her help. She'll soon come round. Meantime, I've something to show you, and Evelyn. And Edward. Come.'

Beatrice led them up to the room now housing both Edward's portrait and Catherine and Evelyn's. In the last couple of days Beatrice had them both framed and they stood on the settee.

'I haven't decided where to hang you girls,' said Beatrice, 'but you look beautiful. Don't they Edward?'

'Beautiful,' Edward repeated.

Evelyn and Catherine's portrait showed them at a table. Catherine was seated, Evelyn was opposite, standing but leaning on a chair. They were both smiling out from the painting. On the table between them was a half finished chess match but from their smiles and the bright mischief in their eyes it was obvious they did not take the game seriously though it was equally obvious they could, should they choose. They wore similar dresses, flat in the bodice with skirts finishing at the knee and though the dresses did not cling, their lithe figures were discernible and taut, as if ready for movement. Catherine held a lighted cigarette while Evelyn held a glass half filled with a clear liquid. There was an energy and life to them suggesting they might walk from the canvas and into the room. It was, '… enchanting …' as Edward said and Beatrice agreed, adding,

'Alice is very talented. We must go to see her tomorrow so you can tell her how thrilled you are.' She turned to Catherine. 'I mean, assuming, you are, thrilled, that is. And how can you not be? Look at the two of you. Such a pair, such a pretty pair.'

Catherine looked at Evelyn. Edward thought her smile nearly matched the portrait's.

'If you are going to see Alice tomorrow, can I ask a favour, or, actually two?' said Edward.

'Of course,' said Catherine.

'Can you ask Alastair if he has considered my thoughts on the return of the sinking ship painting and the use of the steamer tickets to pass Dungeness? If he doesn't feel able to use them then I may have my own use for the tickets.'

'If the moment seems right I'll ask, but I'll not promise anything,' said Catherine.

'I understand, oh and one more favour?' Edward looked to Beatrice saying, 'Your aunt has found the address for the Palmers, where Kayst's parents might be in service. It's close, St. Peter's. Would you drive me there tomorrow, after visiting Alice? Or if you're busy, I could take the tram, but I thought a day out …?' Edward let the question hang.

The Blue Bench

Edward, St. Peter's, Thursday 4ᵗʰ November 1920

In the morning Edward waited impatiently while the ladies went to thank, and congratulate, Alice on the portrait. He had slept well with a decent dose of morphia solution but when he woke imagined he felt the shrapnel move and pain grow, so, against his better judgement, injected again, missing breakfast. He managed to dress and by mid–morning was at the piano. Though he didn't play or compose, the room was filled with light from the day's bright sun and, rather than nerves at possibly seeing Kayst's parents, there was a sense of perhaps bringing something to completion. And in the next few days, he hoped to turn his attention to other matters.

He waited until gone eleven, fighting the growing head pain, before deciding he could wait no longer. Carrying his coat, he walked to the tram stop at the bottom of Athelstan Road, the breeze was cool and welcome. On the way he made two stops. The first was at the post box to drop in his ticket application for a reserved space in Whitehall for the coming Armistice Day ceremony – he hoped to see the cortege for the unknown soldier. The second was at a pharmacy, not the one he had broken into, was it three months ago? and bought a small bottle of laudanum.

At the tram stop he was the only person waiting. He lit a cigarette and found himself watching the house over on Athelstan Road where Tosh's body had been found. He wondered if he'd done enough to make sure Evelyn hadn't been too upset, remembering the first shattered body he had seen. Just a day into the front line one of the men had been careless. The sharp crack of a German Gewehr 98 rifle burst across the broken landscape. The victim fell back into the trench, the ragged hole in his neck spurting blood. He was dead in seconds. Edward ordered the body to be covered with tarpaulin while they waited for stretcher bearers. He wasn't sure if he did that out of respect or to hide the body from the other men but soon learnt it was naïve to the point of embarrassment. The men were already inured to violent death and they laughed at the gesture. But Evelyn was … Evelyn. Should he have done more? Or could he? As Evelyn might say. The image of Tosh's mutilation did not haunt him, he had seen worse, of course, but he prayed Evelyn didn't dwell on it.

He turned away from Athelstan Road on hearing the tram approach and dug into his pocket for change. It was an open topped tram and though it was November, because the sun shone, he climbed the stairs to sit. The conductor followed him up to take payment but his bland conversation stopped when he looked up from his change holder to see Edward's face. As quickly as he could, but not smartly enough, he continued. Edward pretended not to notice, asking to be put off at Albion Road, St. Peter's. When the conductor went back to the lower deck Edward took the bottle of laudanum from his coat's inner pocket and swigged.

The three mile trip passed, no other passengers joined him on the top deck, when the conductor, half way up the stairs, called that Albion Road was the next stop. Edward was the only passenger to disembark. It was a quiet, residential street with a few large Victorian houses, well spaced from each other. He was looking for Flinting Villa, where the Palmer family now lived. Edward started walking as the tram left. Here, away from the coast, there was no breeze and the sun unseasonably warm so he carried his coat but was uncomfortably hot and his head, which had eased with the wind on the top–deck of the tram, began to hurt badly again.

Flinting Villa was towards the end of the road. Edward stood at the entrance to the drive, looking up to the large house. The gardens were laid to lawn with a few trees, bare after the autumn except for the large sycamore. It dominated the driveway entrance and, it being early November, still held leaves. Its shade appealed to Edward. His head was hot under the homburg, which he was reluctant to remove despite the road being without pedestrians or traffic.

He rested under the tree for a minute or two, sipping from the bottle of laudanum though it had little effect on the pain behind his missing eye. His pulse was fast and his stomach churned; he was reminded of the minutes before an attack, the terror of the known and unknown, the pretence of calm before the chaos. He checked his watch. Back then, he had reason to but today there was none. He took no notice of the time; ignored the Elgin's inaccuracy.

From the side of the house came a man struggling to push a barrow, loaded with earth. The man concentrated on the effort of moving the load down the driveway, towards Edward's tree, and didn't look up. He was not a big man. Edward recalled neither was Private Kayst.

Edward's pulse raced faster and when the man was in hearing range called, 'Excuse me. I'm looking for Mr. Kayst?'

The slight figure looked up and rested the wheelbarrow back down to the floor. Edward thought how heavy it looked for such a small man to be pushing. He was still some twenty yards away and Edward realised that in the shade of the sycamore and under the rim of his hat, his face was not yet visible.

'That's me.' The man said. Though it was

November he wore no jumper or jacket. The sleeves to his now muddied white shirt were rolled and his face red with exertion. He was almost bald but the little hair he had was not well tended. Edward remembered Private Kayst had thick back hair.

Mr. Kayst stepped towards the tree, leaving the barrow. Edward moved from the tree's shade and as his mask became noticeable Mr. Kayst stopped and hesitated, looking at the small bottle in Edward's hand before saying, 'What can I do for you? Mr and Mrs. Palmer are away at the moment and I've no instructions to pay creditors. They've not paid me for a month.'

Edward slipped the laudanum into the pocket of the coat he was still carrying and stepped a yard closer, his head banging with pain. 'I'm Edward Thompson. I … served with your son.'

'With Joseph?'

'Yes.'

Mr. Kayst thought for moment. 'Thompson? His lieutenant was a Thompson.'

'Yes. That was me.'

Kayst stood to his full height and stared into Edward's painted eye. 'Ha, he wrote he was happy to be serving with the Lucky Lieutenant. Don't look so bleedin' lucky to me. What do you want?'

Edward tried to take another step but his foot caught on the uneven ground, his head was tight with pain and he was bound with the sudden realisation he had nothing to say which could make any difference.

Mr. Kayst looked at Edward, waiting, but his patience was thin. 'Lucky Lieutenant my arse … you …' Mr. Kayst started to speak but two voices interrupted. From the house came a young woman, laughing as she trotted after a small boy, calling after him, 'Teddy, be careful.'

The young boy was caught in his own excitement, shouting, 'Grandpa, Grandpa,' as he ran and laughed.

The boy ran to Mr. Kayst who stooped to pick him up.

'Easy lad.'

The young boy stopped laughing as he realised there was another man there and, on seeing the mask, looked back for his mother. She stopped running to walk towards them. She was petite and wore a pair of men's dungarees that hung from her but didn't detract from her beauty. As she joined the scene Mr. Kayst said to her, 'Lily. This is the Lucky Lieutenant. Joe's lieutenant. 'cept he don't look so lucky now. He's probably here to tell us Joe was a hero …' his sarcasm was heavy but then he looked to the boy he held, adding more softly, '… and he was. Isn't that right lad?'

The boy nodded, checking on Edward with sideways glances.

Edward felt his neck and the right side of his face flush, the surge of blood bringing even more pain to his head. He tried to smile at Lily but knew it was more a grimace. He wanted to make a joke of not knowing young Private Kayst had such a beautiful young wife and handsome boy, but that could never be amusing. The young Teddy looked at him with questions. The beautiful Lily just looked at him; Edward couldn't read the emotion. He had nothing of consequence to say. He was sweating in the sun and felt a dribble form on his forehead. He wanted to take off his hat and wipe his face, to stop the bead trickling behind the mask. His head hurt. His heart pounded. He looked back to the shade of the tree and took half a step back there before passing out.

Edward rested against the trunk, embarrassed at the attention. He didn't know how long he had been unconscious but his head was a little easier, though heavy, and he wanted to sleep. The young boy stood some yards away, staring; his mother and grandfather were closer, whispering. Edward tried to check his mask and hat were in place without being noticed but they saw and looked to him.

'Thank you,' said Edward, assuming they had moved him into the shade and against the tree. He reached for his coat and found the bottle of laudanum but as he tried to undo the top Mr. Kayst said, 'Do you not think you've had enough?'

Edward didn't know why he'd passed out – the pain, the laudanum, the heat, the morphine earlier, some combination – but he did know for a precious few moments he was free of the pain. He wondered how long and looked to his watch but the numbers made no sense.

'No more than a minute or two,' said Lily, guessing his thought.

Edward tried to stand but his left leg would not take any weight and he got no further than sitting a little more upright. 'Do you have a telephone? Could you call … Mrs. Blundell. Do you have a telephone?'

'Call who?'

'Mrs. Blundell, Margate. The exchange will know her.'

Lily went inside the house, taking young Edward. Mr. Kayst sat next to Edward under the tree and offered him a cigarette. They smoked in silence and were still sitting there forty–five minutes later when Catherine drove Edward's Wolseley up the drive, Evelyn in the passenger seat.

Evelyn, Margate, Friday 5th November 1920

The night was cold and the walk from the tea shop in darkness, lit occasionally by a sudden flare or burst of coloured light above the roofs, followed by a sharp, violent crack. Evelyn remembered Guy Fawkes nights before the war when the fireworks were busier and louder and the smell of the gunpowder drifted on the smoke through the narrow streets of Spitalfields. The celebration had been banned for the duration of the war and the year after had been muted. This year there seemed a little more enthusiasm for it but it was still lacking the excitement she could recall.

Evelyn had spent most of the afternoon in the tea shop, at Alastair's request, because Alice was feeling poorly and he feared Isabella might be running a fever. Evelyn sat a while with Alice and then, when Alice slept, sat with Isabella, occasionally holding and rocking her when she seemed unsettled. Her temperature was normal, though Alastair pointed out Evelyn was not a nurse, let alone a doctor. Evelyn recalled similar criticism on the day Isabella was born. She took a slow breath before offering to fetch either if that was Alastair's preference but he calmed down as Isabella fell into a peaceful sleep. Alice woke a little later, feeling brighter. Evelyn stayed for tea and until Alice felt comfortable. It wasn't until she was walking home and the fireworks started she remembered the date. Her first thought was to hope Isabella would not be woken by the explosions and outbursts that seemed so close. The second thought was for Edward.

Back at Beatrice's, Edward sat in the drawing room, a tumbler of Hennessy in one hand, his music score in the other.

'Beatrice and Catherine have gone up to see the bonfire,' he said to Evelyn as she entered. Evelyn stood by the fire, enjoying the warmth seep through her woollen dress. 'I'd hoped to go with them,' she said, 'but didn't want to leave Isabella.'

'Are she and Alice all right?'

'Yes, I think so.'

'And Alastair?'

'Hmmm, his usual self. Oh, and Alice mentioned you paid her ten pounds, for your portrait. That was generous.'

'I don't know about that, but it seemed the right amount. Did Alastair mention the sinking ship painting?'

'No, why? Did you take it back as he asked?'

'I offered, again, but again with the condition it wasn't to be displayed around Alice or Isabella, though of course that's not my business.'

'And Alastair didn't agree?'

'No. And I know it was sanctimonious of me but …'

'Well, for what it's worth I think you're right. And anyway, I heard Beatrice say her friend told her the painting's practically a copy of something Turner did years ago.'

Edward nodded, 'I heard something similar. Though, of course, those that went down with the *Gurkha* were closer to being free men.'

'What do you mean?'

'Nothing, I was being facetious. I'm sorry. Anyway, I don't suppose Alastair mentioned the steamer tickets again?'

'No.'

'Good, I've decided on another use for them.'

'Oh, and what's …'

Evelyn was interrupted by the sudden shriek of a rocket followed by the bang as it exploded. They both flinched. She looked at Edward. He raised his glass to her, 'It's all right. The first few did make me jump, a little, but they're nothing like the real thing.'

'I don't know why Beatrice went with Catherine to see them, she said she hates the noise and smoke,' said Evelyn.

'Will the other Ladies of St. John's be there?'

'I expect so. Had Beatrice calmed down?' Evelyn asked. For much of the day Beatrice had been cross at Edward, starting at breakfast when she berated him for going to St. Peter's on the tram the previous day, on his own. Edward had said little in his own defence and Evelyn could see he was embarrassed at having to rely on Catherine and Evelyn to bring him home. Beatrice was also angry at William for not responding positively when, after receiving the call from Mrs. Kayst she had asked William to go there and he had refused. Evelyn wondered how Edward felt about that but he had said little in the morning and she had been out of the house, at the tea shop, for the rest of the day.

There was a loud bang that rattled the glass in the bay window as a firecracker burst somewhere close.

When the noise subsided Edward said, 'Beatrice was more relaxed this afternoon but I was well and truly told off this morning, wasn't I?'

'Good. But are you feeling much better? After yesterday?' On returning from the Thanet Royal hotel, Evelyn had found her concerns about Edward and Margaret still troubling her, but, as his attempt to make contact with the Kaysts showed, he was still very much the Edward she had come to know.

'Much better thank you.' Edward put down his music score on the side table next to his chair and lit a cigarette. 'And I'm sorry you had to come and … rescue me, yesterday.'

'Catherine jumped at the chance to drive.'

'Well that's something I suppose. And the car can remain here from now on. Not that I expect Catherine to drive me about. Not at all. I just mean, as William is going back to London the car might as well stay here and if Catherine wants to drive it, well, why not.' He drew on the cigarette. 'And you too, of course, if you want to learn how to drive.'

'I'd like that.' Evelyn said then sat on the settee opposite Edward's armchair. 'But I still don't know how you got on yesterday, with the Kaysts.' After she and Catherine had brought Edward home he had retired to his room, saying little.

'I'm afraid I don't remember it properly. After I ... passed out ...'

'Fainted ...' interrupted Evelyn, smiling as she teased, remembered the previous time.

'... passed out ...' Edward repeated with his practised smile. 'They dragged me under the tree and when I came to we sat together and smoked, but said little.'

'You told them what happened to their son?'

'Not really. Kayst's mother wasn't there and his widow and the boy stayed in the house. Mostly it was just me and Kayst's father, sitting, smoking.'

'Oh.'

'I think I mentioned to him, we, the men, spent a lot of time just sitting and smoking, in the war. Which is true.'

There was a flash and a bang from outside.

'Bloody Guy Fawkes,' said Edward.

'So that's enough of looking for Kayst then?' Evelyn made it a question.

'I suppose. I'd had it worked out, once, a long time ago, what I would say, but when I was there it just didn't seem enough.'

'So what did you say?'

'I'm not sure. I thought the father might like to

know about the Reverend Railton's idea for the grave, for the unknown soldier, but I don't know if I explained it properly or even if he was interested. For the most part we just sat … and smoked.'

'Sat and smoked?' Evelyn repeated.

'Maybe that's as much as it ever could be, do you think?'

'It's true sometimes just being there is enough, or, should I say, just making the effort to get there is worth much.'

'You see, I knew you'd make me feel better about it.'

Evelyn shrugged. 'And how's your head been today. Have you needed any … relief?'

'It's been better and I've taken … just a little today.'

'Well that's good.'

'Oh, and a brandy or two, of course.'

Evelyn returned his smile. 'How is the score coming along?' Evelyn indicated to the paper on the table.

'The first movement is finished. The orchestration isn't complete but the foundation is there.'

'Well you seem much happier about it.'

'It may not be much good, but it is mine.' Edward smiled again.

Evelyn hesitated before asking, 'And the letter, from the Royal College, was it … was there … news?'

'Letter?'

'Last week?'

'Oh, yes. It was just an acknowledgement of my enquiry. It is … or, rather, I … am … under consideration.'

'Which is a good thing, isn't it?' Evelyn said with enthusiasm masking her relief it hadn't been bad news – though good news would mean Edward leaving them to go back to London and that suddenly felt a bad thing. She didn't want to imagine not having Edward around.

'Talking of last week …' Edward stood and went to

the drinks cabinet to refill his glass, '... I'm sorry about Tosh's funeral.'

'It went well I thought. The Reverend Railton found just the right tone.'

'No, I didn't mean the funeral, I just meant Tosh, and how we, you, found him. I was concerned it might be on your mind, at the funeral. You were ... distracted. I'm sorry I let you come with me to find Tosh. And perhaps you shouldn't have come to see Tewson either. Sorry.'

'That's all right Neither was your fault. My mind was on other things, I'm sorry.' Evelyn wondered if, or how, to broach the subject of Edward and Margaret coming down the stairs together again. Though she had mentioned it to Edward a couple of days earlier and he had made nothing of it, still it nagged and she had not confessed to actually seeing them. 'At the funeral I think it was Margaret's reaction which upset me.'

'Margaret was drunk.'

'But even so, didn't you, don't you, feel sorry for her?'

'No. Margaret is ... resourceful. I wouldn't be surprised if she spends the winter here, looking after that guest house once William and Georgette go back to London.'

'Oh, and you'd ... visit her there?' Evelyn felt jealousy that she knew was irrational and then guilt, as if betraying Catherine.

'Visit Margaret? Why?'

'I don't know.' Evelyn hesitated to admit to having seen them come down the stairs together but now was the time, if ever it would be. 'I just wondered if you and Margaret had ... become close?'

'Good grief no. What makes you think so?'

'The other day, when I said I'd heard you had help carrying the painting ... that's not quite the truth. Last Thursday, when you were at William and Georgette's, I was ... passing ... and saw the two of you come down the stairs, and then something Georgette said, made me think … you and Margaret …' she paused, then, 'I'm sorry, it's none of my business.'

'Me and Margaret? Why would you, or anyone, think such a thing? She merely brought down the sunset painting. What did Georgette say?' There was anger in Edward's voice.

'Nothing, it doesn't matter,' said Evelyn.

There was a short silence which might have become awkward if not for the next explosion outside.

'Bloody Fawkes,' Edward said, 'They'll be burning the effigy by now. Where did Catherine and Beatrice go?'

'I think the bonfire was to be set on the allotments, up by Trinity Church. I saw some lads carrying the guy that way earlier. The mask was quite terrifying.'

'Really?'

'Oh, I'm sorry, I didn't mean to imply …'

'Evelyn, it's all right, I'm teasing, I know you didn't mean anything, you wouldn't.'

The gas lights on the wall were dim and their light only just exceeded that from the coal burning in the fire. Edward rose to stoke the fire. His mask was dull in the poor light.

'Speaking of masks,' said Evelyn, feeling relieved to know there was nothing between Edward and Margaret, but keen to change the subject, 'did you give any more thought to letting Alice repaint yours, and perhaps repair the nick inside that catches your cheek.'

'Not much, though I suppose it could do with it.'

'You know how good Alice is. Just look at your portrait. Have you bothered since it was first here?'

'No. Have you looked at yours and Catherine's?'

'No, but … that's different. Besides, don't change the subject. We're talking about you, not Catherine and me. Your portrait is a very good likeness.'

'Probably not. After all, the right side of my face is much older than the left.'

Evelyn frowned.

'After Major Gillies, God bless him …' Edward raised his glass, 'had done all he could, which was much, it was down to Derwent Wood at Wandsworth. He and his men made the masks. They took months and, in part, based it on my joining–up photograph, at the start of the war. So you see, my left side looks a good six years younger than the right.'

'That was at the tin nose workshop?' Evelyn asked, pleased with herself for remembering.

'Yes, but for true likeness, without the mask, we'd probably need to find my drawing by Henry Tonks.'

'Henry who?'

'Tonks. When I was at Sidcup he drew pictures of … us. He was determined to show us as we really are, despite the genius of Major Gillies, or, rather, because of it. But it doesn't matter. Perhaps it's a question for Alastair when he's in a better mood, I believe he and Tonks studied together, though their careers took dissimilar paths.'

'Edward, you're prevaricating, trying to avoid the point, again. Alice would do a good job on your mask, I'm sure. She does a fine portrait.'

'I suppose.'

'You suppose? Really? You paid ten pounds for yours. A strong endorsement, wouldn't you say?' Evelyn smiled, feeling a new sense of mischief.

'But does it look like me? After all, your portrait shows you drinking a tumbler of neat gin.'

'I beg your pardon, I don't think so. That would be inappropriate.'

'I can assure you it does.'

'I don't remember that. You're teasing.'

Edward shrugged.

'All right, let's go and see,' said Evelyn.

Edward followed her from the drawing room and up to the first floor room containing the paintings. Evelyn lit the gas lamps on the wall. Both paintings were still resting on the settee, looking out into the room.

'You see, a fine portrait.' Evelyn pointed at Edward's picture.

'You see,' mimicked Edward, 'you've a full glass of gin in yours.'

Evelyn moved closer to see. 'No it's not. It's soda water. No one puts that much gin in a glass and look, there's even a bottle of Schweppes on the table behind.'

Edward also moved closer to see. Their shoulders brushed. 'I apologise unreservedly, though my eyesight is poor so I'll take your word for it.'

'And so you should, after all I'm a reverend's daughter. And do you now agree to let Alice repair your mask?' Evelyn turned to look at him but Edward was pretending to concentrate on Evelyn and Catherine's portrait.

'Two such pretty ladies. Prettiest in Margate,' said Edward and Evelyn heard no sarcasm in his tone.

'True. Catherine is most attractive,' said Evelyn and had a flashing memory of lying in bed, with Catherine, in the Thanet Royal hotel. She was grateful for the poor light as she could feel herself blush. Edward was close enough she could smell both brandy and tobacco on him, but also something else, something more base, something she didn't recognise, something very different from Catherine's lavender scent.

'You are both most attractive,' said Edward.

'More than Georgette, or Margaret?' asked Evelyn, but before Edward could respond Evelyn continued, 'Oh my goodness. What would my father say? Such vanity is an awful thing, please, Edward, ignore it.'

'Wouldn't it be vanity on my part, to ask Alice to touch up my mask? Is that … acceptable? Besides, I've said before, I couldn't be without it for even a day.'

Evelyn stepped nearer to him, staring at his face, inspecting the mask closer than she had before. Though the light was poor she thought she saw his right cheek flush a little.

Edward tried to joke, 'Though I suppose I could ask Alice to paint in some stubble. It's a nuisance to only shave half a face in the morning, though it does save on razors.'

'It wouldn't be rough though, would it?' Evelyn said, reaching to touch Edward's right cheek. He didn't flinch, not even when she passed her fingers to the other side of his face, stroking the mask but being careful not to press or make it move. She was surprised to feel it wasn't cold but nearly as warm as his real cheek. Edward took in a deep breath and seemed to hold it as she ran her fingers over the enameled metal, tracing the line a cheek bone once held. 'Does that hurt?' she whispered.

'No, but …'

'Can you feel it?' Evelyn interrupted.

'In a way.'

Evelyn smiled, 'Good.'

With a sudden movement she hadn't expected but didn't resist Edward reached to place an awkward but gentle kiss on her lips. Instinctively she moved to meet him. She didn't kiss him as she had Catherine, just days before, and Edward's lips didn't form to hers as Catherine's had, nor did his tongue play on hers, but he leant forward, and she let him control the pressure. She felt a part of her own cheek touch his mask and made sure not to pull away. Edward put his hands on her waist and pulled her tight to him. Evelyn stretched her arms around his shoulders. Their lips parted and Evelyn rested her head against him. They stood that way for a minute or more, Evelyn feeling the rise and fall of Edward's chest as he breathed heavily, then she pulled away. She couldn't be sure that what she felt for Edward was love, but thought she loved him no less than she loved Catherine. And what if Edward should love her? Would it be wrong to lie with him, as she had with Catherine? There had been an innocence and spontaneity with Catherine that had overtaken them, and she had no regrets. But here, with Edward, she felt a desperate need to know him better and to hope he could understand her.

Without speaking, Edward closed and locked the door and returned to her. She held him again and nuzzled his neck, as Catherine had shown her, and Edward first sighed, at which she wondered, then moaned quietly, at which she smiled to herself. Edward turned his face down towards hers but it was awkward with the spectacles and mask. He stepped back and took her hand, leading her to the other side of the room. Edward sat on the bed, took her hand and guided her to sit beside him.

'I'm sorry if I seem a little … nervous. It's just I am, a little, nervous, that is.' Evelyn said, wanting to add she was also excited.

'So am I,' said Edward.

'Really? I thought you might have known many women.'

'No.'

'But, as a soldier you must have …' she paused.

'Must have … what?'

'I'm sorry,' said Evelyn, 'I was thinking about the … what did William call them? The blue–light houses. I'm sorry it's nothing to do with me. It's really not my business.' She thought about Catherine and the days they'd spent together at Thanet Royal hotel. Having her secret with Catherine meant she could hardly expect Edward not to hold on to his.

'I wouldn't mind if it was your business. The houses in France were … a diversion. We needed such.'

'Diversion?'

'There was a house, in Le Havre. The officers went there, when we had a few days leave and not enough time to come home. I was there, once, in seventeen, before, this …' he indicated to his face, 'and there was a girl, a pretty young French girl. We went to a few bars together, then

505

back to the house, where we drank more and laughed with the others, officers and women, and the spring sun was warming and no one cared who anyone was, we were all … the same, I suppose. All escaping, for a few hours. And we found a bed upstairs and … slept.'

'Slept?'

'Too much brandy or scotch or absinthe I expect. But the afternoon sun was low, the shutters were closed and the air was still and heavy. We lay down and I didn't mean to, but I slept. I woke first, the sun wasn't quite down, and was holding her, like a child, and she didn't wake. I could just hear the party downstairs, there was always a party downstairs, but it was faint and distant as if in another time and place and the girl didn't wake. I watched her and she was lovely. Then she woke and thanked me for letting her sleep rather than … and she thought it was special, so we stayed like that, until the sun didn't come through the shutters anymore and I had to leave.'

'What was her name?'

'She called herself Camellia, after the flower I suppose, but they always lied or used nicknames, so I know that wasn't her name, but that's all right, I didn't need to know it and it's better without one. My Camellia can never be found or denied or spoiled.'

'Camellia.' Evelyn repeated. 'Lovely name. I'm sorry, I shouldn't pry. What did she look like?'

'I can't recall. I have a memory of her but I don't know if it's true. I think it's more a vision of what I hope she looked like.' He looked over to Evelyn's picture, on the settee. 'Hazel eyes, dark hair, almost exactly your height and just as slim. Oh, and a sweet smile that makes me want to smile back, as best I can. Come to think of it, my vision looks like you. Beautiful. Unspoilt.' He kissed her again, with a little more confidence but kept his arms to his side, then stood from the bed, repeating, 'Unspoilt,' and turned away.

'Edward? Are you all right?' Evelyn asked.

'I'm sorry. You deserve so much more, so much better. And someone who can be with you far longer.'

'What do you mean? Is it something I've done, or said?'

'God no, never. You are … unspoilt and I'm … well I'm not.' He tried to laugh, 'And, of course, you're right. I should ask Alice to repair and repaint the mask. Would you speak to her about it?'

'You're changing the subject Edward.'

'I'm sorry. And I feel quite stupid and expect I'll feel a fool in the morning.' Edward walked over to his portrait.

'Do you mean a fool for what has or hasn't happened?' Evelyn stood, confused at Edward's reluctance and a little scared and a little angry.

'Almost certainly more for what hasn't.' Edward tried to laugh.

'You know, if I have done something wrong, you should tell me,' said Evelyn

Edward shook his head. 'No, but would you speak to Alice for me, about the mask?'

'You've changed the subject again.'

'I know, but I can't be without the mask for more than a day, there are no blue benches in Margate,' he tried to joke, 'and it must be ready for next Wednesday.'

'Why Wednesday?'

'The remains chosen for the grave of the unknown warrior will arrive in Dover. I need to be there.'

Evelyn made sure the portrait room showed no signs of disturbance before extinguishing the lights. Edward had gone to his room and she waited in the drawing room for Beatrice and Catherine. They came back late, excited by the fireworks and happy from the cocktails they'd enjoyed afterwards, with the Ladies of St. John's. Evelyn tried to listen attentively as Beatrice told of the evening's events and desperately wanted to tell of her own, to garner advice, but knew it could never be shared, and had no doubt Edward would not speak of it to others. As Beatrice talked and Catherine encouraged her, Evelyn's thoughts wandered to the confusion caused by Catherine and Edward. There was guilt for betraying Catherine, satisfaction at attracting Edward, concern over what Edward's future might hold and fear at how unknown and unknowable were the days ahead. There was anxiety at not understanding what Catherine might need and excitement at what she might hope for.

She would not be asking her father to offer any wisdom on these last few days. For all the sudden and welcome recent intimacy there was a growing sense of isolated responsibility.

Edward, Margate, Saturday 6th November 1920

Edward was the first to rise on Saturday morning, apart from Cook, obviously. The sky was clear and he left the house quietly, making sure not to disturb Cook who would be in the kitchen by now. He wore his heavy winter coat, walked down to the seafront and out to the end of the harbour pier, smoking incessantly. It was the morning after Guy Fawkes night and he remembered, as a boy, this morning was for finding spent banger and rocket carcasses and catching the occasional scent of gunpowder still in the air. But even if the sea breeze hadn't blown the air clean, his sense of smell was lost. He wondered what Evelyn had smelt like last night but had no doubt it was both fresh and enticing – a bittersweet thought. His head hurt a little but he had a bottle of laudanum in his pocket should it worsen and, besides, he'd be using the morphia solution later, as had become his habit, regardless of the degree of pain. But despite the nagging headache he was feeling more content than he had in days. The previous evening, in the bedroom with Evelyn, had been both joyous and frustrating, but he allowed himself to take a little pride in his behaviour, hoping it was as Evelyn would expect from a gentleman. It was sad to think he had resisted further intimacy and he wondered what Evelyn made of that, but he was sure it was the right thing, though the vision of Evelyn sitting on the bed was easily and readily called to mind. He lit a cigarette and sipped from the laudanum. It was also a matter of pride, though only a little, that he'd spoken to Kayst's father. It had taken longer than anticipated to find him, though there was embarrassment at fainting. There was a time, lying in Queen's hospital Sidcup, waiting on Major Gillies' next visit, when he had planned the conversation with Kayst's father to the word. But the visit hadn't been anything close to his imagination and he doubted Mr Kayst was any more calmed – he hadn't even seen Kayst's mother. But the little boy, Teddy ... Edward ... looked strong and bright. Perhaps one day, in a few years, Edward would seek him out and tell him about his father. Perhaps he would make a better job of that.

Perhaps.

One day.

He winced at a sharp stab of pain behind his left temple.

One day? In the future? Who was he fooling? But it was nice to pretend, for a little while.

The sea wind was welcoming. He checked his watch and deducted ten minutes. Another hour and a half and he could wander up to The Winter Gardens. He had agreed with Mr. Taylor to try his concerto on the grand piano there. Of course, only the first movement was, sort of, finished, but it would be interesting to hear it in a concert hall, albeit a small one, and Mr. Taylor had agreed.

He wondered what Evelyn was doing and lit another cigarette before leaving the harbour pier. He turned left and onto the jetty, wandering to the extension, out at sea, needing to check the steamer timetables.

Saturday brought an afternoon of letters, parcels and visitors at Beatrice's guest house.

Edward had returned from The Winter Gardens just after lunch and insisted Cook needn't prepare anything. He was keen to sit at the piano in the drawing room and make some changes to his musical score, changes inspired by hearing the concerto played in The Winter Gardens earlier, changes he knew had to be noted or he would forget. But after making only a couple of minor amendments he was struggling to remember the ideas evoked by playing at The Winter Gardens that morning – though it was possible sharing a half bottle of Hennessy with Mr. Taylor afterwards hadn't helped.

Then Evelyn and Catherine had come to see him and though Evelyn seemed more reserved than she might have considering the previous evening's intimacy, Edward assumed Catherine's presence to be the cause. Evelyn passed Edward two letters received in the afternoon post. Edward turned the first over and was disappointed there was no return address, as there would be had it come from the Royal College of Music. He opened it and read the contents. It was from Reverend Railton. Understanding Edward's interest he thought Edward would like to know the remains of the unknown warrior would be selected in the next few days and it was still the plan to bring them into Dover on Wednesday. The *Verdun* would dock at Admiralty Pier in the afternoon, Edward told Evelyn and Catherine.

'And you'd like to be there?' asked Catherine.

Edward realised she and Evelyn must have been discussing him. Evelyn looked down to her own letter.

'Of course, and also when they take the coffin to Westminster Abbey, though so far I've not received a response to my request for a ticket in the ballot to attend at Whitehall,' said Edward. He thought it might prompt some conversation but both ladies were quiet as they opened their post. As they read, Edward watched. Evelyn looked perplexed but said only,

'It's from Father.'

'So is this,' said Edward holding up the second letter he'd received and having recognised the handwriting on the envelope.

'From my father?' Evelyn was confused.

'No, sorry, I meant mine. It's from mine.'

Evelyn nodded her understanding while Catherine

appeared a little more concerned, saying, 'Mine is from from Eugene. And he's sent over another book by an American, *Sister Carrie*.'

'Is that the author's name? I've never heard of her,' said Evelyn.

'No, the title of the book.' Catherine held it up but before she could say any more there was a heavy knock at the front door. Catherine went to answer it and came back with William.

'Good afternoon all. How are we? Enjoying the weekend? How's that masterpiece coming?' He was cheery as ever, though Edward knew that counted for little.

'The first movement is finished, though the orchestration will need lots more work, of course,' said Evelyn with authority.

William looked from her to Edward who smiled and nodded.

'Well that's good,' said William, 'and I can't wait to hear the first performance.'

'You may have to wait a long time, but if nothing else, hopefully it will help persuade the Royal College.'

'Of course. And speaking of performances,' William said, not listening to Edward, 'I need to pop down to Brighton, for a few days. There's a chance of a booking for Georgette at the Theatre Royal, but they want to hear her, so we're going to see them, and while I'm there I can see if there's anything for you.'

'I don't want any bookings. You know that.'

'Of course, but even so, doesn't harm to remind them you're still about. Anyway, can I borrow the car, to get there? It's much quicker than train. Unless Catherine has plans for it, this weekend?' William looked at Catherine who shook her head.

Edward nodded, 'In which case, all right.'

'Thank you,' said William with unusual manners. 'I can't stay, we need to get a move on.' He stood to leave.

'Is Patrick going with you?' Catherine asked.

'No.'

'He can't stay on his own,' said Catherine.

'He won't be. Margaret's there.'

Catherine looked to Evelyn, saying, 'He should stay with us.'

Evelyn agreed.

'No, it's all right. He'll be fine with Margaret.'

Evelyn looked at Edward and caught his eye.

'No,' said Edward. 'It's a condition of borrowing the car. Patrick stays with us.'

'Well, I don't care where he stays.'

'And nor, I doubt, will Georgette,' added Catherine.

William laughed and looked at Edward, but he wasn't smiling. 'All right, I'll go and ask Georgette.' William moved to the door. Edward followed him and when they were at the bottom of the steps, on the pavement, tapped William's shoulder.

'I hear Georgette has been spreading rumours, about me and Margaret. Tell her to mind her own business.'

'Ah, there's the rub. It's not like it's my business to tell her to mind hers, is it? Oh, and by the way, I heard you found Kayst's old man. Did you tell him all about the day he died?'

'You didn't want to come and collect me from St. Peter's. That's what I heard, causing concern to Mrs. Blundell.' Edward ignored William's question.

'I expect it wasn't easy for Kayst's old man to hear. Or did you not get round to telling the full story?' William ignored Edward's question in turn. 'I'll be back in a few minutes with Patrick. Is the car ready to go? Oh, and by the way, remember that contact I had in Brighton? If he's still there shall I get some more of your ... supplies?'

Edward was silent for a few seconds but as he started to speak William interrupted with, 'Yes, I'll do that then,' and walked away before Edward could respond.

The Saturday evening was frustrating for Edward. He had hoped to find time alone with Evelyn, but Beatrice, Catherine or Patrick, or all three, were around. After dinner, Constable Simms called and Beatrice brought him through.

'Constable Simms is hoping we can be of some assistance, in a matter involving William,' said Beatrice. She sat next to Catherine on the settee. Constable Simms stayed just inside the door. Evelyn was in the armchair, Edward on the piano bench, as usual, though he had not been composing or playing.

'There's been a complaint against Mr. Burrslow, again,' Constable Simms said, calm as ever, though Edward could imagine he was suppressing frustration. 'Do you know where he is?'

'What has he done?' Edward asked.

'Perhaps I could speak to his son. Patrick is it? The lady at Mr. Burrslow's guest house said he could be found here.' Despite the calm manner, Constable Simms ignored Edward's question.

'Patrick is in bed. He's only six,' said Catherine. 'There's no need to disturb him. Besides, Mr. Thompson can probably help.'

'I don't doubt it Miss Burton.'

'Mr. Burrslow has gone to Brighton, on business. But what's he supposed to have done?'

'For how long and to what address?' Constable Simms again ignored Edward's question.

'I'm afraid I don't know the address but he can be contacted via the Theatre Royal. And he indicated he'd only be gone a few days,' said Edward.

'On business,' Constable Simms repeated.

'Yes. But what's he done?'

Constable Simms hesitated. Edward saw Beatrice catch his eye and give an almost imperceptible nod.

'There was an altercation, earlier today, out on the beach. Apparently, while helping the boy fly a kite he argued with another man, and that man is now in the cottage hospital. He was beaten quite seriously. A complaint has been made. It appears it started over a minor disagreement when strings became tangled but your Mr. Burrslow does seem to have a quick temper and fists.'

'He's not my Mr. Burrslow,' said Edward.

'Perhaps not. Anyway, could you bring the boy to the station, tomorrow morning? He may be able to shed some light on the matter. Meantime, if you hear from Mr. Burrslow please insist he return immediately and come to see me. I'll be contacting my colleagues in Brighton in the morning. So, in any event, I expect we'll see him back here soon.' He turned to Beatrice, 'Sorry to have troubled you Mrs. Blundell.'

'It's no trouble at all Constable, though it is Sunday tomorrow so would you prefer to see the boy before or after church?'

'It's all right, I'll take him,' said Edward. 'I doubt Patrick's been attending regularly, and neither have I.'

Beatrice saw Constable Simms to the front door. Edward excused himself, saying he had the beginnings of a headache, though in truth it had been nagging all day.

The Blue Bench

Edward, Margate, Sunday 7th November 1920

Patrick ate a big breakfast which included freshly baked biscuits; Cook, despite her complaints of extra work, was pleased for the excuse to spoil the boy. Patrick was at ease, sitting next to Catherine who insisted on accompanying Edward and Patrick to the police station. She was trying to make the trip an adventure and apologised to Beatrice for not going with her to St. John's for the Sunday service. Evelyn gave a similar apology, saying, 'I thought I'd join Alice at Holy Trinity this morning and ask when she can make a start on Edward's mask.'

She said it openly and cheerfully, as if repainting a disfigured man's face was no more a task than repairing a cracked vase.

'There's no rush,' said Edward.

'But there's no benefit in delay either, is there?' said Beatrice and, with Catherine nodding, Edward again felt there had been a conversation in which he'd been the subject but to which he'd not been party. Evelyn smiled at him and he had not the heart to complain further.

'I don't want to be considered vain. What would your father say?'

'I don't think even Father would consider it an act of vanity.'

'And how was your father, from his letter?' Edward asked her.

'All right, for the most part,' said Evelyn, but Edward saw her glance at Catherine. 'And how was yours?' Evelyn referred to the letter Edward had received yesterday. 'You rarely receive family letters.'

'It was more a business thing. You know my father is a solicitor? I had written to him with some instructions regarding my affairs and he was letting me know all has been taken care of. But he did say he and my mother are well, though, of course, in a letter what else would he say.'

'My late husband took the view that letters should only be used to communicate business and all other matters should be face to face. That way there was always a record of matters of fact while matters of opinion, including, dare I say it, the heart, would be confined to personal conversation,' said Beatrice.

'But what if the correspondents are far away from each other?' asked Catherine.

'It's true to say there is a flaw in my dear husband's views and, besides, he, himself, did write letters to me which were quite … amorous, I think it's fair to say.'

'Do you still have them?'

'Of course.'

'May we see them?' Catherine indicated to herself and Evelyn.

'Of course not. But when I'm dead you'll find them with my more personal effects. And speaking of more … personal letters, you received such from Eugene yesterday?'

Catherine looked at Evelyn and hesitated before nodding.'

'And how is he?' Beatrice asked.

'All right, I think.'

'You think?'

'His letter didn't say much.'

'He's written a long way to not say much.'

'There was one thing,' Catherine shifted in her chair. 'He has invited me to visit him in America.'

Beatrice put down her spoon. 'And why not. And you should take Evelyn. A young lady should not travel alone. Perhaps I should come too.'

'Dear Aunt. If I go, so will you,' said Catherine.

'And we should at least take some time to enjoy the excitement of planning such a trip before we finally decide whether to go or not,' said Beatrice.

Edward finished his porridge, listening as the conversation unfolded, occasionally glancing at Evelyn. Unusually, he felt an outsider – they talked of a future of which he felt unlikely to be part.

In the morning morning Beatrice attended St. John's. Evelyn attended Holy Trinity. Edward and Catherine attended the police station with Patrick.

Constable Simms took Patrick to see the Douglas motorcycle Simms had rescued after the war and rebuilt. The constable lifted Patrick to sit him astride the motorcycle then gently questioned him. Edward and Catherine listened as Patrick, though vague on details, alluded to a fight on the beach involving William. Constable Simms didn't dwell on the event, speaking to Patrick for less than five minutes. Once outside the police station Edward could sense Catherine's relief that there had been no tension for Patrick. Edward suggested they see if any steamers were due and Patrick needed asking only once. He ran ahead of Catherine and Edward as they wandered along the jetty. Edward recalled the incident when his mask had slipped, scaring two young girls. The memory was unsettling but there were few people on the jetty today. Half way along, Catherine shouted at Patrick to slow down then half turned to Edward.

'You will be careful not to hurt Evelyn, won't you?'

Edward stopped walking.

'Evelyn told me about Friday, how you … were closer.'

'Did she? I wouldn't do anything to hurt her,' said Edward, 'which is why I told her she deserves more.'

'But that doesn't help. The way you put it places the

519

burden on Evelyn. You must see that.'

Edward hesitated.

'Especially in light of the letter Evelyn received from her father yesterday,' Catherine added.

'I don't understand.'

'Reverend Coughston's letter made reference to a conversation he had with you, regarding marriage and Evelyn.'

Edward began walking again, slowly. 'He did speak to me, but wasn't clear. I didn't say anything to Evelyn of my conversation with her father.' Edward thought the reverend had practically offered Evelyn's hand but he didn't want to say as much to Catherine and he had asked Reverend Coughtston not to tell Evelyn of the conversation.

'Well, whatever was said, Evelyn is now wondering if her father is expecting her to marry you.'

'I would never expect that.' Edward repeated.

'Again, Edward, you must see that by saying it that way you are burdening Evelyn. And so is her father.'

'Burden? You're right. I'm sorry.'

'So what's to be done?' asked Catherine, but before Edward could reply there was a tug at his hand.

'Lieutenant, there's a steamer coming in, come on.' Patrick pointed to the east, 'I can't tell which one, come on,' and pulled Edward along, keen to be at the jetty extension. There was a heavy mist out on the sea and Edward could only just make out the funnels, cruising toward them.

Few passengers disembarked from *Royal Sovereign* and fewer still queued to replace them. Edward, Catherine and Patrick watched the coming and going on the gang plank and Patrick pointed out the various parts of the steamer, explaining how the two funnels could be lowered for the smaller bridges upriver on the Thames.

'And when I leave school I'm going to be a captain on a steamer. Uncle William says his father used to be one and so can I,' said Patrick.

'And he's right,' said Edward, 'there's no reason why not.'

'When you finish school,' added Catherine. 'And you have been going, haven't you?'

Patrick didn't answer.

'A steamer captain is a fine profession,' said Edward, 'and I've an idea. Would you like to come on a trip with me on the steamer, on Wednesday? To Dover. I've already got tickets.' Edward took the small paper from an inside pocket and gave it to Patrick who looked at it with wonder, turning it over and back again several times.

'There, see?' Edward pointed to the words. 'It's going all the way to Hastings but we'll get off at Dover, on the way. It's not far.'

'Can I, Aunt?'

Patrick looked to Catherine. She looked at Edward then back to Patrick's pleading eyes.

'We'll need to ask your mother, but if she says so, then why not, and perhaps I should come too. Better two grown ups than one when travelling with a little one, eh?' Catherine said to Patrick but Edward understood it was for his benefit.

After lunch Edward took Patrick into the garden and they persuaded Catherine, Beatrice and Cook to play French cricket. As usual, with French cricket, the rules were vague and served to ensure Patrick was the most frequent batsman and, in time for tea, the winner. Evelyn joined them as play finished. She had lunched with Alice and Alastair after church at Holy Trinity. Cook and Beatrice took Patrick into the kitchen to choose a cake while Evelyn joined Edward and Catherine in the small summer house at the bottom of the garden. They sheltered from the growing wind, and Evelyn spoke of her lunch with the Trenters, saying to Edward, '… Alice seemed quite excited at the prospect of working on your mask.'

'As long as it's ready for Wednesday,' said Edward.

'In time for the trip to Dover, I suppose,' said Catherine, going on to explain to Evelyn all four of them were taking the trip.

'Has anyone checked the weather forecast?' asked Evelyn.

'Does it matter?' said Edward. 'I'm sure the weather won't stop the *Verdun* bringing back the body from Boulogne and if the steamer's running then it'll be fine.'

'Surely the other way around. If it's fine the steamer will be running,' said Evelyn, 'and is it a good thing to be taking Patrick? Isn't the occasion a bit … sombre?'

'He'll love it. He's desperate to go on a steamer and just wait until he sees the *Verdun*, a full size destroyer. She'll be magnificent.'

'Hmmm. I thought the idea was to reflect on the heavy sadness of war, not glorify its machinery,' said Evelyn.

Edward shrugged. 'Yes, I'm sorry. But he's only six. Anyway, it would be good for the mask to be a bit cleaner and brighter. But I can't be without it for more than a day.'

'Alice said she could do a little at a time. It would spread the work over longer but each time would be just a day. She understands.'

'Good.'

'One other thing. Alastair still wants the ship painting back. We were talking of the plans for the memorial to be erected outside Holy Trinity, next year. And of course he expects Curtis's name to be there. However, he's adamant a memorial is all well and good but it's not a strong enough reminder. He wants to understand, to share the pain …'

'… by looking at the painting,' said Edward.

Evelyn shrugged. 'As if it might somehow relieve

poor Curtis of the fear he must have suffered. You can't blame Alastair for wanting that.'

Edward lit a cigarette, watching Evelyn's face and thinking on Alastair's words.

'I think I understand. I'll take the picture back this afternoon and perhaps tomorrow you could take my mask to Alice. And Catherine, I'll be in my room all day tomorrow, without it, but could you make sure Patrick is kept away. I'd hate for … you know.' Edward gestured to his face then turned to Evelyn. 'And thank you, for another problem solved.'

Edward returned the painting to Alastair that afternoon, resisting the urge to remind Alastair again that he'd rather Isabella not see it until old enough to understand. Alastair took it with no thanks but they shook hands on parting.

The Blue Bench

Edward, Margate, Monday 8th November 1920

On Monday morning, straight after breakfast, Edward went up to his room, Evelyn and Catherine following. He asked them to wait outside while he removed his mask, then opened the door just sufficiently to pass it back out to them without his face being seen.

Patrick was downstairs, helping Beatrice with a new jigsaw puzzle.

As he heard the ladies walk downstairs, Edward's pulse increased and sweat formed on his brow, though it was a cold November day. He fought the urge to shout out to Evelyn he'd changed his mind and tried to slow his breathing as the vision from his right eye blurred. He paced the room in a panic, grabbed at a bottle of laudanum but dropped it in the sink. The bottle shattered and he cut himself on a shard of glass. The laudanum disappeared down the plughole and his panic grew. He drank from a bottle of scotch, embarrassed it was so early to be drinking and then ashamed. He paced the room again, pressing a handkerchief against his palm to stem the blood, careful to avoid the mirror and when he thought he might faint lay on the bed but his pulse wouldn't abate. Within a minute he stood again, pulling deep but fast and unsatisfying breaths and then drank more scotch. It was to be a long day. Edward understood but had no control save for the lock on his room's door.

The knock on the door was not hard but still enough to

make Edward, sitting on the bed, start. His morning panic had faded slowly, to be replaced by the pain in his head, not merely headache pain, but the wound pain he feared the most, the pain that screamed there was something malevolent and spiteful gnawing through his brain. He had injected a little morphia in the early afternoon, but the effect seemed minimal. He knew he would resort to a heavier dose later but hoped to wait until after Evelyn returned with the mask. The door was knocked again. He opened it a little.

'Alice hasn't done much today, and there's a couple of places not quite dry but …' Evelyn passed the mask through the gap.

'Thank you.' Edward took it, placed it on his face and went to the mirror. The light in the room was not good and at first it wasn't obvious what had changed, but he studied his reflection.

'Is it all right?' Evelyn called from the landing.

'The eye, it has more … life, and the eyebrows, they are darker, more a match for my own.' Edward went back to the door and opened it fully, allowing Evelyn to enter.

'Alice said she hasn't done anything to the cheek plate and thinks that might need her to keep it for a couple of days, but one step at a time.'

'And the small nick on the inside, I can't feel it anymore.'

'There was a small mark in the metal that had rusted. Alastair had some emery paper and rubbed it down.'

'It's much better. Thank you. I'll write to Alice. What do you think?' Edward turned to see Evelyn. She studied both sides of his face.

'I think it looks, like you, but more so, though Alice has hardly touched it, so I'm looking forward to see how it will look after she's worked on the cheek.' Evelyn stepped closer to him, the closest she had been since the Friday night.

'In which case, Alice can have the mask again, in a week or so. I can spend a couple of days in here.' Edward desperately wanted to repeat the kiss from Friday night and stepped toward her.

'Are you all right? You look a little pale, and unsteady.' Evelyn said, before Edward could reach out to her. She looked in the sink behind him. The shards of the broken laudanum bottle and used syringe from earlier were still there. 'And what have you done to your hand?'

Edward put out his hand and was surprised himself to see the handkerchief wrapped around it, a dark red stain in the middle of his palm.

'You should lie down.' Evelyn took his arm and helped him to the bed.

'My head … today … has been bad.'

'When's the last time you took some medicine?'

'A few hours. I can have more. I was waiting for you.' He tried to sit up but Evelyn easily kept him flat with a hand rested on his chest. He was so weak.

'I'll do it,' said Evelyn. She went back to the sink, cleaned and prepared the syringe and took it back to the bed. Edward went to take it from her but she said, 'Let me.'

'Not in a vein.'

'I remember,' said Evelyn, pressing the needle against the side of his bicep. There was resistance, so she pressed harder, ignoring the short intake of breath taken by Edward, and, when the needle was half an inch into the muscle, depressed the syringe.

As his body grew heavy Edward felt Evelyn lie beside him on the bed.

Evelyn, Margate, Tuesday 9th November 1920

Evelyn, Margate, Tuesday 9th November 1920

Evelyn knocked on Edward's door a couple of times during the night and again on Tuesday morning. Though each time there was no answer she went in anyway, making sure he was covered and warm. As far as she could tell he slept untroubled. Each time Catherine had said she'd go in with her but she went alone as she didn't think he'd want anyone else to know about the morphia solution – he had placed confidence in her and that she would not risk.

Evelyn had already spoken to Catherine of the Friday evening intimacy when she and Edward had looked at the portraits. When talking to Catherine, Evelyn had spoken of the kiss. Catherine asked if Edward had declared his love for her, but he had not been so clear, said Evelyn. Catherine had not seemed at all surprised at the kiss and the letter from Evelyn's father, in which he hinted at having suggested marriage to Edward, had seemed to subdue Catherine. Since returning from Thanet Royal they had occasionally slept together but with little sexual context or contact and Evelyn sensed Catherine was as confused as she was – confused but in no way guilty, she hoped.

And now, since receiving Eugene's letter, Catherine had seemed preoccupied.

After the third visit to Edward's room, during which she changed the dressing on Edward's hand without waking him, Evelyn thought to catch Catherine on her own and talk more about Eugene's letter but as she came down the stairs she saw the two figures through the glass

529

of the front door – William and Georgette. Evelyn opened it before they could knock but didn't invite them in.

'We're back,' said William.

'So soon?'

'There's no place like home. Can we come in?' William took a step forward but Evelyn didn't open the door wider.

'Perhaps later. But first you need to see Constable Simms. He's expecting you. Something to do with the kite and a fight on the beach and a poor man in hospital.'

'Ah, I'd rather hoped that had blown over. The fight I mean, not the kite.'

'That's not funny.'

William shrugged.

'Where's Patrick?' Georgette asked. Evelyn thought for a couple of seconds. Patrick was in the garden, with Catherine.

'He's upstairs, taking a nap. It's been a busy few days.'

'Well go and wake him,' Georgette said.

'Why don't you go with William to see the constable first and, as we didn't know when to expect you, we've arranged to take a trip to Dover tomorrow, to take Patrick on a steamer. He's very excited about it. And we can bring him to you afterwards.'

'Dover?' said William.

'And Patrick will not only get a trip on a steamer, he'll see the destroyer, *Verdun* is it? bringing back the unknown soldier from France,' said Evelyn.

'Edward's idea, no doubt.'

It was Evelyn's turn to shrug.

'He's bloody obsessed.'

Evelyn smiled. 'Anyway. You better go and see the constable. We'll bring Patrick round tomorrow evening.' She shut the door before there could be a response.

Edward, Dover, Wednesday 10th November 1920

The steamer's paddles churned noisily through the heavy swells off the Kent coast. The engines clattered and banged, belching steam and smoke from the funnel while the ship pitched and rolled awkwardly. It was not a good day for a sea voyage and half an hour into the trip Edward was wishing they had taken the train or car; Catherine could have driven. But then Patrick would not have journeyed on the steamer and Edward would have missed the vicarious excitement.

Patrick had been patient throughout the morning, asking Edward only a few questions while Edward was reading in the papers of the plans for Armistice Day, tomorrow. Edward tried hard not to be impatient or show his disappointment at not having received a ticket to attend at Whitehall. An early lunch had fuelled Patrick's anticipation and he was insistent they be on the Margate jetty extension in plenty of time to meet and board *Eagle*, the steamer from London that would take them to Dover. There were few passengers on such a dreary November day but the rain held off and Edward sat up top with Patrick, the wind making it impossible to finish reading the paper, while the ladies sat in the aft saloon. Patrick ran from side to side and fore to aft, engrossed in and swamped by, the sound, smell and feel of the small steamer; Edward could imagine how alive it must feel to the boy, how the movement was more organic than machine like and how immense must seem the grey sea stretching endlessly before them. He recalled his first trip over to France, with his regiment, and being almost overwhelmed by the vastness of the seas, even though they were never out of sight of land. It had been a relief to dock in Boulogne for that first campaign at the front. He laughed out loud to recall such naivety and Patrick looked at him. Patrick was back and forth, dispensing knowledge and asking questions until Catherine came on deck, looking more than slightly queasy, and said she'd spoken to the captain and did Patrick want to meet him. The joy in the boy's face was a delight and the captain was a winning combination of benevolence, stern authority and generosity of spirit. Edward had a brief recollection of the first captain he'd served under in France, but it was a hazy recollection of a brief encounter, just a week before the captain was lost in a flooded shell hole. He was a good captain; a young captain, perhaps two years older than Edward? Probably not more. Edward wondered if he was already dead when he sank down into the putrid waters at the bottom of the crater, or if he'd drowned, as so many wounded had; then he thought of Curtis – Alastair and Alice's son. Edward would leave the steamer before it passed Dungeness and perhaps it was better Alastair had not taken the ticket. The grey skies and seas were oppressive and weighed heavy and ominous; it would be easy to imagine them pressing Curtis to the depths.

Edward lit a cigarette and tried to concentrate on the steamer captain's explanation to Patrick of winds and tides before leaving Patrick and Catherine there to go and find Evelyn, still in the aft saloon. Edward thought they should have much to talk about – the previous Friday's intimacy and kiss, the morphia solution injection Evelyn had given him – but he didn't know how to start the conversation. As he sat next to Evelyn she turned away from the window, smiled as openly and warmly as he had ever seen, and patted his forearm. She looked at him and said nothing and though he didn't know what to take from the silence he was both peaceful and grateful.

The rocking of the steamer was less pronounced down on this deck and they sat that way for ten or fifteen minutes until, a few miles out of Dover, when Edward thought they were heading due south, he saw the flotilla of seven warships. At such a distance, and with his poor eyesight, it was hard to be sure of their direction and he went back up to the top deck to find Patrick to both show him and ask his opinion. The steamer captain dismissed Patrick with a proper salute and Patrick was keen to share his new learning with Edward, until Edward pointed out the ships. They were closing.

'What do you think they are?' Edward asked.

'Scout cruisers or destroyers,' said Patrick with a confidence that made both Edward and Catherine smile. Ignoring the growing coldness of the wind up on the top deck they squinted into the greyness and watched the flotilla grow slowly closer until Patrick declared, 'Destroyers!'

'In which case let's hope if the *Verdun* is there we land in Dover first,' said Edward, checking his watch and compensating for its fast running – just past three p.m.

At Dover the Prince of Wales pier was ready to accept the steamer, though it was crammed with sightseers watching for the *Verdun*. Outside the harbour the sea was growing rougher; inside the harbour the steamer captain was able to gently berth his ship. The few passengers disembarked. Edward took Patrick's hand, the ladies walking arm in arm behind, and led the way through the crowd and off the pier. They crossed Wellington swing bridge, Edward looking behind and out to sea, then he started at the crashing roar – a field marshal's salute, nineteen guns, rang from Dover Castle, the smoke drifting over the hills above the port.

Patrick laughed at Catherine covering her ears in case of another salvo.

Edward looked back out to sea. 'That must be the *Verdun*,' he told Patrick, pointing at the sole destroyer passing the breakwater and progressing slowly towards Admiralty Pier on the western edge of Commercial Harbour. They turned left on to Strond Street and followed the quayside.

Patrick pulled Edward along and on to Admiralty Pier. There were two sets of railway tracks running the length of the pier. Parallel to the tracks, flanking them, were two single rows of soldiers. The men faced each other and each held a rifle, reversed, with its muzzle resting on their boot. Suited dignitaries, senior clergy and uniformed officers stalked the quay. There was a small crowd on the pier to welcome the *Verdun's* precious cargo and a regimental band, Edward couldn't tell which, played *Land of Hope and Glory*.

Edward, Patrick and the ladies found a discreet place from where they could watch. HMS *Verdun* was close to docking, sailors were throwing ropes to shore so the ship could be secured. Edward had thought this might be a moment of quiet celebration, a homecoming, but instead there was an atmosphere of sombre tension. He watched as the coffin was unloaded. Patrick was asking questions to which Catherine or Evelyn whispered answers but Edward was transfixed. The two rows of soldiers were called to straighten their lines and bow their heads. Six soldiers carried the coffin, draped with a Union Jack, on their shoulders, flanked by senior naval and army figures. Behind them came more officers, dignitaries and two files of slow marching soldiers, though Edward thought the display lacked precision. The cortege moved at a steady pace and, as it neared them, Edward passed his newspaper to Evelyn so he could pick up Patrick. They watched the procession shepherd the coffin into Marine Station. The coffin was followed into the station by soldiers carrying the huge wreaths that had accompanied it from Boulogne and would continue with it to London – each wreath needing at least two men.

Edward put Patrick down and they went into the

station. The coffin was placed into a carriage together with some of the wreaths, while the larger ones had to be carried in another luggage van. Edward took back his paper from Evelyn, saying, 'I should go.'

'Don't you want to wait until it's on the way to London?' she asked. 'I'm sure Patrick would like to see the train leave.'

'No, I meant to London.'

'Oh. Why?'

Edward shrugged. 'I feel I should. I don't know why but now, seeing the coffin ...' Edward nodded to the open carriage and the coffin inside, still draped with a Union Jack.

'Hmmm.' Evelyn was sceptical.

'I just think I should go and then I can see it in Westminster Abbey, tomorrow. I may not have the chance again.'

'You do know you're not in the army anymore?' Catherine offered. 'Did you get a ticket in the ballot then? You didn't mention it.'

Edward forced a laugh. 'No, but even so, anyone can see the procession on other parts of the route and go into the abbey afterwards.' He waved his copy of *The Times*, as if the ladies might understand the itinerary and timings were all there, then bent down to talk to Patrick. 'Now you'll look after the ladies and make sure they get home safe, won't you.'

'I'd rather come with you.'

'I'd like that, but I need someone I can trust to look after our ladies.'

Patrick nodded.

'Good lad.'

'Should I come with you?' Evelyn asked.

'No,' said Edward. 'Not necessary.'

'I don't mind. I feel I should.' Evelyn said but looked to Catherine, who first shrugged then nodded, almost imperceptibly.

'Really, I'll be fine and it's been a long day already. Don't worry so.'

'As if she can help herself,' said Catherine.

By just gone four, Edward was sitting in a passenger coach, two back from the steam locomotive. He stowed his coat in the rack above and sat facing forward, on the west side, his mask nearer the window. Two carriages behind were the van containing the coffin and the saloon coach bringing the honour guard. The train was scheduled to depart at 16:25 and at 16:17 he saw the pretty young woman walking down the aisle, checking the seats. It took him two looks to realise it was Evelyn. She stowed her coat next to his and sat down, pre–empting the question.

'I thought you shouldn't go alone. Catherine understands and would have come also, if not for Patrick. She'll take him home by train. We've missed the last steamer back to Margate.'

'I'm glad of the company,' said Edward.

As the train left Dover in the early winter darkness the conductor came through the carriages explaining they would be travelling slowly through the stations en route to London; it was expected crowds would gather on the platforms to pay respects to their special cargo and the roof of the funeral van had been painted white in order that it would be easy to identify. This would, of course, add greatly to the journey time. No passengers complained.

True to the conductor's word, shortly out of Dover the train slowed at the first station. The platforms on both sides of the train were lined two or three deep with onlookers, the men removing hats as the white roofed funeral van passed. The stations were poorly lit but well enough that Edward and Evelyn could see the pale and drawn faces. Evelyn watched them pass and Edward thought their presence went some way to justifying his reactionary decision to follow the coffin to London, though he would not say as much. On clearing the station the train gathered speed but was soon slowing again for the next station. The platforms were again crowded.

'Railton was right,' Edward said quietly.

The train pulled into Victoria, platform 1, shortly after 8 p.m. Evelyn had said little on the journey and, now he was here, Edward had no plan. They were almost last off the train and stood on the platform watching as the funeral van and coach were detached and shunted to another platform. An honour guard was placed at the door to the carriage holding the coffin – soldiers and marines with rifles reversed and heads bowed. Edward and Evelyn stood at the entrance to platform 8 for fully twenty minutes before Evelyn asked, 'What now?'

Edward lit a cigarette. 'Do you wonder? I mean you must, surely? Who is it?'

Evelyn followed his gaze to the funeral van and the coffin which could be seen through the open door.

'Yes, a little, but it's far, far better not to know, isn't it? That would ruin it for thousands, tens of thousands.'

'You're right, of course, but still …' Edward's voice tailed off.

'Anyway, we can't stay here all night. There's a train back to Margate in twenty minutes,' said Evelyn.

'I thought I might stay here, as I want to see the procession and interment, tomorrow,' Edward said but realised as he spoke how naïve seemed the idea of standing there all night. 'Sorry.'

'Is that necessary?'

Edward nodded.

'Really?'

Edward shrugged.

'So stubborn,' said Evelyn. 'All right, but why don't we stay with my father tonight. It's only a bus ride away. I'm sure he'll be happy for you to sleep on the settee. He'll probably try to give you his bed, but you'll say no and he'll insist. Oh, but we must send a telegram so Catherine and Beatrice don't worry.'

'Of course. Dear Evelyn, always a solution,' Edward said with no irony.

Evelyn, Spitalfields, Wednesday 10th November 1920

They ate at a café outside Victoria station then Edward insisted they take a taxi rather than wait for a bus. Evelyn pointed out her father's house in Elder Street to the driver as they pulled into the short street of terraced properties in Spitalfields. The street was ill–lit and no lights were visible in the house. This wasn't unusual as Evelyn's father would often be out on parish business in the evenings. The houses opened on to the street and Evelyn knocked at the door next to her father's. It was opened by an older woman, wearing a heavy coat, who welcomed Evelyn warmly, and, on introduction, didn't flinch from Edward's mask. The woman explained Evelyn's father had gone away for a couple of days, to see a colleague in Birmingham, then nipped back into the house to get the key for Evelyn.

Evelyn let herself and Edward in and lit a couple of gas wall lamps while Edward waited in the hall. The house was cold and seemed even darker for the shadows cast by the lights. She apologised for her father's absence, though she knew there was no need, and asked Edward to start a fire while she put on the kettle. She found some stale biscuits and took them into the parlour with the tea tray. Edward sat on the settee. Evelyn sat in her father's threadbare armchair. The fire was welcoming and soon warmed the small room.

'So this is where you grew up? It's very cosy.' Edward looked around the room.

'Thanks to my mother. We didn't have much, the

539

church may be rich but the working clergy scrape by as best they can.'

'You must miss your mother.'

'Of course.'

'Were they married long?'

'Not long. I was born just a year after they married, so they only had nineteen years. She was nine years younger than him, twenty three when they married. Not an old spinster like me.' Evelyn joked.

'You'll not be a spinster,' Edward said and Evelyn thought of the letter from her father in which he hinted she might consider marriage to Edward an option. She still didn't understand how she felt about Edward, or Catherine, but her father was right about so many things.

There was an awkward silence until Edward said, 'This settee is very comfortable. I'll be fine here tonight.'

'I'm sure Father won't mind if you take his room. He would be offended if you didn't.'

'No, that's all right. I've slept on far worse beds. Would you mind if I settled down for an early night?' He rubbed his left temple. 'I've a bit of a head and need a good start in the morning, to get to Westminster.'

'You're determined to see the grave tomorrow. Too much so?' She let the question hang. Edward shrugged.

'Let me check Father's medicine cabinet, he's likely to have a bottle of laudanum,' said Evelyn, grateful for something to do. She returned with a small brown bottle. 'Lord knows how old it is but there's a little left. I'm sorry we've no scotch or brandy, but there's probably a little sherry left, upstairs. Sweet if I know Father. I'll see if I can find it and a blanket or two.'

Edward stood to take the bottle and glass from Evelyn, nodding a thank you, and emptying the bottle's contents into the tumbler. There were little more than a couple of mouthfuls which he turned away from Evelyn to drink. He was facing the fire and the flames played a gold tint on his mask. Evelyn watched him and when he turned back asked, 'You will let Alice finish touching up your face, won't you?' Evelyn went back to him and took his empty glass, placing it on the sideboard.

'I suppose. Would you bring me a blanket, and I'll put out the fire before I settle down. I'm always careful when it comes to fires, especially after one of the men, Shiner, I think it was, set one in his sentry box and forgot about it when he had to …'

Evelyn interrupted. 'Another change of subject. It really is your forte. Or rather, shield.' Evelyn smiled and went to find a blanket and pillow.

Evelyn's room smelt old, damp and not at all familiar. She lit the gas lamp on her dressing table. Her copy of *Pride and Prejudice* still lay there. She looked in the drawers, the few clothes she hadn't taken down to Margate were there. The bed was still made up with the last sheets and blankets she had used and the picture of her father and mother on their wedding day was still on the dresser. But it no longer felt like her home. She heard the back door open. Edward went outside into the garden and down, she assumed, to the toilet at the end of the small yard. Her room looked out over the back and she peaked through the gap in the curtains but it was too dark to see anything bar Edward's dark, hunched outline. Before going into the toilet shed he stopped and lit a cigarette. She watched the glow bloom and fade as he drew then exhaled. She thought about Guy Fawkes night and their intimacy in the portrait room at Beatrice's and wondered if he might come up to her room tonight. Would that be a good thing or not? Did she want him to? and should Catherine know? As far as she could tell Edward didn't look up to her window.

The room was cold and though weary, she didn't think sleep would come easily so she sat on the bed, against the headboard and tried to read. Before the first paragraph was complete she heard Edward come back to the kitchen and the creak of the stairs as he made his way to her room. The door was ajar. He knocked softly and waited until Evelyn said, 'Come in,' then entered slowly, sheepishly. Evelyn stood from the bed.

Edward breathed deep and said, 'Evelyn, I just wanted you to know, I understand you think I'm … obsessed with this unknown soldier thing and you may be right but I don't want you to think less of me because of it.'

'Oh Edward. Of course not. It's true I might not understand but I would never think less of you. You should know that.'

'Thank you. Sometimes things need to be said, don't they?'

'Yes.'

'Good night.'

'Good night Edward.' Evelyn took a step so she could peck his right cheek.

Edward smiled and half–turned, then stopped, saying, 'Evelyn, when we kissed, just a few days ago, was it the same as kissing another man?'

The question surprised Evelyn. 'I don't know, though it doesn't matter.'

'You don't know? But you have kissed others?'

'No, I'm perhaps a little embarrassed to say.'

'Not Tewson. Poor Mr. Tewson?'

'No, not even Mr. Tewson.'

'So when we kissed was …?'

'The closest I have been to a man, yes. Which perhaps reflects more on me than the men.' Evelyn joked weakly.

Edward smiled. 'No, that reflects very badly on all us men.' He stepped back to her and pressed his lips gently against hers. She responded and flicked her tongue over his lips as Catherine had shown her. Then she let him pull her close. She felt his erection grow and press against her lower belly. It was a shock, quickly replaced by no small pleasure that she should have such an effect and she moved against him, enjoying his quiet moan. Her breath shortened. She thought of her abandonment with Catherine a little over a week earlier and then the confusing excitement and disappointment of her intimacy with Edward in the room with the portraits. This moment, here with Edward, was even more exciting but before she could wonder what that meant Edward stepped back. She wore a simple dark blue jersey knit dress with a straight bodice to a low waist and a pleated skirt. The bodice was buttoned from the waist to its round neckline. Edward unbuttoned it from the top down; Evelyn thought his hand was shaking but it may have been her own body trembling. Standing still, being undressed, was as unnerving as it was exciting and when the last button was undone she shook the dress free from her hips and legs. Under the dress she wore her usual simple white chemise and, with a flash of recollection, wished she had borrowed some of Catherine's more exotic lingerie, though of course, how could she have foreseen? She blushed but with such a dim gaslight in the room she doubted Edward would see. She helped him remove his waistcoat and tie and watched as he unbuttoned his shirt. At the base of his neck, on the left hand side, were three lines of scar tissue, stretching out to the collar bone. Evelyn touched the scars lightly. 'More wounds? I had no idea.'

'Not from the battle front, I'm afraid. When they were trying to rebuild my face they needed skin tissue.'

'So they took it from ...' she touched the scars.

'Sort of. But they left it attached, where it is now scarred, while it grew to the face.'

'Oh,' Evelyn removed her hand imagining a strip of living, growing flesh torn from the chest but still attached and somehow merging to his face. 'It sounds so painful and ...'

'Grotesque? Yes, it was, but Major Gillies is a genius. If not for that I would have even less ... here.' He indicated to his face. 'But it doesn't matter now.'

'No, not now,' said Evelyn, moving to the bed. She lay and watched as he removed the remainder of his clothes, deliberately turning her thoughts from the agonies he must have endured in the hospital. He turned away before taking off his underwear. She slipped under the bed cover, shivering at the touch of the cold sheets, before removing her chemise, so she too was naked. Edward lay next to her under the sheets and pulled her close. Catherine's body had been soft and pale, giving and yielding but Edward's was taut and marked, tense and ready, and as much as she wanted to touch him, she wanted to be touched. He was breathing heavily and pushed his mask and spectacles a little higher on his nose before kissing her, simply, lightly, but it was no less passionate for that. She nuzzled at his neck and gently ran her fingers across his shoulders and down to his lower back. He copied her but went further, cupping her bottom and squeezing gently. She knew she was ready and reached to pull Edward onto her. He took his weight on his arms and started to ease himself across her but hesitated. Evelyn pulled him a little more strongly but he resisted.

'What is it?' she asked.

'I'm sorry, you're so … beautiful, and I so want to … but …' he gestured to his face.

'I don't care. I want to, very much. Don't you?'

'Of course.'

'Are you worried I might fall pregnant? I would douche straight away. A reverend's daughter doesn't live in the East End without knowing such things.'

'Evelyn, always a solution. You must know that doesn't work very well but you'd take the chance?'

'Yes. Wouldn't you?'

'I suppose.'

'Then …' she took his hand and rested it on her breast. He caressed gently for a few seconds but stopped and pulled away again.

Evelyn said, 'We've been in a similar position before, haven't we? And did you feel a fool the next morning? I know I did.'

'Yes, for what didn't happen, and I know I'll feel a fool tomorrow. And it would be different if we were to marry. But we can't. I can't ... expect you to. I should not have come up here. I had no right and ...'

'It's all right.' She put a finger to his lips. 'I know my father expects me to marry you. I don't know what I want but I don't expect you to ask me. Is it something to do with Camellia, in Le Havre?'

'No, nothing happened with Camellia, though she was the last woman to see me, in a sense.'

'Then let me be the next.' She leant over to kiss him but he resisted, sitting up. She sat upright likewise and took his face in both her hands. She drew it close to hers then, without speaking, carefully tugged at the spectacles holding the mask, pulling them away from Edward's head.

'No,' he muttered.

Evelyn's, 'Yes,' was firm and she steeled herself for what might lie behind. By unhooking the spectacles from behind Edward's ears the mask came free. She cradled it and stared at the half face in her hand then rested the mask on the pillow. With a deep, slow breath she looked up at Edward, determined not to flinch or react. From the half face of the mask she looked to the half face of the man, placing her hands either side of Edward's head so he could not easily turn away. Though the light was poor she saw the concave bowl where there should have been a cheek and a sheet of red scarred flesh where there should have been an eye; there was not even a socket to show an eye had once been there. There was no brow and no lower forehead, just flat, scarred skin. The jagged scars still looked fresh and raw and she wondered what was beneath the skin and was afraid there was nothing, that should she move her right hand from the side of Edward's head to the missing cheek the skin would fold softly inwards, offering no resistance. So she held his head tighter and stared harder, desperate to make sure he knew she could look at him, anxious he should understand such a terrible maiming was nothing to her. She could not imagine what he had been through, the agony he had endured, the shock of understanding what had become of him, the seemingly endless operations and weeks of frustrating waiting before bandages could be removed and always the fear of what might still befall and how he might still be himself. And it was for those reasons she wanted to sob for him, not for the abhorrent mutilation in front of her, but she swallowed hard and fought to control herself. His right eye was open wide, staring back. He spoke quietly,

'Back in eighteen, when I was at Queen's hospital and the major was … operating, they painted the benches around the hospital area blue. Bright blue. The people of Sidcup knew that if a patient was sitting on one of the benches they should be ready, prepared, for the wounds and abomination they might see. But those benches didn't make us invisible and I hated them and I loathed the people that avoided them and resented as much those that steeled themselves to look and offer a greeting as they passed. I was so angry for a long while and I never thought there would be someone who would see me again.'

Evelyn kissed him, first on the lips but then where the cheek bone was gone and only scars remained and then where an eye should have been but was not.

'Shhhh,' Evelyn whispered, 'lie with me.'

'I'm sorry. The man who makes loves to you first should be the man you marry and that can't be me.'

They sat in the bed for two or three minutes, Edward without his mask but looking to the ceiling so Evelyn could not easily see the left side of his face. Evelyn felt anger; he didn't know what it had taken for her to be undressed with such apparent ease in front of him, and yet also relief and joy Edward had been so open. She was excited at what had so nearly been and still might, but disappointed the fulfilment she had felt after lying with Catherine eluded her.

Edward spoke first. 'I'm sorry. I hadn't planned for this. I don't deserve you and you deserve so much better.'

'You talk a lot about what we, you, deserve, as if there's a set of rules and a list somewhere. There isn't. And I don't know that feeling guilty for what hasn't happened makes anything better.'

Edward drew her into a tight cuddle, pulling the sheets and blankets to their necks. He sighed heavily.

'Tell me again about Le Havre,' said Evelyn, 'and the warm afternoon shadows and how the innocent sleep.'

The Blue Bench

Edward, Spitalfields, Thursday 11th November 1920

Sometime during the night Evelyn had woken and placed Edward's mask on the bedside table. At first he hoped it had been during the dead of night when darkness cloaked his face, but then he remembered how she had looked at him … at his face … maskless, and kissed him and lain next to him. They had held each other for … he had no idea … but he hoped, through the night. He checked his watch again. There was much to be done today and he pushed himself to sitting up. He was about to put on the mask when there was a knock at the door and Evelyn called, 'Good morning,' but didn't enter. He returned her greeting as he put on his mask and Evelyn entered slowly to give him time, he thought. She carefully carried a bowl of hot water with a flannel resting on the side. She wore a white cotton dressing gown and thick bed socks. As she bent to place the bowl on the dressing table her dressing gown gaped slightly and Edward saw her chemise, stretched over the swell of her breast. He felt an instant regret that he, they, had only slept the night, then some relief they had slept, fully, the night.

'I thought you'd want to wash, here,' said Evelyn.

'Thank you.'

Evelyn sat on the bed. 'Did you sleep well?'

'Yes. You?'

'Yes.'

'I'm sorry if …'

'It's all right. I think I should be sorry as well and yet neither of us know why. So maybe let's not? Not fully

549

understanding someone isn't the same as not knowing them.'

He didn't know what to read into that, but it didn't matter, now he had only one secret from her.

Evelyn, Westminster, Thursday 11ᵗʰ November 1920

'What's the time?' Evelyn asked as Edward came into the kitchen.

'Seven forty, or thereabouts,' Edward said.

Evelyn stood at the table next to the small stove and gas hob, pouring boiling water from the kettle into two plain white china mugs. 'Tea?' she asked, 'though I can't find any more milk and there's little choice for breakfast. It looks like Father may not be looking after himself as well as he should. I did wonder last time I was here. Perhaps I should come back more often, or for good?'

'I don't think that's a good idea. Catherine is going to need you, isn't she?' Edward lit a cigarette. 'Anyway, drink up and dress, we've a lot to do today and time's getting on.'

Evelyn nodded, unconvinced by Edward's enthusiasm.

'And while you're doing that, do you have a pen and some paper? I need to write a letter,' he asked.

'Of course. Who to?'

'Royal College of Music. While we're here I'd like to drop off a reminder of my previous letter.'

Evelyn found the writing materials, prepared a fresh bowl of water so she could wash and took it upstairs.

'I don't suppose there's any more laudanum around?' Edward asked as Evelyn came down the stairs.

'I don't think so. Are you in pain?'

'Not to worry, it's not as if the laudanum helps much anyway. We'll stop off at a pharmacy on the way to RCM.'

'RCM?'

'Royal College of Music.'

'All right. I just need to leave a note for Father, to let him know we were here.' Evelyn left Edward in the hallway. 'By the way,' she called from the parlour, 'what's the plan for today. You don't have a ticket for the Whitehall ceremony.'

'Well, after we've dropped the letter off at RCM we'll watch the coffin procession through Wellington Arch then walk down to get as close as we can to Whitehall. After the ceremony at the Cenotaph we can go into the abbey to see the grave. The day's itinerary is here.' She heard the sound of Edward clapping yesterday's copy of *The Times*. He was trying to sound excited but there was an underlying anxiety.

'Good. And is there time in the itinerary for us to talk about last night?' Evelyn tried to sound lighthearted.

'Yes, we should. We must. But later.'

They stepped out into a misty November morning. The air was still, almost unnaturally so, thought Evelyn, as she breathed deep, reminding herself of the smell of home – damp and soot, stale alcohol, rotting rubbish and clogged drains, coal bunkers, burnt oil and, most of all, people. She posted her father's door key through the neighbour's letterbox and led Edward to the top of the road where they joined the bus stop queue. Evelyn nodded hello to one or two recognised faces and Edward flagged down the first passing taxi. Evelyn was reluctant and complained at the extravagance of another taxi journey, following the previous evening's, but Edward insisted and helped her board. She blushed a little to think of the bus stop queue watching her.

Edward started to give the destination to the driver but was interrupted.

'You do know sir, most of the west of the city is closed off today. I say that in case that's your route.'

'Royal College of Music.'

'Prince Consort Road. I'll have to detour a bit. It'll cost more I'm afraid.'

'And can you find a pharmacy on the way please,' added Evelyn.

They travelled west, into the City and past St. Paul's, then north west through Soho and Mayfair to approach Hyde Park from the north. As they crossed Kensington High Street the driver commented on the growing traffic and pedestrians. It was eight fifty–five. The taxi left them at the Royal College of Music. Edward tipped generously.

The red bricked Victorian building faced Prince Consort Road. The regimented windows were dark and few people entered or left. Evelyn did not feel welcomed but Edward stood watching for perhaps a minute before leading the way. He stopped inside the door and looked around, as if something was different, until his gaze rested on a memorial on the wall. A grey rectangle of marble, with white stone surround, held a list of names in black lettering – a list of students and staff who had died in the war. Above the memorial was inscribed the motto: PRO PATRIA. Edward repeated it quietly in English, 'For Country.'

Evelyn wanted to ask if he had known anybody on the list but before she could, he took a few quick steps across the hall to the reception hatch where he handed in his letter with a brief explanation. The woman took it and Evelyn had no indication whether Edward might have known her, who shied away at the sight of his face.

Edward went back to the memorial on the wall but only briefly before indicating to Evelyn they should leave. She touched his arm. 'Why don't we look around, it's a beautiful building. You could show me the place and perhaps you might come across a tutor you know.'

Edward checked his watch. 'We've not time. The procession will be at Wellington Arch by ten.' He led her back outside.

They headed to Knightsbridge but Edward's initial fast pace slowed as the number of pedestrians going their way increased and, Evelyn thought, Edward tired, though it was only just past nine o'clock. Half way down Knightsbridge the road was blocked and police turned back traffic. The black and greys of the pedestrians, many wearing black armbands, were a sombre reminder of their purpose and there was a determination in their steady pace. At Hyde Park Corner the crowds grew and slowed while others joined the throng heading down Grosvenor Place towards Victoria. The mist had lifted a little but was still a fine veil across the pale sun and, though it promised warmth later, Evelyn felt a chill. She and Edward meandered through the crowd to the top of Grosvenor Place and a position from where they could see both down towards Victoria and across to Wellington Arch. They waited as the crowd grew around them and many passed to make their way on to Whitehall. Edward stood straight and though his favourite homburg was pulled low he didn't avert his face from those who looked his way. Though Evelyn may have imagined it, she thought there was many a nod of recognition and respect and she was proud to be standing next to him.

At twenty to ten the guns in Hyde Park barked. The crowd started but calmed quickly and though there was little conversation, there was an air of expectation. As the noise of the guns faded into the cold air the sound of pipe and drums began to build – a solemn march. It came from the south as the funeral procession made its way along Grosvenor Place. The road was lined with soldiers. A command rang out – they reversed arms and bowed heads. The quiet hum of the crowd faded. Evelyn took Edward's arm, raising herself to her full height to see better over and around the surrounding heads. The dull thud of a bass drum marked time as the bands of the Foot Guards and Scots Guards came into view. Following them were six horses pulling a limber and gun carriage, holding the unknown warrior's coffin, draped with a Union Jack. The flag was tattered and stained with blood and mud but still drew the eye as flashes of colour in a sea of black and grey.

Behind the coffin Evelyn could see the ranks of uniformed men, four abreast. But this was no self–serving or conceited parade, no call to self–congratulation, no celebration of victory. The crowd's expectation was riddled with grief and anxiety – a painful realisation of years of waiting and fear for the changed years to come. They shared, and fed off, each other's desire for comfort yet understood the need for individual and private pain to be respected, almost encouraged.

The coffin neared. The crowds went silent. Men removed their hats and bowed their heads but not before Evelyn saw the tears, though they did not bring life back to their eyes. Many of these men and women were as dead as the man they came to venerate. Edward looked at her and she saw the same hopelessness in his face, the mask somehow extending its lifelessness, almost to Edward's soul. She stifled a sob. It was not for the unknown warrior; his time was past and he was in God's hands; it was not just for Edward, she hoped to help him confront the war still threatening him and to welcome the peace that was yet to comfort him. No, it was mostly for her countrymen and women, still swamped with the pain of missing loved ones, the pain of their country's sacrifice, the terrifying realisation fathers, sons and husbands would never return, the fear that their Britain had changed beyond understanding and their place in their world would never be safe again.

The coffin was level with Evelyn and Edward and she saw the helmet, webbing and side arms resting on the stained flag. She could hold her tears no longer. Edward placed his hand over hers, on his arm, and looked at her. There was a half smile of encouragement on his face, as if asking her to cry for him, also, not for pity, but because he had no tears of his own left to give.

The coffin was flanked by field marshals and admirals and air chief marshals. Then came the navy, then the soldiers, then the air force, then the former servicemen wearing civvies. They passed the silent crowds.

Edward looked up as the head of the procession turned sharp right towards and under Wellington Arch. The bands compressed to fit and then expanded on the other side, leading the way down Constitutional Hill. The gun carriage with the coffin passed easily then the marching ranks squeezed through. The crowd remained silent. As the cortege marched away and the music faded the crowd remained still and silent. And even when the last of the procession had passed, the crowd was silent save for occasional sobs and choked cries. Evelyn was accustomed to congregations in church respecting the silence of service but this was no organised ceremony. This was an instinctive sharing of emotion almost shocking in its strength and crushing in its depth. This was a land pressed under the weight of hundreds of thousands of souls. This was a country praying for peace for the solitary soul in a coffin draped with a flag covered in battle mud and blood and desperate that, as that soul might find peace, so might they. Evelyn sensed, rather than heard, Edward's quick gasp, as if some realisation had come to him, and he squeezed her hand tighter.

It was ten or fifteen minutes before the crowd around Evelyn began to disperse. The procession was passing down Constitution Hill, the music growing quiet with no breeze to carry even the occasional refrain.

'Are you all right?' Edward asked.

'No, not really. I didn't know, didn't realise, so

many people could share so deeply. Such a shared instinct. I'm sorry.' Evelyn dabbed at her eyes with a handkerchief. 'And you? Are you all right?'

'I suppose.' Edward sighed and shook his head, as if to clear an image. 'Do you think Alastair should be here? Would it help him to know he's not alone?'

'I don't know. Some of these people still look very lonely, despite such common grief. I don't think I understand what's happening anymore.'

Edward nodded. 'Let's try to get closer to the Cenotaph, to see the unveiling.' He took the bottle of laudanum acquired that morning from an inside pocket and sipped as discreetly as he could, though not hiding from Evelyn.

Much of the crowd was heading through Green Park.

They were still linking arms as they walked down Constitutional Hill. The air was still cold. The sun was still faint behind the mist, still struggling to break through.

The funeral procession had moved from Constitution Hill onto The Mall and was twenty minutes ahead of them, though they could no longer see it. Edward led Evelyn through St. James's Park. They headed towards Horse Guards Road where he hoped to cut through to Whitehall, but hundreds, perhaps thousands, had the same idea and there was no way through. Edward checked his watch and deducted ten minutes: 10:40. The crowd around them was full of murmur which quietened at the sound of the bands. Though the Foreign Office buildings stood tall between them and the Cenotaph, the music was just audible. Evelyn strained to hear and caught *O God Our Help In Ages Past*, with a choir singing faintly, but so faint that she may have imagined it. Then the silence returned and the crowd around her became restless, checking pocket watches, confirming times with each other. The funeral procession had reached The Cenotaph. There was a frustration at not being able to see the events then the first chime from Big Ben was heard and a heavy hush settled on them. The men removing their hats, all bowing heads.

'Edward,' Evelyn whispered. 'I don't want to go through it again. Can we leave?'

Edward looked at her and she thought he was about to agree when the bell rang again and it was too late. The bell chimed eleven times and the crowd was silent. The last chime drifted away but not a person moved, not a voice whispered until there was a screaming sob from somewhere, Evelyn could not say from where, and some of the crowd tensed, though not with any sense of condemnation, and some did not notice, lost in their own dark, oppressive grief. Evelyn wanted to find the woman who had cried out, to hold her and tell her it was all right, to offer some comfort. But she had no comfort to offer and there were too many women to reach out to. She felt Edward looking at her and turned and, though he faced her, his gaze was elsewhere.

From somewhere in Whitehall, out of their sight, a bugler played *The Last Post* – sad, mournful, embracing.

A shouted, indistinct command signalled the clattering of the funeral procession and marching ranks regrouping, but, as at Wellington Arch, the crowd around Evelyn did not move. Hats were not replaced, quiet tears were not dried, sobs were still choked.

Evelyn was lost in the dark mass of shared grief. Then a sharp guilt pricked at her – a guilt she had no right to feel as so many others did. Yes, she had known many who hadn't come home, including cousins and friends, but, in truth, none she had loved as a husband or son. How could those so bereaved stand it? She looked again at Edward, who had not brought home those he had served with and, in a way she couldn't appreciate, loved. How did he stand it?

Evelyn sobbed again for the people around her and

for Edward.

'Edward, I need to go, somewhere. I'm sorry, I can't … it's too much.' Evelyn had lost track of how long they had been standing there. Many were now leaving.

'I'm sorry. You didn't need to come. I shouldn't have expected it.'

'Of course I did and you shouldn't be sorry, you're not to blame.'

Evelyn was desperate to hold him and, perhaps even more desperate, to be held. She took a step toward him, regardless of the people surrounding them. Edward held her and for a brief few seconds it made a difference, but only briefly as Edward pulled away.

'But there is one last thing. The grave in the abbey, before I go.' He took out his bottle of laudanum and sipped long.

'No Edward. I can't. Not yet. And I don't know you should either. You don't look well. You're pale. Do you feel well?'

'I feel … small, and shrinking.'

'And your head?'

'Hurts, but …'

'Then we need to sit and you need to eat. Come.' Evelyn forced a smile, taking a little pleasure at deciding a course of action. She led him back towards Horse Guards Parade then hailed a taxi and asked to be taken to the Lyons Corner House, on Coventry Street, just down from Piccadilly.

Many of the roads north of Whitehall had re–opened but the pavements still heaved with people. The taxi dropped them off a few yards from the restaurant and Edward passed his wallet to Evelyn for her to pay the driver. Not far from the door Evelyn saw the young woman. She was trying to light a cigarette but her hands shook. Her eyes were red from crying and her lipstick smudged.

'Catherine!'

Catherine started on hearing her name and turned, smiled but then sobbed with an outburst of relief, dropping her cigarette. Evelyn held her, waiting for her to calm. Catherine pulled away, 'I'm sorry, it's just, so many people, everywhere and it's been such a ... hellish difficult journey to get here, and I didn't imagine it would be so ... just, so ... many people and I lost a glove and then caught a heel and I thought I was lost and I was stupid to come here and ...'

'Here,' said Edward, handing her a cigarette of his own, already lit.

'Thank you.' Her hand was still shaking but she took it and drew heavily. She looked at Evelyn, returning the smile which steadied her, then looked at Edward, 'Are you all right? You look a bit peaky.'

'It's been a long morning but first, what are you doing here?' said Evelyn, leading the way into the restaurant. They were led to a seat on the first floor balcony area.

After ordering, Catherine explained, 'I wanted to come up with you yesterday and when we received your telegram to say you weren't coming home, well then I knew you Edward would be ... keen to see the funeral procession and, this morning, it just seemed important, so important, I come too and I did, but when I saw so many people I had no idea where to go or where you might be and then remembered what you'd said about this place,' she gestured around her. 'So I came here. In fact, I've been here ages. I've already had two coffees and a scone. They asked me to leave, for the lunchtime trade, and I was outside just, waiting. Oh Lord, it sounds so stupid of me. I'm sorry.'

Evelyn leant forward and rested a hand on Catherine's forearm.

'But I missed it all. Everything. I panicked and didn't know where to go. How stupid.'

'It's all right. I'll tell you all about it later. It was …' Evelyn looked at Edward, '… moving.'

Edward nodded. He still wore his homburg.

Catherine seemed to understand and didn't press for details, excusing herself to visit the bathroom.

Their sandwich lunch was brought and eaten in silence, though Edward ate little and took two or three sips from his laudanum, with no attempt at discretion. After the first one Catherine started to enquire but Evelyn shook her head subtly.

Edward insisted on paying the bill, though without his usual humour. It was clear to Evelyn he was in pain. Catherine sought to lighten the tone, saying, 'Well thank you kindly. I'm glad I came, after all.'

'And so am I,' said Evelyn, and now we can take Edward home, sooner rather than later, I think.'

'After the abbey,' said Edward.

'Do you really think you're up for it?' Evelyn asked. 'I don't. What do you think Catherine? Edward wants to see the new grave, in Westminster Abbey, but …'

'You don't look well Edward. It's a long way to Margate. Evelyn's right. We should go home.'

'Home?'

'Margate,' said Catherine.

'Margate? No, not home. But it doesn't matter. Not everyone deserves to come home anyway, do they? Some … one … gets chosen, one lucky sod gets chosen, but the others don't get to come home.' Edward muttered then lurched forward and held his head. 'The abbey,' he repeated.

Edward walked unsteadily between the two ladies and Evelyn was embarrassed some might think him drunk, so she took his arm and chatted as brightly as she could, with Catherine's help, until Edward hinted the noise hurt. It was half a mile to Trafalgar Square but took fifteen minutes and when there Evelyn's heart sank. The square was full of people and, at the south end, the exit to Whitehall, was a horde queuing to be let through a barrier. It wasn't clear where the queue started or where to join it. From the steps of The National Gallery Evelyn could see the line of people stretching down Whitehall, towards the Cenotaph and Westminster beyond.

'Edward, there are thousands, tens of thousands, of people. It will take hours to reach the abbey. It's not a good idea.'

Edward nodded but began walking anyway. Catherine whispered, 'Obsessed. And what's all that with the laudanum?'

Evelyn nodded, adding fearfully in a whisper of her own, 'Stubborn too. And is he limping?' She avoided the question about the laudanum.

Catherine watched Edward walk a few yards. 'I think he may be.'

'He is missing a toe. He once told me.'

'Is he?'

'Yes. Perhaps it's a problem today?'

'It's never been one before, has it?' Catherine said.

Evelyn and Catherine flanked Edward, each taking an arm. Edward seemed happy to be steadied but was not to be diverted and ignored Evelyn's question about the limp. With little conversation they passed under Admiralty Arch and made for Horse Guards Parade. There were still many people around, meandering with little obvious purpose. On reaching Birdcage Walk they rested, for Edward's sake, before turning east towards Parliament Square. On the far side of the square was the broad queue of people, mostly women, waiting to pass through the north door of Westminster Abbey. Inside lay the unknown soldier in his new grave. At the front of the queue, controlling entry into the abbey, was a small contingent of police and clergy. Catherine pointed their way, 'We could go and ask if they'd let Edward to the front. After all, he's a war hero and you're a reverend's girl.'

'It's not like the queue for the Hackney Empire. They've been waiting hours and there are thousands of them.'

'There's no harm in asking.'

'I had no idea there would be so many. Evelyn's right, we can't walk up and expect to be let in,' whispered Edward.

'Perhaps we can't, but surely you should?' said Catherine.

'No.'

'Then why did we come down here? You're not looking well and we could be going straight home.'

'Catherine has a point,' said Evelyn.

Edward nodded, took a swig from his laudanum and crossed the road, walking around the west side of Parliament Square, still with a slight limp and Evelyn wondered if he realised. As they passed the square Evelyn stopped to look up at the wonder of Westminster Abbey. The towers on the west side stretched far into the sky. Its size alone was awe inspiring and there was an authority to its presence impossible to deny but Evelyn wondered if it was more to glorify the ingenuity of man than the God her father served. The towers above the north door were shorter but broader, more imposing and, to Evelyn, not welcoming as a church should be. The steady stream of mourners passed through the arched doorway into the darkness behind. Edward didn't stop to look but went around to the west side. Whilst the people entering through the north door were controlled, here they wandered out through the west door with no order. Some were crying, others pale and dumb with shock, perhaps, or numb and drained from the emotion of the day and finally seeing the grave after hours of queuing. Many, now back in the cold November air, seemed to be lost, not ready to move away from the abbey but not knowing what they should be doing and unwilling to go home. The sense of grief was now exaggerated with a sense of helplessness.

Edward threaded a path through the crowd, keeping his head down, towards Dean's Yard, just past the abbey. Evelyn and Catherine caught up with him as he approached a doorway to the south side of the cloisters. A policeman stood in front and Edward hesitated. Evelyn went to him. 'Excuse me officer. I know this is most unusual and I'm embarrassed to ask, but my brother, the major had a ticket for the funeral today but was not well enough. He is feeling a little better now but is distraught he was not able to attend the interment of one of his comrades. My sister and I wondered if there was any chance you could see him through, just for a few minutes?'

Evelyn's plea was heartfelt and the policeman wavered but then refused, politely, but firmly. Catherine took a step forward but Edward coughed and put an arm on her shoulder. 'No, it's not fair to ask the constable to desert his post. I'm sorry officer. We shouldn't have asked,' said Edward, raising his hat. The police officer saw Edward's face.

The policeman did not leave his post but let them through the door into the cloisters, with instructions on how to find the passage to the nave. Evelyn was oddly elated at having been part of the deceit but then guilty as they went through. To their right, by the choir, was the front of the queue that stretched to Trafalgar Square. A policeman and member of the clergy were managing the movement of people from that leading edge to the grave, just to their left. The grave was surrounded by the last batch of visitors to have moved on from the main queue. Without hesitation Evelyn took both Edward and Catherine's arms and they went to the grave, joining the mourners there. The coffin had been placed in a grave just inside the west door and covered with a silk pall and Union Jack. The grave was bordered with wreaths and flowers. Wooden railings kept the public a yard or two back. At each corner was a member of the armed services, their rifle reversed. The mourners at the graveside milled in disorganised fashion and there were murmurs and hushed sobs. Some bowed their head, others looked to the vaulted ceiling, as if for comfort or wisdom, and others looked blankly at their companions, before hugging or taking another's hand to hold tightly. The atmosphere here, in church, seemed less intense to Evelyn than when the funeral procession had passed. Perhaps the church itself brought some peace or perhaps being closer to the man in the grave was a comfort? For those that knew where a loved one was buried the soul in the coffin was a proxy – and if your loved one had never been found he might lie in that coffin. It was a shared belief, a common truth.

Edward took off his hat and edged to the railing, the crowd parting as he brushed past, and gave a quiet moan of disappointment, barely audible over the solemn organ music drifting through the vast spaces of the abbey.

'What's the matter?' Evelyn was at his side and whispered.

'Nothing. I … just hoped it, the coffin, wouldn't be covered yet, that I might see it.'

'You saw it in the procession.'

'Not properly, not uncovered. There was always a flag on it.'

'Why does that matter?' Catherine had joined them at the railing.

'I don't know. It doesn't. But I just thought, I don't know why, there might be something, an indication, a clue …'

'You do know the chances of it being anyone you knew, let alone Kayst, are remote, to say the least. Thousands and thousands died,' Evelyn whispered.

Edward nodded. Evelyn touched his shoulder and

tried to turn him but he resisted. 'I know, it's stupid of me. I'm sorry, I'm not thinking straight.' He rubbed his left temple, just above the top of the mask and reached inside his pocket, as if for the bottle of laudanum, but his knees buckled and he sank to the cold stone of the abbey's floor.

Evelyn, Westminster, Thursday 11th November 1920

The taxi pulled up outside Reverend Coughston's terraced house in Elder Street just before midnight. Evelyn saw the dim yellow light through the gap in the curtains in the front room and was grateful. Her father was home; she had not wanted to wake her neighbour for the key. She knocked on the door while Catherine helped Edward from the car. The curtain twitched as Reverend Coughston peeked before answering. He opened it and Evelyn went in without speaking. She hugged him close. Catherine and Edward came in behind her. Reverend Coughston freed himself from Evelyn's hold, shut the door against the November cold and ushered them into the front room – in silence until he prompted Evelyn to, 'Put on the kettle while I start a fire.' Evelyn knew he would have been reading in the cold, reluctant to spend money on expensive coal.

Catherine and Edward sat on the small settee.

'I'm sorry, Father,' Evelyn was back in the room, 'for disturbing so late, but we've had a … difficult day and it's too late to take Edward back to Margate.'

'Not to worry, I saw your note when I came home this morning. I'm sorry to have missed you last night. You all seem a little … worn. I'm sure I'll hear all about it, but first, would Mr. Thompson like a drop of sherry? Sweet, I'm afraid.'

Evelyn watched Edward as he nodded. He had said little since they left St. Thomas's hospital. Now she thought of it, he had said little since the abbey. After fainting at the grave of the unknown soldier he had been unconscious for but a minute or two, not even long enough for one of the clergy supervising the abbey to call for help. Evelyn had put Edward's hat back on him before helping him stand and the mourners around had kept a respectful, perhaps fearful, distance. Edward had murmured wanting to get to 'Major Gillies at Queens,' but Evelyn knew that was too far and besides, St. Thomas's was just over the river. They'd hailed a taxi, Evelyn again embarrassed at the extravagance, and had reached the hospital in minutes. But that was over eight hours ago. She was weary.

Reverend Coughston brought Edward a sherry and Catherine lit a cigarette for him. He alternately sipped at the glass and drew on the cigarette until both were finished and Reverend Coughston suggested, firmly, he should sleep in Evelyn's bed and helped him upstairs.

Evelyn and Catherine made tea, waiting downstairs.

'I'm sorry I wasn't here earlier this morning,' said Evelyn's father when he came down. 'I can guess where you've been today and would have liked to have joined you, but I only returned at lunchtime.'

'Is Edward in bed?' Evelyn asked.

'Yes, but I don't know how easily he will sleep.'

'The hospital gave him morphine, I hope they didn't insist on injecting direct into the vein. Edward doesn't like that.' Evelyn stared into the fire as she spoke and was then aware of Catherine's quizzical look.

'He is in pain again?' Reverend Coughston asked.

'Always, not again. But yes. And the doctor at St. Thomas's said the xray showed there were still fragments of … God knows what … in …' she gestured to her own head, 'but then we knew that. They would not have released Edward if not for his insistence and, besides, there's nothing they can do anyway.'

'They gave us more tablets,' Catherine said, pulling a small box from her handbag.

Reverend Coughston insisted Evelyn and Catherine take his bed while he took the settee. The bed was cold and though Catherine held Evelyn tight to ward off the winter, there was nothing she could do to ease the tears Evelyn cried for the women and men whose grief she had shared that day.

The Blue Bench

The Unknown Warrior, Westminster

The unknown warrior lay in a coffin, within an oak casket. The casket lay in Westminster Abbey, in soil brought with him from France. He had died in a foreign land to protect his country, his family, his friends. Now he lay in an abbey to comfort those same loved ones, still serving his country. In this service he was held in the highest regard, with the utmost respect. He held a position exceeding that of any King, Queen or other servant of the land. No son or daughter of the Empire, no matter how high born, would pass over his grave – all would step to one side and bow.

The soldier lay there in darkness and quiet and was there for all and only one.

At the end of that first day's service the city above and around him sighed deeply, drawing breath, still swamped with emotion. In the days to follow thousands of mourners would come to him and he would turn away none. He could not prevent grief but could provide for it and, in time, offer solace.

The Blue Bench

Evelyn, Margate,
Friday 12th November 1920

The next morning Edward slept late. They were careful not to disturb him, especially Evelyn when she checked on him every half hour. Catherine went to buy cigarettes leaving Evelyn and her father the chance to speak but the silence was awkward until he said,

'Has Mr. Thompson mentioned the conversation he and I had relating to your … marriage prospects?'

'No.'

'Would you like him to?'

Evelyn hesitated and before she could answer her father said,

'Because, seeing him last night, I think I may have been wrong to even hint at the idea. I'm sorry. He is not well and pity is no reason.'

'You think he may pity me for being a spinster?' Evelyn tried to joke and he hugged her tight.

Edward came down after lunch and his first thought was to dissolve some of the morphine sulphate tablets the hospital had given them the previous evening. He downed the cloudy drink in a couple of swigs and apologised as he wiped the dribble from his chin. Catherine and Evelyn considered sending a telegram to Beatrice and asking her to tell William he must drive to London to collect them but Edward was still fragile and, modern as Edward's car was, the train would be warmer, more comfortable and reliable. Reverend Coughston hinted that Evelyn need not return to Margate and Evelyn pretended not to notice.

At Victoria Station Catherine telephoned Beatrice and when they arrived at the station in Margate William was waiting for them. He almost carried Edward to the car. By six thirty Edward had eaten one of Cook's scones and lay on the settee in the drawing room at Beatrice's, covered with a blanket, with a tumbler of Hennessy within reach, though untouched. Beatrice was teaching Patrick how to play her favourite form of patience. Evelyn and Catherine were reading.

Edward, Margate,
Saturday 13th November 1920

Whether it was the drugs or the pain or the travelling or the emotion of the funeral Edward couldn't say – some combination of them all, he guessed – but in any event he rose early on the Saturday, not feeling rested, but no longer wanting to sleep. The house was quiet and he felt guilty for having caused so much disruption to so many to whom he was close, in the last few days. He washed and dressed slowly and crept from the house. His head hurt a little less than it had for days and he found that he had missed the sea and his morning walk to the front. It was cold but he was wrapped up warm and kept his hat low with a gloved hand. It was a bright day and the brisk wind stopped the few clouds from building. He walked steadily but nearly tripped when his foot dragged, though it wasn't until the third time that he thought anything of it – not that it mattered.

William was waiting for him under the light house at the end of the harbour pier.

'How did you know I'd be here?' Edward asked as he declined the offered cigarette in preference for one of his own.

'I didn't, but I've taken to wandering down here in the mornings myself. My old man would be pleased. He loved the sea.'

'What, a miner?'

'No, why do you think that? He was on the barges, in and around the docks.'

'No he wasn't.'

575

'Wasn't he? Oh well.' William smiled.

'Hmmm. Anyway, I'm glad you're here. Thanks for picking us up from the station.'

'I had little choice. Beatrice made it quite clear after the last time I'd refused, I was not to make the same mistake. She's a feisty one, for one so petite. You know, if it wasn't for Georgette I might ...' William let the sentence hang and laughed.

'Yes, I believe you just might. What happened about the fight on the beach, over the kite?'

'Constable Simms has run out of patience. I don't blame him. Fortunately the other bloke is too scared to press for charges.'

'You're an arse sometimes, you know.'

'It's easier not to be when you've a few bob.'

'Not even you believe that.'

William laughed and they smoked in silence until William said, 'I'd have come with you yesterday, to see the funeral at Westminster, if you'd asked.'

'You didn't need to be asked. And you should go and see the grave. You never know, it could be ...'

'... one of our boys? I don't believe that. For all we know it might be empty, just a cruel joke on us all. The poor and stupid and guilty and bereft.'

Edward shrugged. 'Perhaps, but you should go.'

'I'll see. As it happens we're moving back to London sooner than I thought. Next Wednesday. I've got Georgette a couple more auditions and it doesn't make sense to be toing and froing.'

'Catherine will miss Patrick.'

'Georgette's going to see her today, to ask if Patrick can stay here, while we get settled.'

'Oh, that's probably a good thing.'

'I'll miss him but ... anyway. Oh, there is one thing I'd ask. The Wolseley. Can I take it? You don't need it down here.'

'No, I've sort of promised it to Catherine.'

'I thought so. Fair enough, but worth the question. Anyway, I better get back, need to think about packing. And you might as well have this. I've filled it up and need to start a new one.' William handed Edward the small notebook into which he had made so many notes over the years. 'I always thought one day there'd be something good enough there for you to put music to. But there isn't. It's all bollocks.'

He walked away before Edward could look in the notebook, pausing to shout back. 'When you're back in town look us up. We'll be staying at my old man's place for a while. Oh, and the bloke with the kite that needed a lesson? His kid was bullying Patrick and we ain't 'avin' that. Anyway, stay lucky, Lieutenant.' He gave a salute.

Edward watched him go before leafing through the notebook. The pages were crammed with scribblings of unfinished poems, rhymes and couplets, many with suggestions alongside as to the tempo and mood of the music that might accompany them.

Edward stood and watched the sea for a while, smoked two cigarettes, then wandered up to The Winter Gardens, leaning into the strong onshore breeze as he made the hill. The doors were open but there was no one there. It was only eight thirty. He went through to the auditorium. Still wearing his coat and hat he sat at the piano and removed his gloves. For a blissful hour the pain could be ignored and the image of the coffin being pulled through Wellington Arch forgotten and the dream of a life with Evelyn could be imagined while his fingers brought the piano to life. With no music to follow and no need to compose and no desire for structure, he played.

Rachmaninoff, Liszt, Chopin, Mozart, Beethoven and Grieg came and went, merged and flowed. His mind was free, his hands instinctive, his heart flying.

Edward was sitting on a bench, close to the barren allotments below Holy Trinity church when Patrick found him. Catherine was just a few yards behind, puffing from trying to keep up.

'Lieutenant Thompson, we've been looking for you everywhere,' Patrick said, 'you've visitors.'

'Yes,' added Catherine, 'and do you know the time?'

Edward looked at his Elgin. Just gone four. The light was fading and a light drizzle was settling on his heavy coat. He had been out for hours.

'We have been so worried. You should have told us,' Catherine said.

'I'm sorry, I lost … time.'

'I hope you haven't …' Catherine indicated to the houses across the allotments where Mrs. Capais lived.

'Absolutely not. She … it … is irrelevant now.'

'What does that mean?'

'I don't know.' He turned to Patrick. 'Visitors you say. Who?'

'The Kaysts,' replied Catherine.

Edward let Patrick take his hand, pull him down the hill and back to Beatrice's but as he neared he wished not to be so easily drawn. It had been difficult enough to see Kayst's father when he thought he was prepared, but now, with no time for forethought, he was all too aware how he might say the wrong thing. Evelyn was already back, having looked for Edward on the front and at the Trenters' tea shop. He could see she was angry with him but now was not the time. Beatrice was in the drawing room, entertaining the Kaysts – the father he had already met and a woman he assumed to be Kayst's mother. Beatrice welcomed Edward and made the introductions. Kayst's mother stared at Edward's mask but he did not look away.

'Cook's bringing more tea and scones. Mr. and Mrs. Kayst came from St. Peter's on the tram this afternoon and found us quite easily, thanks to a word with Constable Simms in the police station, who came round with them, just to make sure all is well, naturally, and he is a proper gentlemen. Constable Simms I mean, though of course, I do not imply Mr. Kayst is otherwise, and his good wife and I have already found we have several acquaintances in common, though it turns out the Palmers aren't the Palmers I thought they were, at least, we think not, isn't that so?'

Mrs. Kayst nodded. The Kaysts appeared ill at ease, sitting on the settee in the bay window. Behind them the November daylight was all but gone and the rain was heavier. Beatrice went around the room lighting gas lamps. Catherine added coal to the grate and lit a fire starter.

'I'm sorry for causing you inconvenience last time we met,' Edward said, 'especially passing out like that. I'm a little embarrassed, to tell the truth.'

'You needn't be, Sir,' said the older woman. 'When I heard you had visited I was sorry not to have been there. Are you feeling better now?'

Edward glanced towards Evelyn and nodded. 'As well as can be expected.'

Cook entered and served tea, the noise of crockery and cutlery unduly loud. Beatrice conducted some small talk, based largely on the weather and the propensity of the local dairy to deliver later in the day during the winter, despite the fact Cook was up at her usual time. Then, on finishing her tea, she let the conversation falter and found an excuse to tidy the records lying near the gramophone. Catherine went to join her. Evelyn also half stood to leave but took Edward's nod at the armchair as a hint to stay. Edward filled the silence.

'Mr. and Mrs. Kayst, how can I help you?' He offered a cigarette which Mr. Kayst took but not his wife. It was she who spoke first.

579

'Mr. Kayst wasn't able to explain why you came to see us, week before last, and I can't help but wonder.'

'It's not Mr. Kayst's fault in the slightest. I'm afraid I was vague and poorly and did a bad job of introducing myself. I am sorry.'

'But there was something unsaid,' Mrs. Kayst said, looking to her husband who nodded,

'It seemed so.'

'Your boy was a fine soldier Mrs. Kayst. A man of whom you can be very proud. A man who was well—regarded by his platoon and kept up our spirits in many a hard place. A man who was brave and complained not once and was respected by all. A fine young man.' Edward spoke formally. He had to; the words were true but if he could not deliver them formally, he would break down and not be able to deliver them at all.

'But he wasn't a man, was he?' said Mrs. Kayst. 'He was just a boy. He was eighteen when he died.'

'He was as much a man as any.'

'And how old were you, his Lucky Lieutenant?' Mr. Kayst asked, but with no sarcasm.

Edward looked to Evelyn then back to Mr. Kayst. 'Twenty three when he … when it happened.'

'Twenty three,' repeated Mrs. Kayst, 'and what did happen?'

Edward stood with his back to the fireplace but looked out at the dark rain.

'Vimy Ridge was mostly a Canadian show but there were British regiments supporting, including us. There had been the usual bombardment, unrelenting, but by then we knew better than to think the Hun would be devastated. When the guns stopped and the whistles blew we stepped up to walk into the smoke as usual. Your lad was but six or seven yards to my left, walking steadily, a true soldier, as brave as any. Then the German barrage and guns opened on us and the noise was, unheard of, except we'd heard it before, and walked on, especially young Kayst, he didn't falter and then others around started to fall but he walked on, just yards away but by my side and then he turned to shout something but I don't know what, I couldn't make it out, I think it was a warning of some sort and then something hit me and I spun round and down to the ground. You'd think the pain would keep you down but it didn't, there wasn't any, not immediately, and I got to my knees to look for Kayst and he wasn't there.'

'What do you mean, he wasn't there?' Mr. Kayst asked.

'Just that, I'm afraid. In the second I was put down and scrabbled back to my knees he was gone. There was a lot of smoke and shell holes and he may have walked on untouched. For all I know he may have made it all the way to the German line, but I never saw him again. Then I was down again and didn't come to until the field hospital.'

'He was ... gone?' Mrs. Kayst said, holding a handkerchief to her face. Mr. Kayst took her hand. Evelyn went to sit beside her and put an arm around her, but she watched Edward, who looked away.

Mrs. Kayst took a deep breath but the sobs would not be choked and she rocked into Evelyn as the tears flowed.

Edward turned to Mr. Kayst. 'He walked into battle as brave and proud as any man I served with. It was an honour to serve beside him.'

Mr. Kayst swallowed and sighed. 'A good boy?' He asked.

'A very good man,' said Edward, 'and Vimy Ridge was taken.'

'But there's no grave,' Mrs. Kayst blurted between sobs.

'None I know of,' said Edward, 'and if there was then the War Office would have told you. But I believe they are finding ... people all the time, so ...'

'And there are tours of the cemeteries you can take,' Evelyn said.

'Why would we, if we don't know he's there?' Mrs. Kayst asked.

'Besides,' added her husband, 'we could never afford that.'

'Then what about the grave of the unknown warrior? I read about that,' said Mrs. Kayst.

'That's a load of old rubbish. My boy gave his life and they can't even give him his own grave.' Mr. Kayst was quick to condemn but Mrs. Kayst was looking at Edward.

'It's ... possible, but, even if he's not there, it's still his place,' said Edward.

'I don't understand.'

'I'm not sure I do either Mrs. Kayst. But I think you should go and see how it makes you feel. In any event, you will find many others like you. I would urge you to go.'

It was a further half–hour and a cup of tea before the Kaysts were settled enough for the journey home. Edward asked Catherine if she would drive and suggested that he went back with them to St. Peter's, though he excused himself for a few minutes before the trip. Evelyn followed him to the kitchen and helped him undo the box of soluble morphine sulphate tablets so he could take a heavy dose before the drive, though it was only a ten mile or so round trip. Beatrice lent Mrs. Kayst a heavy winter coat and she sat by the door on the back seat. Evelyn sat in the middle and Edward next to the other door. Mr. Kayst was in the passenger seat up front. Catherine didn't enjoy the drive in the dark but they were soon home, having politely refused Mrs. Kayst's offer of tea.

'Next time Edward, buy a bloody car with windows,' said Catherine as she parked outside Beatrice's guest house. Edward forced a smile though his head hurt – and she was right, the cold wind ripping through the car could hardly have helped.

'With my next inheritance,' he tried to joke. Catherine smiled and led them up the stairs and into the hall. Beatrice was waiting for them. While Edward and the Kaysts had been talking she had remained calm but evidently, once they were gone, her tears had flowed.

'That poor mother,' she said, going to Catherine and holding her close.

Beatrice said good night. Catherine led Evelyn and Edward into the drawing room.

'Well, what a few days it has been. The poor Kaysts.' Catherine said.

Evelyn nodded but Edward stood in front of the dying fire, looking at the mantelpiece. 'Edward, are you feeling all right?' she asked.

Edward grunted.

Catherine sat on the settee and tapped the cushion next to her, indicating to Evelyn to join her. She did, saying, 'It wasn't quite as you told, was it?'

'What makes you say that?' Edward turned back to the room.

'There is more to it, isn't there? I feel it.'

Edward shrugged. 'Kayst was as brave as I said. More so. He was as brave as any of them, but I wasn't.'

'What do you mean?'

'I just wasn't. I couldn't be, not any longer.'

'I don't understand,' said Evelyn.

'And, if I was, perhaps Kayst might still be alive.'

'That doesn't make sense. How much of what you said to the Kaysts is true?' Catherine asked.

'The beginning is as it happened. And it was an orderly advance, just as I said. Kayst was five or six yards to my left, William to my right. The rest of the platoon was spread out on either side of us, but after fifty yards they had our range and the men, my men, were being cut to pieces. Not just shot, not just a bullet, or two, or ten, but being shredded, machine guns and shrapnel. They were disintegrating while I watched, while I did nothing but walk alongside them, holding my bloody revolver as if it was some talisman, the Lucky Lieutenant, such a bloody Lucky Lieutenant. And still they walked alongside me and I couldn't hear the screams as limbs were torn and flesh ripped but I saw them exploding into bursts of skin and blood and guts and the guns were crashing and the noise was beyond hearing and I walked and they walked with me, my men, and Kayst. They were obliterated, devastated and I couldn't watch it any more, I couldn't stand it, I'm sorry. So sorry.' He took a step forward, turned and slumped into the armchair. Evelyn left the settee to kneel at his feet and took his hand. 'But none of it was your fault. Kayst wasn't your fault.'

'I faltered and thought, imagined, I heard silence, thought for a second the guns had stopped, as if that was possible, and I knew, just knew, it was a sign and we couldn't take anymore, I couldn't, wouldn't take any more. I screamed to the few of us left to fall back, to abandon the attack but William screamed louder, to continue and I looked to him, and he screamed again and I looked to Kayst, he stopped, he didn't know what to do, who to obey and William screamed something and I turned to shout he should stop. Then there was a flash to my left and I turned back and Kayst was gone. Nothing was left, not half a man, not a quarter. There was just nothing, he was … nothing … in a second, less, he simply disappeared. But if he hadn't hesitated, stopped, and hadn't heard my screams he wouldn't have been there, I wouldn't have been there, and then, when the next shell exploded close, perhaps this,' he gestured to his mask, 'wouldn't be.'

'But it wasn't your fault.'

'Had I not been a coward, if I hadn't tried to call off the advance, Kayst might have made it. I shouldn't have hesitated.'

'And William called you to carry on?'

'He understood if I took what was left of the platoon back I'd be court martialled and shot. I wish I had been. It's what a coward deserves and I'm still too much a coward to even tell the Kaysts the truth.'

'The truth was Kayst was a hero, and a good man and he believed in you, because you're a good man and his father and mother need know no more.'

'Dear Evelyn, some things can't be made right just by saying the right things. He was just eighteen.'

'And you were just twenty three. And William knows all this?'

'Of course. The shell that ripped away half my face punctured his ribs but it was him carried me back to our lines. He should have left me to rot in the mud. I'm sorry.'

Evelyn rocked back from her knees to sit on the floor. Her tears matched Edward's. How had she not known this? How had she not felt such torment? How could men live with such thoughts?

Edward lurched forward, holding his head and cried in pain.

The Blue Bench

Evelyn, Margate, Saturday 13th November 1920

Evelyn and Catherine helped Edward to his room and his bed where he reached for the box on his bedside table containing the morphia solution and syringe.

'Is it ... does it ... feel like it's moving? The shrapnel I mean?' Catherine asked but Edward was rocking back and forth as he sat on the edge of the bed, fumbling to open the box.

'How much have you had already today?' asked Catherine.

'Not enough.' Edward nodded towards the half empty box of soluble morphine sulphate tablets. 'They ... don't do much ... these days.'

'Perhaps you should wait, just a little longer.' Evelyn said, and bent down to take the box. Their faces were close and Evelyn kissed his right cheek. 'I'm so sorry, about Kayst. I had no idea. But you're not to blame. Why didn't you tell me before?'

'And have you think less of me? I wish I hadn't told you at all. I'm sorry.' He fumbled again with the box. Evelyn took his hand and kissed him again, this time on his lips. 'I could never think less of you. Here let me.' Evelyn composed herself, took the box and looked to Catherine, who had retreated to stand in the doorway.

'I'm sorry Evelyn,' Edward apologised again, 'it hurts badly this evening. I need a vein.'

'I understand. Roll up your sleeve,' Evelyn said, though without conviction.

'I'll need a tie.' Edward pointed to his wardrobe.

587

Evelyn slowed her breathing and stemmed her tears as she pulled the tie tightly around his upper arm, looking for a vein to bulge. Then she prepared the syringe, waiting for Edward to say when to stop on the volume of solution drawn. Her hand was shaking as she brought the needle to his arm.

'Here, let me. Is there any alcohol?' Catherine stepped back toward the bed and took the syringe from Evelyn.

'You've done this before?' Evelyn asked.

'No. So I'm sorry, Edward, if this hurts.'

Evelyn found a bottle of scotch and used a handkerchief to rub some over the vein standing proud in the inside of Edward's left elbow, then held the arm tightly. Catherine did not hesitate and though the insertion was not pin–point, it was sufficient to find the vein. She ignored Edward's moan as she pushed the needle through the skin.

'Thank you,' Edward muttered.

Evelyn found a dressing gown to pull over Edward as he lay on top of the covers then the women made to leave.

'Wait,' Edward called, 'Evelyn, I'm sorry about that night, at your father's. So sorry. But would you, could you, put my mask on the bedside table?'

Evelyn looked at Catherine and gestured she should wait outside while Evelyn went back to Edward. 'Of course. And now you can rest properly.'

Edward nodded. 'Evelyn, thank you. This has been the summer I'd hoped for and you have been the friend for whom I'd dared wish.'

'You knew about the laudanum, and the tablets and, now, the injections?' Catherine was waiting outside and asked Evelyn as she closed the door to Edward's bedroom.

Evelyn nodded.

'You might have told me.'

'I'm sorry. Edward didn't want anyone else to know.'

'He's in such pain?'

'Or that he'd taken to ... well, most days he was taking some.'

'And what's that about the night at your father's?'

'We ... we spent the night together. Sleeping. We kissed, then we slept.' Evelyn didn't want to elaborate but Catherine was owed some explanation. 'He was poorly and ... I think he just needed to be held.'

'You kissed and just slept?' Catherine asked.

Evelyn shrugged.

'You do know how ... attractive you are? Actually, silly me, you don't, do you. And you expect me to believe Edward didn't even try ...?'

Evelyn shrugged. 'He has suffered ... suffers ... so much.' Tears came easily.

Catherine hugged her.

The Blue Bench

Edward, Margate, Sunday 14th November 1920

Edward woke before sunrise and checked his watch for the time but didn't take notice. His thoughts were muddled and his focus blurred. He had a memory of Evelyn lying beside him on the bed, holding him, and it was easy to imagine. So easy it may not have been true. He couldn't tell, but the memory, false or not, was so pleasing, so restful, he didn't care. Then he remembered she once lay naked next to him and he'd felt her softness and warmth and touched her smooth skin and she was perfect. And she had seen his face and not turned away and he'd told her about Kayst. There were no secrets and he didn't feel so old.

His head hurt less than it had the previous evening but it was only a matter of time. He pushed himself up and, clumsily, managed to draw some solution into the syringe. He looked for the tie that had been used the previous night, thinking to inject into a vein again, but couldn't find it. He would go into a muscle instead, but that was less effective, so he went back to the syringe and drew some more solution, then a little more; the syringe was full. He held his breath as he pushed the needle into his arm and depressed the plunger. He withdrew the needle carefully and laid it back on the bedside table, next to the box. He took up his mask and put it on, being careful for a good fit then lay back down on the bed, waiting for the memory of Evelyn to lie beside him. She came to him quickly, with love and calm and this time he smelt her – soap and flowers, possibly roses, then a little of

591

new sweat, but sweet. She was naked again and her skin glowed as she gently stroked his brow. Her breasts rose and fell as she breathed easily. Her hazel eyes shone and were fixed on his. She was so perfect he didn't need to touch her and, as the morphine seeped into his body, so her skin glowed more brightly. As his heartbeat slowed and his breathing became more shallow, he felt lightheaded and dizzy and not scared or ashamed. He need never be afraid again. He called her name quietly and she smiled.

Evelyn, Margate,
Sunday 14th November 1920

Evelyn lay in Catherine's bed. Catherine lay on the settee. Both were still clothed in yesterday's attire but covered by blankets. Evelyn was not sleeping well and stirred at the noise, or imagined noise. She had no idea of the time nor how long she had slept. She left the bed, as quietly as she could, but stopped to make sure Catherine was covered, before going to Edward's room.

She listened at the door but there was no sound. She went in. The new sunrise gave little light but she could see Edward lying on the bed. There was no movement. He was not covered by a blanket and the morning was cold. She went to him. His masked eye looked up at her – the glint Alice had put there seemingly real, while his right eye was open but blank. In death his metal cheek held a colour and tone his other, frighteningly pale cheek, did not.

Evelyn lay beside him, her face wet with silent tears, and prayed for his peace.

The Blue Bench

Evelyn, Margate, Saturday 5ᵗʰ March 1921

'There's a review in the paper of that new play Georgette is singing in. It says she's very good.' Evelyn looked up from her newspaper. She was sitting in the tea shop. Although it was still closed for the winter Evelyn, Catherine and Beatrice had developed a routine of visiting on Saturdays to see Isabella and Alice. They always took Patrick with them, of course, and if Alastair was there he would often take Patrick up to the cliffs near Hodges Bridge, to fly kites, if the weather was good enough. Catherine hated the idea of Patrick, a kite and cliffs, though in truth they were not big, but without William around Alastair had offered and Catherine knew it was right for Patrick. She worried a young boy surrounded by women might not learn that which he should. Patrick had turned seven in the January and was a joy: polite, considerate and funny – so perhaps a house full of women wasn't such a bad thing. He still missed Georgette and William, occasionally, but they visited, occasionally, like at Christmas, and all were agreed he was much better off staying at Margate, where Catherine had insisted he start full time schooling at St. John's. He was behind the other children his age in reading and maths, but seemed popular and his teacher, another young woman, was sure he'd soon catch up, especially with Catherine and Evelyn's help in the evenings.

'Pardon?' said Catherine, looking to Evelyn from Isabella.

'There's a review of that play Georgette's in and it's complimentary.'

'Good.'

'Though I still think you've a better voice,' added Evelyn.

Catherine smiled and turned back to play peek–a–boo with Isabella. She was as bright and beautiful as ever and Alice was the proudest of mothers. Alice and Beatrice sat at another table, sharing the latest gossip from the Ladies of St. John's.

After another pot of tea Catherine reminded Evelyn they, 'needed to stop by the hardware store on the way home, to check on the bench they'd ordered.' Beatrice assured them she'd bring Patrick home later, when he returned with Alastair.

On the way to the hardware store Catherine and Evelyn detoured via the gramophone dealer in town. Mr. Foulks, behind the counter, saw them approach and went to the drawer behind him to retrieve the records. 'Good morning ladies. Here we are, as ordered.'

He handed over two brown cardboard envelopes. Each held a black disc, each with an exposed label – a white dog looking into a gramophone's horn. The print underneath showed:

Papillion (Grieg)
Little Bird (Grieg)

… on one and, on the other:

Prelude in G–flat major, Op.23 no.10 (Rachmaninoff)
Prelude in C–Sharp minor Op.3 No.2 (Rachmaninoff)

Edward Thompson was credited as the pianist; the recordings were from The Winter Gardens back in September. Evelyn turned them over in her hands three or four times, nearly crying but not wanting to embarrass herself in the shop.

'Thank you Mr. Foulks, my aunt will be thrilled

when she sees the surprise,' said Catherine.

Outside, Catherine passed Evelyn a handkerchief before taking her arm to lead her to the hardware store.

Over the winter they had been expanding and refurbishing the new guest house, it was now more a hotel, and, in truth, both had been grateful for a reason to be kept so busy. The work was going well. They should be open in good time for the new season and had become good customers of the hardware store and local tradesmen. Beatrice had provided most of the investment and Edward the remainder – after his death they learnt he had changed his will so that Evelyn benefited from his modest estate; there was a small town property in Lincoln he had inherited from another aunt, which Evelyn sold. The extra money was welcomed. Evelyn could partner Catherine in the hotel venture and they could afford to decorate and furnish the hotel as they'd dreamed. The small touches were important – the latest was for the garden; just a simple thing, but Evelyn needed it to be right. A bench. A wooden bench for four people, in bright blue. The manager at the hardware store took them out to the yard at the back. Evelyn wasn't happy with the colour. Though she didn't know what colour it needed to be, somehow she knew it wasn't the right one, yet. The manager took them back in and they looked through the catalogue of colours he could order–in but they would need to pay for it to be repainted.

They returned to Beatrice's guest house in time for lunch and listened to the new records, Evelyn reminding Catherine how Edward, 'had so loved to play Rachmaninoff, even though the rest of us didn't understand a note of it.'

Catherine said how she missed singing *Danny Boy*, but they both suppressed any tears.

The second post had been received. Catherine had received another package from Eugene, in America. As usual he had sent a book: *My Antonia*. Eugene's letter repeated his suggestion Catherine visit him in Margate, New Jersey – the third time.

'He may get fed up with asking,' said Evelyn. 'Perhaps you should go this time?'

'And leave you to look after our hotel, without me? I don't think so.' Catherine laughed. 'I'll write him again, later.'

'He is persistent and I don't blame him,' said Evelyn. 'By the way, I was thinking this afternoon, we could clear out Edward's room. Beatrice will need to get it ready for the season.'

Evelyn went in first. The room was clean and tidy, Evelyn made sure it was aired at least weekly, but there was still a musty odour. There wasn't a great deal to sort and the first decision was on Alice's portrait of Edward. It was on the floor, resting against the bottom of the bed.

'He looks so young,' said Evelyn.

'He was. Should we hang it in the new hotel, next to our portrait?' Catherine asked. Against Evelyn's better judgement they had agreed to hang Alice's portrait of the two of them behind the new reception desk.

'I don't think so. I think we should hang it in the basement bar, next to the piano.' They had plans to move the piano from Beatrice's drawing room.

'You don't think it might be intimidating for the player, when we can eventually afford one.'

'Edward intimidating? No,' said Evelyn. She moved the picture better to catch the light. Alice's golden sunrise was eternal, Edward's face as whole as it could ever be. She went over to the desk. On it was Edward's joining–up picture – a fresh face and a fresh uniform. They had found it among Edward's personal letters and had it framed. It was the face of a serious young man and Alice had captured his thoughtfulness but also, in both real and painted eyes, the compassion she had known.

'I've been thinking,' Catherine pulled Evelyn's attention away from the photograph. 'Do you think Patrick should have piano lessons?'

'Let's ask him over tea.' Evelyn placed the photograph into a small suitcase, together with a few other effects and papers, including the letter received from the Royal College of Music in December, complimenting Edward's score and inviting him to resume his studies.

She moved on to clear the cabinet over the basin. There was a bottle of Old Orkney scotch in there. She took it out, together with two glasses and poured small measures into each. She handed one to Catherine and they raised their glasses.

'To Major Gillies.'

The Blue Bench

Patrick, Westminster Abbey, Friday 14th November 1941

Evelyn and Catherine had lunch at the Lyons Corner House on Coventry Street, as usual, then went on to Westminster Abbey. Isabella was with them. The grave of the unknown soldier was well tended as ever.

They were subdued and holding back tears. I felt guilty I couldn't be there though it is a place they will always find me.

END

Author's Note 1

Though the main protagonists are fictional there are a number of references to historical figures without whom this novel would not be possible:

Sir Harold Gillies
Reverend David Railton MC
Bishop Ryle
Francis Derwent Wood

Sir Harold (Major) Gillies was a figure of truly historical importance, instrumental in the development of innovative and creative methods to improve the treatment of badly injured soldiers, especially those with horrific facial wounds – wounds that are beyond imagination in their severity. Not only was he a dedicated and skilful surgeon, he was a man of great compassion and vision, able to persuade and motivate others (and the establishment) to support and join his crusade to help the wounded. He was a man determined to do his best for his patients and engendered great loyalty from those he treated and those with whom he worked. Working alongside Sir Harold Gillies were many expert surgeons, doctors, nurses and technicians – such as Archie Lane, who became well-known for using his dental knowledge to assist in both facial surgery and re-building.

Reverend David Railton MC served as an army chaplain on the Western Front during World War One, where he was awarded the Military Cross for saving men under fire. The idea for the grave of the unknown warrior came to him after he had seen a simple cross pencilled with the words 'An Unknown British Soldier' in a back garden near Armentieres in France in 1916. He understood the potential for a formal grave recognising the sacrifice of so many which could provide a focal point for the country as a whole but also provide hope for the bereaved that their loved one had returned. Thus the grave is not only a symbol of sacrifice at a national level, it also an actual grave for one man that may provide solace for many whose loved ones never returned. In this way it is a uniquely powerful concept. In addition to serving bravely and initiating the idea for the unknown warrior Reverend Railton also worked hard after the war to support the returning veterans, represent their interests and raise awareness of the difficulties of reintegration into civilian life for both disabled and able bodied veterans. Mention should be made here of Bishop Ryle, Dean Of Westminster, who took up Reverend Railton's idea, was able to engage with Prime Minister Lloyd George and King George V, and was instrumental in its completion.

Francis Derwent Wood was a talented and influential artist and sculptor able to use his skills to help hundreds of injured soldiers by crafting masks. He managed teams of skilled craftsmen seeking to aid their rehabilitation. Whilst the medical teams on the battlefields and in the hospitals were developing new techniques to keep the men alive and rebuild them, the work of Francis Derwent Wood and men like him was an essential part of their integration back into society.

Author's Note 2

The Great War (1914-1918) and its aftermath is well documented in fictional and historical texts, photographs, motion pictures and museums. As a work of fiction The Blue Bench does not include footnotes or a bibliography with further information on such sources. However, readers may be interested in the following texts that I found invaluable during research and preparation for The Blue Bench and my thanks go to their authors for their work which was comprehensive, informative and enjoyable.

The Great Silence – Juliet Nicolson
Singled Out – Virginia Nicholson
The Story of the Unknown Warrior – Michael Cavanagh

Additionally, I would like to thank the compilers of The Times archive for making available on-line their editions which include coverage of the interment of the Unknown Warrior.

Finally, I would encourage readers to seek out footage of Armistice Day 1920, when the permanent Cenotaph was unveiled and the Unknown Warrior interred in Westminster Abbey. There is not, as far as I know, any measure of the impact public ceremonies may have on a nation's collective consciousness (should such a thing exist). But, by any measure, 11th November 1920 will surely feature high and the importance of the grave of the Unknown Warrior as a cultural and yet uniquely personal symbol cannot be overestimated.

Author's Thanks

Deep and sincere thanks are due to the following:

'Early' readers whose feedback, help and support was gratefully received as I tried to make The Blue Bench the best I could - Howard Fletcher, Chris Troughton, Debbie Marriner.

Paul Swallow for helping me realise my ambitions for The Blue Bench. Without Paul's expertise and encouragement it would not be the book it is. Thank you Paul and thanks to Ann Polhill Walton for the introduction.

Those that have kept me sane through the years and believed in me as I kept trying: Linda Laurie, Eve Marriner, Alex Marriner, Ray Munro, Peter Olive, Angie and Paul Sherritt, Jim Murphy, Tony Thornton, Neil Rendall, Chris Downs.

An entire generation whose sacrifice made it possible for someone like me to come along nearly a hundred years later and try to capture a small part of their stories.

And, most importantly, The Unknown Warrior, Westminster Abbey.

.... by Paul Marriner and available through www.bluescalepublishing.co.uk .

Sunrises

… moving, poignant …

The story of a family learning how to love, lose, mourn and, ultimately, find peace. When Anthony and Christine's daughter dies the void is unimaginable and unbearable. Grief is driving their family apart and they struggle to find peace. Mark, their son, is growing to manhood not sure of his place and seeking his own way forward. Big questions have no answers and important truths hide hard lessons.

Only by learning to share can they find a way to re-build hope for a future.

.... by Paul Marriner and available through www.bluescalepublishing.co.uk .

Three Weeks In The Summer

... innocence lost ...

1976. Richard (16) has finished his exams and a long, hot summer beckons, but his crush on the new girl in town is unrequited. He leaves the stifling suburb to spend time in The New Forest with Dudek, his Czech uncle. Dudek is being cared for by Anika, a vivacious young Czech woman. Anika introduces him to village life and when he meets Jennifer, a girl his age, he finds his attentions torn between them. Teenage emotions and needs are laid bare as relationships with the two girls develop.

The summer's experiences intensify as forest fires threaten the village and Richard learns more of the events that led to his father's death. As the summer break ends, Richard has been touched by love and death and understands more of his father's history.

The story concludes the following New Year when Richard returns to The New Forest, needing to pick up where the summer ended.